A STORY (
AND ALL

A STORY OF GOD AND ALL OF US

COMPANION TO THE HIT TV MINISERIES
The Bible

ROMA DOWNEY
AND
MARK BURNETT

New York Boston Nashville

FaithWords
Hachette Book Group
237 Park Avenue
New York, NY 10017

faithwords.com

Printed in the United States of America

RRD-IN

First trade edition: March 2014

10 9 8 7 6 5 4 3 2 1

FaithWords is a division of Hachette Book Group, Inc.
The FaithWords name and logo are trademarks of Hachette Book Group, Inc.

The publisher is not responsible for websites (or their content) that are not owned by the publisher.

The Library of Congress has cataloged the hardcover edition as follows:

Library of Congress Control Number: 2012954984

ISBN 978-1-4555-2559-1 (pbk.)

For our parents
with gratitude for lessons learned, values taught and love shared.

Maureen O'Reilly Downey
Patrick Joseph Downey

Jean Scott Burnett
Archibald Wilson Burnett

CONTENTS

AUTHORS' NOTE

In the spring of 2011 we began work on a ten-hour television mini-series: *The Bible*. It would begin with the Book of Genesis and end with the Book of Revelation. As you can imagine, we were immediately faced with a massive creative challenge: how do we tell this story? More specifically: how do we transform a sacred narrative that spans thousands of years and features hundreds of individual stories into just ten hours of television?

We had one of two choices: either select dozens of short summaries and tell many brief stories; or, choose fewer characters and stories but make a much deeper emotional connection.

Clearly, we had to go with the second choice.

So we began the TV scripts, written by a team of writers under the guidance of many theologians, advisors, and biblical experts. Their combined expertise brought forth vivid spiritual and historical images. To our great joy, when we showed the scripts to others for technical and creative feedback, the resounding messages we heard over and over were "I've never been able to imagine these Bible stories so clearly in my mind," "I'm going to reread the Bible," and "You really should publish these scripts."

Initially we were resistant, but then we started researching. We came across startling facts like: half of Americans cannot name the first five books of the Bible, 12 percent of American Christians believe that Noah's wife was Joan of Arc, and many believe that Sodom and Gomorrah were a married couple. If our scripts had provided an impetus for people to want to reread the Bible and given them a clearer picture of these stories, then maybe by novelizing the scripts we could spark even more people to pick up the Bible.

Thus, we began the novel *A Story of God and All of Us*. We feel very inadequate to teach the Bible, and we are certainly not theologians. We are television storytellers. It will be easy for people to focus on how we have "compressed stories" or to find "theological inaccuracies." But on this point, we must be clear: we are not retelling the story of the Bible; it has already been told in the richest, fullest possible way, from the mouth of God and through His chosen prophets, students, and apostles. Instead, we are dramatizing some of these beautiful stories from our scripts.

We owe a huge debt of thanks to all the small army of script writers, our amazing production team, and all of our advisors and biblical experts. We also want to thank you for holding this novel in your hands. Our television miniseries will be seen by millions around the world, and it is our hope that the series together with this book will inspire many more millions to read and reread the greatest story ever told: the Bible.

Roma Downey and Mark Burnett
California, 2013

PROLOGUE

Until now, nothing exists. No universe. No life. No light. No dark.
No breath. No hopes. No fears. No dreams. No shame.
No sin.
Nothing.
There is only God. And God is Love.
Then, in an instant, God becomes the Creator.
"Let there be light!" His voice booms out over the great void.
A bolt of infinite brightness vanquishes the nothingness, creating the
heavens. And with that light comes wind, a raw blast sweeping across
the brand-new universe. Then water, unformed and seemingly endless,
soaks everything.
God parts the waters, creating the seas and sky and the land.
He decrees that plants and seeds and trees cover the land and that
there should be seasons. And stars in the sky. And creatures throughout
the land and waters.
Then God creates man in His own image. Then woman, because man
should not be alone. Their names are Adam and Eve, and they inhabit a
paradise known as Eden.
All this takes six days in God's time.
On the seventh day, God rests.

But God's perfect creation becomes flawed, despoiled by men and
women who turn their backs on their Creator. First Eve, then Adam,

then Cain, and on and on. Generations pass, and devotion to God has all but disappeared. Evil rules in the hearts of men and women. This does not please the Creator, who loves the earth and its people and wants only what's best for them.

So God is starting over. He is destroying mankind in order to save it.

Which is how it came to pass that a large wooden ship now bobs on a storm-tossed sea. It is night. A howling wind and pelting rain threaten to sink the homemade vessel. The scene inside the ship is one of complete chaos. An oil lamp swings from the ceiling and illuminates a birdcage filled with two brightly colored parrots. An old man named Noah struggles to maintain his seat on a bench that is affixed to one wall. His wife sits next to him. On the other side of the cabin, Noah's three terrified sons hold tight to their wives as the great ship heaves in the night. These bouts of terror are a daily fact of life for this extended family, but no one ever gets used to it.

Noah is suddenly hurled to the floor. He is not a sailor and has only reluctantly taken this journey. He hears, from belowdecks, the bellows of oxen, the whinnies of horses, the bleatings of sheep, and countless other animal cries of distress. There are precisely two of each type of beast and bird. Try as Noah might to muck out the stalls daily, the hold of the ark is a foul place, with little ventilation. Only a small row of windows on the upper deck of the vessel releases the stench of rotting grain and animal waste. It mixes with the dank humidity to form a cauldron of foul aromas. Those smells waft up through the decks to every clammy, claustrophobic room on the ark. The smells have not only seeped into the air that Noah and his family breathe, but into the fabric of their robes, the pores of their skin, and the simple meals they eat. If the storm would end, Noah could open a hatch and let in a fresh breeze. But this storm seems like it will never end.

A geyser of water spurts through a new leak in the hull. The women scream. Noah battles to stand and plug the hole. Outside the ship, a blue whale breaches. It is an enormous animal, and yet it is still dwarfed by Noah's ark.

Noah is a strong leader, a loving husband, and a good father. He keeps his terrified family calm by telling them the story of creation. A story he knows well.

"On the third day," Noah says calmly, "God created the land, with trees and plants—"

"Will we ever see land again?" asks the wife of Noah's son Shem.

Noah ignores her. "...with trees and plants and fruit. And—"

"Will we?" the woman insists. She is beautiful, and the fear on her face is made all the more distressing because of her innocent look. "Will we see land again?"

Noah's faith is at its very limit. Yet he puts on a brave face. "Of course." He continues his narrative, if only because it gives them comfort. "And on the fifth day...all the creatures of the sea..." He chuckles to himself as he hears the cries of the two monkeys belowdecks. Their cage is next to that of the peacocks. Hardly creatures of the sea! "And of the air," Noah adds, thinking of the doves and hawks living uneasily next to one another. "Then on the *sixth* day, all the creatures of the ground—which includes us! And we were granted paradise. Amazing isn't it? Paradise. But then..." Noah pauses, gathers himself. The thought of what he is about to say confounds him. Mankind once had everything.

Everything. But then...

"But then Adam and Eve threw it all away! They ate from the one tree in paradise from which they were forbidden to eat. That was all God asked. Nothing more. Don't—eat—from—this—tree. What could be easier?" Noah's soliloquy is hitting its stride, even as the storm grows fiercer. Thunder booms loudly, as if an explosion has punched a hole in the ship. "Wrong choices," he says bitterly. "Wrong decisions. This is the source of all evil—disobeying God. That's why, with one simple act of willful disobedience, Adam and Eve caused evil to enter the world. That's why we are on this ship. Because the evil that Adam and Eve introduced has spread throughout the world, and God is cleaning the earth so mankind can start all over." He looks around the small cabin at the few people who fill it. His story has taken their minds off the storm, and he feels encouraged to keep talking. "That's why God told me, 'Build an ark.'" Noah pauses, remembering the humor in that moment. "I asked, 'What is an ark?' God told me, 'It is the same as a boat.' And I said to God, 'What is a boat?'"

Everyone laughs. They have lived in a desert their whole lives—not much water, let alone a need to build a special craft to float upon it.

God described the ark to Noah. It would be designed and built according to specifications that God dictated. This enormous ship would hold two of each animal. Once it was complete, God would soak the world in a massive storm, flooding all the lands and killing all of God's creation. Only the people and animals aboard Noah's ark would live.

Noah built the ship, even though his friends mocked him and his own wife thought him a fool. Why, he was miles from the nearest water, with no way to launch his vessel. Yet Noah kept building, one nail and one board at a time, constructing pens to house the tigers and elephants and lions and rhinoceroses. His great ship towered above the desert floor and could be seen from miles away. Noah and his ark were a great joke, told far and wide, and many a man made the journey to see the ark—if only to shake their heads and chuckle at Noah's folly.

Then the first drop of rain fell. That first drop was not an ordinary trifle of rain, for it hit the earth with a mighty splat that portended the coming of doom. The skies turned from the clearest blue to gray and then to black. "Go into the ark," God commanded Noah. He obeyed and brought his family on board.

———

"I didn't need to be told twice," Noah reminds the rapt audience inside the small cabin. Each of them instantly remembers the race to get on board—while also remembering the heartbreaking sight of friends and neighbors now clamoring for a spot on "Noah's folly." But there was none.

The rains that poured down were unceasing. The waters grew higher as subterranean rivers burst up through the earth's surface. Great tidal waves surged across the land. Flash floods wiped away homes, markets, villages. People died by the thousands. The lucky ones were those who could not swim and drowned instantly. Those who knew how to stay afloat had time to ponder their fate, and that of their loved ones, before the waters pulled them under.

And as the land slowly disappeared, to be replaced far and wide by only water, Noah closed the hatch, knocked away the supports. Soon the water lifted his massive ship—which floated quite well, much to his relief—and they bobbed away, bound for only God knew where. But one thing was certain: God would save them from destruction, no matter how bad the storms and how high the seas.

Noah's story has had its desired effect. Everyone in the small cabin is now calm. Noah goes up on deck alone, and for the first time in what seems like months, the seas are calm. He knows the waters will soon recede.

The world starts over, thanks to Noah and his ark. God thinks of him as an upright man, and through him humanity is being given a fresh start. Through him, faith will be born. Through Noah, God will continue to embrace the world. Through Noah, God will execute his plan for mankind—a plan designed before the earth was created.

But before embracing the world, God will focus on a single nation of people who fear Him and honor Him and worship Him. In that nation will live a man upright and faithful, as is Noah. His name will be Abram. But that is all still to come.

Noah now revels in the warmth of the sun on his face. The ark is bobbing toward land, and he can already feel the floodwaters receding. Then he hears God's voice loud and clear, and he knows his journey is over.

"Come out of the ark," God commands.

The great door on the side of the ark is lowered. The animals pour out onto the dry land and quickly scatter.

God has saved the world by nearly destroying it. Noah was chosen to continue God's plans for humanity. But mankind is fickle, and destined to make the same mistakes once again, turning their backs on God and His all-encompassing love.

But God will act once again to save the world. For all time. But next time He will not need a Noah.

Next time He will send His only son.

This is a story of God and all of us.

PART ONE

A MAN NAMED ABRAHAM

Thousands of years ago, in the city of Ur, in modern-day Iraq, lives a man named Abram. He is a direct descendant of Noah, eight generations on, through the lineage of Shem. Abram is a vigorous seventy-five years old, with broad shoulders and a flowing beard barely flecked in gray. His wife Sarai is known far and wide for her great beauty, even though she is of the same generation as Abraham. The one sadness of their otherwise charmed life is that Sarai has not been able to bear children. One could never detect this sorrow from Abram's behavior. He is always quick with a smile, and forever has a "Peace be with you" on his lips.

Abram enters the great temple in Ur, where he is greeted warmly by friends. Ur is a city of many gods, and the temple walls are covered in elaborate symbols—an owl, a crescent moon, a snake, and the peaceful smile of a goddess. All around Abram, noisy worshippers gyrate and sway, consumed by the rhythm of a procession entering through the grand doors. A brightly painted wooden statue carried atop a litter is set down on a low altar, to which a live goat is tethered. The crowd chants louder and louder as a temple priest draws his sacrificial knife. The noise is deafening—shrieks, chants, thunderous cheers. The priest grabs the back of the goat's head and pulls it upward to expose the neck.

Abram would normally be absorbed in the ritual, but on this day, he hears a voice he has never heard before. It is speaking only to Abram; no one else in the temple can hear it.

"Abram." It is the voice of God. "Leave your country, your people, and your father's household, and go to the land I will show you."

Abram gazes up to the sky, his mouth open in shock as the unmistakable voice of God makes spectacular promises in exchange for the enormous demand.

The priest has cut the goat's throat, and presses his knife deep into its soft belly to reveal its liver. Abram sees none of that.

"I will make you into a great nation, and I will bless you. I will make your name great, and you will be a blessing. I will bless those who bless you, and whoever curses you I will curse. And all the peoples on earth will be blessed through you."

A lesser man would be puzzled. Or perhaps fearful. But Abram hears the call, which is why God picked him for the task He has in mind, just as He once chose the upright Noah. Abram stands in the frenzied temple, where the priest now holds aloft the goat's liver, not an ounce of doubt in his veins.

"Yes," Abram softly tells God, in a voice brimming with passion. "Yes."

It's one thing for God to instruct a man to leave his homeland, his friends, and the very lineage that has coursed through his family for generations, and it is another for a man to deliver this stunning news to his wife. Abram races home from the temple, eager to tell Sarai. He steps into their courtyard and sees his beloved nephew, Lot.

"Abram," Lot greets him.

Abram slaps a friendly hand on his shoulder and steps briskly toward the front door.

Lot's wife stands to one side of the courtyard, cleaning, as Abram sweeps through. She and her husband exchange curious looks: they recognize something is different about Abram. Very different. They both shrug.

Inside, Abram calls, "Sarai," and then yells: "Sarai!"

He finds his wife in the back of the house, kneeling before a small clay figurine.

Abram's voice is tender and comforting. "Fertility dolls? Fertility dolls? Do we really have need of fertility dolls? What use have they been? Have they brought us children?"

Sarai weeps, thinking she hears disappointment in his voice. "Abram, I've failed you. It is my fault we have not been blessed."

Abram remembers his good news, and takes his wife into his arms. "Sarai, we *are* blessed. Today, God has spoken to me."

"Which God?"

"*The* God."

Sarai pulls back, confused. Theirs is a world of many different gods and idols, each designed to fulfill a specific need. Placing faith in just one god is a tremendously risky act.

"I speak the truth," Abram promises. "He has chosen me. Chosen *us*."

"For what? I do not understand."

"He wants us to leave here."

"Leave? But our whole life is here."

"Yes, Sarai. Leave. We are going away from this city to a new land. And we will have children in that new land. Of that I am sure. God has promised."

Sarai wants to believe Abram. She desperately wants a child, and she would do anything to present her husband with a son. But the prospect of leaving their home and setting off into the wilderness is almost more than she can bear. She looks hard at Abram, torn by her love for him and her fears of what might happen if they leave the safety and security of Ur.

Abram understands. He is a compassionate man who loves his wife more than life itself. But he also knows they must do God's will. "Believe me, Sarai. Believe me. He spoke to me. Sarai, He promised. Think about that: God made me a promise. A covenant. And God always keeps His promises. We must have faith that He will lead us to a land of wonder."

Sarai has always believed that there was something remarkable about her husband. He is not the sort to make delusional claims. Although he is asking her to do something extraordinary, something unimaginable, she knows she must trust him.

Sarai squeezes Abram's hand and smiles. "Take us there."

Abram sets out with Sarai, his nephew Lot and his wife, and a small army of friends and servants that form their extended family. Among them is

Sarai's young servant girl, an Egyptian named Hagar. They travel north and west, following the ancient roads of what we now call the Fertile Crescent, trusting God to lead them to the land He has promised Abram. Their journey takes them through a city known as Haran and finally to a bountiful land of water and palm trees that offers a green oasis in an otherwise barren desert. But the land is not enough for all of Abram's party and their animals. Making matters worse, seeds of dissension are sown by Lot's wife, a jealous and small-hearted woman who chafes at Abram's authority for forcing her to relocate. It soon becomes a standoff, with Abram and his followers on one side, and the followers of his beloved nephew Lot on the other.

The situation finally explodes when two shepherds start a fight. Each believes the other is intruding on his grazing land. They roll in the dust, punching and gouging at one another. Lot sees them first. He races to the fight, his wife a few steps behind.

"Lemuel!" Lot yells to his shepherd. "Stop! Now!"

Lemuel reluctantly releases his hold on Amasa, one of Abram's shepherds. Amasa sneaks in one last punch and then dances back before Lemuel can retaliate. Both men gasp for air, their robes covered in dust and their faces scratched and bloodied.

Abram has heard the commotion and arrives on the scene. "What is happening here?" he asks.

"Your shepherd is stealing our grazing land," Lot's wife hisses.

"We need grazing land to feed our families," Amasa insists.

"So do we," argues Lemuel, who clenches his fists, ready to fight once more.

"This land belongs to all of us," Abram calmly tells the men. "God gave it to us to share."

Lot's wife is furious. She glares at Abram. "Then He should have given us more of it," she tells him. A stunned silence settles over the group. Not only is Lot's wife mocking Abram, she is also mocking God. She should apologize, or at the very least ask forgiveness. But she's not done.

"This can't go on," she tells Abram, before giving her husband a hard look. "Tell him what we've decided."

Lot is uncomfortable. He loves Abram like a father and cannot bear the thought of disappointing him. He swallows hard before saying what he must say. "Abram," he mutters hesitantly. "There are too many of us. And there just isn't enough land."

"But the Lord will provide," Abram replies, trying his best to appear upbeat. "Have faith!"

"In a God we cannot see?" laughs Lot's wife.

Abram pretends he doesn't hear those words. He looks into Lot's eyes.

His nephew will not meet Abram's gaze. "It's time to go our separate ways," Lot tells him.

Abram is horrified. "No. We must stay together."

Lot is about to speak, but his wife interrupts. "Stay and starve, old man? Stay and watch our shepherds kill each other over a blade of grass?"

This time Abram acknowledges Lot's wife, but only with a steely gaze. As loving as Abram can be, and despite his gentle reputation, he is also a hard man. Lot's wife withers under his glare, and her cutting tongue is instantly silent.

"Uncle," Lot says reluctantly. "We're leaving. We have no choice."

"But where will you go?" Abram says pleadingly.

"To the greener pastures, closer to Sodom."

"Lot, that is a cruel and wicked city. Those people have turned their backs on God."

"But at least they are not starving," Lot's wife snarls.

Abram stands alone on the top of a hill from which he can see miles in every direction. He is building an altar to honor God. Stone by stone, he builds, lost in the quiet meditation of labor. He sees the tents of his people in the half-empty valley below, the flocks settling in for the night, the great forests. He also sees Lot and his tribe in the distance snaking their way to the east, toward Sodom. It is a sad moment. The great land is bathed in the red light of dusk. Abram sighs. He loves this Promised Land that God has provided for him, and he revels in its many beauties. God spoke to him again after Lot's departure. Abram had listened like an obedient servant. "Lift up your eyes from where you are, and look north and south, east and west. All the land that you see I will give to you and your offspring forever."

Abram did as God told him, and building the altar for offering a sacrifice is a way to give thanks. But there is still a great deal of conflict in Abram's heart. He is deeply troubled by the departure of Lot, and of Sarai's recent use of fertility idols once again. Doubts about his leadership torment him daily.

To Abram, being chosen by God had seemed like a blessing. But now he knows it also means struggle. Abram places one last stone at the foot of the altar and then kneels in prayer. Weeks pass, and Abram continues to miss Lot. One day while in prayer at the altar, he gazes down upon the valley again, and is surprised to see a lone figure walking his way. It appears to be Lemuel, Lot's shepherd. And while he's still far away, Abram can see that he's limping and clutching his side.

Abram races down the mountain and walks quickly to the approaching figure. Lemuel staggers toward him, close to exhaustion. His clothes are in tatters. Dried blood covers his skin. His face is bruised and dirty. When he sees Abram, he stops and sways on his feet, as if about to collapse.

"What happened?" asks a stunned Abram.

"We didn't stand a chance. There were so many of them." Lemuel groans, sinking to the ground. "We got caught in a fight between local warlords. My flock is gone. Every last one."

Abram takes his goatskin from around his neck and hands it to the shepherd, who greedily drinks the water. He waits until Lemuel is through before asking his next question. He stares deeply into Lemuel's eyes, not once pausing to look away.

Lemuel knows what is on Abram's mind, and as he hands back the goatskin his voice becomes choked in grief. "Lot is alive," he says. "But he is their prisoner."

Abram is horrified.

"He helped me escape," Lemuel continues, "so that I could find you and come beg for your help."

Hagar, bright with youth and vitality, arrives with a bowl of water. She drips a cloth in the water and wrings it out, then opens Lemuel's tunic and swabs a gash in his side. As Lemuel winces with pain, he does not turn away from Abram. "You are our only hope," says the shepherd.

Later that night, Abram holds a council in his tent with Sarai and the families that came with him in search of their new home. The subject is war. "We will fight. We have many trained men among us," Abram tells the gathering.

"But Abram, my beloved," Sarai interrupts anxiously, "you are hardly soldiers."

"It doesn't matter. I made Lot come with us. I told him to trust in God."

"But Lot and his wife had their pick of the land. It was their choice to leave!"

Abram's mind is already made up. "They are family," he tells Sarai. "We have to help them."

The wife of Amasa, the combative shepherd, shakes her head. She is about to speak, to tell Abram that rescuing Lot would be folly. But before she can say a word, Amasa places a finger to her lips. He then stands and walks to Abram's side. The other men join him.

"We will return," Abram promises Sarai. He glances around at his brave men as they quickly prepare for battle and say good-bye to their families, not knowing if they will ever come back. Sarai is anxious and wraps her arms tightly around Abram's waist. She has tears in her eyes.

"I love you," she says.

Abram pulls away without saying a word. His love for Sarai is understood.

He is a solid man and a good husband. Abram reaches for his sword, whose sharpened blade gleams in the firelight. He holds the sword aloft to examine it for signs of weakness. His fists are strong and his forearms powerful. Seeing no imperfections in the sword, he slides it into his belt. "God will take care of us," he assures his wife.

There is power in his words, and the confidence in Abram's eyes makes Sarai's heart swell with pride, despite her fear. She places her hand softly on his face and pulls her to him. She kisses him desperately, knowing that this might be the last time.

Abram looks deeply into her eyes, then pulls away and steps out into the night. There's no time to waste.

Abram and his ragtag army creep carefully toward the enemy encampment. There would be guards posted if this was wartime, and the cooking fires would have long ago been extinguished. But these soldiers have just routed their foes, sending them fleeing into the hills and tumbling into the Valley of Siddim's tar pits. This is a time to make merry. They sit around their fires laughing and drinking. The prisoners they have elected not to kill sit in a circle on the ground, hands tied behind their backs. Lot's wife is being prodded with a spear by their guard. She cries out in pain, which only makes the soldiers leer in delight. Their time away from home and the comforts of a woman has been long. One, perhaps many, of these men will have their way with her tonight. Lot is tied up, his mouth tightly gagged, and forced to watch these men ogle and humiliate his beloved wife. His attempts to cry out in protest are fruitless, and only amuse the guards.

Abram sees all this from the perimeter of the camp. The size of his household has grown since he followed God's orders and set off in search of a new land. His army is made up of shepherds, some 318 of them. They are hardly soldiers of war, but are all skilled with a knife or an axe from years of chasing wolves away from their flocks.

Their enemies, on the other hand, number in the thousands. They are hard men, with scars and muscles earned from long days on the march and countless hours in hand-to-hand combat. These foes are trained and disciplined, and have just conquered the kings of Sodom and Gomorrah and their armies. Their bellies are full, and they are well rested. An attack on their camp would be suicide.

But Abram knows that his men have two things on their side: the element of surprise, and his deep faith in God.

As his men spread out along the camp's perimeter in the dead of night, Abram prays. He asks for God's blessing on their battle, and that he might have strength and confidence as he leads his brave men. As he prays, he can smell lamb being grilled on cook fires, wood smoke, pungent unwashed men, and the heavy, dusty aroma of the night itself. The smells make the battle more immediate. A still, small voice in his head reminds him that there is time to turn around and leave. Lot and his wife made a bad choice by abandoning Abram. No one would call Abram a coward for turning back now that the odds are apparent. Abram quiets that voice and finishes his prayer. He draws his sword, raises it into the air, and slices it in a forward motion—the signal for his men to stealthily launch their attack. A silent wave of shepherd soldiers floods into the enemy camp.

"Trust in God!" Abram roars. His army attacks. Abram and his men are clearly illuminated in the cooking fires. Abram draws first blood, plunging his sword deep into the stomach of an enemy soldier. The soldier cries out in agony, in an instant every head in camp turns their way. "Raaaaaaghh!" Abram screams, pulling his sword from the dead man and swinging immediately at another enemy soldier.

Others join the battle cry. A sword cuts the air next to Abram's face, missing him by inches. He pulls back, then plunges his sword into the man's side. The camp breaks out in chaos, as the enemy soldiers race for their weapons. In the confusion, the enemy cannot reach their tents to get their swords or knives. Abram and his men mow them down like grain being harvested, slashing and punching at the enemy. Abram was right about his surprise attack.

Abram steps over a pile of bodies toward where Lot is being held prisoner. "God is with us!" Abram whispers in his nephew's ear, as he slices the rope binding Lot's hands.

By now, the battle is turning into a rout. Enemy soldiers are running into the night. Many are chased down and killed by Abram's men, who know all too well that if these men are not slain they will ultimately come back and exact their revenge.

Lot's wife comes to her husband's side. She pulls him close and whispers to him, avoiding Abram's gaze.

"Lot," cries an ecstatic Abram. "Now do you see? So few against so many! This is a triumph for our mighty God."

But now Lot cannot meet Abram's gaze.

"What is it?" asks Abram. His gut tells him bad news is coming. But what bad news could they give him now, after this great victory?

Lot pauses, then looks downward at his wife, who nods. "Abram . . . Uncle . . . ," Lot stammers. These are the toughest words he has ever had to utter: "We're carrying on."

Abram looks from one to the other in confusion. "To where?" he asks. "Sodom."

"Sodom! You can't possibly be serious."

"We're going back into the city to live. We're better off there."

Abram's face darkens. This is not a look Lot has seen often, and he knows to fear it. Abram sweeps his arm wide, showing the bodies of the fallen. He knows them all by name. He knows their wives and their children, and knows that upon returning he must personally deliver the news of their deaths. They all fought well. It was a good fight. A just fight. Lot's decision renders it all in vain. Abram feels a deep sadness in his heart when he speaks: "Lot, hear me when I say this: men have died to save you."

"I know! And there is no way I can repay their loss. But I have lost men, too," rationalizes Lot.

"You would have been dead by morning," Abram tells him. "Your wife would have been the trophy of some unwashed soldier—and many of his friends. Don't tell me about the men you lost."

"Uncle, look, your God has not kept His promises. We can't eat faith. We can't drink faith. Faith will not clothe us."

"But it will, Lot. And God *is* fulfilling His promises, Lot. Didn't you see? My small army of untrained shepherds defeated a mighty force. How else would this be possible? I beg of you: come with us!"

"Why?" Lot's wife boldly steps forward. "What has your God promised?"

"A nation! A future! A family! A son!" replies Abram. He believes every syllable.

"Your wife will never bear a son," she sneers.

The words pierce him, and a devastated Abram remains silent.

Lot's wife continues: "What about food? Water? Shelter?"

Abram ignores her. He is exhausted. The battle rattled his nerves. And now this? He places his hand on Lot's shoulder. "Nephew. This time. We must stay together."

Lot's eyes are downcast, but his mind is made up. He places his hand on Abram's, and then gently removes it from his shoulder. "No, Uncle. We must go."

As the bodies of the wounded are loaded onto carts for the ride back home, Lot's wife tries to rationalize with Abram. "Come with *us*," she offers.

Abram looks deep into her eyes for what seems like an eternity. Then he turns in disgust and walks past his men. "Let's go," he orders them over his shoulder. Abram and his soldiers leave.

The air is heavy. Lot and his wife stand silently amid the slain enemy, knowing Abram will never again trust Lot.

Abram doesn't turn back. Instead, he sets his mind to the grieving widows he must console and the dead friends he will have to bury. The hardest part will be facing Sarai, and trying to explain to her how he could have let Lot and his wife continue on to Sodom after the staggering cost his men paid to rescue them. She has always trusted in his wisdom, but this time, Abram knows, he has let her down.

God has promised Abram a land flowing with milk and honey, and descendants as numerous as the stars. Abram's faith never wavers. He immediately does as God asks. He truly believes in God and His promises. Yet he has become frustrated by God's timetable. When will Sarai bear him a son? Or any child, for that matter? Abram's beard is now almost completely gray. And though aged, Sarai's beauty is still beyond compare—she is the living embodiment of a princess. The shared adventure of their nomadic lifestyle is enhanced by their many attempts to have a child, but the idea that Abram will truly be the father of many nations seems hopeless.

Abram stands alone in the cold desert night, staring up into the sky. A campfire burns down to its final embers. Wind rattles the tent behind him, where Sarai shivers as she sleeps. He thinks of the men slain in battle while rescuing Lot, and the futility of their loss.

"Abram," whispers Sarai, shivering as she emerges from the tent. The firelight illuminates her beauty. She is wrapped in a thick blanket woven of coarse fabric that protects her from the desert winds. But even covered by a blanket, her beauty takes Abram's breath away. "Come inside," she says lovingly, holding open the tent flap.

Abram is shivering. He sees the inside of the tent, and their bed, so warm and safe. But instead he turns from his wife, gazes up into the sky, and considers the enormity of the universe above and its millions of stars, as if comprehending the vast scope of God's creation for the first time.

Then he collapses.

"Abram!" Sarai screams, racing to him. When she looks into his eyes she sees nothing but his deep belief in God's promise.

"All the stars. Count them! Count them!" he shouts.

Sarai cradles his head, terrified that her beloved husband is losing his mind. She strokes his beard to calm him.

"Our Creator, who made the stars, will give us that many descendants!" he says with complete faith, reminding himself as much as Sarai of God's promises. The fire in Abram's eyes grows brighter as his revelation continues to unfold. "To populate our land! For us! And for our children!"

Now it is Sarai's turn to be downcast. "How long have we been praying for children?"

He doesn't answer.

She looks straight into his eyes and says three very hard words: "I. Am. Barren."

"But he has promised! You will have a child! You will!"

She shakes her head. "I can't. I won't. There is no chance for me to carry a child."

They hold a look between them. The silence is deafening. Finally Sarai speaks, slowly, softly, deliberately. "It is too late for me, but you are a man. For you there is still a chance." Sarai bites her lip. She pulls her husband closer. "God's plans are many, and His promises will always be kept—but in His own way. Who is it for us to say how God's plans will be fulfilled?"

"What are you saying?"

"I am saying that God has promised that you will be a father. He has not promised that I will be the one to bear your children."

Sarai nods toward the tent of Hagar, the beautiful Egyptian servant. The light of a candle flickers inside the tent. "Go to her, Abram," says Sarai. "Go with my permission."

Abram looks at his wife in disbelief. "No," he says firmly. "No. No. No."

Sarai nods, looking resigned. "Yes," she says, kissing him gently. "You must."

Abram is torn. He has always been faithful to Sarai, believing it to be

God's will that he sleep with no other woman. He has noticed Hagar's beauty but never once imagined sleeping with her.

Sarai cannot look at her husband as she gently pushes him toward her tent. "You need an heir," she says softly. "God has promised you a child. Now go."

Abram pulls Sarai's face to his, kisses her full on the lips, and pulls her body to his, so that she knows without a doubt that she is his true love. Then he slowly rises to his feet and walks to Hagar's tent. It is small, befitting her lower social status, the fabric not as bright or durable as theirs. She is from a different land, of other gods. Abram does not know God's ways. Perhaps God wants Abram to unite these other nations by fathering a child whose blood is mixed and whose lineage will blend the two separate religious traditions. He pulls aside the flap to Hagar's tent and steps inside.

The beautiful, barren Sarai takes a seat by the fire. A tear slowly falls from her cheeks as she stares into the flames.

As Abram emerges from Hagar's tent Sarai can see through the open flap that Hagar is asleep. Sarai is still sitting by the fire, slowly rocking herself back and forth. Sarai's eyes meet Abram's. Hers are puffy, and tears still roll down her cheeks. Both Abram and Sarai feel something is amiss, a heavy wrong weighs upon their hearts. Despite their best intentions, they may have been hasty, not trusting God.

Abram sees his wife's tears of jealousy and regret. She is not happy to have shared her husband with another woman. If he has indeed planted a child in Hagar, Sarai will never have Abram to herself again. Every time she looks at that child she will think of this night, this raw feeling of loss beating within her breast, and know she would give anything to do this night over again.

Abram is distraught. *What's done is done,* he tells himself. Momentarily, he sets aside the hard truth that he has forced God's promise of a child to take place on his own timetable, rather than trust in God's plan.

He pulls his shirt tight around his body and walks into their tent. His path takes him right by Sarai, who continues to stare into the fire.

His short time in Hagar's tent on this clear desert night will alter the world forever.

—————

Fourteen years pass.

Ishmael, the son of Abram and Hagar, is now thirteen years old. The boy is everything a father could want from a son: compassionate, loving, funny, strong, and handsome. Sarai doesn't always share Abram's joy. Whenever she looks at Ishmael she is reminded of that night so long ago when both she and Abram showed their lack of faith, tried to force God's promise and take matters into their own hands. What has gone through Sarai's mind again and again since that night is: God can do all things. That means He can make a barren woman pregnant, no matter what her age. She has known this all along. She should have trusted God's promise. She should have waited.

Abram is now ninety-nine years old. Sarai is ninety. They now live in an oasis near a place called Mamre—amid palm, cedar, and fig trees, and clear running water—still dwelling in the tents they have called home for so many years. This is not paradise, nor is it the land Abram envisioned when he and his followers struck out on their own so many years ago. There is plenty of dissension among his people, beginning with Sarai and Hagar. Everytime Sarai sees Hagar and Ishmael she feels a searing stab of pain in her heart. She is bitter. One hot afternoon, as Abram sits before his tent, the Lord appears to him. "I am God Almighty," he tells Abram, who falls facedown on the ground.

"I will confirm my covenant between me and you," God continues. "And I will greatly increase your numbers."

God orders that Abram change his name to "Abraham," which means "father of many nations." From now on, Sarai will be called "Sarah," for "princess." God also orders that all males of his tribe, which some call "Hebrews," be circumcised. The circumcision is a sign of the covenant between God and man, and a daily physical reminder of God's presence in their lives. Even Abram, at such an old age, must now have the foreskin sliced from his penis.

And then God makes an outrageous promise to Abraham: Sarah will give birth to a son. "She will be the mother of nations. Kings of peoples will come down from her."

Abraham laughs at the idea. He does not believe that Sarah can give birth. But God insists, and says that a long line of earthly kings will be brought forth from this lineage.

The words settle on Abraham's heart, filling him with a joy he has never known. He cannot wait to tell Sarah. And even though it feels utterly impossible that a man his age can father a child, Abraham also reminds himself that God can do anything—even bring this child into the world.

Abraham turns to God to offer his thanks. But God has already gone.

One day not long after, Abraham is practicing the bow and arrow with his son. Ishmael is a good shot, and he hits the target with ease.

"Well done, my boy," Abraham says proudly. He calls to Sarah: "Did you see Ishmael, Sarah? Did you see my boy?"

" 'My boy.' Not 'our boy,' " she whispers disdainfully under her breath. The old lady storms off into the tent. Abraham sighs. He has gotten used to the constant tension.

"Run along, Ishmael," he tells the boy. Hagar is off to one side, watching the scene with a mother's pride. She is happy that her boy will be Abraham's rightful heir, and she cares little about the tension between herself and Sarah.

Abraham stops to pick up the arrows and sees three powerful and mysterious men in the distance walking toward his camp. They wear robes made of fine fabric. On two of the men he can see the outlines of weapons beneath their garments, yet they do not appear menacing. Instead, they have the quietly intense presence of holy men. Abraham feels an instant connection with them, and as is his custom, he enjoys playing the part of the good host. Yet these men are somehow different, and he treats them with more respect. Travelers—mostly wanderers, wayfarers, vagabonds—pass through Abraham's camp all the time and receive only water and basic hospitality.

Abraham's instincts are correct. Two of the men are angels. The third is God disguised in flesh. Abraham has heard God's voice but does not recognize Him.

"Welcome," says Abraham. "You are most welcome. Please sit down." He indicates a spot where they can rest in the shade.

"Are you hungry?" he asks. Without waiting for an answer, Abraham orders a servant to bring food.

"Have you traveled far?" Abraham continues.

"Yes, a very long way," answers one of the angels. A long silence ensues.

"Where is your wife?" asks the other angel.

Abraham points to their tent. "In there."

Inside the fabric walls of their tent, Sarah hears strange voices, but she is weary and in no mood to entertain travelers.

The Lord then speaks and makes an audacious prediction: "I will surely return to you about this time next year, and Sarah your wife will have a son."

Sarah laughs to herself as she overhears this. Surely this man, whoever he is, does not know that Abraham's wife is very advanced in age and barren.

"Why did you laugh?" the Lord says to her.

Sarah almost jumps out of her skin. She whirls around to see who is speaking to her, but no one is in the tent. *I didn't laugh*, she thinks to herself.

"You did," the Lord says. His voice is kind. Once again, Sarah spins quickly to see who is playing this trick. But she is alone.

God continues: "So you will never forget how you doubted me when you have a son, you will name him Isaac, which means 'laughter.'"

Sarah feels the power of God and is overcome with hope. Tears stream down her face. She rushes to where she hides her fertility dolls, and grasps one tightly in her hands until it crumbles to dust. As the grains of clay slip through her fingers, she falls to her knees and thanks God.

The time comes for the three strangers to leave. Abraham has treated them with extreme kindness and deference. He has brought them water to wash the road dust off their feet. He has cooked them a fatted calf and fed them a sumptuous meal featuring curds, milk, and thin loaves of bread. These powerful, mysterious strangers are special, and Abraham has reveled in the honor of their presence. He referred to himself as their servant, and even stood off to one side as they dined, waiting to be summoned. The men have maintained their air of mystery, saying little else after their audacious prediction, as they enjoyed the food and the cool of the shade. As the afternoon sun grows cool they stand to depart.

"Where are you going?" Abraham asks cautiously, still unaware of whom he has been entertaining.

One of the angels looks to God for permission to answer.

God nods.

"We are going to decide the fate of Sodom," the angel replies solemnly, pulling his hood back up over his head. The other angel does the same, and they depart, leaving God alone with a concerned Abraham, for Lot lives in Sodom.

God walks with Abraham to a mountaintop, where they can look out and see Sodom in the distance.

"Shall I hide from you what I am going to do?" the Lord wonders aloud. "You will surely become a great and powerful nation, and all nations on earth will be blessed through you. For I have chosen him so that you will direct your children and your household after you to keep the way of the Lord by doing what is right and just, so that I will bring about for you what I have promised."

Abraham is stunned to realize that he stands in the presence of God. It can be no one else. This is the manner in which God has spoken to him so many times—honestly, and as a trusted friend and servant. And

Abraham is just as stunned to realize that the destruction of Sodom will mean the death of Lot. Despite their differences, Abraham loves Lot like a son, and is in dread for his safety.

Abraham musters up his courage and speaks to the Lord. "Will you sweep away the righteous with the wicked?"

"If I find fifty righteous people in the city of Sodom, I will spare the whole city for their sake," replies God.

Abraham considers that for a moment. He knows the ways of Sodom, which is the most evil of cities. He doubts there is a realistic chance of God finding ten righteous people, let alone fifty. So he takes a deep breath and speaks once again. "Now that I have been so bold as to speak to the Lord, though I am nothing but dust and ashes, what if the number of righteous is five less than fifty?"

The Lord loves Abraham, and their covenant is a powerful bond. So for the sake of Abraham, he relents. "If I find forty-five good men, I will not destroy it."

Abraham grows bolder, striving desperately to save Lot. "What if only forty are found there?"

"For the sake of forty I will not do it."

"May the Lord not be angry, but let me speak," Abraham says uneasily. "What if only thirty can be found there?"

"I will not do it if I find thirty there."

On it goes, Abraham bargaining for the people of Sodom while the Lord gently concedes, until Abraham reduces the number to ten righteous people. The Lord leaves. Abraham stands alone on the road, despairing for Sodom and his nephew. Because he knows, just as God knows, that his bold haggling with God is for naught. For there are not ten righteous people in all of Sodom.

In fact, there is just one.

Of course, God knows that. He has only bargained with Abraham as a testimony to their covenant. Abraham's fears about seeing Sodom destroyed show the depth of his compassion, and God is honoring that. Now it is up to that one righteous man to save himself and his family.

Lot sits alone at Sodom's city gate. Evening has fallen. The desert outside the walls is pleasant and fragrant, and a stark contrast to the city streets, which smell of stale urine and vomit. Lot loves to breathe the night air just out beyond these city walls. The breeze is cool after the long hot day, and he basks in the calm on this side of the city. He and his wife have two lovely daughters now. The city is infamous for its vice and depravity, a place of idolatry that has not only turned its back on God but celebrates that fact. Lot's wife finds the city very much to her liking, and has refused his numerous requests that they leave. He feels that life is too short to be so distant from God. Lot fears for his daughters, terrified that they will grow up to become as lascivious and faithless as the women of Sodom. It breaks his heart to imagine his gorgeous young girls living a life defined by lust instead of love, of fear instead of faith.

Lot sighs. There is nothing he can do about that. What will be, will be. Until the day his wife chooses to leave Sodom—a day that he believes will come—Lot must simply endure his life, rather than live it to its fullest.

As Lot sits alone at the city gates, gazing out into the vast desert, he can hear the music and raucous laughter spilling out of the taverns. He can hear the moans of men and women having sex in the dark, dingy alleys. Were he to turn around right now, he would be able to see a barely dressed young couple groping one another, nearly nude prostitutes pushing their wares, a band of drummers entertaining a group of drunks, and a feral dog tied to a post—snarling loudly at all who walk past, and more than eager to bite into human flesh. Hardly the place to raise a family. Lot is an honorable man, which makes him unusual in Sodom. The wickedness of the city troubles him greatly. It is why he comes to the city gates to gaze out into the desert.

Two men in great hooded cloaks march through Sodom's city gate. They are powerfully built and have the placid look of warriors who fear no man. They walk with purpose, as if they have come to Sodom on business. What type of business, Lot can hardly imagine. The two strangers look out of place on these streets. Lot's heartbeat quickens.

For the first time in quite a while he senses he is not the only righteous man in Sodom. Lot rises quickly and hastens to them. "Gentlemen," Lot exclaims, "welcome to Sodom. I invite you to spend the night at my home. You can wash your feet and enjoy a meal."

"No," they answer. "We will spend the night in the square."

Lot will not take no for an answer. And soon these spiritual warriors are entering his home, where he feeds them a simple feast before showing them where they will sleep.

Inside Lot's house, a dim oil lamp glows, illuminating the faces of Lot, his wife, his two teenage daughters, and these mysterious strangers.

Lot hears a huge commotion in the streets outside and suddenly, fists hammer on the door. Lot's wife and daughters hug one another, scared. "Open up! Send out the strangers!" screams a voice. "Or we'll burn the place down!"

"They've done you no harm and they are guests in my house. Leave them be," Lot yells through the thick wooden door.

"Where are the men who came to you tonight?" yells the voice, louder and more insistent than before. "Hand them over to us!"

Then Lot finds great courage within himself. He steps outside to face the people of Sodom, young and old in a mob, one man against many. He tries to reason with them, but they become even more aggressive. Inside, the strangers stand silently, listening to every word and admiring Lot's bravery. His wife clutches her daughters, wishing that she had never seen these strangers. Her life has once again been turned upside down.

Lot realizes his attempts to negotiate have proven futile and starts to retreat to the safety of his house, but the mob attacks. They surge past him and try to break down the door. Lot fends them off with a shepherd's staff, wielding it expertly. He's like a new man, full of fighting spirit. When the mob's leader grabs the staff and pulls it toward him—a sadistic look in his eyes—Lot doesn't let go, but his courage is no match for this man's strength. "Stay out of this, foreigner," the mob leader says, and spits in Lot's face.

"Stand aside," says one of the angels. He steps forward and closes his eyes, as if in prayer. The second angel joins him. A sudden, rushing wind fills the room and then spills out into the streets, accompanied by the low rumble of thunder. Fear replaces the snarl on the mob leader's face. Lot steps back, unsure of what is happening. The mob leader scratches wildly at his eyes, rubbing and prodding, until tears of blood stream down his face. "I can't see," he screams. "I can't see!"

But he is not alone. One by one, the other members of the mob scream in horror as they, too, are blinded. Those who can still see are even more enraged, and they push forward to exact their revenge. But hardly have they taken a step when the two angels shed their robes, revealing the most incredible suits of armor—honed by a craftsman, stronger than any lance a man might want to thrust through it.

One angel pulls two short swords from his scabbards and wields them like a man who more than knows his way around a blade. The other angel has no need for such subtlety. A great broadsword dangles from his hip, and he knows how to use it. With a single, swift move this angel slides the thick sheet of sharpened steel from his sheath with two hands and makes one of Lot's tormentors pay for his behavior. The man falls to the ground, and the other angel grabs for Lot and his family. "We must go!" the angel says calmly, implying haste.

Lot and his family hesitate; however, they have no choice. The angels forcibly drag them out of the house and pull them along by their shoulders through the mob, not giving them a chance to turn back or slow down. "Don't stop running!" screams the first angel. "Not for any reason." He leads Lot's family through the streets, and the other angel protects them from behind. The angels slash at the mob with their swords, felling one man after another in their mission to get Lot's family to safety. They know, as God knew when He bargained with Abraham, that the only righteous inhabitants of Sodom are Lot's family. God is about to destroy Sodom. Everyone in the city will die a horrible death, and the city itself will be lost to the ages. Unless Lot and his family get out quickly, they will also suffer this fate.

Suddenly, flames rain down from the skies. A fireball slams hard into the streets with a sudden wail and clap of thunder. Lot's wife is almost paralyzed with shock and feels the white heat of this incredible explosion, as the second angel forces her to stagger onward.

The mob continues to pursue them as another fireball slams into Sodom. And then another. The second angel stops running and uses the sharpened tip of his sword to draw a circle around him in in the dirt street. As Lot and his family continue their desperate race to freedom, he takes on all comers, hacking at them as if they were kindling wood.

Meanwhile, on a hillside overlooking Sodom, a horrified Abraham witnesses the flames shooting upward through the buildings as the city begins to burn. Fireballs continue to rain down from above, joined by lightning and the unnerving boom of thunder.

He fears for Lot and his family as he watches the terror and prays that his nephew will get out alive.

Behind him, unseen, stands God.

Back in Sodom, stone buildings are beginning to collapse. Fire has burned through the wood and the thatch of roofs. Falling beams have trapped many families in their homes, and the screams of those experiencing the agony of flame on bare skin pierces the night.

The second avenging angel has finally defeated all challengers and caught up with Lot's family. The first angel says, "In saving us, you saved yourself. Your decision to help us was a godly test of your righteousness. Run from the city and continue running. But remember this: Don't look back. Never look back. No matter what."

The angels disappear before the eyes of an amazed Lot and his family. They now stand in complete darkness, save for the light of the moon and the distant fire of a burning Sodom.

"Keep going," shouts Lot, "and don't look back."

They run and run and run, their feet kicking up the desert dust as they race on to a new life. A monumental burst of lightning suddenly illuminates the sky, cracking down into the remains of Sodom. Then, in one last brilliant explosion, the city is gone. Lot hears his wife gasp. He loves her dearly, but he knows her contrary and prideful behavior. Before she can make the one mistake the angels warned them about, he pleads with her, "Do not look back!"

But her curiosity is insatiable. She absolutely must see for herself what is happening to the city she has called home for more than a decade.

Her last sight is an explosion of light. Her eyes are blinded, her body becomes paralyzed, and she turns into a pillar of salt.

A hard wind blows. Lot stares in disbelief at what used to be his wife. He watches with an all-consuming grief as gusts of air blast the pillar of salt, and pieces soon chip off and disappear into the night. That gale does not stop blowing until the entire pillar is turned to dust and carried away.

Fearing the same fate, a terrified Lot and his daughters run for their lives. They don't dare look back. As if chasing them from behind, the continuing screams of the people of Sodom carry across the desert. The dawn breaks as they run. It's the start of a brand-new day, and a brand-new life, for Lot and his daughters. They run and they run and they run, across the desert and up into the safety of the hill country, where they will live for the rest of their days.

———

Time passes: from Abraham's camp comes the painful howl of a woman enduring the agony of childbirth. Sarah squats inside their tent, tended to by a midwife. Abraham paces nervously outside. He is ecstatic that his wife is bearing him a child.

Sarah's screaming stops, replaced by the sound of a newborn infant breathing its first gulps of air, then squealing so loud that its cries can be heard across the valley.

As Abraham steps forward to enter the tent, his eyes meet those of Hagar and Ishmael. The teenaged Ishmael is strapping and handsome, and bears a strong resemblance to them both. If the baby is a girl, Ishmael remains first in line of inheritance. If the newborn child is a boy, Ishmael will no longer be Abraham's rightful heir, according to Hebrew tradition.

Abraham pulls back the tent flap. A beaming Sarah holds their child to her breast. Abraham leans down to her. Without saying a word, she hands him the child. Tears well in the corners of his eyes as he holds the baby.

"A boy," Sarah whispers. She is radiant.

"Just as God promised," Abraham marvels. "Just as God promised. Only the Almighty can do the impossible."

Abraham holds the child aloft. "His name will be Isaac." He and Sarah burst into joyous laughter.

Outside the tent, Hagar and Ishmael hear the commotion, and know the baby is a boy without having to be told. Hagar wraps her arm around her son's waist, seeking to comfort him.

A year passes. The tension in Abraham's encampment grows by the day, though not between Ishmael and Isaac. The silent war for Abraham's attention and affection is between Sarah and Hagar, and each one begrudges every single instant that he spends with the other. Abraham walks a fine line each day as he tries to keep the peace between these two strong-willed women, but it is never easy. The tent of Abraham and Sarah is always pitched close to that of Hagar and Ishmael, so that the teenage boy can be close to his father. Every single word and gesture that Abraham makes is scrutinized.

Sitting in the shade outside her tent, a most content Sarah softly sings a lullaby to baby Isaac. The air smells of wood smoke from the cooking fires and the dusty tang of the desert. Isaac can walk now and is beginning to form words, but at this moment he is asleep in his cradle. Sarah feels that he is the most perfect creation in the world, and she cannot take her eyes off of him. Then she sees Abraham walk into camp and embrace Ishmael when he jumps to his feet and rushes to show off his new bow and arrows. Abraham turns the bow over in his hands, studying it for imperfections. Seeing none, he musses Ishmael's hair affectionately. "Good," he tells him, "very good."

Hagar sits on a pillow across from Ishmael, gazing at her son with the same loving expression that Sarah shows to Isaac. For Ishmael, she will do anything.

"Sarah!" he cries out, walking quickly toward their tent. He doesn't see the hurt look on Ishmael's face as he abruptly shifts his attention from the boy to Sarah.

Abraham ducks into the tent and steps inside. Sarah is facing the tent entrance, still hugging Isaac as she sits on a thick pillow. She is in a dark mood—that much Abraham can tell in an instant. "What's wrong?" he asks innocently, even though he knows quite well what's troubling Sarah.

"That woman thinks her boy is going to inherit what rightfully belongs to Isaac," she hisses.

Abraham once again feigns naiveté—as if the question of inheritance has never crossed his mind. "What do you mean?"

"Who is to be the first of all our tribe, Abraham? The first star of all those stars in the heavens?"

Abraham steps to within inches of his wife so that their words can be private. "This is not something we need to discuss right now."

"Oh, yes we do. Is it to be *our* son? Or hers?"

Abraham struggles to respond. "Sarah, I—"

"You decide! Now! Do you understand me?"

Isaac gurgles the word "Ma-ma," as is if he is eager to join the conversation.

Sarah looks hard at her husband. They have been through so much together, but it is as if she is looking at him for the first time. "Either you decide," she tells him in a steady yet angry voice, "or let God decide." She storms out of the tent, carrying Isaac on her hip.

Abraham, feeling the considerable weight of that long-ago night with Hagar, sits down and ponders the fate of his two young boys. He prays for God's guidance and receives it. Though he overflows with sadness at the mere thought of it, he knows that he must follow the instructions that God is now placing upon his heart. God tells Abraham to listen to Sarah. The inheritance will go to Isaac. That is God's decision. It means that there is no more place for Hagar and Ishmael in his camp, but God reassures Abraham that they will be taken care of, and that the children of Ishmael will also become a great nation.

Abraham is devastated as he delivers the news that Ishmael will have to go out into the world and make his own fortune, but that does not compare with how he feels as Ishmael and Hagar prepare to set out into the wilderness. It's morning. Flat bread is turned over a low cooking fire. Hagar slips the two warm loaves into a small sack. Ishmael comes to help. He is quiet and sad, but devoted to his mother. Ishmael will travel in just sandals, a scarf atop his head, and a knee-length robe. Hagar is dressed much the same, but with a hooded smock that will keep away the desert chill.

Abraham waits at the edge of camp, holding a skin of water. He places the strap over Ishmael's shoulder and let's his hand linger tenderly on his son for a moment. "Good-bye," he mumbles, overcome with sadness, then looks Ishmael in the eye. "My boy, God will one day bless you with many children." His own eyes fill with tears.

Ishmael says nothing, though his eyes study Abraham's features, memorizing his father's appearance. The boy is stoic. Sarah stands off in the distance. This is being done at her insistence, and she knows full well that her demands might lead to the deaths of Hagar and Ishmael. She knows she created this problem in the first place by insisting that Abraham sleep with Hagar. So this is her solution. She is surprised to find that she does not take delight in forcing Hagar and Ishmael out. Sarah knows it needs to be done. This may be a cruel act, but she is not a cruel woman. For if this is not done, grave trouble could arise when Abraham's two boys grow to be men.

Abraham and Sarah watch as Hagar and Ishmael begin their journey. One moment, they are specks in the distance, then they disappear.

"Be brave," Hagar tells Ishmael, though she is saying it to herself as well. The two of them will wander out into the desert alone, yet she trusts God to protect them. Hagar prays to God for help, and God provides it. Less than a week into their journey, they will run out of water, and Hagar will fear for their lives. An angel of the Lord will appear to them at that time, promising that Ishmael will one day become the leader of a great nation. When the angel departs, a well filled with water will suddenly appear to Hagar and Ishmael, saving their lives.

Ten more years pass.

Isaac emerges from his family's tent, with its tasseled doorway and striped fabric walls. He yawns and stretches as he makes his way past the goat pen and over to the cooking fire, where Sarah grinds grain to make flour for the morning bread.

Abraham has been awake for hours. His age is truly beginning to show, and though he slept the night through, he is extremely tired. Weary. Life has not been the same since he sent Hagar and Ishmael away. Abraham sees his life slipping away. He doesn't feel like the leader God intended him to be. He doesn't feel worthy of God, of the Promised Land, or the prospect that his descendants will be as numerous as the stars. His faith has not wavered, nor has he veered from God's plan since that long-ago night when lack of trust sent him into Hagar's tent. As he gets older with each passing day, Abraham ponders his purpose.

The wind picks up and blows the grain into the fire. The wind grows louder. Abraham looks all around, and notices that he is all alone. Everyone in the camp, including Sarah and Isaac, has disappeared.

It has been a long time since God spoke to Abraham, but he still knows the voice well. "A sacrifice?" he whispers to God.

It is common for Abraham to offer sacrifices to God. In a ritual slaughter, an animal's throat is sliced, and then offered up as a sign of thanks. The animal is then burned over an open fire.

God continues telling him the details.

At first Abraham doesn't comprehend what he's hearing. Then, as he realizes what God is saying, he becomes horrified. "No," he whispers. "Please, no. Haven't I shown enough faith? Dear God, I will make any sacrifice You ask. Anything"—now he can barely speak—"anything but Isaac."

It is God's will. With a heavy heart, Abraham retrieves his best knife from his tent. He and his people are camped at the foot of a great desert peak, Mount Moriah. As the sun rises higher and higher in the sky, Abraham sets off in search of Isaac, his knife firmly secured in the sheath on his waist.

He finds him eating bread with Sarah. "Eat more," she encourages the boy. "How will you ever grow if you don't eat?" But she stops talking as Abraham draws near. She sees confusion in her husband's eyes—confusion laced with determination. Something is about to happen, of that she is sure.

"Abraham?" she says cautiously.

"God wants a sacrifice," Abraham says, offering a hand to Isaac. He trembles as the boy places his palm in his father's meaty fist. "Come with me," he commands.

"Of course," Isaac says brightly, and then rushes off to gather his bag for the long and arduous trip up the mountain.

Abraham leads his son up Mount Moriah, leaving behind a confused Sarah, who assumes that Abraham will take a sheep from one of the pens to offer as a sacrifice.

Storm clouds are rolling in, and Abraham and Isaac can hear the faint boom of approaching thunder. The two gather wood for a fire along the way, and with each twig and branch that Isaac presents to his father,

Abraham finds himself more and more distraught about what he is about to do. Isaac, the trusting and obedient son he believed would begin a dynasty, must be killed. Isaac, the son he and Sarah prayed for, must be killed. Isaac, the handsome and brave apple of Abraham's eye, must be killed. God has demanded this beautiful, innocent boy as a sacrifice.

"Father?" Isaac asks, handing him a new handful of twigs.

Abraham takes them. "Good work," he tells his son. "Let's get more."

Soon, the bundle is so thick that Abraham wraps it in rope and straps it to Isaac's back so they can carry it easier. Abraham soon makes another bundle, which he shoulders for the hike to the summit. "Enough sticks," he tells Isaac. "Let's just get up there."

"But why are we going directly the top?" Isaac asks. "We have the firewood for the sacrifice, but we still need to go back down and get the lamb."

Abraham sighs. His heart is heavy. "God will provide the sacrifice, my son."

At the camp, Sarah has become so troubled that she goes to the sheep pen and counts the flock. They are all there. Suddenly, horribly, she realizes Abraham has not taken a lamb with him. She falls to her knees. Could the sacrifice be their beloved son? Could Isaac be the Lamb of God? She rises to chase after them.

Up on the mountain, the storm grows more fierce. The sun, strangely, is completely white, then the sky turns black. Winds swirl. Clouds seem low and thick enough to touch. Abraham knows there can be no greater sacrifice than for a father to offer his son. This is the most difficult test of faith he has ever endured. Abraham loves God, but he is not sure he can do it.

Hands shaking, Abraham sets down the wood and begins making a stone altar. Using the rocks that litter the mountaintop, he carefully arranges a structure on which to lay the sacrifice. Stone by stone, Abraham builds the altar. He has done it countless times in the past, so the work goes quickly.

Once again, Isaac asks, "Father, where is the sacrifice? Will it be a lamb today or a ram?" He is puzzled because they have not brought a small animal with them, and he sees none atop the mountain.

"*Jehovah-jireh*," responds Abraham hopefully, invoking a common phrase meaning, "The Lord will provide."

When the time comes to do what he must do, Abraham powerfully grips his son's hands and begins tying them together with rope. Isaac struggles, but only for a moment. Abraham fixes the boy with a gaze that freezes Isaac on the spot, making him too scared to disobey.

"You must trust God," Abraham says, choking in anguish on the words.

Isaac, in all his confusion, nods. Abraham continues binding Isaac's hands. He then lifts Isaac and sets him down upon the altar. A fierce wind blows at Abraham. Isaac looks at the knife in his father's hand, terrified. Abraham looks to the sky, uncertain of why he must do what he is about to do. He lifts his knife with two hands, and raises it high above his head. He pauses, knowing he is about to plunge the blade deep into his son's throat.

Isaac looks up, breathing in short, sharp gasps. His eyes are open wide in horror.

Abraham feels his hands tighten around the knife handle. He wants this to be over quickly and painlessly. Isaac must not suffer.

He takes a deep breath and plunges the knife downward.

"Abraham!" a voice calls out to him.

He stops midstrike, the knife precariously frozen a few inches above Isaac.

The voice is that of an angel, whom Abraham sees standing off to one side of the altar, near a bush. "Do not hurt your son," the angel tells him. "You have proved that you have faith in God. The Lord will bless you with descendants as numerous as the stars in the heavens."

Abraham turns from the angel to look at Isaac. Father and son are both crying as he unties the ropes. Isaac looks off to where the angel stood. But the angel is not there anymore.

Instead, as Isaac and Abraham stare in disbelief at the bush, they are stunned to see a small white lamb tangled in its branches. God has delivered the sacrificial lamb.

Sarah, meanwhile, is racing up the mountain to try and stop Abraham before it is too late. But she is old, and her pace is not fast. In her heart, she fears that the outcome is inevitable, and that she will never see her beloved Isaac again. Her beloved boy, for whom she waited one hundred long years, will be no more. Yet she pushes onward, never once stopping to rest. She breathes heavily and prays for the life of her child. Finally, she takes one final step and reaches the top.

Sarah sees the head, the eyes, and then the beautiful beaming smile of her Isaac. He is alive. Isaac runs to his mother, followed by Abraham. Sarah envelops her boy in her arms, all the while sobbing and shouting praise to God.

Abraham joins in the embrace. His faith in God has been tested, but he has most definitely passed that test.

Years after his death, Abraham's grandsons will found the twelve tribes of Israel—so called because their father, Jacob, is also known as Israel. This does not ensure harmony throughout the land, or even a powerful kingdom, for there is great bitterness and rivalry among the brothers. The greatest portion of that interfamily envy is directed at Joseph, the eleventh son. Jacob makes no secret of that fact that seventeen-year-old Joseph is his favorite. The other brothers are secretly plotting ways to edge him out.

A symbol of Jacob's love for Joseph is a splendid and expensive multicolored robe. Jacob lacks the sense to treat all his sons equally. Just as Abraham once discovered, every group, large or small, needs wise leadership—and this is where Jacob is found wanting. Given to Joseph as a gift, the robe has come to signify all that the brothers loathe about him. It would be wise for Joseph not to wear the robe at all, but he cannot help himself. This only makes his brothers more furious.

Now, in the fields outside the family estate, the brothers gather around

Joseph. They trip him, and then circle around him as he lies in the dust. Simeon, one of the older brothers, angrily pulls at the elaborate coat.

"We'll have that," he demands.

"No," Joseph answers defiantly.

This is followed by the sound of fabric being ripped. All the brothers laugh and pull eagerly at the coat as Joseph cries out in anguish. They push his face down into the dirt. Their sandaled feet kick dust upon him. The situation is rapidly spinning out of control as it becomes obvious that Joseph's brothers mean to do him even greater harm. "I'm going to kill him," vows Simeon.

"No," says Reuben, another of the brothers. "We must not spill our brother's blood."

No one knows what to do, but they also know they cannot stop what they have started. Joseph is dragged by the arms across the rocky ground, choking on dust and fearing the worst.

"Look!" cries Judah, yet another of the brothers.

Joseph peers into the distance, and instantly knows his fate. For he sees a line of pack animals and a single-file line of men roped together. This is a slave caravan, headed through Israel on its way to Egypt with a fresh cargo of men to sell.

Soon, an incredulous Joseph watches as a bag of coins is thrust into Simeon's hands. The slavers grab Joseph and slip a length of rope around his wrists and neck. Now dressed in nothing but a ragged loincloth, he stumbles in the sand. But that rope around his throat soon yanks him forward.

Joseph's brothers feel no sadness as they watch their sibling being led into a life of slavery. What's done is done. Now they must find a way to conceal their vile act from their father.

Joseph's tattered robe lies on the cracked earth. Simeon and the other brothers drop the blood of a dead goat upon the robe until it is drenched.

Then, adopting their most solemn and forlorn faces, the brothers approach their father with some very bad news.

Simeon pulls back the flap to Jacob's tent and presents the robe to his father. "No...," Jacob says, a smile vanishing from his face. He puts his hand through one of the holes in the fabric. "A wild beast did this?"

Simeon shrugs helplessly. "It must have been. We didn't see what happened."

"Why?" Jacob yells to the heavens. "Why, O Lord?"

He buries his face in the robe. Benjamin, at ten years old the youngest of his sons, looks on helplessly. He has been sworn to silence and knows better than to cross his brothers. Jacob's face, now smeared in blood, is soon riven by tears. His son is gone. Forever.

Joseph is sold to a wealthy Egyptian family, and would appear to be ensured a life of ease. But when he resists the romantic advances of his owner's wife, she lies and tells her husband that it was Joseph who was being improper—not she. Joseph's life seems to go from bad to worse. He is cast out of the house and thrown into prison. Time passes, and he becomes gaunt and filthy from months in the squalid and barbaric conditions.

Yet Joseph is an optimistic and a warmhearted man, even in the toughest of times. He soon becomes friends with his cellmates, both of whom once worked in the royal palace—one as a cupbearer, the other as a baker. Joseph has a gift for listening to God, prayerfully and intently. This allows him to interpret the meanings of dreams. During his time in prison, Joseph is not afraid to share this gift by deciphering the dreams of his two companions.

"And what does my dream mean?" the baker asks him one morning. The three men sit on the grubby cell floor, chains clanking whenever they try to move. "The one with the birds and the baskets?"

Joseph closes his eyes to concentrate. "You were carrying three baskets of bread?"

"Yes! Then the birds attacked me and ate the bread!"

Joseph focuses. "In three days' time..." He lifts his head and looks hard at the baker. "You will be executed," Joseph informs him solemnly. And to the cupbearer, "You will be freed."

The execution comes to pass, just as Joseph predicts. The cupbearer is soon released from prison, leaving Joseph alone in his cell. He spends his days on his knees in prayer, trying to divine God's plan for his life. Man's relationship with God seems impossible to fathom, but Joseph feels as if God is watching over him.

Light floods into Jospeh's cell one day, as a jailer steps in to wash the filth from his body. Joseph's heart sinks, for he knows that being bathed can mean only one thing: an appointment to see the Pharaoh—which, of course, also means execution.

Soon Joseph's hands are bound behind his back. He is led out of the jail and into the Pharaoh's throne room. A foreigner, a prisoner, and a slave, Joseph knows that his life has no value to the Pharaoh. And yet he stands tall, placing his faith in God.

Pharaoh enters the room and sits on his throne. He nods and Joseph hears the clank of a sword being pulled form its scabbard. But instead of feeling its sharp tip press against his back, Joseph is stunned to feel the ropes being cut from his wrists. The flat of the sword then smacks against Joseph's legs, driving him down onto his knees.

The cupbearer whom Joseph knew in prison steps forth and offers the Pharaoh a drink. Pharaoh accepts, sipping slowly and thoughtfully from the gold goblet before clearing his throat to speak. "I've had strange dreams," he tells Joseph. "My magicians can't explain them. But I'm told that you can."

"No," Joseph says, his face pressed to the ground. "God can. Through me."

"Whose god?" Pharaoh asks, his voice dripping in scorn. "Your God?"

Joseph dares to look up. "What is your dream?" he asks boldly. The flat of the sword smacks him on the back of the neck, forcing him to gaze down once again. This is where he stays as he listens to the Pharaoh describe his dream.

"I was by the Nile," begins the Pharaoh, "when out of the river came seven cows, fat and healthy. Then seven thin, ugly cows swallowed them whole. Then I had a different dream. Seven full heads of wheat, glowing in the sun—then quickly eaten by seven rotten ones, thin and scorched by the wind." He drinks thoughtfully. "Can your God explain that?"

Joseph is silent, lost in prayer. He waits patiently for the voice of God. Just as Pharaoh is about to lose all patience, Joseph speaks, his gaze still directed at the stone floor. "The cows and grain are all the same," he says.

"What do you mean?"

"There will be seven years of plenty. But then seven years of famine. You must store food in preparation for that day."

"There will be no famine," the Pharaoh says imperiously. "The Nile always feeds our crops. Every year, without fail."

"You don't understand: there *will* be famine." Joseph stops abruptly, almost choking. The tip of the sword is suddenly under his chin. It forces him to raise his face and gaze upward at a most furious Pharaoh.

"You contradict the Pharaoh?"

Joseph speaks carefully, knowing that his next words could be his last. "You contradict your dream."

"Go on."

"Store grain. Store a portion of the harvest when it is plentiful. Otherwise your people will starve. This is the meaning of your dream."

Pharaoh rises and steps down from his throne. "I am impressed by your conviction. You are set free, but on one condition."

"What is that, Pharaoh?"

"You will be in charge of telling the people to store their harvest."

Joseph's prophecy is proven correct. Thanks to the supreme power given him by the Pharaoh, Joseph is able to force farmers throughout Egypt to store their crops. This averts a national famine when hard times come.

For Joseph, this dramatic change of fortune is divine providence. He will forever remember it as a reminder that there is always hope, even in the darkest moments. Thanks to his success, he assimilates into Egyptian society. A signet ring is place upon his finger. Eyeliner decorates his eyes, preventing the sun's strong rays from burning them. He wears a black, straight-haired wig, and his chin is always smoothly shaved.

Joseph soon becomes one of the most powerful men in Egypt, second only to Pharaoh in prestige. He even takes the Egyptian name of Zaphenath-Paneah. Thanks to Joseph, Pharaoh's wealth increases massively—though at the expense of many Egyptians, who are forced to sell their land to survive the famine.

And it is not just Egypt that suffers through the seven-year drought. The people of neighboring nations feel the pain as their crops wither and die. Thousands upon thousands of foreigners flood into Egypt, which has become legendary for its well-stocked granaries. Among them are Joseph's brothers, sent there by Jacob to purchase grain. To do anything less would mean the end of their lineage, for they would all starve in Israel.

So it is that Joseph sees his brothers in a crowd as he makes his way by chariot through a crowded city street one day. He immediately orders that they be sent to his palatial residence. Joseph has never talked about the painful method in which his brothers changed his life, but he has also never forgotten. Now he has the ability to change their lives—for better or worse—as they once changed his.

Joseph's brothers are led into a formal drawing room by armed guards. The flat of a sword strikes Simeon on the back of the legs as a reminder to kneel. Joseph enters the room with all the regal grace he has learned during his long rise to power. In his black wig and eyeliner, he is unrecognizable to his brothers.

They cower as Joseph studies their faces. He can do anything he wants to them right now: imprison them, enslave them, and even have them killed. Yet Joseph's thoughts are always upon God. He shows his brothers the same love and mercy God has always shown him, particularly when times were so hard that hope barely flickered in his soul.

"Feed them," Joseph orders.

His brothers are incredulous. This act of kindness goes beyond their wildest dreams. As soon as they are able, the brothers make their way out of the room. Outside, their donkeys are being loaded with heaping bags of grain to take home to Israel. Not once do they suspect that Joseph is their brother.

But Joseph is not done with them. His kindness comes with a price, for he wants to know whether or not his brothers have changed their ways and learned compassion for others. Joseph has contrived a test: hidden within one of those bags of grain is a silver goblet. Guards have been instructed to slice open the bag and reveal this cup and charge his brothers with theft. This is where the test begins.

Everything goes according to plan. Simeon, Judah, Benjamin, and the others wait patiently as their donkeys are loaded with sacks of grain. A guard pretends to notice something suspicious when it comes time to leave, and slices open a bag to examine the strange bulge. When the silver cup falls onto the ground, Joseph's brothers are grabbed and immediately marched back to stand before Joseph.

The ten brothers kneel once again, this time even more terrified than before.

"I am told that this man is the guilty party," Joseph tells them, staring at Benjamin. He has carefully selected this youngest brother to blame, for he alone among his brothers was blameless when Joseph was sold into slavery.

"Benjamin would never steal," Simeon begs.

"Silence!" barks Joseph. "Go home. All of you. But this one stays—as my slave."

The brothers all raise their faces, begging together. "No!" they cry out. Please! We beg of you!"

Joseph surveys them with amusement. "We cannot leave him," protests Judah.

"It would kill our father!" agrees Simeon.

"I will be your slave instead," adds Judah. To which Simeon protests that he should be the one taken into slavery.

"Silence!" Joseph commands once again. He struggles to remain composed. All the brothers fearfully press their faces to the floor. With a wave, Joseph dismisses all his guards. They leave. He stands alone, towering over his brothers.

"Bring our father here," he says in a hoarse whisper.

A mystified Simeon sneaks a look at Joseph, who has removed his Egyptian wig.

"Joseph?" asks a stunned Simeon. The others raise their eyes.

Joseph has longed so many years for this moment. "What you did to me was wrong," he tells his brothers. "But God made it right. He watched over me. I have saved many lives, thanks to Him."

———

The brothers do as they are told, returning home and bringing Jacob to Egypt so that he might be reunited with his son. The entire family is together again—all of Israel's children. But they are in the wrong place, and they know it. For while they now live in luxury, this is not the land that God promised Abraham.

Even worse, over the generations that will follow, the drought that Joseph predicted means that thousands upon thousands are forced to leave. The people of Israel willfully travel to Egypt in source of food, then adopt this terrible new lifestyle just to stay alive. They build the great palaces and monuments of Egypt, working all day under the blazing desert sun. They are slaves of a great Pharaoh.

But they will be saved by a murderer, an outcast, and a man who will have the most extraordinary relationship of all with God.

This man's name is Moses.

PART TWO

EXODUS

Almost five hundred years have passed since Abraham died. The banks of the Nile River are drenched in blood. The descendants of Abraham are hundreds of miles from the Promised Land, and a generation from ever setting eyes upon it. They are slaves in the land of Egypt, but they are also a proud and hard people. As God promised, they have become as numerous as the stars in the skies—so numerous, in fact, that a new form of evil is visiting them: infanticide. The Egyptian Pharaoh has become fearful that his many Hebrew slaves will rise up and rebel against his authority. So he has sent his soldiers throughout the land—village to village, house to house—to kill every Hebrew boy.

Mothers wail as their infant sons are snatched from their hands and carried off in broad daylight. The grisly sight of pushcarts filled with screaming baby boys is commonplace. But they will not scream for long. Egyptian soldiers merely throw these swaddled young infants into the Nile, where they either drown or make a quick meal for the legendary Nile crocodile.

Yet one brave Jewish woman is taking extraordinary measures to save her child. For three long months she has successfully concealed her boy from the Egyptian soldiers. Now she fights for her baby's life by wrapping him in a blanket and concealing him in a basket. The simple basket, known as a *tevah*, which means "ark," is this nameless mother's version of Noah's ark. Just as God sent Noah to save the world, she has fashioned a second ark that will carry a boy who will become a man and continue the job that Noah had begun.

Then comes the hard part—so hard that she cannot bear to witness it herself. Instead, she sends her daughter, Miriam, to hide the basket in the reeds along the Nile's edge, knowing that the number of terrible things that might happen to her child is almost endless: crocodiles, six-foot-long cobras, the deadly asp. And, of course, the infant boy could be swept away on the current, leaving Miriam to helplessly stand on the shore and watch her brother float off to his death.

Miriam doesn't want to do this, but she has no choice. Either she hides her brother in the reeds, or he is sure to die at the hands of Egyptian soldiers. Better to do something—even something foolish—than to let her brother be pulled from her mother's breast and hurled into the dark blue waters of the Nile. Now she watches helplessly. She tries to remain calm as she follows the little ark along the water's edge.

Every morning, the Pharaoh's daughter Batya is in the habit of stepping down to the Nile with her maids to bathe. There she removes her diaphanous robe and steps into the water. On this morning her face is serene in the morning light. Miriam, who has been watching the progress of her brother's basket, bites her lip in anticipation as the tevah holding the boy bobs nearer and nearer to where the princess wades.

The current carries the basket right into Batya's head as she glides through the water. Miriam, hidden behind the reeds on the water's edge, follows the ark. The princess covers herself as she stands up in horror and backs toward the shore. Her maids are hysterical, which is quite a cacophony, for there are more than a few of them, and they are all prone to squealing and wailing.

Miriam cannot rush to her brother's defense, but knows that unless someone retrieves the basket, it will be swept downstream.

A startled Batya does nothing. The tevah slips farther and farther away. Then she hears a baby cry. "Be quiet, all of you," she commands her maids, as she makes a long, stretching reach for the basket.

Miriam's heart soars as Batya lifts the young boy from the basket and clumsily attempts to cradle him. Batya is too young to have a child of her own, knows nothing about holding or taking care of a baby, and immediately grasps that this child is not an Egyptian, but an Israelite slave.

"Please put it back, my lady," beseeches a maid, as if the infant is a dangerous being.

Miriam, a girl of great faith, knows nothing of Batya's character, and begins to pray. If the princess is mean, evil, or simply goes along with Pharaoh's wishes, she could hurl the child out into the current. Miriam prays for intervention, that God would touch Batya's heart and spare her brother's life, so that she can bring her mother good news. "Please God," begs Miriam. "Please don't kill him. Please don't kill him. Please God...help him."

God hears Miriam's prayer.

Batya smiles at the baby boy. "This one lives," she proclaims, pulling the child to her bosom.

"But what will the Pharaoh say?"

"Let me deal with the Pharaoh. This is my boy now. And I shall name him Moses." *Moses*, the Egyptian name meaning "drawn out of the water."

Miriam approaches, driven by the fear that she will never again see her brother. "If it pleases you, Highness, I can find a wet nurse for the boy," she says. For the enslaved to even speak to a member of the royalty is absurd, so for Miriam to be so bold is astounding.

Yet the Pharaoh's daughter sees the wisdom in this plan. "Do this at once," she commands.

Miriam rushes to her mother and tells of Moses' new home and the need for a wet nurse. Her mother cries out in joy. Her son will live.

Eighteen Years Later

Prince Moses stares straight forward as his maidservant applies the black kohl eyeliner that will protect his eyes from the sun's rays and harmful desert dust particles. Moses is a muscular young man, full of ideals and optimism. He has grown up in the Pharaoh's court as a surrogate grandson and never known a day of fear, worry, or hardship. His every wish is granted and every whim catered to—most unlike the Hebrew slaves who toil for Pharaoh, from whom he is unknowingly descended. Few know Moses' true story, least of all Moses himself.

The servant moves behind Moses to fasten the amulet around his neck, as he does every morning. This talisman will guarantee safety and good luck, though given Moses' luxurious surroundings, wearing it is more of a ritual to appease the many gods of Egypt.

Batya, his mother, enters his dressing room looking very worried. She is no longer the teenage girl who brought Moses to the palace so many years ago, but she has not lost her great beauty. "Moses," she says wearily, "I hope you're not going to fight again."

The prince stands, dressed for combat. He towers over her, his rippling biceps and bronzed chest a reminder that he has spent many an hour training in the art of hand-to-hand fighting. "He keeps challenging me, Mother," Moses says calmly.

"So refuse him!"

"I cannot, Mother. Even though he is family and of equal age, he is still Pharaoh's son." A sword leans against a nearby bench. Moses lifts it up and grips it with two hands. "I have no choice."

The clang of swords soon echoes through the palace courtyard. On one side of the arena is Moses, a skilled and careful swordsman with a deep competitive streak. On the other is a son of Rameses and heir to the Egyptian throne. Both are armed with a sword and shield. They are both nothing more than teenage boys, but someday they may be called upon to lead great armies into battle, and thus it is vital that they prepare for the art of war.

"I've been practicing," young Rameses cries with false bravado. His teeth are gritted as he warily circles Moses, eyes fixed on his opponent's sword.

"We don't have to do this," Moses says evenly.

"Yes, we do," Rameses vows, feeling the thick beads of sweat coursing down his forehead and into his eyes.

The sound of sword on sword alerts Pharaoh to the duel. He is annoyed as he hurries through the columns and statues filling his palace.

Batya walks with him, struggling to keep up. "They're fighting again," she explains to her father.

"I can hear that."

"Do something!" Batya says anxiously.

"I told you to control Moses," Pharaoh says curtly. "You didn't. And now you expect me to sort it out?"

"They'll kill each other! Father . . . please . . ."

An impatient and weary Pharaoh looks at Batya. Moses has been a welcome, though unnatural, addition to his court, but now Pharaoh has grown weary of him—particularly since Batya's adopted child has more strength, insight, and ambition than his own son. If something were to happen to Rameses, Moses might become the heir to his throne, thanks to Batya's considerable influence. That cannot be, and things are about to change. "You want me to deal with it? I will," he says coldly.

Back in the arena young Rameses is growing more confident. It is a fool's confidence, not based at all in fact. But he chooses to taunt Moses. "You may be my sister's favorite, but I am the next in line to my father's throne—and don't forget it." He lunges, thrusting his sword at Moses' side.

Bored, Moses deflects the blow, and all that is left of the attempt is the *clang* ricocheting off the smooth rock walls lining the combat pit.

When Rameses sees that Moses has no intention of fighting back, he attempts attack after attack, hacking down hard on Moses' shield with his sword. Moses even falls to one knee as a sign that this duel is senseless, but the attacks continue.

"Ha!" cries Rameses. "I made you kneel!"

Moses stands. He holds up his shield but lets his sword dangle uselessly to the ground. "Enough. I don't want to hurt you."

"Fight me, Moses. I command you!"

But Moses turns his back. An enraged Rameses runs at him, and attacks Moses from behind. This violates every rule of combat, and both men know it. Fed up with his cousin's behavior, Moses turns and fights.

Moses strikes blow after blow on Rameses' shield and says, like an older brother to an impetuous younger sibling, "I will not tolerate this foolish behavior any longer."

Rameses falls to one knee and cowers behind his shield, hoping Moses doesn't take the next step and kill him.

Pharaoh arrives just in time to see Moses embarrassing his son, making the future Pharaoh look weak and unfit. Batya and several palace courtiers are at his side, witnesses to Rameses' shame. Word will soon spread in the palace and throughout the nearby villages, and make it apparent that Moses should be the next Pharaoh. "Stop!" thunders Pharaoh's voice.

But Moses has worked up a righteous lather. He hurls himself at young Rameses again, slamming him into a wall covered in hieroglyphics.

"Enough," insists the Pharaoh. "Leave him alone!"

Moses never intended to go in for the kill, but young Rameses is winded. In the concluding fray and confusion of the moment, Moses' sword blade cuts sharply across Rameses' cheekbone. A gash opens, and blood pours forth. Rameses will not die from this wound, but it will become a horrible scar once it heals.

"*Moses!*" Pharoah barks.

A chastened Moses turns from Rameses and looks to Pharaoh.

Rameses screams at Moses in pain. "You will pay for this! I will be Pharaoh. I will be God!" He then turns to his father. "It is your fault. You should have never let her keep him," Rameses screams, spitting blood at the ground. Then, a final jab at Moses: "You're not even one of us!"

"He's right," Pharaoh tells Batya.

Moses stares at his mother, who looks away. The truth is starting to dawn on him. "What's he talking about?"

"Tell him," Pharaoh orders his daughter. With that, Pharaoh and a smirking Rameses leave the arena, followed by a small army of unnerved courtiers.

A most confused Prince Moses is left alone with Batya. "Tell me what, Mother?" he asks, not sure if he wants to know the answer.

Batya bows her head but says nothing.

"What?" Moses pleads. "Tell me. Who is my father?"

A tear falls down Batya's cheek. "Moses, I love you like a son. But you are not my blood."

"Then who...is my mother?" he mumbles in shock. "Where did I come from?"

Batya starts talking, and the words spill forth. "You were the child of slaves," she begins, tenderly cupping his face in her hands. "Father killed all the male children of your people—because they were too many, and a threat."

"Just as I am now a threat to Rameses."

"Yes."

"What do you mean when you say, 'my people'?"

Batya takes him to a window. In the distance they can see the Hebrews laboring in the hot sun. "The slaves, Moses. You were a slave child. I saved you. You also have a brother. And a sister. But they are not like you and me. They worship the god of their ancestor Abraham, and he has deserted them."

"And my real mother? Where is she?"

Batya falls silent. Moses rushes out of the room. He must see these people—*his* people—for himself.

Moses walks, haunted. He is horrified by the sight of slaves being beaten, and then kicked once they fall to the ground. He watches men, women, and children labor in the blazing sun. The heat is like an inferno. Their faces are weary and their spirits are broken. His people are without a hope or a future. In his eighteen years in the Pharaoh's court, Moses has never paid these people any heed. They have always been beneath him, a separate people he never noticed. Until now, he has never known nor witnessed the cruelty they suffer in daily existence. His heart is in conflict, for this could easily have been him. Somewhere among them is a family he has never known.

Moses hears an anguished shout: "No!" He turns to see an Israelite slave being dragged into the shadows of a nearby building. "Please, no," the slave screams. Moses follows the sound into a blind corner, where he finds a slave master beating a young man with a large club.

"Filthy slave," sneers the overseer, spitting on the Hebrew.

He lands blow after blow, even though the man cowers and tries to cover his face. Moses doesn't know what to do. This is not his business. The slave surely did something to deserve these painful blows. As the stick rises into the air and comes down again and again, Moses can no longer be an innocent bystander. Without fully realizing what he is doing, Prince Moses—a resident of the great Pharaoh's palace and recognized throughout the land as the son of Batya—walks back toward the slave master and picks up a large stone. He approaches the slave master from behind and raises the rock high over his head.

The slave master turns just in time to see Moses preparing for the blow that would crush his head and kill him instantly. He reaches out and in the confusion grabs instinctively the golden amulet dangling from Moses' neck, somehow managing to curl his fist around it. It offers him no protection from the blow. But as he falls dead the amulet is still curled inside his fist.

Moses is stunned, as he looks at the dead Egyptian at his feet. He is not sure what to do next. He runs.

The slave master has been hastily buried by other slaves to hide the crime. Rather than a grand stone tomb like the Pharaohs or wealthier members of Egyptian society, his body has simply been placed in a hole scraped from the hard desert sand, and then thrown inside. The Hebrew slaves have done the backbreaking word of digging the grave, and as might be expected when burying a cruel man they have long loathed, the hole is so shallow that it can barely hold the body. A thin layer of dirt was kicked over the body.

Later that night, a hard rain begins to fall, a welcome relief from the oppressive heat. It washes dirt away from the grave, revealing the dead overseer's hand, clutching the gold amulet he ripped from Moses' neck. Neither vultures nor wild dogs find the slave master first, but soldiers from the Pharaoh's palace, who bring Prince Rameses.

A soldier's torch illuminates a shiny piece of metal in the overseer's dead fist. Rameses leans over out of curiosity and is rewarded with a piece of gold he knows all too well: Moses' amulet necklace. Rameses smiles. This is all the proof he needs. There is no more guessing to be done: Moses is the killer. Rameses does not feel a single drop of the rain. "Welcome to your new life, Moses!" he exults. "You are nothing now. Nothing. And you never will be . . ."

By nightfall, word has spread throughout Pharaoh's kingdom about Moses' heinous crime. In the dark of night, torches are used to search the desert for clues to the whereabouts of Moses, who is now a fugitive from the Pharaoh's law.

"We can catch him," one of Pharaoh's top commanders says to Rameses.

"No. Let him run," replies Rameses. His humiliation from the sword fight with his cousin is still fresh, and it fuels his thirst for vengeance. "There's no water out there in the desert. No food. He will die soon enough."

———

Four decades pass.

Rameses now sits on the Egyptian throne, that scar given him by Moses a daily reminder that his nemesis is out there somewhere.

Although Moses escaped that night long ago after murdering the overseer, he never got a chance to say good-bye to Batya or to thank her for saving his life when he was an infant. Life as a prince is a distant memory. Now he is a shepherd, living in the land of Midian, on the Arabian peninsula, destined to spend each moment of each day alone with his flock. It is a hard, lonely life. His beard is long, and his face is dry and bronzed by the sun. His body is hard and strong from having survived the elements.

On this day, he holds on to his tent for dear life, and the canvas flaps violently in the desert wind. Sand blasts every bit of exposed skin, and he shuts his eyes hard to avoid the sting. His tent is about to blow away. He lets go the canvas and moves from tent post to tent post, hammering them deeper into the soil with a large flat stone. With each crack of his strong arms bringing the rock down hard on the wooden pegs, Moses finds his thoughts drifting back to Egypt. The sound and movement are very much like those long ago when he crushed in the overseer's skull. The land of his birth haunts him.

Crack—he sees the slaves in the building site.

Crack—the unknown faces staring at him in the crowd of slaves.

Crack—the bloodied face of the man he killed.

Crack—a woman carrying a water jug. Could that be his sister?

Moses' hands are bleeding now. He forces himself to forget Egypt in order to save his tent. The wind is blowing harder, and it has created havoc all around him. A small bush, uprooted by the gusts, tumbles past and then comes to a stop, seemingly pinned on a rock just a few feet away.

Moses grabs a rope to secure the tent, but the cord whips from his calloused hands. It doesn't matter—the tent finally appears to be secure. With a last look at his sheep, which have pressed their bodies to the ground nearby, he staggers inside his tent to weather the storm. The wind continues to blow. Moses wraps himself in a rough blanket. He tosses and turns, trying to get a few hours' sleep as lightning flashes outside. The night goes white, just for that instant.

And then, silence.

But Moses does not find peace. The sudden silence after hours of noise is jarring. His eyes blink open. He rises to his feet and stumbles outside to see if the storm has truly passed.

He expects to see darkness. Perhaps a patch of starlight in an otherwise cloud-filled sky. He expects to see lightning crackling on the horizon. And, worst of all, Moses half-expects his flock to be scattered, which would mean yet another endless night wandering through the wilderness to find them and bring them back to the little hardscrabble patch of dead grass and stone that he optimistically calls a pasture.

But he sees none of that.

What he sees is far more unnerving: the small bush that had tumbled past earlier in the day is now completely ablaze. Yet the leaves and branches do not burn. And there is no smell of smoke. It is just a flame, brilliant as the daytime sun.

Moses approaches cautiously, wary of the intense heat. As he does, the flames begin to roar with a distorted and disembodied sound. Moses walks closer. He shields his face with his hand, lest the heat burn him and the light blind him.

In the distance, thunder rolls in a low growl. But in that growl, Moses hears a voice. "Moses! Moses!"

"Here I am," he replies cautiously.

A deafening clap of thunder. Moses raises his hands to his ears, exposing his eyes and face to the intensity of the fiery bush.

"You are real?"

The fire burns so bright that Moses must shield his eyes.

"*I AM*," a voice tells him. "I am the God of your father. The God of Abraham. The God of Isaac. The God of Jacob."

Moses hides his face, because he is afraid to look at God. "What do you want with me?" he asks.

Another clap of thunder. This one makes Moses jump back in panic.

"I understand the misery of your people—*my* people. I hear them every night in my dreams. They cry out for freedom," says God.

A loud wind rages. The flames on the bush roar to a new and larger height. But this time, rather than panic, Moses approaches the bush. He hears his instructions, but he is mystified. "Free? How can I set them free? I am not a prince now. I am nothing. Why would they listen to me? I think this is a mistake. There must be someone else."

The fire grows higher in response. Now the flames reach out to Moses, enveloping him. Yet he is not burned. Rather, he feels a new strength course through his veins. He is overcome with a new sense of purpose.

"I'll do it," he says, his voice now resolute. "Who shall I say sent me?"

Moses hears the answer on the wind. In that instant, the fire goes out. The bush, still unburned, lies on the ground.

"Lord," he marvels, rolling the word around on his tongue. "Lord...I will do it, Lord. I will set Your people—*my* people—free."

Moses sleeps soundly the rest of the night. In the morning, as the sun rises high in a sky as clear and blue as any he has ever seen, Moses leads his flock into Egypt. He will sell that flock the first chance he gets. For his God—Yahweh, the God of Abraham—is about to give him an entirely new kind of flock.

But tending them won't be as easy.

Rameses has now become Pharaoh. Out of habit he absentmindedly touches his scar as he enters his throne room to the fanfare of trumpets and the beating of drums. Courtiers trail behind him, careful never to walk abreast or stand taller than the Pharaoh.

To make sure such a calamity never happens, the throne is on a raised dais. Lackeys who dare not look in his direction are soon carrying a smaller throne up onto the dais, which they place next to the larger throne. This royal chair is reserved for Rameses' son, who will someday earn the divine status of Pharaoh. Ruling Egypt will require years of patience and training, as Rameses himself is well aware. His is the biggest empire on earth, and to be Pharaoh means to be worshipped as one of the gods.

Rameses' ten-year-old son is escorted to the lesser throne. He looks intimidated, and he gazes anxiously at his father for signs of how he should behave. But Rameses offers no affection in response, no guideposts of how a great Pharaoh must rule. Instead, he beckons to a courtier, who quickly steps forth and hands the boy a gilded toy chariot. The child looks up to his father, who smiles and assures him, "One day you will have a whole army of these chariots—real ones."

Meanwhile, in a brickworks far outside those throne room walls, a gray-bearded and muscular Moses has walked across the desert and returned to the scene of his capital crime. He smells the fine dust of the Egyptian air and feels a stir of nostalgia as he gazes at the palace in which he was raised in splendor and luxury. Now he sees before him dusty, exhausted slaves guiding carts laden with bricks. Egypt's magnificence is built upon their labor, and is vital to the kingdom's continued growth.

Moses, now an old man, has been given an impossible task: persuade Pharaoh to let those slaves go. They must be set free, even if it means the potential end to Egypt's magnificence. "So much suffering," Moses mumbles under his breath, gazing upon men and women who have never known freedom. Caked in dust, emaciated, beaten. These are his people. They are wretched and broken, and have no idea what freedom actually means. To them it is an ideal, a whisper of hope, a long-ago promise from a God who has not spoken to them in ages. How is Moses, a wanted murderer who has never lived among them, going to persuade Pharaoh to let them go? And if he does, how is Moses supposed to lead them? The task isn't just impossible. It's unthinkable. Moses is afraid, but he was called upon by God. Only the memory of that burning bush helps him fight his urge to turn around and return to his quiet Sinai mountain.

"Hey, old man," barks an overseer, before jarring Moses back to reality by shoving him. The slave master raises his whip to beat him, but a powerfully built slave named Joshua intervenes on Moses' behalf just in time.

"Don't worry, sir. Don't worry," Joshua assures the overseer. "I think he's a little confused. Let me take care of this. I am so sorry."

The overseer looks at Moses and Joshua as if they were the dirt itself. He spits a great gob of phlegm into the dust and saunters away, cracking his whip as he goes.

Joshua pulls Moses around a corner. When they're out of sight Joshua confronts this stranger who has suddenly appeared in his midst. "Do you want to get us all a beating?" Joshua hisses at Moses. "I ought to beat you myself."

Moses only stares at him.

"Who are you?" Joshua asks.

"My name is Moses."

A stunned Joshua takes two steps backward. His eyes glaze over in wonder. "Moses? You are Moses?"

"Yes."

"*The* Moses?"

A deep breath. A reminder that he has not been forgotten. A call to battle. "Yes. *The* Moses."

———

Later that day it becomes obvious that not everyone is happy to see Moses.

"What do you want from us," demands a slave named Ira.

The Israelite elders stand in the small communal square allotted to the slave community. Moses has been brought forth by Joshua and introduced. A few young men stand nearby, careful not to speak.

Moses takes in the scene as he ponders the best way to answer that question. It is an answer he has sought throughout his long walk back into Egypt, and he knows what he must say. But Moses doesn't answer immediately. Instead, he looks up to the heavens, where a bird flies free overhead. It inspires Moses at a time when he desperately needs inspiration. When he finally speaks, something about his tone of voice commands attention. "I am here to set you free."

He hears gasps of surprise. A few look embarrassed.

"That's very kind of you, Your Highness," says the mocking voice of Ira, the self-appointed spokesman for the group.

The comment draws immediate laughter, and Moses feels a surge of self-doubt. But he does not give in to his fears. Instead, he searches the men's faces. Despite the laughter, some of the men are very much intrigued.

"God has sent me," Moses adds.

"God . . . ?" asks Ira, whose voice is just the smallest bit less sarcastic.

"Yes. God sent me to speak to you. Remember God? Your Creator? The God of your ancestor Abraham?" Men step out of the shadows to listen. The laughter and derision has temporarily subsided. Moses has their attention—and he means to keep it. "Well, even if you have forgotten about God, He has not forgotten about you."

"In case you had forgotten, Pharaoh is the only god we have to fear," Ira shoots back.

"Who created the earth, the seas, and the sky?" Moses insists. "Or more specifically, who created you?" Before Ira can say a word, Moses adds to his question: "Was it God? Or was it Pharaoh?"

From behind Joshua, Moses can see a woman join the crowd. This is most unusual, for women routinely leave these discussions to the men. With her is another man, roughly Moses' age, though with a slave's haunted eyes and hollow cheeks. This man's eyes are fixed on Moses. His name is Aaron, and the woman's name is Miriam.

Joshua joins the argument. "But why would God send you? And why would Pharaoh see you, let alone listen to you?"

Now Moses is on sure footing. He smiles knowingly. "Oh, he'll want to see me. And I am quite sure he will listen to every word I say."

Aaron speaks for the first time. "He's right."

Moses looks into Aaron's eyes and has a sense that they know one another.

"God sent me a dream," Aaron continues. "He said Moses was coming. And that we must help him win our freedom."

And then, to Moses' great surprise, Aaron is sweeping past Joshua and wrapping his powerful arms around Moses in an enormous hug. "Welcome home, my brother. I am Aaron. And this," he adds, pointing to the woman, "is Miriam. Your sister."

"Brother," she says lovingly, taking Moses' hands in hers.

Moses stares in shock. He can't speak. He feels his emotions rising. "My family," he says, gently touching the side of Miriam's face. Then, searching the eyes of everyone in the room, he adds, "My people."

Everyone else watches in amazement, unsure of what will happen next. It is Aaron who takes control, even as Moses now falters, searching the eyes of each man in the room, challenging them to defy him.

No one does.

Moses sends word to the palace that he would like to meet with Rameses. As Moses predicted, the mere mention of his name is enough to produce an audience with the Pharaoh, and soon he and Aaron are escorted up the grand stairway toward Rameses' throne, past ornately carved pillars and statues. The air smells of perfume and palm fronds. This is all new for Aaron. He tries desperately not to show it, but he is deeply fearful of every aspect of Egyptian royalty. This is the seat of the power, the people who have crushed the Israelites. Aaron cowers as he walks past the Pharaoh's guards, remembering the many times a whip has bitten into his flesh. He tries to walk tall and to feign bravado, but deep inside, Aaron is quite sure that he and Moses will never leave the palace alive.

Moses walks to this homecoming with a gnarled wooden staff in one hand, as towering and imposing as the day he scarred Rameses for life. Memories flood back as he recognizes every statue, every hieroglyph, and every door. As he strides toward the throne room, he nods now and again at an old friend, exchanging a smile or a tilt of the head now and again. In these halls where he played as a child, he reflects on the odd path his life has taken. To be back home, in these hallowed corridors, under these circumstances, is almost surreal.

A courtier marches the two Israelites into a large hall. Rameses sits before him on a large golden throne. His son sits by his side in a smaller, identical version of the same regal chair. Moses smiles at the boy, who smiles back.

"You have a son," Moses says to Rameses.

"An heir. My family's dynasty will last forever."

Moses smiles again at the young boy, who shyly looks away. Moses notes the scar on Rameses' face, no less visible for the passing of the years. The Pharaoh has a hard look in his eyes. The two men stare at one another, remembering the past.

"Have you come to beg forgiveness?" says an expectant Pharaoh. He has waited years to hear an apology.

The palace guards step forward. If Moses shows disrespect, a simple snap of Pharaoh's finger will see Moses and Aaron thrown to the ground. If Moses tries to approach Pharaoh, he will be killed.

Instead he stands his guard and speaks. "God saved me," Moses explains. "For a purpose."

All around the court, the mood has darkened, for it is clear that Moses is not talking about an Egyptian god but the God of Abraham—a god the Egyptians do not know or worship.

"And what purpose would that be?" the Pharaoh says with a bemused expression.

"To demand that you release his people from slavery."

"Demand?" Rameses says, absentmindedly running one index finger down his fight scar. He steps down from his throne and approaches his adoptive nephew. The two men stand eye to eye, a Pharaoh and a Hebrew. In any other situation, Moses would have been instantly struck down and killed for daring to look in Pharaoh's eyes. But there is a deep history between these two men, and this is no ordinary moment.

Moses does not back down. "Let my people go."

"You always were a fighter, but you never knew when you were beaten."

Moses weighs his words before responding. "That's because you never beat me. If you defy God, you will receive a punishment more severe than anything I could have ever imagined inflicting upon you."

"I have a good mind to slam my fist hard into your face, Moses," Rameses hisses, "but I will not revisit our childish matches where you always played unfairly. You kill an upstanding Egyptian, escape a fugitive, and return, after all these years, to threaten me? Tell me, dear Moses, is it your invisible god who's going to punish *me*? The one who abandons his people? The one who runs from his responsibility, his past... his family?" Rameses beckons to the guards. "Show them who god is!"

The guards, large and imposing men, wrap their fists around the necks of Moses and Aaron, then shove them to the hard stone floor. Pharaoh's son watches as Moses and Aaron are beaten. The sights and sounds are shocking to the young boy. Rameses is showing his son, by example, the way of the Pharaoh: take no half measures when dealing with insurrection.

"I am god!" Rameses shouts in their wake. "I. Am. God."

"No, Rameses," Moses cries out, "you are not God! You are just a man. And you *will* set my people free, so that they may worship with me in the desert!"

A hard kick in the head silences Moses, but his words echo around the throne room like a portent of doom.

A week later, Moses walks along the banks of the Nile with Ira, sister Miriam, and brother Aaron at his side. He knows that his first real test is upon him. He has made the Pharaoh angry, but God has protected him, ensuring that Pharaoh will not kill him. He must now convince the Hebrews that God is with them. The Hebrews are a people of faith, but they feel that God has deserted them. Unless God sends a sign, Moses knows, these people will not allow him to speak on their behalf, for fear of the punishment that is sure to follow.

"Moses. You've made Pharaoh angry," Ira warns. "He'll punish us. Don't make it worse."

Moses pauses and looks to the sky. He is lost in his own world for a brief moment, studying a flock of geese flying low and straight above the Nile. "God has spoken to me," Moses answers, conviction in his tone. "He will make Pharaoh free us—by force, if necessary." Moses turns to Aaron. "We are His agents now, you and I. Are you ready?"

Aaron nods. "That is why He has brought our family together again."

Miriam moves closer to her brothers. "What should we do?"

"We must trust in God. You will see. He will show us the way to go," Moses responds. He finds his way down through the reeds toward the river's edge. His hands touch the rushes and he hesitates a moment. God is talking to him, and Moses knows what to do next. Moses draws himself up, raises his arms to heaven, and points his staff to the sky. Then he turns to Aaron and slowly lowers his staff until it points at his brother. "Put your staff to the water," Moses commands him.

Aaron is mystified. He hasn't heard God's voice, and Moses appears to be acting strangely. But he does as he is asked. Aaron drops the tip of his staff in the Nile, barely touching the surface. But from that simple point of contact, the water starts to radiate red. No. Not red. A darker hue. Something more akin to the color of blood. In fact, that's what it is. The waters of the Nile, the greatest river on earth, flowing thousands upon thousands of miles, have turned to blood.

Meanwhile, downstream, Rameses swims in the royal bathing area. He dunks underwater and feels the cool liquid against his skin, a sharp contrast to the scorching desert air. His feet touch the bottom, and he stays under until his lungs feel as if they are going to burst. He stands, lifting his head above the surface. He hears a scream, and looks up at the faces of his courtiers along the banks—hands covering their mouths, eyes wide with horror.

A shocked Rameses looks down to see that he is completely coated in blood. Behind him, the Nile stretches away, still and calm—and bloodred. He hears a voice inside his head. It is the voice of Moses: "You are not God! You are just a man. And you will let my people go!"

Rameses ignores the voice. He stumbles to the bank, where his slaves wrap him in clean white cloth, through which the blood quickly soaks. One unwitting courtier tries to clean off the blood by reaching into the Nile for a bucket of water, only to dump more blood on his Pharaoh.

Moses gazes at the Nile, not at all surprised by what has just happened. Joshua comes to the bank and looks across, not sure what he is seeing. Is this all real?

"Do you doubt?" Moses asks him gently.

Joshua's confusion evaporates, replaced by a sense of purpose.

"All my life," Joshua tells Moses, "I've belonged to Pharaoh. But I will never be a slave to a man again."

"God is with us," Moses assures him.

"So surely, Pharaoh will now let us go. Right? He can see for himself what God can do."

"It won't be that easy." Moses hopes the Israelites can maintain their faith through what is sure to be a long, tough battle. "This is just the first plague, Joshua. God is sending ten plagues to change Pharaoh's mind. Ten. Prepare yourselves."

The next attack soon follows.

Pharaoh's son is one of the first in the palace to notice. He is playing on the floor of his bedroom with his toy chariot when a frog hops past. Then another, and another, all croaking. Until a tide of frogs fills the palace. Terrified, the boy climbs onto his bed to escape this horde.

In the throne room, Moses is once again standing before Rameses, repeating God's command that his people be set free. And though the Pharaoh can clearly hear the screams of his son above the croaking, he refuses to back down. "I will not free my slaves," Rameses says, as he stands up and sweeps out of the throne room, followed by anxious courtiers.

Moses merely shakes his head, for he knows the many trials the Egyptians are about to face. And he knows that with every refusal by Pharaoh, there will come another, more destructive, plague.

Next comes the death of all Egypt's livestock—cows, sheep, and goats, the source of their meat and milk. The Egyptian people begin to starve. And still Rameses refuses.

Then the people of Egypt are attacked once again. Hideous boils break out over their skin, even as the Israelites are left unscathed. And still the egotistic Rameses refuses to see the truth. A plague of locusts descends from the heaven, plucking the fields clean of every crop, every bit of grain, and every last morsel of food in the land. Plague after plague visits Egypt, and with each plague, Pharaoh grows more resolute in his refusal to back down.

God then finally does to Egypt what Pharaoh once did to Moses' people: He sends His Angel of Death to kill every firstborn son throughout the land. Just as Pharaoh killed all the firstborn sons of Israel, now God's Angel of Death will do the same to the Egyptians. But to ensure that the Angel of Death won't pay a visit to their homes and families as well, God instructs Moses how to spare the Hebrews from God's vengeance.

Joshua holds a struggling, bleating lamb in the courtyard. His knife flashes and the bleating stops. The lamb's blood flows into a bowl. The man holding the bowl leaves the courtyard and is immediately replaced by the next man in line. He also fills a bowl and leaves, and then is replaced by the next man. A long line of men wait their turn, knowing that time is of the essence. And if they have forgotten this simple fact, Joshua makes sure to remind them. "Hurry! Don't spill! Remember: use the blood to mark the entrance to your homes. The lintel and the doorposts."

Moses told them that splashing this above their doors will cause the Angel of Death to pass over their homes—and spare their firstborn children.

Even as Joshua works quickly and methodically, men throughout the Hebrew settlement are using crude brushes to daub blood above their doors. Moses and Aaron go house to house, ensuring that all precautions are being made. For after the nine previous plagues, no doubt whatsoever remains that God will do precisely as Moses has prophesied.

"God's word is clear—the blood of a firstborn lamb is His chosen sign," he lectures the occupants of one home who have not heeded his warning. "It is the sign that you are chosen people. Every single house must be marked with blood. Every one!"

Moses looks into the faces of his people, many of whom are holding their children tightly. Their faith in God is being tested to the breaking point.

Even Aaron is confused. "We promised that God would free our people. Yet now He sends death. How can this be?"

Moses glances at Aaron, the strain of leadership etched in his face. He is an introverted man, more comfortable in solitude than taking charge. But this is what God has commanded him to do, so he works his hardest to be the leader that God needs him to be. It is not easy at all. But he has chosen to honor God. God has spoken directly to him.

The sky above is darkening to a bloodred color.

"We must trust in Him," Moses whispers to Aaron.

At midnight, as God has promised, the Angel of Death approaches, seeking to destroy every firstborn male in Egypt. Young and old, it makes no distinction. Aaron, for instance, is a firstborn son. He now huddles inside his home with Moses, fretting at the ominous sight of that awful bloodred sky, praying that the lamb's blood above his doorframe is enough to spare his life.

At the Pharaoh's palace, Rameses is not a firstborn male—but his son is. The ten-year-old stands at his bedroom, staring up in awe at the red sky. He is heir to the throne. The future of an entire dynasty. Rameses' hopes and dreams rest on his shoulders. But in the royal palace, no one knows about the blood of the lamb. They are not aware of the sign that will save lives. Once darkness falls, the Angel of Death travels through the land. He finds every Israelite house marked with the blood of the lamb—and passes over. But the Egyptian homes that do not display this sign are visited with tragedy after tragedy.

Especially the palace.

Rameses' son is asleep, his beloved toy chariot resting on his chest. A gust of wind blows the curtains open, and a faint red mist enters the room. Lit torches burn by the doorway, for the child is afraid of the dark. But as the red mist makes its presence known, those torches go out. The room is completely dark and silent, save for the breathing of Rameses' precious son.

The breathing stops.

The toy chariot topples to the ground.

Blood trickles from the nose and mouth of Rameses' son.

Vengeance doesn't take long. The morning sun is a low red ball on the horizon as half a dozen soldiers, led by a captain of the imperial guard, drag Aaron and Moses from their beds. The soldiers have not been trained to be delicate, and they seethe with rage at the terrible news that is traveling throughout the land. Many of them woke to find their oldest sons dead. And among the phalanx of soldiers, there are many missing—grown men killed by the Angel of Death.

Every firstborn son in Egypt is gone. Every last one. All of the grief is expressed in manhandling Moses and Aaron.

"Leave them be," screams Miriam. "They've done nothing!"

But her words fall on deaf ears, and soon Aaron and Moses are being led through the towering palace doors. Soldiers shove them into the center of a dark, pillared room, and then force them to their knees. Moses and Aaron press their faces to the floor, knowing that to look up at Pharaoh right now would be a grave error.

Then they hear Rameses' voice. The sound of grief is unmistakable. "Why?" he cries. "Why should lowly Israelite slaves have life . . . when my son is dead?"

The captain of the guards grabs Moses and Aaron by the hair and lifts their heads. Rameses is walking toward them, the limp and lifeless body of his son draped across his arms. "Is your God satisfied now?"

Moses and Aaron say nothing.

"I asked you a question."

Moses says nothing. He takes no joy in the death of a child. He only looks at Rameses with sadness, as if to remind him that all of this could have been prevented. If Rameses had only listened.

Rameses lays his son on the floor. "Take your people and your flocks and go! Leave my land. And take your wretched God with you!"

Moses and Aaron say nothing, eager to get out of the throne room as fast as possible. "Thank God," Aaron whispers once they are finally out of the throne room.

"Yes," Moses replies. "We must."

It is time to leave captivity and travel to the Promised Land. Three million Hebrew men, women, and children are in captivity. The Egyptian people are so eager to see them leave immediately that they freely give gifts of silver, gold, and cloth to encourage them to be on their way. Everywhere in the Israelite settlement, carts are being loaded. People are packing their life's possessions onto donkeys.

Amid the preparations for departure, people can't help but celebrate. The Hebrews seem to have permanent smiles on their faces, and they spontaneously sing and chant songs of joy. When it comes time to depart, Moses is carried through the city streets on the shoulders of men who were once wary of his presence. The impossible promise Moses made is coming true.

"Put me down!" Moses tells the group of men carrying him through a packed street. Children are running and jumping to get a better view of their new hero.

Aaron is one of the men carrying Moses. "No, brother. We won't put you down yet—we're carrying you all the way to the Promised Land."

It all seems so simple to the Hebrews: they are leaving a land that has held them hostage for centuries and heading toward a new home where milk and honey are theirs for the taking. God has appeared to Moses and told him the specific route he must follow to reach this Promised Land.

Only Moses, the most unlikely believer among them—raised as an Egyptian, exiled into the desert for decades, and only late in life finding a relationship with God—sees the broader importance of their journey: the Hebrews are fulfilling Abraham's covenant with God. "We are going to live in the Promised Land," he marvels, "with descendants as numerous as stars. . . ."

As the Israelites travel east out of Egypt, Rameses is having second thoughts. He stands in his throne room, where his son's body lies in state. Incense burns from ornate bowls. A cotton sheet covers the child's torso.

"My son," says a grief-stricken Rameses, placing a hand gently on the boy's forehead. He can't help but notice that the body is cold to the touch, and that the skin, which had been deeply tanned from hours playing in the hot Egyptian sun, is now ghostly pale. "How could slaves do this?" Rameses mumbles, his broken heart hardening into resolve. He takes his son's dead hand in his own, and crouches down. "I vow to you," he promises his son, "here and now, that I will bring the Israelites back and make them build you the greatest tomb the world has ever known." The toy chariot has been placed next to the boy, so that once he is mummified the toy will travel with him into the afterlife. "And I also vow that the body of Moses will be buried beneath that tomb's foundation, crushed through all eternity by the weight of your death."

Rameses pivots to his left, to where the captain of the guard stands watching along the wall. "We will bring them back," Rameses orders. "I will lead the way, Commander. The Hebrews want freedom? They're free to choose: crawl back to me as slaves—or die."

Pharaoh takes one last loving look at his son. What a beautiful boy. His heart fills with rage at losing the life that could have been.

"Get my chariot!" he roars. "We leave immediately."

The line of Hebrews refugees extends to the horizon. Theirs is not an orderly exodus. The sound of bleating sheep commingles with complaints about blisters, sunburn, and thirst. Moses leads the way, deep in thought, as always. Miriam, Aaron, and Joshua follow close behind.

"I still can't believe Pharaoh just let us leave," Joshua wonders aloud.

"But he did," Aaron says proudly.

"You're right: it's what God demanded. Only a madman would defy God one more time after what He just did."

Moses doesn't join the conversation. He feels a deep responsibility for the safety of the entire group, and he will be more than happy to finally kick the dust of Egypt off his sandals. But he knows Rameses all too well, and he is quite aware that the Hebrews will never be completely safe from his wrath until they are safely beyond his borders.

He groans out loud as he walks up and over a large sandy ridge and looks below to a vast sea, spreading across the land in all directions. He cannot see the other side. More important, he cannot see a way to get across.

Aaron sees it next. "Brother, what now?"

Moses stares at the sea in disbelief. How could this be? How could God lead them to the Promised Land yet throw a roadblock like this in their path?

"God will provide a way," Moses insists.

Ira the elder arrives, looking agitated and doubtful, as always. "Moses," he says, as if talking to a child. "Why have you brought us here? This is insane."

"God has brought us here."

"And what does God say about getting to the other side?"

The Hebrews reached the Red Sea after a week's journey. To be truly out of Egypt, and free from the Pharaoh's power, they must cross to the far shore, a distance of many miles. They have no boats or other watercraft.

Finding the wood to build enough boats to ferry millions of people to the other side is an insurmountable logistical challenge. Swimming is out of the question. There is always the choice of walking several hundred miles north to the mouth of the sea, but the way is mountainous and the rugged journey would take weeks, perhaps months. Small children and the elderly would be pushed to their mental, physical, and emotional limits each and every day. Bandits are known to hide in the mountains, and this long caravan of travelers would be plundered easily and often. But most of all, should Pharaoh change his mind and wish to enslave the Hebrews once again—a fear foremost on everyone's mind—the north-ward path would make it easy for Rameses to catch them. They don't know that this has already come to pass. The Hebrew dilemma comes down to one simple choice: trust in God. There is no other option. But trusting God requires courage. For there is clearly no possible way that the Hebrews can get from one side of the Red Sea to other. For if God is to rescue the Hebrews it will take the sort of impossible miracle of which only He is capable. The freed slaves make camp and wait on God, lulled to sleep each night by the small waves lapping the seashore.

Trouble is fast approaching from the west. Horses' hooves pound the desert floor. Charioteers scream at their mounts, flicking their whips to coax an extra burst of speed. Rameses is expert in the chariot, and he rides tall and true, his face impassive. He wants his slaves back. Neither Moses nor his god can stand in his way.

The chariots and the lines of soldiers following close behind kick up considerable dust—so much that their progress can be followed from miles away. A small band of Hebrew men, including Joshua, stand on an oceanfront ridge, horrified at the sight of Pharaoh's approaching army. As the reality of their predicament sinks in, he runs to find Moses.

"Horses!" Joshua screams as he sprints into the encampment. "Chariots!"

"Fool! Now what do we do?" torments the always irritating Ira, who still chafes at the leadership he believes he has lost since Moses arrived. Joshua surveys the terrified crowd before him, and sees with sadness the faces of the women and children who will surely die. "We fight," he barks.

"Against Pharaoh?" scoffs Ira. "With what?"

"With our bare hands, if we have to," replies Joshua.

The Hebrews panic. They begin packing their belongings as quickly as they can.

Moses looks at them in dismay. What is the use of packing if there is nowhere to go?

An exasperated Aaron comes to Moses' side. "This is hopeless, brother. What do we do?"

Moses is deeply disappointed in his brother's lack of faith. He looks Aaron in the eyes, then turns and walks toward the water's edge.

Ira chases after him. "Was it because there were not graves in Egypt that you brought us here to die? Because that's what you've done."

"Do not be afraid," Moses commands.

Ira looks bemused and frustrated as Moses plants his feet in the sand, and sinks his staff into the ground. The surf washes over his feet. Moses clenches his gnarled old wooden staff tightly, then closes his eyes and lowers his head until it comes to rest on the staff. His breathing deepens. Moses shuts out the chaos and panic surrounding him. He hears nothing. The world around him slows.

Moses prays. "God, we need You now. Your people need You."

Above and behind him, Pharaoh's chariots arrive on the ridge. Rameses' face lights up with anticipated revenge as he looks down and sees the trapped, terrified, huddled masses. "We have them," he exults. "They're trapped." Rameses looks to his left and to his right. As far as he can see in either direction, an Egyptian charioteer awaits his signal to charge. Their horses paw at the ground in anticipation. Below them, certain that their fate is in Pharaoh's hands, are the terrified Hebrews. Pharaoh utters one word: "Charge."

Moses continues to pray, eyes closed, the thunder of hooves not intruding on his conversation with his Maker. He remembers the moment when God appeared to him and told him the specific route he must follow to the Promised Land. Moses knows that he has done just as God commanded, so even as he prays, his faith is strong that God will find a way to deliver the Hebrews from this coming evil.

The sky is growing black, and a hard wind whips at his robe, sends his long hair flailing about his shoulders. "Lord, I know You have a plan for us. And I believe in Your plan. And I believe that this is not the end You planned for us."

The strong wind whips up clouds of sand. Shelters are blown away, and children cry. Aaron gathers Miriam and her children.

But Moses sees none of it. His faith is in God, and he continues to pray. "We have watched You bring terror on our enemies..."

Ira crouches in the sand, rocking back and forth in despair.

The long line of chariots races down the road to the beach.

Moses' hand grips his staff ever tighter. "You kept death from our doors..."

Joshua stands defiantly, glaring at the coming Egyptians, ready to fight.

Then Moses' eyes suddenly open as God speaks back to him. "Lord!" Moses says in shock.

The wind is now almost at hurricane strength. A funnel cloud touches down on the sea before Moses, hitting the water and then exploding back up into the sky. The shock wave flattens the Hebrews, and they stumble around on hands and knees, disoriented and momentarily unable to hear.

Only Moses is left standing upright, not letting go of his staff as he raises his face to the heavens.

Before him, the sea rises to the sky, a great wall of water stretching from the earth to the clouds. All around him, the Israelites shield their eyes from the mist and spray, stunned at the vast wall of water climbing higher and higher right before their very eyes.

And then the water parts in two, forming a great canyon. The sea floor is completely exposed, with water on either side. The wind rages through that gap.

Moses knows precisely what to do next. "Follow me," he cries, thrusting his staff into the sky. "This is God's work."

Aaron leaps to his feet and organizes the Israelites, hurrying them into the divide in the seas. They scramble toward the entrance, so eager to be safe from Pharaoh that many leave all their valuables behind. As they step inside, faces glance up in awe at the vast mountains of water. Ahead, there is darkness, and Joshua quickly orders the people to light torches. Moses leads the way, in silt and mud up to his ankles. Water from the parted sea drips in the smallest of droplets onto his head. The way is misty, loud, and dark, yet Moses presses on.

"Come on," Aaron encourages the Israelites. "Come quickly."

Joshua joins in, when he sees that the people are terrified of taking that first step of faith into the parted sea. "It's safe. Have faith," he cries.

Yet Ira sputters, "Are you crazy? We're all going to drown!"

"Better to drown than to be a slave of Pharaoh," Joshua replies. "Come on, old man. Let's go."

The Hebrews have all fled into the tunnel of water. Rameses races his chariot through their abandoned belongings, feeling invincible. But he slows as he approaches the sea. All around him, his men gaze up in shock at the terrifying sight. They stop, afraid to go on. But just as Moses stayed strong when the Hebrews showed nothing but fear, Rameses ignores the lack of courage from his soldiers. He steels himself, knowing that they are watching him, and will take inspiration from his action. "After them," he cries, holding back on his horse's reins as his army charges forward. "Bring me Moses!"

Inside the tunnel of water, Miriam and Aaron are helping families with small children. "Keep going—that's it," Miriam exclaims.

"This way. Follow Moses," encourages Aaron.

Up ahead in the darkness, Moses trudges forward. His pace is measured, and his staff picks through the sediment to keep his footing sure. Behind him, the Israelites scramble along the seabed; their way is now miraculously dry, thanks to a path of smooth, dry stones. They shout at their pack animals and strain to move the heavy wheels of their handcarts.

Back on shore, some of the Egyptian horses balk at entering the watery tunnel. The Egyptian commanders orders their men to dismount and grab their weapons. God has not made their path dry. They stumble into the great chasm, their eyes adjusting to the darkness, even as they stumble over the rocky slime in their search for the Hebrews.

Moses trudges over sand and rocks. Ahead, he can see something new and quite miraculous: the sun. It is merely a faint disk right now, burning through the wall of mist. But the mist soon begins to part, and the sun burns brighter and brighter.

Joshua breaks ranks and charges toward it, a broad smile spreading across his face. "We're almost there! Come on!" he yells.

Lit by the sun, Joshua charges forward. Others soon follow, their peals of laughter echoing up and down the canyon. The wind still howls. Mist sprays their faces. But the fury is not as intense right now, and against all odds, it looks like the Israelites may succeed in crossing the Red Sea—on foot.

The light increases as the ground becomes total desert again. In ones and twos the Israelites finally step onto the sand of safety. Then by tens and twenties. And then by the hundreds and thousands. Moses is the very last man in the tunnel as the last wave of Israelites reaches the beach, keeping his pace even and calm. Then he, too, steps into the sunshine. He is greeted by the sight of hundreds of thousands of rejoicing men, women, and children, amazed by the fantastic journey they just took.

Now Moses turns around and faces the sea once more. Yet again he raises his staff to the sky. In the depths of the tunnel, he sees Pharaoh's army rushing forward.

The darkness is intense, but there is light on the faces of the Egyptians. Then they feel another sensation: raindrops. But this is not rain.

The Egyptians glance up to the sky, just in time to see the great walls of water collapsing down onto them.

From shore, the Israelites stand in stunned silence as they watch the ocean descend from the sky and drown Pharaoh's army. A great whoosh of wind is shoved from the chasm as it closes shut, but then the seas and the skies are calm. A moment of sad realization passes, as the Hebrews realize that so many men are now dying. But this is followed immediately by the natural joyfulness of freedom, and the end of slavery for the Hebrews.

"Thank you, Lord," shouts Joshua. "We are free at last."

Moses takes it all in, then speaks quietly to the waves. "You are not a god, Pharaoh. There is only one God, and He is here, with us."

As if he can hear Moses, Pharaoh watches the devastation from the far bank of the sea. He is surrounded by the belongings of the Hebrews and those horses too reluctant to gallop into the tunnel—just as he himself was reluctant, despite his show of bravado. He can say nothing, for there is nothing to say. Pharaoh has lost. He lets out a great sigh of horror and disbelief.

"Come," Moses tells the jubilant Israelites. "There is a long road ahead. We must be strong." Their faith in God is strong, and they will follow Moses anywhere God tells him to go. Thus begins forty years of wandering for the Israelite people, always in search of that elusive Promised Land that God promised to give Abraham and his people. The parting of the Red Sea and the escape from slavery marks a new beginning.

God does more than lead them through the great desert wilderness; He gives Moses a set of rules to govern their lives. God's gift of freedom for the Hebrews is being amplified. Moses returns alone to Mount Sinai, where he once tended his flock and saw the burning bush. Here he receives the Ten Commandments, a moral code written in stone. God has passed down hundreds of laws for His followers to heed, but these ten are the most crucial. They provide a road map for health, happiness, and contentment.

Moses descends Mount Sinai, carrying two stone tablets listing these ten all-important commandments, and is greeted by Joshua. These will be placed inside the Ark of the Covenant—the sacred vessel built from specifications handed down from God, and carried with them as their most holy possession. "God has renewed the promise He made to Abraham," Moses says, brimming with a faith greater than ever before. "We must worship no other God...no more lying...stealing...cheating... no more murder or dishonor....If we are true to God, He will keep His promise."

"Abraham's dream. That is our future?" asks Joshua.

"*You* are the Israelites' future now, Joshua. Don't look back. You must take the land promised to Abraham. And to all his descendants—as numerous as the stars."

Moses' face is radiant as he speaks, because God appeared to him in all His glory during the presentation of the Ten Commandments. This was God's way of showing that He was pleased with Moses and what he had done for God's people.

God never allowed Moses to enter the Promised Land. His good and faithful servant only saw it, in all its glory, from the top of Mount Nebo, on his 120th birthday. Then Moses died. God buried him in an unknown grave, as the Israelites crossed into the Promised Land in fulfillment of His covenant with Abraham.

Joshua, Moses' handpicked successor, leads the Hebrews, now that they have finally reached the Promised Land. But this is not the end of their struggles. It is just the beginning.

PART THREE

DEFENDING THE HOMELAND

The massive walled citadel is named Jericho. The word means "fragrant," which is apt, for the aroma of its many palm trees and clear springs carries across the desert in all directions like a sweet perfume. Jericho is an ancient city, settled time and again over the centuries by different cultures. Tall, thick walls that have kept out many an enemy surround it. The Hebrews have crossed into the Promised Land, and this cherished settlement calls to them. For forty years since escaping Pharaoh, the Israelites have wandered the wilderness of the desert. They have brought with them the Ark of the Covenant—the sacred vessel, designed from specifications passed down from God, that holds the Ten Commandments. Their Ark needs a home, as do they. And they are prepared to fight for it.

The great walls of Jericho loom before the Hebrews. It is many years after Moses, and the now-muscular, sixty-year-old Joshua has taken over as their leader. He has sent a pair of spies, Nashon and Ram, into the city on a reconnaissance. In the dead of night, they scale the high walls and witness a scene of chaos. On the outside, Jericho appears impregnable. But inside, its people fear a siege. They hoard food and water, knowing all too well the starvation that will ensue once the Hebrews stop all supplies coming in and out of the city. Jericho's military commanders will certainly put up a fight, but there won't be much they can do if the Hebrews choke the life out of the city, which means a shortage of ammunition and weapons as well as of sustenance.

"Go home," one of Jericho's military leaders, a strapping man with an eye for the ladies, screams as he walks through the darkened city streets, lit only by torches. "Lock your doors. The enemy are close, but they won't get in."

Unbeknownst to the commander, Nashon and Ram are already high up on the city walls. They prowl its darkened parapets, searching for signs of weakness and military vulnerability—anything that will allow Joshua and the his army to defeat Jericho's Canaanite inhabitants.

A lone woman walks down a street inside Jericho, her face radiant in the moonlight. Rahab carries her water jar in preparation for the siege, which nearly falls to the ground when four Jericho soldiers intentionally collide with her. Her beauty is legendary in Jericho, as is her trade—she sells her body to make money. This flawed and fragile single mother is imperfect. God has selected her to see that His will is done. Rather than choose a man or woman who might seem more upright or virtuous, God will prove His strength in her weakness.

As God begins his work with Rahab, it seems like just another ordinary night. Men ogle her as she walks from the well. Wives gaze at her with contempt, jealous of her sensual beauty, angry that their husbands would prefer Rahab's bed to theirs.

A small group of soldiers blocks her path home, jostling Rahab and flirting coarsely. They step aside when Achish, their commander, forcibly stops her. "Rahab, my little whore," he says, as if the words are an endearment. He brings his face close enough to hers that she recoils from his stale breath. "What are you doing out?" he asks. "Those wilderness people are so close that I swear I can smell them from here. You know it's not safe."

"I'm safe enough," she responds, though her voice is shaky.

"No one is safe," the commander hisses.

Encouraged by their leader, the soldiers press in around Rahab. They are no longer playful, but rapacious. Their eyes are hungry and their hands positioned to grope her, as they have on so many other occasions. Yet they defer to their commander, and it is Achish who grabs Rahab, sending her water jar clattering to the ground. She tries to squirm away, but he manages to kiss her face. Only then does she free herself from his oily grasp.

The commander hasn't quite gotten what he'd hoped for, but there will be no more advances in the company of his men. "Go home," he purrs to Rahab. The insinuation is clear: Achish is keeping a close eye on Rahab. His intentions are far from honorable.

He struts down the street, followed by his soldiers. A distressed Rahab picks up her half-empty jug and staggers into the night.

Meanwhile, Nashon and Ram, the two Israelite spies, cautiously throw down a rope and rappel down the enormous city walls. Jericho is still in a frantic mood, with the smell of fear in the air. But the two take nothing for granted, and move with stealth and caution. Nashon wields a battle-axe, while Ram slides his dagger into his belt. At the bottom of the wall, they conceal their rope and move carefully across a broad courtyard. This is the first time they've been in the open since entering the city, and both men are frightened about the danger. The penalty for getting caught will be just enough torture to loosen their tongues, followed by an immediate beheading.

An old woman surprises them. Nashon, the more fearless of the two spies, calmly places a finger to his lips to shush her. He smiles when she seems to comply, thankful that he has had the presence of mind to remain calm. But then she suddenly screams at the top of her lungs. Nashon and Ram run out of the courtyard and leap into an alley. They run with all their might, with each stride and footfall transforming themselves from spies to scared young men who will do anything to get out of Jericho immediately.

They make a hard right turn around a corner, but run only three more steps before spotting the dark silhouette of a Jericho soldier blocking their path. Another soldier steps out of an alley. Nashon and Ram come to an immediate halt, and then turn to sprint back the way they came. A third soldier struts out onto the street, this one pulling a sword from its scabbard.

"Brother," Nashon cries to Ram. "For Israel!"

That's all that needs to be said. Ram knows exactly what Nashon is saying. With a dramatic swipe, he jerks his dagger from his belt and squares to fight.

"Get more men," one of the soldiers calls out loudly, knowing that there are dozens of soldiers within earshot. "The enemy is inside! Sound the alarm! Sound the alarm! They're here!"

Within seconds, soldiers fill the streets. Among them is Achish, the commander. One of the soldiers blows a ram's horn, the signal that battle is imminent. In that instant, Nashon spies a way out. He sprints into a narrow gap between two homes, through a fetid goat pen, and away into the darkness. Ram is right behind him, running for all he is worth. The spies hug the walls, and try each doorway that they pass, but all are locked. The alley leads to another, and more doors. Finally, in the darkness, Nashon finds an unlocked door. He slowly pushes it open and finds the small home empty. He and Ram waste no time hiding deep in the shadows, praying that the soldiers don't conduct a house-to-house search.

Behind them, the soldiers of Jericho mistakenly believe many more members of the Israelite army are within their walls and frantically assemble for battle.

The countdown to war has begun.

Rahab has refilled her water jug when she hears the call of the ram's horn and starts to run home. It is a simple set of rooms built into the city's thick walls, with windows looking out into the street. Rahab's concern is not her own safety, but that of her young son. He is home with her parents, and if the Israelites are going to attack, she needs to be with him. But Rahab moves slowly, bearing her bulky water jug on her head, and she is soon exhausted. Two of the soldiers who taunted her earlier run right past her, no longer interested in a whore when their lives may soon be on the line.

She watches incredulously as four soldiers run down an alley, hunting Nashon and Ram. Despite the weight of her jug, Rahab forces herself to move faster. She is relieved as she approaches home. Rahab places her water jug on the ground and leans back on to the smooth wood of her doorway. Exhausted, she is out of breath, and her chest heaves as she gulps for air. There is no telling if she will live until morning, or what the Israelites might do to her if Jericho falls. But for now she is safe.

Rahab lifts her water jug and pushes her front door open. The room is only half-lit by the moon streaming in the window, but Rahab doesn't need a candle to make the short way from the door to her table. She puts down the jug and tenses up. She notices nothing out of place about the room. She hears no shuffle of feet or deep breath to indicate anything is out of place. She just knows that something is wrong. "Hello?" she says to the darkness.

Suddenly, a knife is pressed to her throat. Rahab tries to scream, but a hand covers her mouth. "Sshhh," hisses Ram.

Rahab's eyes widen in terror as she looks into the shadows and sees the broad-shouldered Nashon holding her son—the gleaming blade of a battle-axe pressed to the boy's throat. In the corner, her mother and father cower in fear. "We are a good and honest people," Nashon tells Rahab. "Help us, and I promise I won't hurt him."

Rahab nods. She has no choice.

Ram releases his grip and takes the blade from Rahab's throat. He slides his knife into his belt once more. At the same time, Nashon puts the boy down and lets him run into his mother's arms. The boy cries out in happiness, but Rahab quickly shushes him.

"You're Hebrews?" she asks.

Nashon nods.

"Don't you have a god who commands the winds?"

Nashon nods.

"And parts the seas?"

Nashon nods again and speaks. "Our fathers were there on that day. God saved our people. We are His chosen flock."

Now Rahab is terrified. "All of us in Jericho have heard these many things about your God. Tell me this: how can we fight a people whose God can do those things?"

"You can't," Nashon tells her.

"Everyone in Jericho knows this, and it fills us with fear. For your God is powerful."

"Yes," says Nashon. "Trust in Him."

They hear soldiers outside pounding on doors, drawing nearer and nearer to Rahab's home. It's only a matter of time before the Israelite spies will be found. There is no way out.

"I will hide you," Rahab tells them.

Nashon and Ram have no right to expect Rahab's assistance. They have entered the city illegally, they have entered a woman's home without her permission, and now they hide in the thatch of her roof, knowing that she might be forced to lie for them. But they have offered her something in return—safety for her and her family and a chance to trust in their God, to learn His ways. Just before she showed them to the roof, from which they can see the Israelites' campfires farther down the valley, Nashon and Ram gave her a scarlet cord to tie in her window. "Tie this scarlet cord in your window. We will convince Joshua, our leader, to prevent the Israelite army from harming you and your family, but only if that cord is hanging in the window."

Below, they hear the soldiers of Jericho banging on Rahab's door. As she opens the door to let them in, Nashon and Ram let down their rope so that it dangles from her roof to the far side of the city walls. The two men rappel down quietly. No sooner do their feet hit the ground than they are running hard toward the Israelite camp.

"Joshua," exclaims a breathless Nashon as he finds their leader.

Joshua is hunkered down over a fire, breathing in the still night air and wondering how God will choose to get them inside the city. He stands at the sight of Nashon, and tightly embraces the spy. "Tell me," asks Joshua, "did you find a way in? Is there a weakness?"

"The walls are solid and thick, and about as impregnable as any fortress known to man," Nashon tells him.

Joshua is crestfallen, but tries hard to hide his disappointment. Nashon has shown great courage, and to disrespect this bravery would be an insult. But Joshua is confounded to see that this same terrible news doesn't trouble Nashon in the slightest. In fact, he seems to be growing increasingly excited about what he is going to say next.

"The walls are solid, Joshua," Nashon exclaims, "but their hearts are not. We met a woman. She thinks that God has already taken the city, and that there is nothing the people of Jericho can do about it. Their people are already melting in fear because they believe God is with us."

Joshua could leap for joy. "He is with us! But we've still got to find a way to get inside those walls."

The Israelites have spent years in the wilderness. They've scarcely seen a town, let alone captured one. Joshua has no plan of attack.

But he claps Nashon hard on the shoulder and wanders away from the fire. He thinks of his old friend, long since departed, and his constant demonstrations of faith. "Moses, old friend," Joshua wonders aloud, "what would you do?"

As he saw Moses do so many times when life was hard, Joshua climbs a nearby mountain to think. He carries a torch to light the way, but otherwise it's dark. A moon hangs low and full in the clear air of the desert sky. A wind blows, and Joshua sees dust in the pale moonlight. Joshua stands alone, remembering the way Moses always returned from the mountain with simple answers to complex questions. Hours pass. It's getting late, and Joshua is feeling old, doubting himself. The deep chill of the night air is settling into his bones. In violent exasperation, Joshua plunges his torch into the ground. Then he falls to his knees and prays. This, he remembers, is what Moses did constantly: pray. When life was uncertain, Moses prayed for guidance. When life was spectacular, Moses prayed words of thanks. When life was mysterious, Moses prayed for wisdom. Prayer was Moses' way. Joshua feels slightly foolish, because he's been standing up here alone in the darkness for hours, and this is the first time he's remembered to actually bow his head and talk to God. "Lord," he begins. "I was a slave when You showed me Your love and Your power...You gave me a new life, a life that I cherish, despite its daily hardships. You have brought us so far, but now these mighty city walls stand before us. What is Your will? What would You have us do?"

Out of the silence comes a whoosh of air. The flames of Joshua's torch burn sideways as a blast of wind levels them. Joshua has seen many things in his life—the plagues in Egypt, the parting of the Red Sea, the drowning of Pharaoh's army, and the many miracles God performed during the Hebrews' forty years of wandering in the wilderness—great and awesome sights, all of them. Never, as long as he lives, will Joshua forget the sensation of walking between the great towers of water after the Red Sea was split.

But he will never forget this next moment.

A great and mighty warrior has appeared out of nowhere and stands before him now. A hood covers his head, but nothing hides his ramrod posture, broad muscular shoulders, and the great sword in his hand.

Joshua is terrified. "Who are you?" he asks very carefully.

The warrior is silent.

Joshua bows his head, overwhelmed. This warrior is mighty. He slowly looks up and asks, "Are you with us or against us?"

The warrior's face is dark, and his eyes unblinking. "I am with God," he tells Joshua. There is no affect to his voice, just power. "I am Commander of the Lord's Army."

Joshua bows his head. This is an answer to his prayer. As terrifying as the warrior might be, Joshua knows God is with him. "What does God ask of us?"

Joshua feels the smooth blade of the warrior's sword press against the bottom of his bowed chin. But instead of harming him, Joshua feels the warrior press upward, forcing him to look up.

"The Lord parted the water for Moses—but for you..." The angel thrusts the blade of that great sword deep into the ground. Instantly, the earth begins to crack. The fissure widens and widens, spreading out around Joshua, but never harming him. "…He will split rock. This is what you must do…"

Joshua listens closely to what the angel tells him. Very closely.

It is daytime. The Israelite army assembles into an orderly formation and marches on Jericho. But they do not attack. Instead, they march around the city's walls, just as the Commander of God's Army ordered Joshua. They will repeat this exercise each day for six consecutive days, as instructed.

Joshua marches with his army, the words of the angel ringing in his ears:

"March around the city once a day with all the armed men. Do this for six days. Carry the Ark of the Covenant around the city. It contains God's commandments, showing that the Almighty is with you."

Joshua sees the men carrying the Ark. Thousands of sandal-covered feet kick up dust. *Yes*, he thinks, *we are doing precisely as I was told*.

But Joshua also knows that the best is yet to come. For on the seventh day, his men will not rest, as God did when creating the heavens and the earth. No, the Israelite army will march seven times around the city walls, after which Israelite priests will blow a special trumpet made from the hollowed horn of a ram—the shofar—and then, with an enormous shout from the Israelite army, the mighty walls of Jericho will fall down.

Joshua knows that up and down the ranks, many of his soldiers are struggling with this plan. It seems ludicrous, and most definitely impossible. To march around Jericho in the hot desert sun, clad in battle armor and coated in the thick clouds of dust produced by an army on the march, is the height of discomfort with no chance for valor. There is a great deal of grumbling, and Joshua knows that if this plan fails, his authority will be in question.

But he follows the plan and does not fear. Joshua has seen for himself what happens when a man has the faith to listen to God and do as instructed. He possesses that faith in great abundance. He marches, his mouth dry from the heat, ignores the cool shade of his tent calling to him, and waits eagerly for the seventh day.

The seventh day arrives. Joshua doesn't even wait for daylight to begin the seven laps around Jericho. The Israelites march by torchlight; the Ark of the Covenant is being carried by the strongest of their men, for its weight is considerable. Great expectation is palpable in the ranks, for after forty years of waiting and wandering, God has promised them a home in this land. The Hebrews think of their years sleeping in tents, and of the babies born in the thick, choking grit of the desert floor. They dream of solid roofs over their heads, and homes where they may raise their families in comfort and cleanliness.

One lap. Two. Jericho is not the size of a great metropolis, but it is large nonetheless. Each circuit around its walls is a minor act of endurance. Four. Five. Men wonder if this far-fetched plan of Joshua's will work. He says it comes from God, and they believe him. But what if the walls don't fall? Will they still attack? Men wonder if this is the day they will die, and with that curiosity comes fear. They think of their loved ones, wondering if they will ever see them again. By the lights of their torches, the Hebrews see the terrified citizens of Jericho peering down from atop the walls. They are starving and scared, yet clinging to the hope that the walls that have protected them from the Hebrews thus far will continue to keep the desert wanderers at bay. Jericho's army stands ready in the battlements atop the city walls with spears, swords, and battle-axes.

Six. Seven. A Hebrew commander holds up a hand to end the march. The men know what to do next, standing still as seven Israelite priests step forth and, in unison, press the shofars to their lips. As one, they sound a long blast.

This is the signal Joshua and his army has been waiting for. The entire Israelite army shouts as loud as possible. The roar of the troops builds as the forty years of wilderness floods out of them. Joshua joins them, tilting his head back and letting loose a primal scream, shouting with all his heart and soul, remembering the words of the angel: "Glory will come."

Suddenly, Jericho's soldiers are hit by a shock wave. Their faces distort under the impact of the roaring sound. They fall backward off the walls and crash into the streets below. The noise floods over the walls and into the streets of Jericho. Her terrified citizens have nowhere to hide from these earth-shaking decibels. They run in circles, ears bleeding. The entire city is in chaos.

The noise fills Rahab's house, penetrating the mud walls and forcing her family to cower in the dark. But while her parents huddle beneath a table, afraid to move, this is the moment Rahab has been waiting for. "Mother!" she screams. "The cord!"

But her mother is too terrified to come out from beneath the table. Rahab grabs the red cord and runs to the door. She flings it open and sees people racing past frantically, none of them sure where they're headed or why they're running. Rahab attaches the cord to the doorframe, as instructed.

A bolt of lightning sizzles down from the black sky. A massive storm swirls overhead. Rahab shuts the door and retreats back into the darkness of her home, unsure what will happen next.

A violent thunder rises from the desert floor. It is even louder than the thunder let loose by the Hebrews, who continue their roaring. The earth begins to shake. The tremors are small at first, and then grow stronger and more convulsive. Inside Rahab's small home, the masonry in the walls falls out and plates clatter to the earthen floor. Rahab covers her son's ears, as he begins to wail in terror. Tears course down Rahab's own cheeks as new noises of destruction from outside cause the room to fill with dust.

Meanwhile, the city walls have begun to collapse.

The earthquake grows more violent. Many citizens of Jericho have huddled in the city's main square to seek protection, only to have rocks and buildings fall and crush them. The city walls are rubble, and the shaking continues.

Then, almost as quickly as it began, the trembling stops.

The lightning stops. The roars of the Israelites are no more.

The voice of Joshua cries out to his army. Without their walls to protect them, all of Jericho hear the words of Joshua ring out: "Jericho is ours! Every man must go in. We give this city to the Lord."

Joshua follows his two spies, Nashon and Ram, through a collapsed section of Jericho's wall. Time seems to slow as he surveys the wreckage of this once-great city. The people and soldiers of Jericho stumble, bleeding from the ears and noses. The city's military is helpless, and the Hebrew army cuts them down easily. God has willed that everything in the city be destroyed, and it is Joshua's responsibility to ensure it.

Everything, that is, except Rahab and her family. For God has said that she must be spared for helping the Israelites.

As Israelite troops beat down doors and enter houses, Nashon and Ram race toward Rahab's home, searching for the telltale and all-important red cord. They sprint through the city streets, hurdling fallen rock and the remains of homes, ignoring the cries of the dying. In the distance, that red cord flutters in the wind, and the two hulking Israelites aim toward it.

They kick in Rahab's front door. The entire family is cut and bloodied from the destruction—but alive.

Time is of the essence. "Our men are coming," Nashon screams, holding out a hand. Rahab cowers on the floor from the noise, unsure who to trust or where to turn for help. She hesitates. The Israelites are the enemy of the people of Jericho. To trust Nashon will mean forever turning her back on the place of her birth and the people she has known since childhood.

Nashon can see her dilemma. "You can't stay here," he reminds her softly.

Rahab takes Nashon's hand. He lifts her from the floor and holds her protectively against his body. This is a new sensation for Rahab—being protected by a man, rather than being taken advantage of. In this moment she leaves her Canaanite heritage and joins with the Israelite people, soon to worship their God and stay with them for the rest of her life.

Ram lifts Rahab's son into his arms and uses the same urgent tones to convince Rahab's parents to flee with them. They all stumble out of the house and make their way to the city's main square. The scene is a warped vision of dust, smoke, the bodies of Jericho's fallen citizens, and exhausted Israelite soldiers. Joshua stands at the center of it all, holding up his arms to heaven. "God has kept His promise," he mutters joyfully to himself. "God has kept His promise." The former slave is now master of the Promised Land. His first thought is to give thanks, for he knows that God cherishes a thankful heart. "Thank you," Joshua shouts to Nashon, the spy who first penetrated these city walls. "Thank you," he shouts to Rahab, who made the Israelite victory possible by hiding the Israelite spies. And, finally, "Lord," he screams to his maker. His heart fills with gratitude and love for God. "Thank You."

Then Joshua hears it, a low and rumbling chant that spreads through Jericho. The words remind him of those days so long ago in Egypt, and the distant dream that someday the Israelite slaves would escape that awful world of toil and strife to create a home all their own. The chant is this: "Is-Ra-El! Is-Ra-El!" and it emanates from the lips of every Israelite soldier standing in the ruins of Jericho. Some are cheering. Some are crying tears of joy and exhaustion. From slaves to a nation. The impossible dream has become a reality: the Israelites are home.

"When we obey the Lord," Joshua tells anyone who will listen, "anything is possible."

Joshua is a man of faith. And for the next fifty years he leads the Israelite army as they conquer the Promised Land. He forges an Israelite nation built upon the ideal of each man and woman putting their hopes and dreams in the capable hands of God.

But when Joshua dies, that faith seems to die with him. Generations of Israelites forget their covenant with the Lord, turning to other gods to meet their needs—gods of rain and fertility, gods of the previous inhabitants of the Promised Land, who they wrongly believe will bless their new way of life.

God is grieved by this betrayal. He reminds the Israelites of the covenant with Abraham, and that the Promised Land is a gift that must be cherished. God uses hard, powerful armies to attack the Israelites, like a father disciplines his son.

The cycle will be repeated for hundreds of years: Israel breaks their covenant; God sends foreign armies to subdue and subjugate them; they learn the lesson and cry out for help; God then raises a deliverer or "judge" to save them; and, once again, the land enjoys peace, until a future generation again forgets God.

Of all the foreign enemies that subdued the rebellious Israelites to this point in history, none was more powerful than the Philistines. They soon conquer the Israelites and claim much of the Promised Land for themselves, yet God has not deserted His chosen people. He longs to renew His covenant with the Israelites and return to them the Promised Land.

Once again, God chooses a most unlikely individual to carry out this plan—an eight-year-old boy named Samson, who has the strength of a lion.

It is 150 years since the death of Joshua. The Philistines, a sophisticated culture, control the coastal regions of the Promised Land, and despite their oppressive attitude, many Israelites find their ways attractive. Some have even stopped worshipping the God of Abraham and instead choose to bow down to Philistine gods.

One day, an angel of the Lord appears to a woman as she draws water from the village well. She is barren, and though she prays daily for a child, her faith has not been rewarded. The angel is in disguise, his face partially concealed by a hood. "Do not be afraid," he tells her. "Though you are barren, God will give you a son."

She is speechless as the angel suddenly disappears from her sight.

Then he stands behind her, his lips uncomfortably close to her ear, and informs her that there are conditions to this childbirth, a strict code of conduct that she must follow throughout her pregnancy and beyond: "See to it that you drink no alcohol and eat nothing unclean. And when your son is born, no razor may be used on his head. This will be the sign that the boy is given to God."

Unable to find words, she nods in agreement.

The boy is soon born and given the name Samson. By the age of eight, he knows the story of the angel by heart. His mother believes that he is destined to free the Israelites from the Philistines.

Ten years pass. Samson is a young man now, with a thick head of hair that flows in great powerful locks, just as the angel requested. He is renowned for his feats of strength, and for the yoke of muscles descending from his powerful shoulders down his back. Some say there is no more powerful man in all of Israel. But Samson has done nothing to free the Israelites from Philistine rule. He has strayed from the God of Abraham and taken Habor, a Philistine woman from a place called Timnah, for his wife.

On the way to the wedding, Samson and his parents approach the vineyards on the outskirts of Timnah. Within the maze of grapes and vines, Samson finds himself separated from his mother and father. Frantically searching for them, he takes a wrong turn into an isolated lion's den. Suddenly a young lion cub leaps at Samson. In that moment, the spirit of the Lord grants Samson the strength to protect himself by tearing the lion apart with his bare hands. After collecting himself from this unexpected attack, Samson sets off to find his parents. As he turns to walk away, he hears the fervent buzzing sound of bees pollinating inside the lion's carcass. This gives him an idea. He will keep the lion's attack a secret.

Upon arriving in Timnah with his parents, Samson can already sense the tension caused by his wedding. The ceremony takes place in the village courtyard. On one side sits his Israelite mother and father; on the other, Habor's Philistine parents. She is a delicate bride, as beautiful and lithe as Samson is strong. It is Samson's wish that his mother love Habor, rather than disparage her son's choice. As the wedding band plays in the corner, Samson gives Habor a peck on the cheek and whispers into her ear, "I will go talk to her."

Samson crosses the room. He is discreet, speaking in soft tones to his mother. "I know that if you had your wish I would have married one of our people."

"Not my wish. That directive came from God, so I certainly hope that God understands your choice," his mother sniffs.

"But it was God who sent her to me. I know it in my heart. Does love not come from God?"

Abimilech, a Philistine warrior, enters the courtyard. He is renowned for his disdain for the Israelites and fondness for taunting their God. His assistant, a deputy prefect named Phicol, accompanies him.

Samson's mother sees Abimilech and points him out to her son. "Will your love protect us from that one?"

Their discussion is interrupted by a chant, "Samson! Samson! Samson!" as the wedding-goers demand that Samson perform a feat of strength. Three Israelites struggle with a heavy clay jar of water. They place it in front of Samson as the other members of the wedding party rush to his side and urge him to hoist it.

The jar weighs well over two hundred pounds. Yet it is as light as a feather for a man with Samson's muscles. He lifts the jar above his head, and tips it back so that water pours into his mouth and spills all over his face. The courtyard erupts in applause. The men all wish they had Samson's power, while more than one woman finds herself admiring the size of his muscles.

Still holding the jar above his head, he carries it across the room to Abimilech. There he places it on the ground and challenges the Philistine to lift it. This is no longer the gentle Samson who gave his wife a loving kiss just moments earlier, nor the doting son who wants to please his mother. Samson is now surly and bullying, a defiant Israelite afraid of no man, determined to show the Philistines that he is the greatest man in their entire kingdom.

Abimilech is humiliated. He cannot lift the jar. Attempting it will make him look like a complete fool. He surrenders.

Not being content with his humiliating strength, Samson decides to further embarrass the Philistines with his intellect. He asks an impossible question.

"Let me tell you a riddle," proclaims Samson to the humiliated Abimlilech. "If you give me the answer within the seven days of the feast, I will give you thirty linen garments and thirty sets of clothes. If you can't tell me the answer, you must give me thirty linen garments and thirty sets of clothes."

"Let's hear it," Abimilech retorts.

Samson's booming voice recites the riddle he had come up with in the lion's den: "Out of the eater, something to eat; out of the strong, something sweet."

Silence falls over the wedding feast. Nobody can solve the riddle. Furious, Abimilech turns and walks away, his every footfall mirrored by the loud beat of the wedding drum. But Abimilech doesn't go far. He and Phicol study Samson from a discreet distance, hidden in the shadows just beyond the courtyard. "Who gave consent for this wedding match, Phicol? I certainly didn't. Any Philistine man would have been a better match than that abomination."

They observe the look on the face of Habor's father, and the way he idolizes Samson. "Her father is weak," Phicol mutters. "But how do we get to Samson? He's too powerful."

Abimilech smiles again. "Leave it to me. We are not going to get to him," he says, then looks hard at Habor. "We are going to get to *her.*"

———

After three days of feasting, the Philistines are still unable to solve the riddle. As Samson rests in privacy, Phicol confronts Habor for the answer.

"I do not know. Samson has not told me," replies Habor.

"Coax your husband into explaining the riddle, or we will burn you and your father's household to death," threatens Phicol.

Horrified, Habor throws herself onto Samson, sobbing, "You hate me! You don't really love me. You've given my people a riddle, but you haven't told me the answer."

"I haven't even explained it to my father or mother," says Samson. But on the seventh day of the feast, with Habor fearing for her life, Samson gives in to her pleading and confides in her the answer to the riddle.

Valuing her life and her loyalty to her people, Habor in turn explains the riddle to Abimilech and Phicol.

That night at the final banquet of the wedding feast, Abimilech stands to address Samson, "What is sweeter than honey? What is stronger than a lion?"

Samson immediately recognizes that the impossible riddle was solved. Enraged and betrayed, Samson flees the wedding party, plotting revenge on Abimilech and his people for humiliating him at his own wedding.

Later on, at the time of the wheat harvest, Samson seizes his opportunity to retaliate. He sets fire to the Philistine fields and watches as the shocks, standing grain, vineyards, and olive groves burn.

Fearful of Samson's strength, Abimilech refers back to his original plot: "If I cannot destroy Samson directly, I can use his helpless wife."

A fist bangs on the door to the home of Habor's parents. It is night. Samson is not home, so his wife opens it.

Abimilech and Phicol step inside. Their eyes scan the room. "Where's Samson?" Phicol demands.

"I don't know. He's not here," she replies.

That's all Abimilech needs to hear. "Do it," he commands Phicol.

The soldiers quickly bind Habor's father and mother, then tie them to one of the home's support poles. Phicol wraps his arms around a struggling and screaming Habor as the soldiers carry straw from the manger and scatter it about the floor.

"You're a disgrace to our people," Abimilech tells Habor, stroking her under the chin.

Abimilech and Phicol leave, locking the door from the outside. A torch is thrown onto the thatch roof, setting it ablaze. Inside, Habor pleads for mercy and pounds on the door. A crowd gathers, watching as the house is consumed in flames and smoke. As Habor's screams slowly fade to nothing, not a single bystander defies the soldiers and attempts to save her life.

Samson's one-man war against the Philistines begins the moment he learns of the atrocity. Nothing can stand in the way of his revenge. The first to die is a Philistine guard standing watch near an alley. Samson merely approaches him, takes his head into his hands and snaps the man's neck. "That's for my wife," Samson tells him.

Unable to control his rage, Samson continues his murderous cycle of revenge. He bursts into the barracks housing Philistine soldiers without warning, brandishing a wooden club. He is instantly attacked by a half-dozen armed men, but swats them away. Soldiers are thrown over the balcony into the courtyard below, and then Samson moves into the jail, opening the cells to release their Israelite prisoners. Just as on that great day when Joshua and the Israelite army laid waste to Jericho, Samson kills every Philistine in sight before storming into the night. Yet he is far from finished getting revenge.

Abimilech surveys the aftermath of Samson's rampage. "One man did all this?" he asks, looking at the piles of dead bodies. Flies buzz over the corpses.

"It was Samson," replies Phicol. "The man who burned—"

"I know who he is," Abimilech interrupts.

The Philistine guards standing nearby know better than to speak. They watch Abimilech as he simmers in a quiet rage, scheming to regain control of the situation. A crowd of Israelites has gathered to witness the commotion. "Where is he?" Abimilech yells to the crowd of Israelites standing outside the barracks. "Where is Samson?" Their mere presence enrages Abimilech, and in his anger he marches over to an Israelite elder and wraps his fist around the old man's throat. The elder, Elan, is known for his wisdom and authority. "*You* will bring Samson to me," Abimilech tells him. "And you will do it quickly, because for every day that I don't see him, two of your people will die." He slowly eases his grip on the old man's throat. "Am I understood?"

Elan gasps for air, nodding all the while as he takes a hasty step backward.

"Starting now," Abimilech adds. He snaps his fingers.

Phicol grabs two hapless Israelites. They don't fight back or even struggle, for to do so might anger the Philistines. Phicol shoves the Israelites into the hands of his bodyguards, and then slits their throats.

Had Abimilech known that Samson's mother was among those in the crowd, perhaps those two men's lives would have been spared. For she alone knows where to find her son.

A shadow falls across the entrance to a cave situated high atop a steep cliff far outside town. A frightening and precarious path leads to this cave. Samson's aging mother now bravely makes the climb, accompanied by Elan and a small crowd of Israelites. They make their way upward, breathing hard from the effort, and take care not to look back down to the valley floor. Small rocks clatter down the slope from above, causing them to press their bodies into the face to avoid being hit.

At last, they reach the cave. The villagers enter, one by one, led by Elan. Samson's mother enters last, unsure whether her presence will anger her son.

"Samson," Elan calls out softly. His voice echoes into the darkness.

Silence. From somewhere deep inside the cave comes the drip of water. Samson's mother steps to Elan's side. "Samson? Are you there, son?"

They step forward. In the corner, hidden from easy view, is the form of a sleeping man. Elan contemplates what tragedy might befall him if he surprises a sleeping Samson; so it is Samson's mother who bends down to awaken her slumbering giant.

But the instant she touches the blankets, Samson's mother pulls back her hand in horror. This is not Samson. Not at all. It is merely a pile of clothes and blankets formed into the shape of a man.

"Mother," Samson says from behind her, as he emerges from the shadows. He towers over the Israelites, who now back away from him in fear. The depth of Samson's grief shows on his lined and weary face. There is a wild look to his eyes, and in the confines of the small cave Samson looks even more imposing than ever before. His long, thick hair rolls down onto his shoulders like a lion's mane, giving Samson the appearance of a predator. He looks capable of killing every man, woman, and child in the land to avenge his wife's grisly murder.

"We're here to reason with you," assures a fearful Elan.

"Reason?"

"You must stop the killing, Samson. Please—for the sake of us all. For every Philistine you kill, two more appear, seeking revenge—on us."

"As they did to me, so I have done to them."

Elan is growing exasperated. "Don't you realize that the Philistines are our rulers now?"

"Everyone," Samson replies, walking a fine line between being respectful of Elan and letting him know that he has a job to complete, "must do what he thinks is right."

"No, Samson. Do what's right for your people and for God. Not for yourself."

Samson's mother steps forward and takes his hand. She has not forgotten the promise the angel made so long ago. She trusts that God has a plan that veers from the logical to the impossible in order for His will to be done. "You must give yourself up, my son," she whispers tenderly.

"Is that what God wants?" replies a crushed Samson.

"Sometimes...you must trust in God. He leads us in ways we cannot see. He will guide the choices you make. We must trust in God."

Samson looks to the sky. It feels like an eternity. Then he bows his head and extends his powerful hands. With great relief, Elan nods, and two men step forward to bind his thick wrists with rope. Samson looks to his mother for support, but she cannot meet his eyes. Samson, the strongest man in the land, allows himself to be meekly led away.

Forsaken by his people, labeled a murderer by the occupiers of his nation, and surrendered by his mother, Samson is now chained to a stone wall in the market square. Vendors' stalls line the far wall, and the bleating of lambs and goats destined for slaughter fills the air. Those powerful arms are secured straight out to each side, and the metal chains bite into his wrists. Samson's thick hair is matted, and his body aches from where his Philistine guards have beaten him with fists and rods, knowing that he cannot fight back. Israelites and Philistines press in on all sides, staring at him and making jokes about his powerlessness. Some spit on him. Others jeer. But they know better than to get too close, for even weighted down with chains, Samson's great strength is evident to all. More than one man wonders if Samson will somehow break those chains and continue his cycle of revenge.

Only Abimilech dares to come face-to-face with Samson. The two men stand inches apart, glaring into each other's eyes. "You have your prize," Samson says through gritted teeth. He suppresses the urge to spit at his captor. That would do him no good. Better to wait, find a way to escape, and deal with Abimilech and his minions in a more permanent manner.

"All I see is a common murderer," replies Abimilech. He is calm, smug, thinking of the day he will slice Samson's body in two and throw his corpse to the scavenger dogs. Then, and only then, will he be sure that Samson will never kill Philistines again.

"It was you who murdered my wife."

"She was a Philistine, not one of yours. We needed to teach a lesson—a lesson that your people will never forget."

"And now that you have me—will you finally leave my people alone?"

Abimilech laughs. It is an insipid chortle, the sound of a man who believes himself omnipotent. "Not until we drive you all back into the wilderness where you belong."

Samson realizes that he has made a mistake. His people are not safe after all. Abimilech nods at Phicol. "Kill him."

A gasp rises from the nearby Israelites. They have been betrayed. In their haste to save their own skin, the Israelites have sentenced to death the one man who can save them.

The Philistine soldiers draw their swords. Abimilech steps back to watch the carnage.

Samson hears a voice. "Lord?" he replies, startled to realize that God has waited until his moment of greatest need to speak to him. Samson gazes at the ground, where the jawbone of a donkey rests in the desert dust, dirty and neglected. A new power ripples through Samson, and he knows that the bone has been placed there for a purpose. The soldiers are mere steps away. Samson is not looking at them, much to the dismay of Abimilech, who has long waited to see a look of terror in the strong man's eyes. Instead, Samson stares at the jawbone and speaks to God. "Lord," he asks more loudly, "is that You?"

"It is."

Samson hears God's voice and is amazed at the power beyond all power coursing through his muscles. Samson snaps his chains as if they were made of twigs. He takes hold of the steel links and swings them around his head to force the soldiers back. Believing that their sharpened swords will save them, the Philistines rush at him, only to have Samson drive them to the ground with the snap of a chain.

Samson then snatches the jawbone from the ground. Chains still dangle from his wrists, thanks to the steel shackles, but now he has a weapon—a length of sun-dried bone no different from any other donkey's jawbone, but Samson wields it like the greatest weapon known to mankind. Part scythe, part sword, part battle-axe, part saber, and part war club. He bludgeons any Philistine foolish enough to attack. One soldier is smashed in the head. Another is hurled backward into a market stall. The stall collapses, and the Philistines scatter. Only Abimilech and Phicol remain, and Samson could slay them with the jawbone in an instant. But Samson has far greater work to do, and after piercing them with a hard glare that says he still has not forgiven them the death of his wife, he stalks off in the opposite direction.

Samson doesn't walk far. The moment he turns a corner into an alley, he falls to his knees. Breathlessly, he presses his hands together and speaks to God. "Lord," he asks, "is this what You want? Please, I beg of You, guide me."

Samson hears footsteps behind him. He leaps to his feet, jawbone in hand, believing it to be yet another soldier. But it is a woman, a most beautiful woman. She is so utterly stunning that Samson forgets his rage and simply stares into her dark eyes. The woman carries a jug of water, which she now places on the ground. Staring seductively into Samson's eyes, she pulls back the scarf that covers her head, then bends to pour a cup of water and holds it up for him to drink.

Samson suddenly realizes his great thirst. Hours chained in the market square have made him parched. He feels the thickness of his tongue, and his lips are dry, chapped. He drinks greedily, never once taking his eyes off this vision before him. She is clearly a Philistine, and Samson remembers his mother's admonition that he find a woman from his own tribe.

Samson gulps the last of the water and wipes his lips with the back of his hand. He notices the woman admiring his massive bare chest, and her gaze has lingered on the definition in his rugged shoulders. "Who are you?" he says finally.

"Delilah," she answers demurely. "My name is Delilah."

Word soon travels back to Abimilech about Delilah. The Philistine commander has retreated from the Israelite village to a barracks in his hometown. Samson's victory against the Philistine army seems blessed. Abimilech seeks his own blessing from the pagan deity Dagon, and burns an animal sacrifice in the dark of the night. Smoke fills the small chamber as Phicol enters with news from his spies.

"We have news of Samson," Phicol crisply briefs Abimilech. "He's got a new woman—a Philistine woman."

"Another one of our women? What's her name?"

"Delilah," answers Phicol.

Abimilech smirks, for once again he believes he is about to gain the upper hand against Samson. "I know her. Bring her to me. I need to talk to her."

Delilah is brought before Abimilech. He stands on a balcony above her so that she does not see him when she first enters his quarters. Abimilech gazes down on her, infuriated that an Israelite would dare touch such a spectacular example of the Philistine people. Her beauty is so great that even that the hardened Abimilech stammers for a moment before regaining his composure. He will do anything to please a beautiful woman. He has thoughts of rapture and ecstasy about her, longings of the flesh that he must put aside if he is to win this war.

"Delilah," Abimilech says as powerfully as possible. But his thin voice betrays his weakness. "Thank you for coming," he adds a little more confidently.

Abimilech disappears from Delilah's view, descending from his balcony via a back staircase. His eyes wander over every inch of her body as he reappears behind her. "As beguiling as ever," he says softly.

Delilah whirls around. "What do you want?"

"For now," he purrs, "let's just have a little talk." The purr turns to a growl as his voice grows cold. "I'd like to talk about Samson. An interesting choice, wouldn't you say? Not one of us. Whatever makes you think you belong with him?"

"Why do you want to know?" Delilah answers defensively.

Abimilech reaches out and touches her softly beneath the chin. "What's that tone in your voice? Don't tell me that you care about him."

Her silence speaks volumes.

"So I'm assuming he's in love with you?" asks Abimilech.

"Ask him yourself," Delilah fires back, not at all afraid of the Philistine commander.

Abimilech steps right up to her, so close that he breathes in her face, then grabs her arms so that she can't step back. "He's butchered hundreds of our people." His spittle coats her smooth, unlined face as he loses control of his anger. "Have have you forgotten that?"

"And how many have *you* butchered, Abimilech?"

"Do not confuse justice with murder."

"Do you really think you're any better?" asks Delilah. "But Samson's changed. He's a different man since he met me."

Abimilech laughs bitterly. "Do you really believe that? The truth is that he will go on killing until we find a way to stop him—for good."

The words are like a dagger to Delilah. Abimilech can see their impact and lets her go. "Do you know what happened to his first wife?" he asks. "She died, shall we say, *young*. Do you want to die young, Delilah?"

He reaches for her chin again, but she turns away. He gruffly grabs her face and snaps it back toward his own. "Where does he get his strength, Delilah? What is his secret?"

"I don't know," she replies meekly. "He won't tell me."

"Find a way."

Now Delilah is terrified, caught between the wrath of the two most powerful men in the land. "You've seen what he's capable of. I don't know if I can do it."

Abimilech gestures to Phicol, who drags a large wooden chest over from the shadows. "Perhaps this will help," Abimilech tells her.

Phicol opens the heavy lid. Delilah, who has never had much money in her life, is stunned to see thousands of shiny new silver pieces gleaming back at her. She stares at the chest, dumbstruck. The money is an absolute fortune, money beyond imagination.

"I like to call this 'danger money,' " Abimilech says, his charm returning. Delilah reaches for the coins and grasps a fistful. It feels so good in her hands—so solid.

Abimilech knows in an instant that she's made up her mind. "It's all for you," he says, watching the silver swim in Delilah's eyes.

Delilah is incredulous. She bends to sweep the silver into the hem of her dress.

But Abimilech snatches her wrist and squeezes it so tight that the coins slip from her grasp and clatter back into the chest. Then he slams the lid shut. "Soon, Delilah. Soon. But not now. Only when we know his secret. On that day, all of this will be yours. So tell me: can you find that secret?"

Delilah takes a deep breath and nods.

The night is late. Samson pulls Delilah's body to his, then kisses her tenderly on the lips. This is the moment Delilah has feared, for she knows that any caution in her kiss might give her away. So she wraps her arms around Samson and kisses him like this could be the last time. Samson does not suspect anything; he picks her up and carries her to bed. She breathes heavily in his ear, anticipating the passion soon to come. "Why are you so special?" she asks seductively. "What makes you so different?"

Samson lays her on the bed without answering. He lies beside her, and they hold each other. "You seem invincible," she says innocently. "Can anyone defeat you?"

A confused Samson turns to face her. "What do you mean?"

"Just curious. There seems to be a secret to your strength. If we are to be together we shouldn't have secrets."

Samson looks into Delilah's eyes for signs of her intentions, but sees nothing duplicitous. Her hands run through his long dark hair as his hands caress the soft flesh of her back. "God is with me, Delilah," he finally answers. "He makes me strong."

"But how? How does He make you strong?"

Samson is actually relieved to bare his soul. The words pour from his mouth without filter, confessing all to his beloved. "My mother was barren. God brought her a child—me. But there are things I mustn't do."

"Like what?" she asks, softly kissing his neck.

"My hair. I have never cut my hair. I'm forbidden. It's my sign of devotion. If I cut my hair, my God will take away my strength. I'll be as weak as—"

"As Abimilech?" Delilah whispers.

Samson can't help but smile, even though the mention of that name troubles him. The lovers say nothing for a moment.

"You don't believe me, do you?" Samson says.

Delilah can almost feel the silver in her hands—its heft, its polish, its power. "I do, Samson," she replies, kissing him with a bold new passion that he has never experienced before. "I believe you completely."

Samson sleeps. It is the deep sleep of the untroubled, and for the first time in months, he hasn't a care in the world. His heart is filled with the joy that comes with physical and emotional love. His massive mountain of a body, which has been tensed in anger and rage since the death of his wife, finally relaxes. He breathes deeply and quietly, lost in the most enchanting dreams he has ever known.

Samson stirs but doesn't awaken at the first snip as Delilah takes shears to his hair. She is cautious, starting at the longest end, far away from his head. But his hair is so long that it is if she has cut nothing at all. Another snip. And then another. Soon it is gone—all of it. And still, he sleeps. The final lock falls to the floor just as Philistine soldiers rush into Delilah's bedroom.

"Take him!" Abimilech orders.

In that instant Samson is up, out of bed, on his feet and ready to fight.

He touches a hand to his head and feels the stubble. A look at the bed—a pile of dark hair. A glance at Delilah—gorgeous, delightful Delilah, the woman of his dreams—as she turns away from him. His heart sinks. The Philistine soldiers easily hold him down. Samson fights back, but he has no strength at all. For the first time in his life, Samson is weak and afraid. "What have you done?" he yells to Delilah.

Abimilech empties the box of silver coins onto the bed, where they mingle with the coils of hair like exotic jewelry.

Samson's eyes dart to Delilah. He is dumfounded by her betrayal and curses his own foolishness.

She doesn't speak.

"Beautiful, isn't she?" leers Abimilech.

Samson struggles, but can't break away.

"So, my friend," continues Abimilech. "Take a good look. A very good look."

Samson doesn't want to look at his betrayer. He can still feel her fingertips on his skin. He loved and trusted Delilah. He can feel her warm breath and remember their words of love. He looks at his enchantress with pain in his heart.

"Now paint that picture in your head," says Abimilech. "For that is the last thing you will ever see." Abimilech bends over, his two hands extended, and Samson expects Abimilech to choke him to death. But instead, Abimilech plunges his thumbs into Samson's eyes.

Within a minute, Samson is blind.

Killing Samson would have shown benevolence. But Abimilech is hardly a merciful man. He orders Samson to be chained again—this time in a prison. Abimilech allows his focus on Samson to slip for months.

Samson's hair grows and is getting longer. Samson presses his forehead against the cool stone of a prison cell inside the soldiers' barracks. He is alone, his eyes covered in bloody bandages. Darkness is his world. But it is in this darkness that he finally begins to see that his destiny will be fulfilled. Behind him, the door creaks as it swings open. "Who's there?" he cries in agony.

No reply, but Samson receives his answer soon enough. Two Philistine soldiers pummel him with fists and clubs, taking great delight in their work. Samson roars in pain as the blows rain against his body, and his chains make a great clanking noise as he waves his arms in a futile attempt to protect himself. But with his strength and sight gone, there is nothing Samson can do. His bare chest and ribs soon resemble a side of beef, bloody and raw.

Only when Samson sags forward against the chains, unable to support his own body weight, do the soldiers unchain him, continuing their kicks and punches as the key turns in the locked manacles around his wrists and ankles.

When Samson collapses they drag him from the cell, rubbing the skin from his knees and feet, and into the temple of the Philistine god, Dagon. The room is packed with hundreds of people. Incense smoke wafts over their faces, and their eyes are watery and bloodshot. Pigs are being roasted. Goblets of wine are filled and refilled. Dogs are allowed inside this great pagan assembly, and their barks and bellows ricochet off the tall stone pillars supporting the roof.

"Samson, Samson, Samson," they chant, spitting on the Israelite as his body is dragged through their throng. Even children are allowed to taunt Samson.

When the Philistine soldiers release Samson, he rises to his feet, confused. Samson hears the ridicule, yet he cannot see who is showering him with oaths and profanities. He senses Delilah's presence in the room and turns in her direction.

She does not chant nor take delight in Samson's misery. But she is there, and he knows it.

Samson falters, on the verge of passing out once more. "I'm weak," he cries. "Stand me up against something."

The guards lead Samson to the building's central pillars. In the distance, Abimilech watches carefully. Samson may be blind, but he is a formidable enemy. "Should have killed him when I had the chance," Abimilech mumbles to himself.

Phicol overhears. "It won't be long now," he tells his superior.

Abimilech nods, breathing a sigh of relief. Yes, Samson will be dead before the dawn. He takes a long pull on his wine and strides over to be near Samson in these final moments.

Samson, meanwhile, is behaving strangely. He seems to be caressing the stone on which he rests. He's even talking to the stone. "Lord God," he whispers, "if I am Yours, remember me and strengthen me once more so that I may have my revenge."

Abimilech overhears Samson's prayer and leans his face close to Samson's. "Haven't you forgotten, Samson? Your hair has gone. You have broken your pact with your God, and now He has abandoned you."

"It wasn't God who took my eyes," Samson fires back. "It was you. But I'm glad you did what you did. The dark has helped me think."

Abimilech has never heard such foolishness. "Your God has deserted you and taken your strength with Him," he scoffs.

A look of complete serenity crosses Samson's face. "No. You're wrong. I can see Him more clearly than ever."

"Really. And what is He saying?"

Samson leans hard into the pillar, suddenly pushing on it with all his might. He closes his eyes and prays a last prayer to God. "Lord, remember me. Please God, strengthen me. Just this once. I pray that I am avenged of the Philistines for my two eyes."

Abimilech shakes his head as he watches Samson pray. "It's over, Samson. I've won. Don't you see that?"

But then Abimilech feels a sting as something hard slaps his hand. He looks down and sees shards of fine stone. Then a cloud of dust seems to lower itself from the ceiling. A disbelieving Abimilech swivels his view back to Samson, whose entire body is flexed as he leans into the pillar like a desert wanderer leaning into a stiff desert wind. The muscles of Samson's back and shoulders ripple; his legs, pushing so hard into the stone, are coiled and taut.

Fear sweeps through Abimilech. This can't be happening. Those locks were shorn. Samson's power should be gone. And then Abimilech realizes the truth: Samson's hair has grown back, but it was never the entire source of his power. It comes from God. Those great locks were just a daily visual reminder of Samson's pact with God.

The power comes from God. The God of the Israelites. And it always has.

Screams echo through the chamber. Philistine guards throw themselves at Samson, desperate to pull him from the pillar, but he swats them away like gnats. The roof begins to cave as great sections fall to the floor, crushing dozens at a time. Delilah is among them. Her mangled body lies in the rubble. The bones of her face are destroyed. Those curves that once enchanted Samson are now but a memory. All that silver cannot buy back her life.

Samson finishes what he started. The pillar topples, and finally Samson can stop pushing. He stands and smiles, nearly invisible in the dust and ruin. All around him the temple is collapsing, and he knows that his time has come. "Lord," he says in surrender. "I am Yours. Let me die with the Philistines."

God answers this prayer. The entire temple is destroyed.

But Samson's victory is short-lived. The Philistines continue to wage war on the Israelite people. In the midst of this mayhem, the God of Abraham, for the first time in history, sends a holy man, a prophet. God will reveal the future of the Israelites to this man, Samuel. Not only will he deliver the Israelites from the Philistines, but he will also become their greatest spiritual leader since Moses.

It has been many years since God has spoken to His people. Again God chooses Hannah—a righteous, barren woman—as his vessel. God answers her prayer for a son, whom she names Samuel, which means "He hears God."

When Samuel is fifty years old, he stands at a sacrificial site atop Mount Mizpah, surrounded by priests and elders. His hair is long and his beard is turning gray. The day has been a disaster for the Israelites, as Philistine soldiers have cut down entire Israelite families on the slopes of this rocky mountain. Even as Samuel now stands at its summit, a new battle rages below. The Israelite fortifications are weak, and though their army does their best to repulse the Philistines, the odds of them holding on for one more hour are slim. It is up to Samuel to save the day, because he is a man of faith. He chooses to wage war by calling on God.

"We must make a sacrifice," Samuel tells the gathering of men. "Where warriors fail, God will triumph." Samuel places a handful of dried twigs on top of a large rock, and then adds larger pieces of kindling. "Lord," he cries out, "hear me in our hour of need."

Phinehas, an elder, isn't watching Samuel pray. He's studying the battle. What he sees isn't good. "Samuel, hurry. They're overrunning our lines!"

Even as the blaze grows larger and the flames seem to lick at the hem of Samuel's robe, the sounds of screaming and death can be heard. How far away are the battle lines? A half mile? Four hundred yards? Why, a swift Philistine could run that distance in minutes and kill Samuel and every other man here gathered. To merely stand and pray is an act of foolishness.

A desperate Phinehas would very much like to flee. He turns, on the verge of doing just that.

Samuel calmly reminds him to hold fast. "God is our only hope," he says.

As Samuel continues to put his faith in God, the Israelite army is being crushed. Their lines have fallen, and Philistine fighters are climbing over the dead bodies. A Philistine victory at Mount Mizpah could mean the end of the entire Israelite nation, and men, women, and children flee from the approaching Philistines.

Samuel lifts the sacrificial lamb onto the fire, scattering sparks everywhere, wreathing Samuel and the priests in smoke. "Lord, please accept our sacrifice and help us. Help Your servant in his hour of need."

He says no more. The clang of swords and screams of the dying grow nearer. Children are crying out for their mothers, and wives keen over the deaths of their husbands. Samuel is not indifferent to those sounds, but he remains focused on God's voice. He lifts his face to heaven and straightens his spine. Samuel's face grows taut and focuses as he listens to God.

A clap of thunder. A bolt of lighting. A single raindrop. And then a great wind rolls across Mount Mizpah, sweeping over Samuel and then down toward the advancing Philistine army, stopping them in their tracks. That single raindrop becomes a deluge, soaking the Philistines and turning the earth to a thick mud that makes their advance impossible.

"Hear your God, O Israelites," bellows Samuel over the wind. "He now comes to your aid."

Phinehas and the priests stand amazed. Samuel quietly gives thanks. On the mountain below them, the bodies of brave Israelite men are strewn as haphazardly as the sticks of Samuel's sacrificial fire. Philistine footsteps once again trample these corpses, but this time those footsteps are racing down the mountain, not up. Lightning strikes at their heels. They are retreating as fast and as far as their feet will carry them, thanks to Samuel and God.

The burden of being a prophet means having to prove that connection with God to the people over and over again. Years later, as Samuel grows old, he appoints his sons as Israel's leaders. Samuel gathers with the elders and priests at his home. His two sons, Joel and Abijah, have also been asked to join them. It was the elders who called this meeting, so Samuel is baffled by their presence. "What troubles you?" he asks cautiously.

Phinehas speaks for the group. "We are grateful, prophet. You have given us great victories."

"God has given us great victories," Samuel corrects him.

"But who will speak to the Lord after you are gone?"

Samuel gestures to his boys. "My sons."

Phinehas is in awe of Samuel, so what he has to say takes a great deal of courage. "But Samuel, your sons are corrupt."

Samuel is not often furious, or even unkind. But now he stands and towers over Phinehas, his face livid with rage. "What? I have brought up my sons to trust in God and obey His laws. Everything I have done for you has been done because I walk in God's ways."

"They take bribes, Samuel. Everyone knows it. They shame your good name."

Samuel stares in horror at his sons. They can't meet his look. The silence is deafening after an eternity.

"So after you are gone," Phinehas continues, "and the Philistines return and we look to your sons to call on God...will God answer?"

A crushed Samuel closes his eyes in anguish.

"Tell me: what do our people want? What will reassure them that God will hear their cries?"

Phinehas speaks just two words—two words that will change the Israelite people forever: "A king."

Samuel is dumbfounded. "A king? This is a most dangerous idea. God is our king."

"Why should we be different from other nations?" demands Phinehas.

"But look what other nations' kings have done to their people. Kings become tyrants. They enslave their own kind," Samuel shouts.

"But never in history has a king been anointed by a prophet of God. That king would be different."

All the elders nod in agreement. Samuel still doesn't see the idea's wisdom. His sons, the two men who have made this meeting necessary, stare at the floor, quite aware that their opinions do not matter. King or no king, their shame will follow them the rest of their lives.

"God has promised us this land," Samuel argues. "It is not right for one of us to become king."

"How do we know that, Samuel?" counters Phinehas. "Have you asked him?"

Samuel is alone atop a desert hill. His thoughts are focused on God. Their partnership has molded the Israelite people ever since the death of Samson. In the many dreams and conversations in which God has revealed His plans, there has never once been mention of an earthly king. So this idea put forth by the elders—an idea that has great merit—is stupefying. Is this an idea of man's or of God's? Samuel needs to know the answer.

"I have given everything," he explains to God. "But if you say I should give them a king, of course I will. But what should I do?"

God tells Samuel that they are not rejecting Samuel when they ask for a king. They are, instead, rejecting God. He tells Samuel to warn the people that an earthly king will be corrupt, and they will be very sorry when they live under the pain he causes them. But despite God's and Samuel's warnings, the people demand a king, so God decides to answer their prayers and give them one.

God plants an image in Samuel's head. It is that of a man who is physically head and shoulders above everyone else. Good with a sword, and at home on the field of battle: Saul.

Samuel bows his head. Then an idea hits him. He looks up at the darkening skies. "He will be the king and I will still be Your prophet, oh Lord. I can guide Your king."

Samuel goes in search of Saul, to name him the first king of Israel. He finds him weeks later, in a small village. Before a crowd of hundreds who chant his name in adulation, Saul is proclaimed the Israelite ruler. Samuel anoints the new king with oil, and the Holy Spirit comes upon him.

But Israel's new king does not rule alone. He is subject to the word of the prophet. So even as Samuel stands over a kneeling Saul, pouring olive oil onto his forehead to anoint him as king, it is understood that they are a team: Saul is the king, and Samuel is his seer, the man to whom God predicts the future. "May I, as God's prophet, help you in any way I can," Samuel tells Saul.

The new king rises to his feet. The crowd surrounding the small platform chants his name. The ceremony has been brief, and no crown has been placed upon Saul's head. But he is king, nonetheless, ruler of all the land. His first and foremost task is to reclaim the Promised Land by waging war on the Philistines and any other nation that seeks to claim it as their own.

Saul has a rebellious steak. He will have trouble letting Samuel play his role as prophet, and both men know it. As the two men now stare into one another's eyes just moments after the modest coronation, it is clear that their partnership will not always be an easy one.

It does not take long for Saul to lead the Israelites into battle. He is a good leader and wins many battles. On the morning of one planned attack, Saul and a small band of Israelite soldiers crouch low and run up a slope that overlooks an encampment of the Amalekites. Saul is short of breath after the brief uphill sprint, but his mind is sharp as he surveys the enemy. He has been told by Samuel to wait seven days, at which time Samuel will come and make the required sacrifice to God. Those seven days have almost passed. Saul is growing impatient.

He sees just one sentry. Time to attack.

"Are the men ready?" he says in a level voice to a nearby officer.

"Yes," comes the reply.

"And Samuel," Saul asks. "Any sign? We must make a sacrifice before we strike."

The officer takes a breath and shakes his head.

There has been no sign, no message, nothing at all to let Saul know Samuel's whereabouts or plans. This is the first test of their uneasy partnership. Saul feels abandoned. There is no longer time to wait. His men are growing impatient. Saul is losing his confidence. There must be a sacrifice before battle. In his impatience and presumption, he believes Samuel won't come, so he takes Samuel's place as priest and prophet and slits the lamb's throat himself.

It is done. Saul holds the bloody knife and the limp corpse as a nearby soldier holds a bowl under the sheep's neck to catch the blood. Suddenly, a voice can be heard shouting angrily at Saul. "May God forgive you," cries Samuel. "May God forgive you!"

Saul looks up to see Samuel striding up the hill toward him, pushing his way through a thick crowd of impatient soldiers. "Where were you?" cries a furious Saul. "Seven days we've been waiting. My men are deserting."

Samuel says nothing. He grabs the blade from Saul's fist and seizes hold of the sheep. "Focus on being a military leader," he orders. "And leave the job of being a priest to me. God will not honor your sacrifice."

"I don't have time to argue, Samuel. Some of us have a fight to win. Some of us might not return."

"Remember, God instructs you to kill everyone and everything in this battle you are about to wage. Do not spare anyone or take any spoil."

Saul only glares at Samuel, then orders his men to assemble.

The attack goes according to plan. Saul personally leads the way, then watches with pride as his men slip quietly into the enemy camp. After a week of waiting, the entire battle takes just ten minutes. His men have even taken a battle-scarred warrior prisoner, and they lead him to a small wooden cage.

Saul has won his first victory since becoming king. "God is with me," he shouts, thrusting his arms to the heavens. "God is with me."

His men cheer Saul, even as they round up the goats and cattle captured from the enemy. The Israelites have eaten little in the past few weeks, and the prospect of a hot meal does wonders for morale.

Samuel watches from atop a nearby ridge. He has seen the battle and hears Saul's delighted cries. "Are You really with him, Lord?" Samuel asks. "Really?"

The prisoner and the spoils are the problem. King Agag, as he is known, is alive. And so are the best of his herds of cattle and goats. Yet Samuel told Saul that God specifically ordered him to destroy everything in the village. Now, as the evening campfires roar and the Israelite army relaxes after a meal of freshly slaughtered cattle, Samuel confronts Saul in front of his army. "You had one task. One simple command from God. And what was that?"

"I have done what God commanded," replies a seething Saul.

"Then what is this bleating of goats in my ears? And who is this pagan king at your feet?"

"He will soon be put to death."

Samuel glares at Saul, then walks to Agag's cage and pulls hard on the rope around the king's neck. Agag crawls out like a dog, then roars in defiance. But it is Samuel, and not Saul, who quiets that roar. The normally placid Samuel plunges a knife into Agag's neck. Death comes in an instant for the prisoner, whose lifeless body falls to the ground at Samuel's feet. Samuel bends down and pulls out the knife, wiping the blade on the dead man's robe.

"When God says kill, you kill," says Samuel.

A shocked Saul struggles to assert himself. He has put up with Samuel's selfishness and tantrums one last time. "Samuel, you are our prophet, but I am your king."

"What the Lord gives, He can take away," Samuel shoots back.

Saul is feeling confident. "Are these God's words? Or are they yours?"

"Your descendants could have ruled for a thousand years, but because of your actions today, God has forsaken you."

Saul grabs Samuel and means to shake him, but the men are watching. Better to maintain dignity than to lose control. "More divine words?" Saul asks through clenched teeth.

Samuel turns away. The fabric of his robe tears off in Saul's clenched fist. Rather than be outraged, Samuel quickly seizes the opportunity to make a point. "Just as you have torn my robe, so God has torn your power from you. He wants a man after His own heart."

Saul storms away, muttering under his breath about Samuel's arrogance. Killing him would be all too easy, though it would anger God. Samuel has sown seeds of doubt in Saul's mind, a feeling this eternally confident warrior has never known. But rather than react with violence, he desires to be alone.

"Bring me wine!" orders Saul as he throws open the door to his tent. A servant pours wine. Saul sits and drinks, staring hard at the scrap of fabric in his hands. "Perhaps I was too hasty," he says, shaking his head. "Perhaps I should ask Samuel's forgiveness."

Saul calls to his servant. "Bring Samuel to me," he orders.

"He's gone, Highness," replies the servant.

Saul storms out, screaming for Samuel, But the prophet is long gone— gone to find a new king.

That king will be David.

PART FOUR

A MAN AFTER
GOD'S OWN HEART

David is just sixteen years old when Samuel anoints him as Saul's successor to the throne of Israel. A thousand years from now his direct descendant, Jesus of Nazareth, will also be proclaimed King of the Jews.

But even though David will eventually take the throne, Saul remains Israel's king for now. Saul knows nothing of Samuel's whereabouts or action, or David's right to his throne. It is the end of yet another battle in the midst of the endless, arid desert of the Promised Land. Once again, Saul's army has won, for he has no equal in waging war. Despite being outnumbered, he continues to defeat the Philistines, Israel's most feared enemy.

A bloodied Saul and his teenage son, Jonathan, walk slowly through the troops. Jonathan congratulates the men; Saul says nothing. Despite the victory, he feels beaten down, overwhelmed. An omnipotent warrior, Saul is an inept ruler once the fighting ends. And even the most epic of battles eventually comes to an end.

"Saul, Saul, Saul," chant his men. They would endure any hardship for their king, fight any foe. "Saul has killed thousands, Saul has killed thousands," they cry, the thunder of their voices carrying across the land.

But inside Saul's head, those cheers are muddled and distorted. He finds no peace in victory and is worn down by the strain of being king. Despite his victories, he still stings from his final confrontation with Samuel. And the question, that infernal question, constantly nags at him: *Has God turned His back on me?*

"Father," exults Jonathan, "this day is ours. The Philistines are crushed."

Of Saul's three sons, Jonathan is the most pure of heart. He is proud of his father's accomplishments and courage. Other men would bask in the praise of such a wonderful young man, but Saul just waves him away and walks alone to his tent. The chants of his men fade to a dull rumble as he pulls back the canvas flap and seeks a moment's peace.

Saul's servant knows this foul mood well, and he is waiting with a goblet of the king's favorite wine. But Saul knocks it flying with a violent swing. "Did I ask for wine?" he growls.

Red wine soaks the walls of his tent and the bright fabric of the pillows covering the floor. Even as his servant rushes to clean up the mess, Saul leans over a bowl of water to wash the blood of battle off his hands and face.

"What's wrong, Father?" It's Jonathan.

Saul ignores him and begins to slap water onto his face, trying to drown out the sound of his beloved son's voice.

"Tell me what's wrong," insists Jonathan.

"Nothing's wrong," bellows Saul.

"Today was a great victory. Why is that never enough?"

Saul dismisses Jonathan and his servant with an angry wave. "I need rest. That is all. A little sleep. Now leave me."

The servant knows to exit as hastily as possible if he wants to keep his head. But Jonathan is not afraid of his father. He holds his ground, hoping that Saul will mumble a word or two that will explain his rage. But it's as if he's not there. Saul lies down top his favorite pillow and falls into a deep sleep within seconds.

But Saul's sleep is not restful. It never is. It's been years since Samuel left, and he has since died. But Saul's fear that he disobeyed God haunts him each and every time he closes his eyes. In his dreams, he relives that long-ago battle with the Amalekites. He winces at the memory of ignoring Samuel. Saul's impatience—his insistence on not waiting those seven days, and his offering sacrifice himself before Samuel could arrive—haunts him. He was so youthful then, so callow, so eager for his first battle to be won.

And when he won, what did Saul do then? Once again, he disobeyed God. Yes, he killed most of the Amalekites. Soldiers, babies, children, women, and the inferior livestock were all put to the knife. But God had demanded that every living thing in the Amalekite fortress be killed. Everything. Saul had failed to do that. The quality cows, sheep, and goats were kept alive. Agag, that wretched king whom Saul should have killed, was alive until Samuel himself thrust a blade into his neck.

Night after night, Saul dreams of how he would do it all differently, if he had the chance. He would wait those seven days and listen closely to Samuel as he shared God's word and then performed sacrifice. Saul would not just run roughshod over the field of battle; he would swing his great sword like an avenging angel, chopping down every living Amalekite and their possessions.

Alone in his tent, Saul cries out in his sleep. "No . . . no . . . Lord, please, I beg of You: forgive Your servant." But he knows what's done is done. Saul has been forgiven, but he must still bear the consequences of his disobedience.

Saul eagerly straps on his battle armor with the help of a young armor bearer. His army is camped in the Valley of Elah, already drawn up in battle array to face yet another vastly superior Philistine force. Green rolling hills surround the valley, and on any other day this lovely and tranquil location might be the ideal place to sit and quietly reflect on God's glory. The Philistines have taken position on one mountainside looking down over the valley; the Israelites on the other. The valley itself is currently a no-man's-land that will soon become the field of battle. A man foolish enough to let down his guard will quickly find his body pierced by the violent end of a spear.

Saul couldn't be happier. Adrenaline courses through his veins at the thought of the action. His spies have brought word of the Philistine defenses, and now Saul's brilliant military mind plans where he will position his forces, and how best to feint and pivot to lure the Philistines to slaughter.

Saul pays little attention to the boy helping him squeeze into his battle armor. The boy's name is David. A shepherd by trade, he has come to the front lines to bring supplies to his older brothers, who are soldiers. They had only laughed at David and sent him away. But he remained, determined to help any way that he can. He now helps tighten the buckles that hold Saul's breastplate firmly in position.

The boy has a secret that he dare not share with Saul.

Suddenly, a breathless Jonathan throws back the flap and steps into Saul's tent. "Father, you must come immediately!"

Saul shakes off young David. He rushes out of the tent, muttering, "What could possibly be so urgent?" David trails behind as Saul pushes his way through the Israelite troops to a broad escarpment looking down into the valley. There they see a man almost nine feet tall standing alone, facing Saul's army. He wears full armor and wields a sword that matches his immense physical size. The entire Philistine army stands behind him.

"Israelites," calls out the giant. "I am Goliath. And I have a proposition for you!"

Saul peers down intently, unsure of what he will hear next.

"Send just one of you to fight me, oh Israelites. Just one. If he wins, then we Philistines will be your slaves. But if I win, you will be our slaves."

When he receives no response from Saul or the other Israelites, Goliath continues his rant. "Come now," he goads them. "Surely there is one of you courageous enough to fight me."

A wave of laughter rolls through the Philistine army at the intimation of Israelite cowardice. They thud the hilts of their swords against their shields as a show of appreciation, and the loud, percussive thunder rolls up the mountainside to Saul and his army. This simple act of defiance brings fear to the Israelite faces, and no man steps forward to take Goliath up on his offer.

"Someone must fight him," cries Jonathan, the lone man in Saul's army eager to do battle. He reaches for his sword.

"No," says Saul calmly. Years of strategizing have shown him the foolishness of letting a man's ego lure him into a trap. Below him, the shield beating continues until Goliath raises his arm as a signal for silence.

"I thought you were 'God's people,'" he roars. "Yet not one of you has enough faith in God to fight me?"

The Israelites' eyes turn downward, ashamed. No one feels he can best the giant. No one wants to bring shame to God and Israel in a vain attempt. The silence is deafening.

"I'll do it!" The calm, sure voice of a boy cuts across the valley, answering Goliath's call. All who hear it are sure it is the cry of a hardened warrior. But it is David, the shepherd, the lowest occupation in the land. He is seventeen years old, accomplished at playing the harp, and a part-time armor bearer for Saul. However, he has never once stepped onto the field of battle.

Saul gives him a patronizing smile. "David. The reward would be great, but you're not a soldier. You're a shepherd."

"Yes," David replies, catching Saul's eye before the king can look away. "And I've protected my sheep from wolves. Just as I've protected my sheep, so God will protect me."

Saul is not swayed, even though Goliath has ratcheted up the tone of his chants, until he is now insulting not just the Israelites, but God, too.

"Where is your faith," chants Goliath. "Where is your God?"

The Israelites continue to cower. But David has deep faith, and the mockery in Goliath's words stirs his anger into a righteous fury. "I will kill him," seethes David. "I will most definitely kill him."

The final straw comes with Goliath's next taunt: "I don't believe that your God is on your side at all. Your God is not as strong as our gods." He beams broadly toward the Philistines, who resume the beating of their shields.

"What will be done for the man who kills this Philistine and removes his disgracer from Israel?" David asks the nearby Israelite soldiers. "Who is this uncircumcised Philistine that he should defy the armies of the living God?"

But the soldiers ignore him. So David takes his argument to Saul. "Let no one lose heart on account of this Philistine," he seethes. "Your servant will go and fight him."

"You are only a boy," Saul replies.

"This boy has been protecting his father's sheep from lions and bears for years," David argues. "This uncircumcised Philistine will be like one of them, because he has defied the armies of the living God."

He chooses to place his protection in the hands of God.

David bends to the ground near Saul's feet. He picks up a smooth stone and examines it. Then another. And another. Until he has selected five perfectly balanced pieces of rock. "The Lord is my shepherd," he says to himself, curbing any fears he might have about what will come next. "The Lord is my shepherd."

He does not ask Saul's permission as he gathers his stones and weaves through the Israelite ranks, each step taking him closer and closer to the valley floor. David is just a teenager, but Saul is impressed. He quickly removes his battle armor and has it hand-carried down to David. But the armor is far too big for the shepherd to wear. He takes it off and heads into battle with just his sling.

"Go," Saul tells him after an instant. "And the Lord be with you."

David emerges from the front of the Israelite line and squares off against Goliath, a grown man and battle-scarred veteran nearly three feet taller than he. David's quiet prayers escalate as the reality of what he has done—and is about to do—threaten to overwhelm him. "Yea, though I walk through the valley of the shadow of death, I will fear no evil. For You are with me. Your rod and staff...they comfort me. You anoint my head with oil. My cup overflows. Surely goodness and mercy will follow me all the days of my life."

Goliath raises a hand to silence the shield beating as David plants his feet and squarely presents himself. David's heart hammers inside his chest. Goliath roars a giant-sized laugh. "Is this Israel's champion?" he bellows, barely able to contain his glee.

David says nothing. He reaches into his satchel, never once taking his eye off Goliath, fingering those five precious stones.

"Don't waste my time, little boy," yells Goliath. "You are too young to die."

"It is you who will die," vows David. "You come against me with sword and spear, but I come against you in the name of the Lord Almighty, whom you have defied."

Goliath sighs and adjusts his armor. "Very well. Then be prepared to be fed to the vultures."

The giant draws his sword and advances, his great strides eating up the distance all too quickly.

David stays calm. He pulls a stone from the bag on his belt and slips it into the cradle of his sling. "For You are with me," he prays. "Your rod and staff . . . they comfort me."

Goliath laughs as he sees David rotate the sling around and around his head. From above, Saul and Jonathan look on without hope, wishing one of them had felt confident enough to face the giant, as they consider their coming enslavement.

David's sling swings faster and faster around his head, the leather and rock whirring louder and louder. Goliath slashes at the air menacingly with his sword, not breaking stride as he bears down on David. There are those among the Israelite army who look away, not wishing to see the young boy butchered. But the Philistines do not turn their heads. They beat their shields and wait for the moment when they will surge forth onto the Israelite encampment. Goliath may have mentioned slavery as the possible outcome of this battle, but the Philistines are in no mood to take home slaves. For a slave can escape to freedom and then come back to claim revenge. Better to kill the Israelites now—all of them.

Goliath turns to give yet another derisive sneer back toward his lines. But young David never once takes his eyes off Goliath.

As Goliath's head is turned ever so slightly, David lets the stone fly from his sling. That flat, smooth rock strikes him squarely on the temple, then falls harmlessly to the ground.

Goliath doesn't know what has happened. His eyes open wide in shock. He stands still as a rock.

Young David does not reload his sling. He merely stands, empty sling dangling from his side, and waits. Waits. Waits.

Then Goliath falls, just as David knew he would. A cloud of dust billows up from the earth, which seems to rumble as Goliath's massive form collides with the battlefield.

The Israelite army roars, even as the Philistines stare in horror.

David slowly inches forward. Goliath struggles to breathe. Using two hands, because the metal weighs so very much, David grabs the giant's sword and lifts it high above his head. Then, with a powerful slice, he severs the enormous head from its body. It is a gruesome moment, but he does not look away. Instead, he raises his eyes to heaven, and then falls to his knees in thanks. David then lifts Goliath's severed head by the hair as a signal for the Israeli army to race forth and slay the Philistines.

Without waiting for a signal from their king, they charge onto the plain past David, racing forth with drawn swords and raised spears to lay waste to the Philistines.

David throws Goliath's head to the ground and stands. He is sweaty, breathless, and triumphant. He beams as Saul approaches and claps him on the shoulder. "A wolf in sheep's clothing is what you are, David. You've saved my kingdom." Saul hands David a sword more befitting his stature. "Come. We have an enemy to conquer."

The Philistines are the first of many enemies that David will fight for Saul. As the years pass, David conquers all the enemies of Israel, always fighting alongside the man he calls his king. The Philistines are driven from the Promised Land, and David forges a deep bond of friendship with Saul and Jonathan. The Israelite army comes to believe that David is invincible, and he becomes a great leader of men—a hero.

What he doesn't tell Saul, or even Jonathan, is that before all this began, at a time when he was just the youngest of many brothers, the prophet Samuel personally anointed him to become King of the Jews. He can still feel the smooth olive oil dripping down from his forehead, and hear the words of Samuel proclaiming that someday he would be Israel's king.

This is David's secret. And, as with even the deepest of secrets, it is only a matter of time until it leaks out.

It is daytime as Saul, Jonathan, David, and his closest compatriot, a Hittite mercenary named Uriah, drive their chariots through the great archway marking the entrance to Saul's fortress. The victorious Israelite army follows them. There are cheers as women, old men, and children come out to greet the returning troops. The women ululate, their high-pitched exclamations drowning out all other sounds. That is, until a chant goes up from the crowd: "Saul! Saul! Saul!"

"Hear that, Father?" says Jonathan, smiling.

"I do," beams Saul.

"Saul has killed thousands!" roars the crowd. A relaxed Saul waves to them. He basks in the praise.

As the chanting continues, Saul and Jonathan lead David and the troops into the fortress. They make their way on foot into a square. Fragrant petals fall through the air around them. But now a new voice rises up from the throngs. "David!" cries a woman. "Look! It's David!"

"David has killed tens of thousands!" yells a man.

This becomes the new chant. "David has killed tens of thousands! David has killed tens of thousands."

Saul's smile vanishes, replaced by a dark, angry glare. Jonathan, as always, does his best to appease his father. "David deserves their praise, Father. He served us well."

"What else does he deserve?" Saul answers bitterly. "Next they'll say he deserves my crown."

"David! David! David!"

The chant continues into the evening, giving Saul the most profound headache of his life. He reclines on cushions in his palace courtyard.

The sounds of the crowd waft in through the open windows. Across the room, Jonathan reclines on a second mound of pillows, as do David and Michal—Saul's beautiful young daughter.

Michal can't take her eyes off of David. He is everything a princess could want in a man: rugged, handsome, sensitive, and intuitively wise.

Jonathan happily gazes at his best friend while they reminisce about their times on the battlefield. "You took out those two Philistines with one swing!" says an awed Jonathan.

"That day was ours from the start," David answers humbly.

Saul gazes intently at David. He glowers at him from the other side of the reception chamber, his mind working over paranoid scenarios, wondering if the laughter coming from Jonathan and David is at his expense. So Saul leans forward, listening more intently. "David," he bellows after a moment. "David!"

David stops speaking. A confused look passes between him and Jonathan.

"Come here!" Saul demands.

David rises and stands before Saul. He bows. Jonathan and Michal, who know their father's moods, share an anxious look.

"So," Saul says to David, a thin smile curling over his face. "You are our champion yet again. You've killed thousands—"

"Tens of thousands," Jonathan corrects.

"Thank you, Jonathan. Tens of thousands. Our people are deeply grateful to you, David." Saul's words belie the menacing intensity writ large across his face. Even as David affects a modest posture, Saul's anger grows and grows.

"The Lord has blessed us all," David says.

"I offer you my daughter, Michal," Saul says suddenly.

"What?" replies a stunned David, his face showing surprise.

"I would like to reward you. I want you to become part of my family. So I am offering my daughter's hand in marriage."

Michal blushes appreciatively.

"Who am I, and who is my family that I should be the king's son-in-law?" David says with a low bow, never taking his eyes off of Saul.

Jonathan rushes across and embraces David. "We are brothers now. This is a great day."

But Saul raises a hand. "In return..."

The room falls silent.

"For the hand of my beloved Michal, you must slay a hundred Philistines—and bring me their foreskins."

David's eyes narrow. His instincts were right.

"Killed by your own hand, of course," Saul adds.

Jonathan leaps to David's defense. "Father! He has risked enough. Do you not remember Goliath? Do you not remember the many times he has bravely fought at your side?"

"You surprise me, Jonathan," Saul says slowly. "I would think you would instantly agree that your sister is worth a hundred Philistines—or maybe ten thousand, as you corrected me a moment ago."

There is silence in the room. Even the chanting outside has stopped. David curls and uncurls his fist, staring Saul straight in the eye. A crushed Michal mourns what might have been, knowing that single-handedly killing a hundred Philistines is an almost impossible task. "But what if he doesn't return?" she softly pleads to her father. "What if David never comes back alive?"

"Oh, I'll return," says David. "God willing."

He's smiling. The time has come. His secret can finally be revealed. But first he has a job to do.

David is up early the next morning. He gathers a small band of men, their horses loaded with weapons and food. David has selected the most elite warriors in the army. Each is a volunteer, told of Saul's demand for a hundred dead Philistines and warned that they might not return. In addition, David has promised each man that it would not tarnish his reputation in the slightest if he refuses this mission. But not a single man has said no. In fact, many were so eager to accompany David that they began preparing their gear immediately. They have fought at his side before, and their loyalty for this courageous man is limitless. Chief among them is Uriah. No man is braver or more loyal on the field of battle. David trusts him with his life, and their friendship runs deep.

Surprise will be David's greatest ally. So, rather than leading his team on a circuitous path around the mountains separating the Israelites and the Philistines, he plans to go straight up and over. The trail is rocky and lined with cliffs, but there is less chance that spies will see them and warn the enemy of their approach.

David leads them out. A simple nod signals that it is time to move. No one has come to see the men off. As warriors have done since the beginning of time, each man has quietly said his good-byes to loved ones. Now they all turn their focus to the mission. The warriors quickly form their horses into a single-file line and trot toward the mountains.

At the last minute, just before they disappear from sight, David turns back to Saul's palace and waves a final salute to his king. Saul watches from the parapets, just as David knew he would. After a moment's hesitation, Saul returns the salute.

Jonathan joins his father on the parapet. "He wants our crown," says a paranoid Saul.

"He is loyal, Father. I swear it. Loyal to both of us."

"You are the heir to my kingdom, my firstborn son, and a man who will lead this kingdom for the next generation. That is why I have sent David on this mission."

Jonathan gasps as he realizes what his father has done. "You don't want him back. You want him dead."

Saul loves his son dearly, but in his opinion, the young man is always too dramatic. More than once, Saul has wished that Jonathan had the calm nerves and the sharp mind of David.

"You love him," Saul tells his son, "as Abel no doubt loved Cain."

He is the king. His word is law. What's done is done. He walks back into the palace in search of his favorite courtesan.

Jonathan drops his head into his hands, appalled that he will see his friend no more. His friendship with David is so close their souls are knit together.

But Jonathan, like his father, underestimates David. Within weeks he and Uriah are guiding their army back into the city's main square. Crowds gather to witness their return, and a sobbing and ecstatic Michal fights her way through to the front, where she throws herself at him.

David dismounts and wraps his arms around her, never letting go of the burlap bag he grasps tightly in one fist. She is his reward for performing an impossible task at the order of his king. But in order to claim that trophy, he must finish the job.

Followed by his men, David swaggers into Saul's throne room. David still clutches that bag, while his men clutch the sword and battle armor taken from the Philistines. He bows low before a most unhappy Saul. "My king," David says. "A few mementos for you."

When Saul first ordered David to slay one hundred Philistines, it was understood that David would provide proof. Now the king stares from his throne at the bag in David's hand. The bottom of the sack is clearly drenched in blood.

"What have you?" asks a curious Saul.

David cannot contain his smile as he holds out the bloody sack to his king. He waits until Saul peers inside before announcing its contents to the small crowd gathered in the throne room. "In that bag, you'll find the mementos that I cut off of each man I killed."

Saul realizes what he is seeing, and recoils at the sight and smell. "These are from a hundred men?"

"Two hundred," David replies calmly. "God was with me."

Taking Michal by the hand, David turns to leave. A furious Saul knows that he's been beaten. Overcome with vanity and rage, he lunges forward and grabs a spear from one of his guards. With the power of a man who has thrown such a weapon for more than thirty years, he hurls it at David's head.

Michal screams as the spear narrowly misses David and sticks into the timber doorjamb.

Nobody knows what to say. Everyone stares at Saul, who stands straight and tall—but who now seems smaller and more insignificant than he did just a moment earlier. He sways slightly. His face is pale and blank. Not only has God removed His favor from Saul, but an evil spirit has begun to torment him, meaning that the powers of darkness are now influencing his behavior.

The next move is David's. All the palace guards position themselves for some sort of attack, knowing that their first job is to protect Saul. Yet David merely pulls the spear from the wood and stares deeply into Saul's dark eyes. David drops the spear to the ground. He leaves hand in hand with Michal.

But David knows better than to remain in Saul's palace and soon leaves his bride. Michal is brokenhearted, but she understands. Her loyalty now lies with her husband. When the soldiers come to take David away on orders of the king, she lies to them, saying that David is sick.

It is a simple lie, and the soldiers see through it easily as Saul's paranoia grows. But Michal's words delay them just long enough for David to escape into the desert, knowing all too well that Saul will go to any length to hunt him down and kill him. The secret is out: Saul believes that he and David are now locked in a fight for the Kingdom of Israel.

David is on the run. Wherever he goes, Saul is just one step behind. The man who was made king to lead the Israelites against the Philistines is now distracted with hunting down David and anybody loyal to him. Saul and his men range far and wide across the broad deserts and valleys of the Promised Land, leaving a cruel wake of violence and mayhem in their wake. At one shrine, a priest is found to have sheltered David. Objecting to the holy man's arguments that God's house is a place of sanctuary, Saul ordered that the priest and all of his acolytes be put to the sword immediately. He is a man who has never minded getting his hands bloody, but his obsession with David takes that to another level.

At the end of a long day of chasing David, Saul's troops are encamped by a river. Tents are erected. Horses are being fed. Saul walks off from the camp. He is alone, and he likes it that way. At the base of a cliff he looks right and left to see if anyone can hear him, and then Saul cries out to the Lord. "I have served You faithfully," he beseeches, "as faithfully as a man can. And still it seems it is not enough. Lord, I ask You, do You hear Your servant?"

He waits, but there is silence. Nothing. He wearily walks on, looking for a cool dry cave to get out of the heat. At length, he finds one. Saul steps inside. He looks around, searching for signs of life—predatory animals, poisonous snakes, or perhaps a desert ruffian who has made the cave a home.

But he sees nothing. Saul lifts his robe to relieve himself in the dim light of the cave.

A hooded figure stands behind a nearby rock. He stays in the shadows and silently extracts a knife from its sheath. Moving with utter stealth, the hooded man sneaks up behind Saul, ready to strike. But something about the breadth of those shoulders is familiar.

The hooded man is David, and he realizes that the man standing before him is a very distracted Saul. But although he is inches from Saul, he chooses not to attack him. He is loyal to the anointed king—even though that loyalty may cost him his life. Instead, he silently cuts a strip of fabric from Saul's robe and steps back into the shadows.

The instant Saul finishes his business, David cries out, "Majesty!"

Saul spins around, recognizing the voice and drawing his sword. "David?"

David removes his hood from his head. "Why do you hunt me down? Why? I have done you no harm."

Saul warily approaches the shadows, sword at the ready. David steps toward him, and his soldiers follow. They draw their swords, but David uses one arm to wave them back.

"I could have killed you just now," David tells Saul, holding up the strip of cloth. Saul looks at the hem of his robe and slowly raises his eyes to David.

"Why didn't you?" Saul asks.

"I will not kill you. Ever."

But this only serves to infuriate Saul, for he knows that it is the truth. "Yet another reason for the Lord to reward you! You will become king!"

David shakes his head. "You are my king. Anointed by the Lord."

Saul laughs. It is low and sinister. His voice crackles from dehydration brought on by fear. "And when you are king, do you promise you will not kill my descendants and wipe out my name?"

"I will not, Majesty. I swear."

Saul considers what David has said. Then he sheathes his sword and looks chillingly into David's eyes as he holds out his hand. "Come then . . . let's go home . . . together."

David is wary. He holds Saul's gaze, and as he does so his men tighten their grip on their swords. Showing grace and a quiet strength, he walks to Saul, shakes his head, bows, and then turns to join his men.

Saul, looking wretched and aged, turns and walks back alone to his camp.

Just an hour ago he beseeched God to speak with him. And now he realizes that God has sent him a very clear message—though not the message that Saul longed to hear.

The dignity of the monarchy now belongs to David. He is the man who will be king. It's just a matter of time.

That night, Saul sits alone in his tent. He uses his dagger to carve the meat from a shank of lamb, letting its blood drip on the table. Outside, he hears the thunder of hooves, signaling the arrival of a messenger. Then Jonathan enters, breathless.

"Father!" Jonathan cries.

"What is it, son?" growls Saul.

"The Philistine army is in the next valley. Near Gilboa—"

For once, Saul couldn't care less about battle. "Jonathan," he says gently, "David is near."

"Forget David! You must defend your kingdom. It is your duty!"

Saul grows anxious. His legendary courage is nowhere to be seen. He prepares to bawl out the orders to prepare for battle, but inside he feels a strange lack of confidence. "We leave at dawn," he mumbles meekly. "At dawn. Tell the men. And now leave me, son. I must seek guidance."

After Jonathan departs, Saul wanders alone into the night. He aims for the raging fire he has seen in the distance these past few evenings, for he knows that it is the camp of a woman who speaks to the dead. She is not an Israelite, a pagan, with no god to call her own. It is yet another example of Saul not trusting God.

Saul is dazed, tormented. He would be easy prey if he were attacked during his journey, for he carries no sword and is incapable of defending himself. Finally, he sees the flames and hears the jangle of shells and bones that hang in a tree, blown by the wind. Saul has the presence of mind to cover the bottom of his face with a scarf, so that the medium will not know his true identity. But when he steps into the light of her fire, he sees that it does not matter. The old woman is in a trance as she sways back and forth, crying out for the spirit world to hear her—and answer.

Saul makes a simple request: "Bring up the spirit of the dead prophet Samuel."

She does not make eye contact with Saul. Instead, the seer speaks to the flames: "We ask you . . . the dead . . . for an audience with the prophet Samuel."

Samuel appears to Saul, sitting on a rock right next to him. "Why? Why do you wake me? Why do you disturb my spirit?"

"Forgive me," an astonished Saul stammers. "I only called you because...because when I speak to the Lord He does not answer."

Samuel looks bemused. "The Lord? Really?" A smile now flits across his bearded face. "You disobeyed the Lord," he reminds Saul.

"I tried to obey," Saul answers. "Really. I tried."

"He has torn your kingdom from you and given it to David." Samuel glares at the man he once anointed king. "Look at me, Saul."

Saul doesn't want to. He doesn't know whether Samuel is real or a ghost. To look into Samuel's eyes is to look into some great abyss that Saul has never seen before. But he looks anyway.

"This battle will be your last," Samuel says evenly.

"No. Please. No."

"Soon you will be with me in the cold earth, Saul—as will your son."

"Take me," Saul begs. "But spare Jonathan."

But Samuel is gone. The only sound Saul hears is the rattle of bones and shells clanging in the wind.

No father should ever outlive his son. The death of a child is the greatest pain anyone can bear. So when Samuel's prophecy comes true, and the Philistines put an arrow into Jonathan as he stands at Saul's side on the slopes of Mount Gilboa, the king can no longer cope with the disaster he has created. His spiral into despair is now complete.

Saul unstraps the battle armor from his chest and kneels near Jonathan. Tears stream down his cheeks. He secures the handle in the ground, pointing the tip at his chest. Then Saul falls on his sword. He screams in agony, but his death is not quick. As the enemy approach he begs a nearby Amalekite warrior to finish him off. Instead, the Amalekite steals Saul's crown, jumps on a horse, and rides away. Leaving Saul to die slowly, with plenty of time to think of all he has done and lament all that he has lost.

David and his men wait for news from the fight. Saul has not asked them to join in his fight against the Amalekites for fear that David will outshine him on the field of battle. David hears the *clap-clap-clap* of horses' hooves and the gallop of a lone horseman. He steps from the cave and draws his sword to challenge the messenger, unsure whether the rider is of the Israelite or Philistine persuasion.

It is the Amalekite who has stolen Saul's crown. He clutches it in one hand.

"A crushing victory," gasps the Amalekite messenger, winded from his long hard ride.

David smiles in relief until he hears the second half of the news: "For the Philistines."

"And the king," David demands. "What of him?"

"Dead." He now holds the crown out to David, who is reluctant to accept it.

"And his heir, Jonathan?"

The messenger smiles as he shakes his head. "Dead." He once again extends the crown to David. This time, David takes it from him.

Fingering the crown, David asks, "How did Saul die?"

The Amalekite lies and tells David what he believes he wants to hear: "He had fallen on his own sword, and as the enemy approached he asked me to finish him off, lest he be tortured. So I slew him and brought his crown to you."

A thunderstruck David takes a deep breath and replies, "You killed the Lord's anointed," and instantly orders that the Amalekite be put to the sword.

As his men pull the messenger from his horse, David looks away. He is truly devastated by the news. He is especially saddened by the death of Jonathan, whom he loved like a brother. David looks off into the distance. Uriah, his trusted lieutenant and confidant, moves toward his friend. David places a hand on his shoulder. "At least we can go home."

"You don't see it, do you?" asks Uriah.

David is puzzled. He has no answer.

"This is the beginning, David. Our time has come."

Now the other men spill out of the cave and walk toward David, realizing that the new ruler of Israel stands before them. "The people will look to you to defend them," Uriah tells his friend. "They will want you to unite the Israelites once again."

David stares at Uriah, taking in his words. He is not used to being lectured, so at first he is numb to the Hittite's comments. But then they wash over him, soak into him, revitalize him. David grips Uriah's arm tightly and embraces him. "Thank you, dear friend. You are right. If God has cleared the way, we must be strong."

Now he looks at his men. He knows precisely what he must do next. "Let it begin," he pronounces.

Uriah pulls away from David's embrace. He looks David in the eye as an equal for the last time, and then slowly kneels. "Yes, my king. Let it begin."

The other men follow Uriah's lead, so that now David is the only man standing.

"King David!" they roar.

In time, all of Israel's tribes come under David's rule. As his kingdom and power grow, he decides he needs a capital city from which to rule, and a proper home for the Ark of the Covenant.

The city he chooses is just five miles from David's childhood home in Bethlehem. It is an inspired choice, situated at the crossroads of the north and south trading routes, with deep valleys protecting it on three sides, and a constant supply of fresh water nearby. Abraham once visited here during his years of wandering, back when the city was called Salem. Now it is ruled by a people called the Jebusites, who call the city Jebus.

David plans to conquer the city and give it a new name: City of David. Later this city will return to its pre-Davidic name: Jerusalem. It is a name that honors God, for it means "God is peace." The last part of the word is *shalom* in Hebrew.

In David's dream, he sees that Israel will finally know peace during his reign. That will one day come to pass.

This ancient fortress is already occupied. And walled. If David is to make Jebus his own, he must take it by force. The king of Israel has a plan to penetrate those enormous and guarded walls.

Nighttime. David's lean, muscular torso is wedged inside a sewer pipe. He emerges into a larger tunnel and lights a torch. Soon, the rest of his army climbs into the light behind him. The sound of dripping water echoes up and down the dank stone enclosure. A river of cold black water rises up to their ankles.

The men crawl slowly through the sludge. They do not speak, and communicate only by hand signals. The tunnel soon opens up into a wider chamber completely filled with deep water. Their way is blocked by iron bars rising from the ceiling clear down into the depths below.

Uriah looks at David and raises an eyebrow. *What do we do next?* he seems to be asking.

David simply hands him his torch and dives into the filthy water. A minute passes. And then what seems like another. Uriah and the others anxiously watch and wait, peering down into the muck to where the bottom of the iron bars might be. It feels like an eternity.

Suddenly, David surfaces and treads water on the opposite side of the bars. "Come on."

Uriah hesitates. He's never been much of a swimmer, even in the clearest of waters. But to immerse himself in this filth and then open his eyes to find his way...the thought is reprehensible. A glance at the other men shows that they are experiencing the same fears. "Leave the torches," David commands. With three simple words and a powerful tone of voice he has reminded the men that he is no mere soldier. He is the king. And he must be obeyed. Uriah sets down his torch and jumps in. The quiet splashes of the other men soon follow.

A passage leads from the sewer into the city's underground reservoir, filled with drinking water. David and the men happily immerse themselves in the cool clear water, eager to clean themselves. They swim onward through the cistern until a thin shaft of light plays on the water.

"A well," Uriah says with a smile.

David merely nods, his eyes searching the narrow stone walls for the one requirement vital to all wells: a rope. He spies it in the cleft between two rocks and swims for it.

Within ten minutes David and his men have all pulled themselves up the rope and out of the well. They are now inside the walled city of Jebus. They move quietly through the nighttime shadows. It is well past midnight, and the city is asleep. Two Jebusite soldiers walk past on a lonely patrol. David and Uriah pounce, silently slit their throats, and drag their bodies into an alley, then move carefully to the city's main gates to open them for his main force.

Only when he and his men are in position, does David yell his battle cry: "Israel!"

The roar of his voice carries through the night. Outside the city, David's waiting army hears him and runs to the gate. Inside the walls, David and his men overpower the guards manning the gates and pull down the great levers that raise the opening. A Jebusite guard slashes at an unaware Uriah. But David saves his friend's life by running the man through with his broadsword.

Nothing needs to be said. Uriah merely nods his thanks. He and David stand back to welcome the army into the city.

By dawn it is done. The gates of Jebus are still open, but where there was darkness there is now sunlight. Where there were fighting soldiers, there is now a happy crowd of Israelites cheering David and the con-

quest of Jebus, which they will rename the City of David—and, ultimately, Jerusalem.

God is honored in a procession that winds through the crowd, and
the morning sun flashes off a moving sheet of gold. Priests in multicolored ephods lead the way. A wooden box plated with gold is carried
through town on long wooden poles. Heads bow as it passes, for this is
the most potent symbol of Israel's bond with God. It is the Ark of the
Covenant, and it contains the Ten Commandments.

Israelite children run gleefully alongside, not realizing the majesty of
this moment. David dances with spiritual fervor in front of the procession, and even invites the children to join him. Once the children have
begun to dance, he invites men and women from the crowd. This is a
masterstroke of kingship for David, combining the joy of his victory with
the arrival of the Ark of the Covenant. He is consolidating his city as the
center of religious and political power. Right now, at this very moment, it
seems he can do no wrong.

But he is a man. And where there is man there is sin. So even in his
moment of greatest of triumph, temptation clouds David's judgment. He
knows better. He knows that God has blessed him in abundance, and
that the sin that is now crossing his mind is no different than turning
his back on God.

But he can't help himself. The woman before him is so beautiful. No, delectable. Every manly urge in his body desires her. She is
sensual, voluptuous, wondrous, and dazzling to behold. And she is
untouchable—Uriah's wife.

"Do you mind?" David yells to Uriah above the roar of the crowd,
extending his hand to Bathsheba.

Uriah nods his acceptance.

"I mind," says Bathsheba, smiling. David takes her hand anyway and
swirls her into a dance.

Uriah watches David. Surely he is imagining it. Can David really be
dancing this close to his wife. He is more than a little uneasy with how
much David seems to be enjoying himself.

No matter whether it is night or day, Bathsheba is never far from David's thoughts as he turns Jerusalem into a thriving hub of Israelite power. As king, it seems only right that he possess anything in his kingdom that he desires—and right now, he desires Bathsheba.

David stands on the roof, surveying a model of his proposed temple in front of him. The sight is beautiful to behold. It is broad daylight. From his palace's rooftop terrace, he can look down into the courtyards of the many homes and gardens that surround its walls.

Suddenly, David's gaze is distracted by another wondrous vision. Down below, two women servants hold up a sheet to conceal their mistress as she washes in her courtyard bath. Too bad for them that the sheets protect this woman—Bathsheba—only from the side. No one ever thought that the king himself might be looking down from on high, watching her naked body as she soaps and oils her skin.

It is just a bath. A simple daily ritual that Bathsheba enjoys. She is merely washing herself. David considers this sight to be the pinnacle of beauty and sensuality. He is out of his mind with desire. This afternoon bath he is witnessing has made him incapable of coherent thought. David, a man after God's own heart, is in the clutches of a most powerful temptation, and drifting further and further from God.

A man clears his throat behind him. "Your Majesty?"

Startled, David snaps out of his trance. He turns to see the robed prophet Nathan strolling tentatively across the terrace, curious as to what sight has David so inspired.

"Ah, prophet!" David enthuses. "Look! My temple...for the Ark."

"I don't understand, Your Highness. You've summoned me to discuss...a temple?"

David beckons to him and points down to the small architectural model of his glorious temple. It is stunning to behold, with towering pillars and the sturdy walls of a fortress. "The world has never seen anything like this, prophet. The Lord will be pleased."

But if Nathan is dazzled, he does not show it. He stands still. Then he speaks in solemn tones. "The Lord came to me last night."

"And tell me: is He pleased with our work?"

"The Lord told me this: the House of David will rule over Israel forever."

"We are blessed," David exults, overcome with joy. As if to punctuate the enormity of his blessings, he sidles back over to the wall and gapes once again at Bathsheba.

"Your son will be king," Nathan is telling him, although David isn't listening.

"Your son," he says louder, making sure that he is heard, "will build this temple."

A stunned David turns around. "My temple?"

"God's temple," Nathan corrects.

"Right, right," David says, temporarily forgetting Bathsheba. "God's temple." He longs for the construction of a great monument to ensure that Israel will always remember his accomplishments. But now God will not grant him that comfort. Instead, it will be his son who will be remembered.

A son. The thought turns David's disappointment to gratitude. *Oh, how wonderful. I will have a son, and to know that my son will be king. And that his son's son will succeed him. And so on. Forever.*

"Thank you, Nathan," David says, dismissing the prophet.

Nathan leaves. David turns back to the vision below and walks to a lower deck where he can see her more vividly. Even from on high, Bathsheba's wet skin glistens in the sun.

David is troubled by the thoughts that this vision produces. He feels so irrational, capable of almost any sin to satisfy the desires now stirring within him.

He tries to look away. But he can't.

It is spring, the time of year that all kings and warriors should be off waging war. But David has chosen to remain in his palace rather than fight. If anyone asks, he explains that affairs of state need his urgent attention. But he knows that those matters can be handled from a battlefield headquarters. He wants the other men to be gone—particularly Uriah—leaving him alone with Bathsheba.

One warm evening he summons her to his bedroom, the one place that makes his intentions abundantly clear. David's servant leads her into the chamber. One never refuses the king's request, but Bathsheba is a reluctant visitor. Her eyes are cautious and her movements stiff. She has never been fearful in the presence of the king, because her husband has always been at her side. But she is a woman, blessed with the intuition and instinct that comes from a lifetime of men gazing at her longingly. She knows that David wants her—Bathsheba can sense it in the way his eyes prowl across the curves of her body, and in the way that gaze lingers a bit too long on her hair or her eyes. She is flattered that the king would find her beautiful, but she is too in love with Uriah—too devoted to his own tender glances and warm caresses—to ever think of King David in that way.

Bathsheba knows she will refuse him, even as she steps into the room and the servant prepares to announce her. What she wonders is whether or not she will tell her husband of David's intentions. Uriah would be crushed to know that his good friend and king has plotted such a great act of disloyalty.

"Majesty," the servant announces, "as you requested."

David reclines on the bed, a goblet of wine in his hand. He is clothed in his finest evening robes and his feet are bare. "Ah, Bathsheba," he exults as he dismisses his servant.

"Majesty," she answers. Her voice is flat, wary.

"Call me David."

"Have you called to give me news of my husband?"

The king smiles and moves to one side, making room on the bed for Bathsheba should she choose to sit. "No. It's nothing like that. He's safe enough, of that I'm sure. Although I would be remiss in pointing out that he's very far away."

"And you, Majesty, if I may be so bold: why aren't you off fighting the enemy, too?"

"There's no need, Bathsheba. I have very competent men to that for me—men like Uriah."

David is on his feet now, walking to Bathsheba. She remains motionless, knowing what is about to transpire. David circles her, like a wolf sizing up its prey.

"I am loyal to my husband," Bathsheba says firmly. And yet inside she quivers, for the closer that David stands to her, the more aware she becomes that he is the most powerful and revered man in Israel.

"And what about your king?" he asks, stopping to look her in the eye. "Are you loyal to me, as well?"

He slides a hand around the back of her neck and pulls her face toward him. When she doesn't resist, David gently kisses her neck. And then her lips.

Only then does Bathsheba pull away. "This is wrong," she whispers.

"No one needs to know," says David, holding her more firmly as he kisses the soft skin where her neck and shoulders meet. He forces himself not to think about God, or that he is violating two of the Ten Commandments—coveting his neighbor's wife and committing adultery. All David wants is Bathsheba.

She is unable to refuse her king. Soon he has her.

Then he sends her home.

For every sin is a consequence—a punishment, a lesson learned, or a slow downward spiral into a personal wilderness.

For David, it is all three. One month after bedding the lovely Bathsheba, she confronts him with the rather troubling news that she is pregnant with his child.

"You're sure?" David asks, digesting the news by staring out the window.

Bathsheba has tears in her eyes. She nods.

"And how long has your husband been away?"

"He's not the father," she says firmly.

But David isn't satisfied. He needs to cover his sin. So after Bathsheba is sent away, he immediately recalls Uriah from the front lines. It takes days, but soon his longtime friend stands before him in the palace. The Hittite warrior's face is battle-scarred and covered in grime.

"Uriah, my friend," David says warmly, pulling him close for a hug. "Welcome."

"You sent for me, Majesty," Uriah says stiffly. He is angry that David has called him away from his men, and he is eager to return to the front.

"How goes the war?"

"Well. Very well."

An uncomfortable pause settles between them. "And your commander, Joab—all is well with him?"

"All is well," Uriah replies.

"And your fellow soldiers?" asks David, running out of things to say.

"They fight well."

"Well, after you wake in the morning you must return and give me a complete report."

David waves a hand, the gesture for Uriah to leave.

"I will not be here in the morning," says Uriah.

"But of course you will. I give you permission. Surely you want to be with your wife."

Uriah's face grows tight. He is growing impatient. It is late afternoon. If he leaves now he can make it back to the safety of the Israelite encampment before dark. "I cannot stay with my wife," he tells David.

"Of course you can!"

"While my men are camped in open country? While my men prepare to fight the enemy? Knowing that, how could I possibly go home and spend the night with my wife?"

David displays a friendly grin—as if they are both in this together. "Man to man, who's to know?"

"*I* will know, Majesty."

David calls for wine, hoping that getting his friend drunk will break his resolve. But Uriah remains true to his word, insisting that he must leave immediately for the front. "Give this to Joab," David says, handing a sealed letter to Uriah. "See to it that he opens it immediately."

Uriah rides into the Israelite camp and takes the fateful letter directly to Joab, who sees the king's seal on the parchment and steps away to read it in private. "Joab," David has written, "put Uriah in the front lines where the fighting is fiercest. Then withdraw from him so that he will be struck down and die."

This is Uriah's death sentence.

Joab looks up from the letter, and stares into Uriah's eyes. He wants to say something, but he has been trained to follow orders without question, so he kneels and places the letter into a nearby cooking fire. "Uriah," he says, "I have news for you. It's an assignment—a very dangerous assignment."

Uriah is savaged on the battlefield. The only person who benefits from Uriah's murder is David. Bathsheba knows nothing of the plan, and while devastated by her husband's death, she takes solace in knowing that Uriah died a hero. She mourns him for an appropriate time, like any good widow, and when David takes her for his wife the act is seen throughout the kingdom as an act of graciousness on his part—the devoted king marrying the pregnant wife of his fallen friend to save her from bearing a child who will not have a father. In time, the Queen of Israel, as Bathsheba is now known, bears a son. David, King of Israel, a man after God's own heart, has committed the perfect crime.

But God knows, and He speaks to His prophet, Nathan, who soon appears in David's palace to confront the king. It is night. The air smells of sage, juniper, and wood smoke. David stands in a courtyard sipping from a goblet of wine, consumed with the pleasure which comes from being king—and having each and every one of his dreams come true. Nathan's shadow falls across the tiled floor, backlit by a large torch.

"There were two men in a certain town," he tells David. "One rich, the other poor. The rich man had a very large number of sheep and cattle. The poor man had nothing but a single ewe that he had bought. He raised it, and it grew up with him and his children. It shared his food, drank from his cup, and even slept in his arms like a daughter.

"Now, a traveler came to the rich man. But instead of using one of his own flock to prepare a meal, the rich man stole the poor man's sheep and slaughtered it to serve to his guest."

David is infuriated by the story. "Find this man! As surely as the Lord lives, the man who did this deserves to die."

"You are that man! Do you think you can just sweep what you've done under the carpet?" Nathan angrily whispers to David. "You took everything from Uriah, your poor loyal servant. He deserved your respect."

"I did respect him," David whispers back, fearing that Bathsheba might hear. She is near, on a wooden bench beneath a towering date palm, nursing their son.

Nathan nods to Bathsheba. "Really? You took his wife. And then… his life."

David's fury grows. "Prophet!" he shouts, shaking a finger at Nathan.

But Nathan is doing God's work. He has no fear of a mortal man. David's newborn son begins to cry, as Nathan steps closer and condemns the king in a loud and emphatic voice. "You think that God doesn't see everything? The Lord has spoken to me. I tell you this: He will soon bring disaster on your house."

"But I am His chosen one," replies a stunned David.

"Yes. You will not die. But you have shown contempt for the Lord, and there will be a consequence."

"I have sinned," David says mournfully, finally realizing what he has done. "I have sinned."

David's son begins to cry.

David, king of Israel, kneels in the tabernacle tent, the Ark of the Covenant arrayed before him. This is not the smug David of just a week earlier, who believed that his chosen status somehow exempted him from God's judgment. He has been fasting for seven days. Now he is dressed in sackcloth, a coarse and drab material that scratches his skin and possesses none of the brilliant colors and precise tailoring of the royal robes. These are the clothes of a slave, the clothes worn by his ancestors during their years in Egypt. And like a slave pleading with a master to spare his life, David is pressed flat to the ground. He begs and pleads, "Anything, Lord. I will do anything You command. Please spare my child."

David's prayer has also lasted seven days. The lack of food and his focus on God give his the face the delusional look of a man who has lost his way.

And then he hears Bathsheba scream.

David pushes himself to his feet and races from the tent, stepping out backward so as not to turn his back on the Ark. He races through the palace, searching for someone who can give him news. He finds a servant. "What news?"

But the man cannot bring himself to speak. David races on, until he hears a soft shuffling noise coming from a long hallway. It is Bathsheba, and she is so pale and drawn that she can barely walk. In her arms is the limp bundle of blankets holding her dead son. Bathsheba's eyes are red-rimmed from crying.

David collapses and wails in agony.

"First my husband, and now my son," says Bathsheba. "We are cursed."

"But I was anointed," David whimpers. "God blessed me."

Nathan speaks next, standing over David. "Then you abused your power, and turned to tyranny. A king is never above his God."

David blinks back tears.

"You were supposed to rule in His name, not your own," continues Nathan.

"We're finished," groans Bathsheba. "The people will all see that God has left us."

Nathan says nothing. David stares at him, waiting for an answer. "Prophet?" he asks.

"God loves you, David. Even though you are weak. You have admitted your sins and asked for forgiveness. You have also forged God's nation on earth. He will not take this away from you," Nathan tells him. And then, to Bathsheba: "And he will grant you another son."

That son's name is Solomon. He builds the great temple in Jerusalem, just as Nathan prophesied. Long after David and Bathsheba pass on, that temple provides a permanent home for the Ark of the Covenant.

Solomon gains a reputation as the wisest man in the world. His rule as king of Israel is a time of prosperity and peace. But like David, Solomon finds it impossible to follow God's law. He is a man easily corrupted by his privilege and passions. After he dies, power continues to corrupt Israel's kings. Maintaining God's kingdom on earth becomes harder and harder as powerful new enemies emerge to threaten the Israelite claim to the Promised Land. Civil war will split the nation in two. Prophets will warn of coming destruction if the kings and people do not turn back to God. They will struggle for centuries. The Northern Kingdom will be destroyed by the Assyrian army. The Southern Kingdom will be carried into captivity.

A new prophet named Daniel will speak in images telling of a dream in which God promised to once again save the Israelites by sending them a new king. "There before me was one like a son of man, coming with the clouds of heaven. He was given authority, glory, and sovereign power. All peoples, nations, and men of every language worshipped him." Daniel is dazzled as he speaks, overcome with the majesty and wonder of the dream that God revealed to him. But he does not know when he will come. Nor does Daniel know that this king will be directly descended from David, nor that his name will be Jesus.

PART FIVE

SURVIVAL

Jerusalem, 587 BC. Since the death of King Solomon more than three centuries ago, the superpower nations surrounding the Promised Land have been squeezing the life from Israel. Assyria has already conquered the northern portion. Zedekiah sits on the throne in Jerusalem as the king of Israel, but he is a mere vassal to the Babylonian empire, which has conquered another great chunk of the Promised Land. In exchange for the privilege of ruling his own people, Zedekiah pays an annual fee to the Babylonian king, Nebuchadnezzar.

Or at least he's supposed to. King Zedekiah has come to believe that the Babylonians are no longer a threat. It's been years since he's paid tribute, and he's even been convinced to conspire with the Egyptians, who promise to come to his defense should the Babylonians ever attack.

Many people of Israel are equally negligent in their respect for the God of Abraham. They ignore God in their search for divine guidance. Pagan gods and idol worship have taken the place of prayer. The act of sacrifice as a means to atone for sins or to seek God's blessing has also changed: instead of merely offering up a sheep or cow, the Israelites now offer up their own children on pagan altars outside the city of Jerusalem. A people that have been saved time and again by great men like Abraham, Moses, and Samson are as lost and arrogant as when God sent the great flood to wipe them all from the earth. Fifteen hundred years after God's covenant with Abraham, a thousand years since Moses led the Israelites out of Egypt, and four hundred years since the reign of David, they remain unfaithful to God.

But God is not absent, or silent. Through a small army of prophets God speaks and reassures the Israelites that He has plans for them—plans to give them a hope and a future. The prophets tell the people of the day when God will send another great king to earth.

The Israelites ignore this good news, and they often treat the prophets as madmen or malcontents, because they are more concerned with the immensely troubling here and now than with the future. King Zedekiah is hard-hearted and weak; his reign is one of fear and oppression. The religious leaders of Jerusalem have perverted the people, turning worship into an act of commerce and enriching themselves at the expense of the faithful. But time has passed, and Jerusalem is now under attack. Armies from the east have come and lain siege to the City of David, just as he once took it from the Jebusites.

Baruch Ben Neriah, a record keeper in the royal court—a scribe—bears witness to this descent into chaos. Baruch works for King Zedekiah, but he is also a man of God. He is one of the few in Jerusalem who have not turned their backs on the God of Abraham. He alone among the royal court admires Jeremiah, a dour, brutally honest man whom no one else cares for. Jeremiah has preached the same message from God to successive kings for forty years. Yet few have had the heart to hear.

Jeremiah is a prophet—one of the greatest of all time.

There is no money in being a prophet. Little chance for a family. Often abuse, scorn, ridicule. Perhaps even death. But then it is incumbent on a prophet to then share with others what God has spoken. That is tortuous, for most in Israel have absolutely no desire to hear what's on God's mind.

Baruch's admiration for Jeremiah is a secret, as is his faith in God. The scribe would lose his job if the king knew that he believed Jeremiah to be speaking the truth. So he keeps it to himself, finding solace and inspiration in the prophet's words, which serve as a regular reminder for Baruch to keep his focus on God and His covenant with Abraham to bless his descendants. Baruch often prays for the strength to reveal his faith.

But God doesn't seem to hear him. So the scribe keeps his secret, even as Jeremiah risks his life for God.

And then one night, God answers Baruch's prayer. Baruch tries to concentrate on his work. Scrolls of parchment rest on the table before him, awaiting the words he will soon write upon them. Baruch is distracted, and with good reason. Just outside the walls of the city in which his cramped office sits, he hears the sounds of a religious sacrifice taking place. The sounds are all too familiar by now: a distraught mother, the cry of an infant about to be put to death, the chanting of the priests, the drums beating a dull and hollow rhythm, the chanting of the crowd so eager to see blood.

Baruch smells the incense and the wood smoke from the sacrificial fires. He stands to stretch his legs. Long hours of writing make his shoulders tight and make him feel a little dull in the head. A few minutes of walking around gets the blood flowing again, and helps him gather his thoughts. As Baruch stands to ease his mind, he finds himself pacing anxiously. He presses his eyes closed and lapses into a frustrated prayer. Sometimes he understands God, or at least he thinks he does. But at times like this, God's absence makes no sense. Where is His power? Where is His enduring love? "God," Baruch whispers, "I know You see all. Not just our actions, but also our hearts. I know that we defile Your name and Your love and Your laws. We do. And for that, there is no excuse. But I beg You, please... help us. Help those who are still true."

Baruch opens his eyes and peers out his window at the sacrifice. He's stunned to see that King Zedekiah has noticed him, and is glaring curiously in his direction. Baruch hastily sits down and unrolls a fresh scroll. Baruch is a timid man, terrified of the world beyond scrolls and scribes.

Suddenly, Jeremiah's loud and annoyed voice pierces the tumult. "Sacrilege!" yells the man. "Faithless people! Have you forgotten the Lord your God?"

Baruch is back on his feet to see, as are all the court officials, the old man Jeremiah fearlessly wading through the crowd to stop the killing of the newborn whose body is laid across the altar on the hillside. Baruch wishes he had Jeremiah's courage, his fearlessness. Jeremiah seems almost eager to risk his life in the name of God. "You feed human life to a lifeless idol," rails Jeremiah. The elderly prophet is bearded, dressed in shabby clothes, and wears a perpetual scowl. For all his faith in the glories of God, Baruch can't remember a single time that he's seen Jeremiah smile. "You turn your backs on the one who gives you life," continues Jeremiah. "Repent. Return to God."

The palace guards hurl him to the ground and pummel him with fists and clubs as the crowd cheers them on. Despite all his passion and righteousness, Jeremiah is a man without power. Most people of Jerusalem fear King Zedekiah far more than they fear God. Good men and women—like Baruch the scribe—do nothing. So evil triumphs. The battle for the soul of Israel is being lost. The chance for the Israelites to avoid God's judgment is slipping away. They have forgotten about Noah and the flood. They have forgotten what became of Sodom. They have certainly forgotten the many years their people were enslaved.

But the words of Jeremiah threaten the men who hold power, who fear that the people of Jerusalem might actually start listening to Jeremiah. So later that night, long after the sacrificial fires have burned to coals, and as Jeremiah struggles to sleep standing up in the palace stocks, Jerusalem's high priests and court officials order that his writings be seized. They read the scrolls by torchlight in the palace. King Zedekiah sits on a nearby throne. This is not the first time that Jeremiah has riled the king.

"Return, faithless Israel," reads one priest in a voice that mocks Jeremiah's writings. "I will not look on you in anger. Admit your guilt—"

"What guilt?" screeches Zedekiah, reaching for his wine. "Angry about what?"

"That you rebelled against the Lord your God and that you have not obeyed His voice," explains the priest. "He's saying that God will let us live in peace if we change our ways."

"Change what ways?"

"By not shedding innocent blood or worshipping other gods."

It never occurs to Zedekiah to heed Jeremiah's words. As king, he believes that his power is supreme. The notion that following Jeremiah's instruction will save the Israelites from a cruel fate has never crossed his mind.

"I don't want to hear from this lunatic again," Zedekiah says. With a wave of his hand, he dismisses the issue forever. The priests know what to do next, and immediately set fire to Jeremiah's writings.

Smoke drifts across the palace courtyard. This was once the home to great kings like Solomon and David, so it is appropriate that a true man of God stands here. But his is not a position of power. Jeremiah is hunched, his head and wrists locked in the wooden stocks. Though he is an old man, deserving of respect, a pulsating wave of people walk past as the sun rises over Jerusalem. They could ignore him as they make their way to the well to fetch the morning water. Or they could easily find an alternate route on their way to the market for their daily bread. Instead, the abuse of Jeremiah has become a game. He is defenseless against the shouts of abuse. His beard is thick with spittle and vomit. Jeremiah accepts it. This is his lot in life. Jeremiah knows he was marked out by God as a prophet before he was even born. "Why does the way of the wicked prosper?" Jeremiah asks God, hoping the conversation will help him endure this humiliation. "Why do all the faithless live at ease when the faithful are hunted down like dogs?"

Jeremiah's will has finally been broken. He no longer has the strength to speak God's message. His body aches each and every day from his many injuries. His head has been shoved to the ground and kicked more times than he can remember. He is a one-man army, fighting a weak king and a wayward people. He is alone. Always alone. Not a friend in the world. But this habit of talking to God has been with him a lifetime. When Jeremiah tires of the fight, God is his refuge and his solace. His comforter. God's words are a lamp unto his feet in times of darkness, showing him the way to go. Jeremiah talks to God, if only out of that lifetime habit. "They will never hear," Jeremiah mumbles. "If I cannot open their hearts with truth, and help them remember the Lord's compassion, what else is left?"

God hears all prayers. He answers them in many ways. Jeremiah is at his lowest ebb, and his prayers to God are answered by his one friend on earth: Baruch. The scribe hurries to the stocks, where he bribes the soldier standing guard to unlock the chains. The soldier is shocked to see a member of the royal court standing before him, wearing the brightly colored robes of his position. He takes the money and looks the other way.

"Why are you doing this?" Jeremiah asks, as Baruch drags him away. "If they find out, you'll lose everything."

Baruch would not ordinarily put himself at such great risk, but God has moved him to act, putting it upon Baruch's heart to help Jeremiah. So as he comes to Jeremiah's aid, he says the words God placed so carefully on Baruch: "I can no longer remain silent. I've seen you before. I've heard you speak. And I've always known that God is with you."

Baruch pulls Jeremiah into a small room in the temple. Finding a cloth and bucket of water, he cleans the scum off Jeremiah's face. But Baruch recoils as he begins to sponge the blood from the prophet's back, laid bare so many times by whips and beatings that thick, ropelike scars crisscross the flesh.

Jeremiah pulls away from Baruch. The scribe is about to apologize, thinking that the scars were Jeremiah's secret, and that he has somehow embarrassed his new friend. But the prophet is clutching his head and struggling to his feet. Baruch instinctively reaches out to help, but Jeremiah waves him away and steadies himself on a nearby pillar. His whole body is convulsed, and his thoughts no longer reside in the present.

Baruch steps back, unsure of what he is seeing. Then Jeremiah begins chanting like a seer, channeling the words of God. "They have set up their detestable idols...defiled my house..."

The scribe is aghast as he realizes that it is not Jeremiah who is speaking. Baruch is listening to the words of God, as God speaks them. He frantically hunts for a scroll to write it all down.

"Prepare yourself. I am bringing disaster from the North," Jeremiah continues. "I am bringing terrible destruction."

Baruch scribbles furiously.

"I will give their children over to the famine, hand them over to the power of the sword," Jeremiah continues. "I will hand all your country over to my servant...the king of Babylon. I will make even the wild animals subject to him."

Neither Baruch nor Jeremiah knows it, but this prophecy of God's wrath is all too real. King Zedekiah's betrayal of King Nebuchadnezzar of Babylon is about to be punished.

"I will lay to waste the towns of Judah so that no man can live there," Jeremiah channels. "I will make Jerusalem a heap of ruins, a haunt of jackals. I will make the people eat the flesh of their sons and daughters."

Hand shaking, heart pounding, Baruch writes down every word. Baruch later tries to help Zedekiah understand the warnings and change his ways by surreptitiously making sure that the handwritten scrolls make their way to the king and his priests, but those words go unread.

Jeremiah's prophecy comes true. The enormous and terrifying Babylonian army is camped outside the walls of Jerusalem. It is too late to repent, and far too late to heed God's warnings. The Babylonians and King Nebuchadnezzar have surrounded them, and the people of Jerusalem hear their battle horns, the bawled orders of field commanders, and the screams of captured spies being tortured. They smell the foreign foods on their cooking fires.

In a last great act of desperation, Zedekiah falls back on the God of his forefathers. He pleads with God to remember him and keep him safe. Zedekiah promises with all his heart that he will never again worship false idols, and that Jerusalem will once again be a city that worships the one true God.

God doesn't answer Zedekiah's prayers. When the king climbs to the highest room in his palace and looks out into the distance, he sees the Babylonian army preparing to lay siege to Jerusalem. Every day their numbers grow larger, and every day their force grows closer and closer to launching the great attack that will doom Zedekiah's kingdom.

One of Zedekiah's priests comes to the king. The priest has noticed that the handwriting on Jeremiah's scrolls matches that of Baruch. The scribe is immediately brought before the anxious, yet still haughty, king. Baruch is neither arrested nor threatened with the loss of his job. Instead, his freedom is guaranteed on the condition that he find Jeremiah and bring him to Zedekiah.

The king terrifies Baruch. But he knows God's power, and he fears for the life of Jeremiah. In his most humble and contrite voice, he tells Zedekiah that he will not betray Jeremiah's location.

"I don't mean to harm him," Zedekiah promises, oozing sincerity. "I simply wish to ask him to speak to God on behalf of me and my kingdom."

A wary Baruch promises to return with Jeremiah.

He finds his new friend unshakable, as always. Jeremiah is determined to deliver a harsh new message to Zedekiah—and in a way that the king will never forget. Jeremiah finds a wooden yoke, the type that is used to tether cattle. With Baruch's help, he hoists it onto his narrow shoulders and staggers into the palace. A stunned silence greets Jeremiah as he enters. The prophet looks preposterous, as if he will crumble under the weight of the yoke. But there is an undeniable fire in his eyes; no trace of fear or weakness is evident in Jeremiah's demeanor when he stands before the king.

"What is this?" snarls Zedekiah, weary that Jeremiah refuses to grovel before his king.

"This is you, as you will be under the yoke of Babylon."

"I will never succumb to Babylon," Zedekiah replies. "I called you here to speak to God on behalf of me and my kingdom."

Jeremiah continues on as if he hasn't heard the king. "If you're wise, you will listen to what I have to tell you."

"And what is that?"

"Bow your neck and serve. Submit to Babylon and you will live."

One of Zedekiah's courtiers springs upon Jeremiah, throwing the yoke to the ground. "Wretch," says the courtier with utter disdain. "How dare you tell your king to bow his neck?"

Jeremiah doesn't flinch. His face flushes in anger as he squares off before his attacker. "No," answers Jeremiah. "How dare *you* question the words of your Lord God."

One of the chief priests says, "You wrote that we should repent and all will be well. That God will be with us," thinking he will make points with Zedekiah.

Jeremiah fixes the priests with a look of pity. He alone knows that Zedekiah's pride has already guaranteed Israel's fall. The Promised Land will now be Nebuchadnezzar's. Her people will be scattered and enslaved. Her temple will be destroyed. This is God's prophecy—this is as God allows. All the protestations of courtiers and high priests cannot stop this from happening.

"Look outside the walls. You're too late," says Jeremiah.

"Take him to the palace dungeon!" hisses Zedekiah.

Many months pass. Babylonian soldiers have been camped outside Jerusalem since the day of Jeremiah's last appearance before the king. The walls are twenty-two feet thick and almost impenetrable. Inside the city, the people of Jerusalem are trapped and starving, deprived of food and much of their water supply by the Babylonian presence. Time has come for Nebuchadnezzar to capture the city. Cooking fires are doused as the men of Babylon strap on their armor and sharpen their knives. Siege engines—those great towers on wheels that will allow soldiers to rain arrows down on the city—soon roll forth. At the city gate, the first wave of soldiers now runs a battering ram into the thick wooden entrance.

Zedekiah's army tries to hold the gate, but they are disorganized and weak from hunger, and they cannot withstand the Babylonians. It has been years since the Israelite army has taken the field. Their battle lines are chaotic and undignified. The Babylonians have drilled and battled without ceasing. Their lines are crisp and their discipline precise.

Zedekiah's pitiful resistance barely registers with the Babylonians. His army is swatted aside and his men gutted where they fall. The only question remaining now is the degree of suffering that King Nebuchadnezzar will inflict upon Jerusalem, and who among the Israelites will find a way to escape it. In the city streets, panic is everywhere. The flames of burning rooftops climb high into the nighttime sky. People desperately run through the streets, having no place to go.

Inside the palace, chaos reigns. Zedekiah has fled, sneaking out through the gate between the two walls near his garden. His wife and children, ministers, high priests, and entire army follow behind. They are bound for the Jordan valley called Arabah.

The palace dungeon has been emptied of all but one prisoner: Jeremiah.

Baruch makes his way through the empty palace. Its walls are lit by the burning city. The footsteps of his sandal-clad feet echo on the stone floor.

Baruch frees Jeremiah and ushers the prophet out of the palace. They race to the temple designed so long ago by David, cavernous, and usually a refuge of calm and tranquility. It is the spiritual home to God's covenant with the Israelites, where the Ark of the Covenant resides. It is about to burn to the ground. The few remaining faithful within the city are inside, working feverishly to save precious scrolls and religious artifacts. The Israelites hide the Ark of the Covenant in order to prevent it from being taken to Babylon. To this day, it has never been found.

Baruch and Jeremiah run from the temple, hoping to find a way to escape the city. They turn and take one last look back at the great building, its rooftop now licked by flames. Smoke billows into the sky. Screaming people fill the streets. Arrows launched by distant Babylonian archers plummet to the ground, killing people at random. The bodies will lie unburied, and vultures will come in the morning to pick the bones clean.

This is what the end of the Promised Land looks like.

Just as Jeremiah prophesied.

King Zedekiah's escape from the city has not gone at all well. The Babylonians pursued him and his army on their way to Arabah. The two sides met on the plains outside Jericho, where the Israelites once famously marched until the walls fell. Now the Babylonians have won the day, scattering Zedekiah's army and capturing him and his entire family. They now stand on a roadside outside Reblah at dawn, in chains, surrounded on all sides by Babylonian soldiers. King Nebuchadnezzar steps before them, a scowling man cloaked in battle armor. There is little that needs to be said: Zedekiah has not only been a disobedient subject, but he has made his punishment worse by forcing the Babylonians to lay siege to Jerusalem for so long. If only Zedekiah had done as Jeremiah warned. Bowing down to Nebuchadnezzar would not have been pleasant, but it would have been much preferable to the sentence that the Babylonian king is about to pass down.

Zedekiah hears the sentence and howls in pain. Then, on a signal from the Babylonian king, the sentence is carried out.

First, Zedekiah's sons are brought before him. Zedekiah is only thirty-two years old, having ascended to the throne at a very young age. His sons are still children. He cherishes them—the sound of their laughter, their handsome looks, their athleticism and intellect. Zedekiah loves when they wrap their arms around him, and that special way they gaze with pride at their father.

On Nebuchadnezzar's command, soldiers step forth and slit their throats, one by one. When Zedekiah tries to look away, Babylonian soldiers grab his head and he is forced to watch.

The deaths of his sons are the last sight King Zedekiah will ever see, for after the murders are complete, King Nebuchadnezzar personally grabs a hold of Zedekiah's head and pushes his thumbs hard into his skull, blinding him. Zedekiah is then placed in special bronze chains and marched on the long and painful road to Babylon, where he will be a slave for the rest of his life.

Accompanying Zedekiah on that long march into captivity are the elite of Jerusalem. They too are now slaves of the Babylonians. Nebuchadnezzar doesn't take everyone to Babylon. It's the cream of Jewish society that he wants; the professional and educated are led off. Among them is a group of young friends named Daniel, Hananiah, Mischael, and Azariah. On them rests the hope that the people of Jerusalem can one day find God and return.

But first they must find each other. For almost as soon as the deportation begins, they are separated in the great throng of refugees, pack animals, pushcarts, and soldiers, destined to make the long walk without the camaraderie of friends.

"Give me strength, oh God," prays Daniel. "Protect me and guide me, and one day, no matter how many years it takes, please forgive us our sins and allow our people to return to the Promised Land."

Just in case they had any idea about turning around and fleeing back toward Jerusalem, a watching soldier draws his sword, itching for the chance to run them through. From this day forward, their every movement will be scrutinized in this manner. Punishment will be swift and sure. Death will always be an option.

Welcome back to slavery, O Israel.

Fourteen generations of Israelites pass from Abraham to his descendant David. Another fourteen generations from David to the great deportation to Babylon. There will be fourteen more generations until the birth of Jesus, a direct descendant of David and of Abraham, with whom God made His covenant. Jesus will be sent to renew that covenant with God's people. The covenant is in desperate need of renewal. But that is fourteen generations in the future. Now, as a long line of bedraggled, weeping Israelites gaze upon the waters of Babylon for the first time, the covenant seems a thing of the ancient past. After a march of five hundred miles, they have finally landed in exile. The vast shining waters of the Euphrates River shine like steel in the sun. No one knows if they will ever see their beloved Jerusalem again.

But even as soldiers prod them to cross the water at a low ford, many of the Israelites fail to grasp why they are here. These people see their exile from the Promised Land in purely political terms, as if it were the natural order of things for one great army to conquer another, and the people of the vanquished land to suffer accordingly.

The faithful, however, know why they're here. When the others gnash their teeth and wail about their plight, the faithful remind them that the Israelites had forsaken God and served pagan gods in the Promised Land. But even the faithful wonder if God has turned His back on them forever.

Daniel, a cheerful, bright young man of twenty who is a distant relative of King Zedekiah, wades into the cool waters of the Euphrates and prays. "God," he asks, "how will we ever find our way back home?" Daniel has always worshipped the God of Abraham, despite Zedekiah's wanderings. He wades in deeper. The water soothes his aching feet and washes away the dust that coats his bare legs. "God," he pleads, "please come back to us."

Suddenly, Daniel loses his footing. The current sucks him under and sweeps him away. His body flails and tumbles in the current, and he swallows a stomach full of water. Daniel is not a swimmer—there was no need to learn to swim back in the dry environs of the Promised Land. So even though he battles to find footing, or at least to push his head above the surface, nothing works. He's been underwater only a few seconds, but it seems like forever. As low and near death as he's felt on the entire journey from home to captivity, those feelings are nothing compared with the terror of this instant.

Then Daniel feels the loving arms of Hananiah, Mischael, and Azariah grabbing him from the water, pulling his body from the current. They help him stand. Then the four of them—coughing, choking, and shivering—embrace.

In the midst of their worry and fear, the four of them find a way to laugh. The relief that laughter brings reminds them that God is there with them, watching over them, keeping them safe, protecting their hearts and minds and bodies from the hard realities of their new life in a pagan land.

They make a pact in the waters of the Euphrates as a hapless Daniel gasps for air: they will stick together. If Daniel, Hananiah, Mischael, and Azariah are to remain alive, their friendship and compassion will be more important than ever. They don't have Jerusalem, but they have each other. And they have God's promise for His faithful, which must sustain them through tests they cannot imagine. Daniel and his friends hug for a moment. Then, cold and wet, but happy to have found each other, they move on again through the flow of the river.

Meanwhile, King Nebuchadnezzar is in no hurry to ford the Euphrates, to sleep in his own bed, or to revel in the delights of his harem, for the comforts of home no longer call to him. The king of Babylon has been two long years in the battle waiting for Jerusalem to fall, and the simple act of leveling Jerusalem and burning the entire city to the ground has whetted his appetite for more.

Nebuchadnezzar is not marching his army back to Babylon. He's guiding his army west into Egypt, that unconquerable desert land that the Pharaohs have ruled for more than two thousand years. But conquer it he does. And still Nebuchadnezzar wants more. With a thunderous sweep he lays waste to the land of the Pharaohs, then doubles back and sweeps through the civilized world. Every nation falls before him. His power is penultimate. Thousands upon thousands of people who don't even speak his language call Nebuchadnezzar "Lord" and "Majesty." His new subjects are not only Jews, but every tribe and nation from the River Tigris to the River Nile; from the sands of the great Arabian Desert to the great mountains that mark the gateway to what will one day become known as Europe. Nations that do not submit are put to the sword. Their women are raped. Their children are enslaved or simply left to starve.

Years pass. King Nebuchadnezzar returns home to enjoy the wealth and spoils of his vast kingdom. His subjects slowly and reluctantly adapt to their ruler and his ways. Generations of children are brought into the world and grow to adulthood never knowing any difference between Nebuchadnezzar's customs and those of their forefathers. The Israelites unwittingly join in the worship of their king's pagan idols, having long lost even the memory of the God of Abraham. Those who do remember feel God has forsaken them. Most don't know who God is at all.

However, one Israelite—Daniel—has been blessed in a strange and powerful way during this time in exile. Now a man, he has adapted and risen to become Nebuchadnezzar's chief advisor. He has a God-given gift to interpret dreams and see visions, and he has chosen to honor that blessing by not defiling his body with the food and drink served at the royal court. His three good friends from home have enhanced their bond in the years since they left Jerusalem, and each of them also follows this diet.

But this gift comes with a certain peril. For once Nebuchadnezzar learned of Daniel's special ability to listen and hear God in all circumstances, the king inquires about the meaning of his own dreams.

On a spectacular morning, long before the desert heat can despoil the setting, Daniel stands at Nebuchadnezzar's side, next to the seated king's throne, in the shade of the palace's outdoor pavilion. Thousands upon thousands of Babylonians and Jews are being herded out of the city and onto a broad desert plain. Daniel watches with regret as the chief priests and soldiers of Babylon assemble on the plain. Drummers and musicians prepare to perform. Trumpeters raise their horns to their lips and await the signal to blow a loud triumphal note.

The subject of all this exuberant commotion is a giant golden statue. It is ninety feet tall and nine feet wide. The idea for the statue had come to the king in a dream, and he chose to test the soothsaying powers of his chief astrologers and magicians by having them describe the dream and what it meant.

The punishment for failure to relate the king's dream was death. None of them had the slightest idea what Nebuchadnezzar's dream meant. Daniel, however, was blessed by God with the ability to interpret the dream. He explained to Nebuchadnezzar that the dream was of a giant statue, which had a head of gold, the chest and arms silver, the belly and hips bronze, the legs iron, and the feet a mixture of ceramic and iron. The different parts of the statue signified the various kingdoms that would come to replace Babylon. Daniel also described a great stone that would fall upon and destroy the great statue, signifying that the Kingdom of God would be the last remaining empire. It showed the fragility of a king's power and the omnipotence of the one true God. To build such a statue would invite God's wrath.

Nebuchadnezzar was intrigued by this God of Daniel's, but he built the statue anyway. He chose to interpret the message as a signal to act more boldly. So he didn't just order that the statue be built, but that it also be made entirely of gold.

Now Nebuchadnezzar raises his royal arm. This is the signal the trumpeters have been waiting for. A single mellifluous note floats above the assembled thousands. Instantly, they all grow silent and drop to their knees in worship. They are paying homage to the statue and, by proxy, Nebuchadnezzar. Everyone bows: chief priests, soldiers, Jews, Babylonians. Everyone.

Daniel's worst fears are made manifest as his friends Hananiah, Mischael, and Azariah refuse to bow. They alone remain standing, refusing to honor any God but their own. "With all our heart, we follow You," Azariah prays aloud to the God of Abraham.

The trumpeters lower their horns. The desert plain is silent save for the screaming of the chief priests, who are demanding that the three faithful Jews fall to their knees.

"We fear and seek Your presence," the prayer continues. This time the words come from the mouth of Mischael.

Now guards are wading into the crowd, eager to beat on the insolent foreign slaves. But the three of them remain standing. Daniel looks on from the distance, his face grim as he knows the fate awaiting his friends. Yet he is proud that they refuse to worship false idols. "Oh, my dear friends. Your faith will be tested now," he marvels to himself.

Nebuchadnezzar is apoplectic with rage. This man who once blinded

King Zedekiah screams at Daniel, "Who's that? What's wrong with them?"

"My Lord," Daniel tells him. "They are only moved by God. They will not bow to any but Him."

Even as Daniel speaks, the guards seize his friends. Daniel follows close behind as Nebuchadnezzar bolts from his throne and makes his way out from his shaded awning. The crowd parts instantly as the king strides toward the miscreants. Daniel hurries alongside. Ahead of him, he sees his friends' hands being bound.

"They will serve you faithfully all their lives, as I will," Daniel reassures Nebuchadnezzar, searching for the soothing words that will calm the king. "But—"

"But what?" Nebuchadnezzar replies.

So Daniel continues. "Please understand, Majesty, that only God can be worshipped."

A chief priest has joined them. He knows that Daniel gained prestige by interpreting the king's dream, and is eager to reassert his own authority. "Is that some nonsense you foreigners believe? That your God has more power than our glorious king?"

Daniel says nothing. This is not the time to argue with a priest.

It's Nebuchadnezzar who breaks the silence. "Your friends will bow— or I will make them bow."

But even when the guards try to force the three Israelites to their knees, they do not utter a word of worship to King Nebuchadnezzar. They seem fearless, which unleashes the king's legendary temper. "King Nebuchadnezzar, we do not need to defend ourselves before you in this matter," they tell him. "If we are thrown into a blazing furnace, the God we serve is able to deliver us from it, and He will deliver us from Your Majesty's hand. But even if he does not, we want you to know, Your Majesty, that we will not serve your gods or worship the image of gold you have set up."

"What do we do with something that won't bend?" Nebuchadnezzar screams, whirling around in anger. "We throw it into a fire."

The words are like a dagger into Daniel's heart. Nebuchadnezzar stares straight at him as he addresses his guards: "Burn them."

A soldier immediately douses them with oil. A second soldier runs toward the prisoners, carrying a torch. Nebuchadnezzar grabs his arm, taking ahold of the torch himself. In one swift moment, he throws the torch at the three Israelites.

Whoosh.

A fireball erupts as each man is set aflame.

Nebuchadnezzar smiles in satisfaction and turns to his priests so that they may share in his joy. All the while, Daniel is praying as hard and fervently as he possibly can: "The Lord hears my weeping. The Lord hears my cries for mercy. The Lord accepts my prayers."

As Daniel prays, his voice grows more steady and sure. He does not fear for his friends any longer, for he knows that God is near. In the midst of the flames and billowing smoke he sees the silhouette of a fourth figure standing guard over Hananiah, Mischael, and Azariah. The fiery silhouette offers a blessing to the three men.

"The Lord hears my weeping. The Lord hears my cries for mercy. The Lord accepts my prayers," Daniel says softly.

This is not an apparition that only Daniel can see. Nebuchadnezzar's face has grown white as he sees this mysterious presence. His chief priests are mumbling incantations, summoning their own gods to protect them. These men have claimed to be spiritual their whole lives, and yet this is the first time they've actually seen and felt the presence of God.

"The Lord hears my weeping. The Lord hears my cries for mercy. The Lord accepts my prayers," Daniel continues praying.

The flames go out. The three kneeling figures of Hananiah, Mischael, and Azariah are wreathed in smoke. As the smoke billows away, the three men rise. They are completely unharmed and do not even smell of smoke. Tears in his eyes, Daniel gives a humble thanks to God.

As his chief priests turn and leave, desperate to escape any wrath that this God of Daniel's might want to inflict, Nebuchadnezzar sinks to his knees. He grasps Daniel's leg in an act of supplication and something else. Something that Daniel has prayed for for many, many years.

That something is faith. Nebuchadnezzar is deeply impressed by the power of God.

In the grandstand of Nebuchadnezzar's folly, God showed up. His power is there for the entire world to see. Guided by Daniel, Nebuchadnezzar soon allows the captive Jews to worship their God in peace.

Time passes. The great king of Babylon is going insane; he is guarded around the clock. His subjects are not allowed to view him in this state, for Nebuchadnezzar behaves like a wild dog. Rational discussion about setting the Israelites free is out of the question. Yet even as he crawls about on hands and knees, his hair matted, and his movement restricted by the size of his royal kennel, he is still very much the king.

Over the more than twenty years that Daniel has been in slavery to Nebuchadnezzar, their relationship has deepened. Daniel is no longer just a servant, nor merely a respected member of the court. He is indispensable to the king, performing a vast number of bureaucratic and ceremonial duties that ensure the Babylonian empire runs smoothly on a day-to-day basis. Even in the depths of his madness, Nebuchadnezzar still feels a deep admiration for this foreigner's faith and efficiency.

So if anyone can persuade Nebuchadnezzar to set the Israelites free, it's Daniel. But Daniel, of course, is now irreplaceable.

It's the middle of the afternoon as a bolt is pulled back on Nebuchadnezzar's royal dungeon. A heavy door opens. Daniel, now in his early forties, enters. As two Babylonian priests watch from outside, he fearlessly delivers a golden chalice of water to the king's cage in the darkened center of the room.

Suddenly, a head lunges into a narrow beam of sunlight. The king bites at a plate of food on the floor, and then he disappears back into the shadows. All that Daniel can see of Nebuchadnezzar is that tangle of unwashed hair and beard, and the pair of dark, malevolent eyes staring hard at him.

"Behold the greatest king and lowliest man on God's earth," Daniel whispers. "See where your pride has brought you. And my people are just as trapped in Babylon as you are in that cage."

Daniel says this last sentence as a heavy lament. This is out of character, for Daniel is known for his cheerful heart. He hears himself speak, and he asks God's forgiveness for not being thankful. Daniel looks down upon his earthly lord and master. Then he carefully places the golden cup onto the floor. The priests still look on, not sure what Daniel has in mind.

"Shh," Daniel says soothingly. "Come here. It's all right"

Nebuchadnezzar slides forward on all fours and laps at the water like a dog. Softly, Daniel informs the king about the new prophecies about the fate of the Israelites—and the Babylonians. "I'm sorry to inform you of this, sire," Daniel says, making sure the chief priests cannot hear. "He will take pity on the Israelites. He says Jerusalem must be rebuilt, and that the temple's great foundations must once again be laid."

The words mean nothing to Nebuchadnezzar. He is too far gone.

The prophecy comes true, but not immediately. Twenty-three years after Nebuchadnezzar's death, during which four weak corrupt kings rule, a new king gallops toward Babylon. He rides a splendid white horse and leads an army tens of thousands strong. This man is from the east, and he wears a heavy gold crown, lest anyone not know that he is king. For three years, this king of all Persia has swept across the land. He has conquered everything in his path, and now he rides forth to take control of Babylon. This is his greatest prize of all: his gateway to the west and the south, possessor of the plundered riches of Egypt and Israel.

High on a tower in a center of the city, Daniel stands among a group of royal ministers, watching the coming army. Among the group are his lifelong friends, Hananiah, Mischael, and Azariah. They are all in their sixties now, and they have spent the vast majority of their lives in this foreign land. But they do not call it home. They never will. They don't fear the new king—they welcome him. To them, he is a liberator. Daniel has studied the new king, and knows that the people in every territory that the Persian conquers have been left free to live and worship in their own traditions. Daniel smiles and says, "He will set us exiles free."

The chief priests have been wreaking havoc on the city. They have banned prayer. They have even murdered Babylon's latest king as a symbol of their loyalty to the Persian king. As Daniel and his friends descend from the tower and walk into the city's main square, they see precisely what the chief priests have done: the king of Babylon swings from a gallows, his neck broken. His legs are bound at the ankles and his arms behind his back. There is no cloak covering his face, he stares at his former subjects with lifeless eyes. The chief priests smirk, refusing to let the soldiers of Babylon cut him down until this new king can see what they've done. The priests hope to curry favor by allowing the new king to enter Babylon without a fight. As Daniel and his friends look on, the chief priests order the Babylonian guards to pull back the giant wooden bars that secure the massive, impregnable doors to the city, and the guards follow their orders without hesitating. With heavy hearts the soldiers of Babylon watch the Persian army gallop in, their swords sheathed, knowing the new king's men will surely cut them down and feed their bodies to the vultures.

The Persian king rides into the city square and gazes upon his latest conquest. No ruler greets him; no one formally hands over control of the city. The chief priests, for all their cunning, are afraid to confront him. The Babylonian soldiers lie prostrate on the ground, hoping this act of subservience will save them.

Daniel, Hananiah, Mischael, and Azariah walk to the center of the courtyard, striding past the assembled Persian soldiers, courtiers, and mounted lords. The chief priests instantly find their courage, not wanting Daniel to speak with the new king before they have their say. Daniel might insist that this bold Persian ruler put them to death. The panicked priests race forward to greet their new king, singing great hymns in his honor, until the new king is swallowed up by his welcoming committee.

As royal advisor, only Daniel has the sovereign right to negotiate with a king. As he makes his way forward, he has every intention of asking that the Israelites be set free from bondage, in fulfillment of the Persians' very specific role in God's prophecy.

But before Daniel can draw near to him, a pair of powerfully built priests take hold of his arms and steer the aging Daniel off to the side. "I must speak with the king," Daniel protests. "He will be expecting me."

"Of course," oozes one of the priests, "but as you can see, the king is busy. We have made special arrangement for a private audience. Please come this way."

Daniel watches helplessly as the new king is escorted away. Then he is ushered into the palace and left there to wonder what the priests are planning.

Twelve long hours later, just as night falls, Daniel finds out. He stands inside the Persian king's new throne room, surrounded by a circle of priests. They point, jeer, shout, and hurl accusations and insults at him.

Daniel turns from one accuser to another, saying nothing but processing every charge directed his way. The new king, who has become wise in many years of conquest, knows better than to interfere with religious proceedings. He listens quietly, studying Daniel and the priests.

One of the priests steps close to Daniel. He looks him up and down, as if examining an exhibit at the zoo. The priests sniffs, and rears his head in disgust. "Sorcerer," he accuses Daniel. "You call on demons. Don't deny it."

This piques the Persian's interest. "How so?" he demands from his throne.

"He infected the mind of his previous lord, the great King Nebuchadnezzar," hisses the priest. "He turned him into a raving animal!"

Daniel's face is impassive. His faith demands that he fear no man. He looks almost bored. These charges are nothing new. "And he's not alone," cries another priest. "Why, his three friends once defied death with the help of a fire demon."

"And he prophesied the ruin brought on by Babylon's rulers. He even told the last king, 'You have been weighed and found wanting. Your kingdom will be divided—'"

Daniel seizes the opening. "'—and given to Persia.'" He turns toward the king. "I prophesied that Babylon would be given to you, King. It was God's will."

The priests won't be denied. "But who's to say you won't call on this demon god to do the same again?"

"God is just." Daniel's eyes are like ice as he cuts the man off. "The righteous have nothing to fear."

The priest seethes. He is a man of many gods. "We don't know this god," the priest fires back, ignoring Daniel to address the Persian king directly.

Daniel's great mistake is battling with the priests instead of appealing to the rational wisdom of a wise ruler.

The priest continues: "Who's to say having another new king, and then another, and then another, will be his god's will, too? Surely I say to you that this man is a sorcerer and not to be trusted. That is why we have banned prayer, an edict we believe you will find wise to let stand."

The king stares at Daniel. This is his chance to convince him of the need to let the Israelites leave. "May I offer one more of God's prophecies?" Daniel asks humbly.

A priest interjects. "No, you demon. No more of your weasel words."

But the Persian king now holds up a hand for silence. He nods his assent.

Daniel approaches the throne. "This is it, sire: there is a king of whose right hand I take hold of, to subdue nations before him and to strip kings of their arms, to open doors before him so that gates will not be shut." He bows.

"Well, he would say that, wouldn't he?" cries a priest.

The new king watches Daniel's eyes carefully, searching for signs of misdirection or embellishment. Daniel's gaze never wavers, and even as the Persian responds to the priest's accusation, the king finds himself intrigued by this Israelite and his ability to remain calm and cool in the face of such rage.

"Yes," the king responds. "Any normal man might—whether it was true or not."

The new king is torn: he has inherited a powerful priesthood, whose cooperation will be crucial to a smooth government. But on the other hand, the priests clearly fear Daniel's God. He must be wise in choosing sides. *Should I fear Daniel's God, too?* the king wonders to himself. *Or are these Jews and their God more trouble than they're worth?* His policy of appeasement, which has worked so well throughout his many conquests, suddenly feels precarious.

Then all the action comes to a screeching halt as Daniel begins behaving in an odd manner. He is still, but his eyes are closed. The king sees him mouthing words, but he is not sure whether Daniel is praying to his God or summoning a demon. One thing is for certain: Daniel is offering absolutely no respect to his new ruler.

The Persian suddenly rouses himself, like a lion waking from his slumber to go on the attack. He rises to his feet and roars his response, shaking up everyone in the room and bringing an abrupt end to Daniel's mumblings. "I am king of the world. Great king. Mighty king. King of Babylon. King of all the Jews in my land. And my judgment is this: from this day forth, the Jews will desist from their practices and rituals." He strides out of the chamber, leaving behind a stunned Daniel and a band of smirking and self-satisfied priests. They gaze with smug happiness at Daniel, who is left feeling crushed and betrayed.

The prophecies of Isaiah have been proven false. Daniel's long-cherished dreams are in ruins—and not just his dreams but those of the entire Jewish population. For more than forty years God's chosen people in exile have clung to this thin strand of hope. Daniel's shoulders slump as he walks from the throne room, a broken man. He finds a spot in the corridor and presses his forehead against the cool stone walls, desperately trying to make sense of what has just happened. He responds to the setback the only way he knows how: "Oh, dear God. I've failed Israel. I've failed you. We're further from freedom now than ever before. How could I not have seen this coming? Why didn't I say more?"

But prayer has been banned in the Persian ruler's kingdom. As Daniel prays in the corridor, the high priests walk past and eagerly take note. Breaking the king's command means an automatic sentence of death, and Daniel is clearly doing just that. The king will hear about this act of disobedience.

Daniel is arrested and thrown in the dungeon. The guards, who normally strut about completely fearlessly, seem skittish and to suffer from a lack of nerve as they quickly open the gate, push him inside, and quickly slam it shut. Their bravado returns only when Daniel is safely locked away. Unlike the chief priests, they do not gloat and instead turn away from Daniel with a look of sadness. They know him well, having observed him in the royal court for years and years. Daniel has never been known to speak angrily, talk down to those beneath him, or gossip. His poise under pressure is legendary. Daniel is humble and upbeat at all times. The guards never see such behavior from other members of the royal court, whose haughty manners and slippery words often make them feel like a lower form of life. Locking Daniel in the dungeon is one of the hardest orders they've ever had to carry out.

Daniel is puzzled. It's just the dungeon. He can endure the solitude of prison. Perhaps the king will change his mind about the death sentence. All things are possible with God. He turns from the door to examine his new home. The only light comes in through the slatted bars of the door. Daniel squints into the darkness. The cell is enormous. At the far end he can make out the sleeping figures of other prisoners. The men seem to be abnormally large, and as Daniel takes a step toward them, he notices that they have an unusual odor. The men are almost feral.

Daniel steps cautiously closer, careful not to startle them. But he suddenly realizes these are not men. This is not a prison cell. A shot of adrenaline courses through his veins and his heart seizes in fear as the shapes make themselves known. A horrified Daniel realizes that he has been hurled into the lion's den. The new Persian king has not just condemned him to death; he is putting an end to all talk of the God of Abraham by having Daniel's body torn to shreds.

Daniel is about to become the example of what happens in the new ruler's kingdom when a man prays. He will be eaten alive. His flesh will be ripped from his bones, even as his screams for help echo through the corridors. Children will be told of this day as a reminder that the Persian is the only king.

Daniel stands completely still as one of the lions stirs. It is a male, his face wreathed in a mane of unruly fur. The animal's body stretches at least eight feet long, and his massive paws are as big as Daniel's head. The lion sniffs the air. He rises and walks slowly toward Daniel, the thick pads of those magnificent paws not making a single sound on the stone floor. Then it roars. The sound is like death itself. Primal wiring in Daniel's brain urges him to turn and run. But he doesn't; that would be madness. A tear forms in the corner of Daniel's eye as the lion saunters toward him. Daniel falls to the ground and curls his body into a very small ball. The smallest he can possibly make. The damp floor of the cell feels calming against his cheek as he awaits the death that is soon to come. The other lions are awake now. Daniel doesn't know how many. Could be three. Could be six, for all he knows. They roar and grunt as they assemble. Daniel squeezes his eyes closed, knowing that there is absolutely no way to fight these beasts.

But then he remembers a way. "Lord, hear me. We do not make requests of You because we are righteous, but because of Your great mercy," he prays to God. A sense of calm fills Daniel as he awaits death. He realizes God is providing this peace. So he continues: "Thank You, Lord. Thank You for my life and its many joys. Thank You for Your love. And thank You, even now, for what is about to happen. For I know that it is Your will, and that some greater good will come from my death."

He pulls himself into an even tighter ball. The lions now stand over him. Daniel knows how prey on the great desert plains must feel as a pride looks down upon it, preparing to enjoy a feast. He feels utterly defenseless. The tears flow now, pooling on the floor. Daniel thinks of the people he loves and whom he will never see again. He thinks of the majesty of a sunrise, and the magnificence of the stars shining in the nighttime sky. All these wonders of life are about to be taken away in a burst of pain and terror.

"Your words are heard," says a voice.

Slowly, cautiously, Daniel raises his head. A tear slides from his cheek.

An angel stands before him. "You are innocent in the eyes of the Lord," the angel says.

That instant, all Daniel's fear vanishes. His tears dry. His optimism returns. He uncurls himself from his tiny ball and rises to his feet. Daniel stands before the lions, completely unafraid. Whatever will happen, will happen. The lions are God's creations, no different from man. And God has dominion over all of His creations.

Daniel is ready for anything.

Daniel and his God are haunting the Persian king's dreams. He wakes in a panic, seeing the truth for the first time, and he quickly gets out of bed. Throwing on a robe, he races through the palace toward the dungeon. He is desperate to save Daniel, knowing that failure to do so will result in God's wrath being brought down on his kingdom.

The king is new to the palace. He runs past walls lit by torches, making wrong turn after wrong turn in his search to find the dungeon. "Your God is real," he chants as he runs, "your God will save you. Your God is real, your God will save you." A long hallway finally leads to the stairwell down into the dungeon. "Open it!" the new king screams into the night. "Open it!"

The baffled guards aren't sure what terrifies them more: the thought of reopening the dungeon, or the spectacle of this all-powerful Persian king running through the night, strangely bent on saving Daniel's life.

"Please," he pleads, praying openly to Daniel's God, "let it be so, Lord."

The thick wooden door is flung open. The king steps inside. His guards draw swords and move to go with him, but he waves them away. One of them hands him a torch, which he accepts. The flames reveal a sleeping lion. They also reveal a sleeping Daniel, his head resting quite comfortably on the lion's chest.

The Persian gazes upon the sight in utter disbelief. Daniel is completely unharmed. The king swings his torch from lion to lion to lion—all are asleep. A dumbfounded king remembers the words Daniel once spoke to him, quoting the prophet Isaiah, "whose right hand I take hold of to subdue the nations before him, and to open doors before him, so that gates will not be shut."

Daniel stands. The king drops his torch and embraces him. Then the two men fall to their knees in prayer.

The years of exile are now at an end. The Persian decrees that the Jews may return to Jerusalem, taking the treasures looted from their temple so that it might be rebuilt.

Forty thousand Israelites soon march westward, back to their Promised Land. As the line of exiles marches into the late afternoon sun, Daniel will not be joining them. This is his life and his home now. He and Azariah watch the Jewish people leaving with the temple treasures. As Azariah sighs with pleasure, Daniel tenses. Sensing his friend's anxiety, Azariah turns to him. "What's wrong?" he asks. Daniel explains and feels a bold new prophecy being revealed to him: There will be enormous tests for the Israelites. They will turn away from God again, and other nations will conquer and enslave them.

Daniel has seen a vision of a great beast, dreadful and terrible and incredibly strong, with iron teeth, that will devour the entire world. But

Daniel has also had another vision, of the son of man, come to save the world, who will be given glory, authority, and sovereign power. Peoples, nations, and every language group will worship him. He will be called Prince of Peace, Holy of Holies, Lord God Almighty. Descended from the lineage of David, this man, like his forefather, will be called King of the Jews. Though he will rule over a very different kingdom.

PART SIX

HOPE

Five hundred years pass. War, conquest, and subservience to the empires of Macedon and Rome. The Israelites have reestablished themselves in the Promised Land but are ruled by a Roman puppet named Herod. This king of the Jews, so to speak, comes from a family that converted to the faith. He has been married ten times, murdered one wife, and will soon murder two of his sons. He suffers from fits of paranoia, has been in power for forty years, and owes his position to none other than Julius Caesar. The Jews live under oppression, which causes fear and tension, but they are allowed to practice their religion without fear of prosecution.

Jews have learned patience during their long years under the boots of the Egyptians, Babylonians, Persians, Greeks, and now Romans. So they pay the austere tax demanded by Rome, knowing the soldiers will go for now and leave them alone. They wait in the hopes that the Messiah will come rescue them. They long for the end of poverty and senseless death at the hands of their oppressors.

The revolution starts quietly and without notice, in the small village of Nazareth. Joseph, a carpenter, sits in a small synagogue as an elder reads from the Torah, the Israelites' holy book. Joseph is a direct descendant of King David, and his life revolves around scripture, work, and family. His time in the synagogue would normally be spent in quiet prayer and meditation, just like the men around him who have come to worship, lost in their communion with God.

But today, Joseph is lost—in love.

A latticework screen separates the men and women. Joseph has purposely seated himself next to the divider, allowing him to sneak a look at at his bride-to-be. Her name is Mary, and she's the most beautiful girl he's ever seen.

"Mary, my betrothed," Joseph whispers to himself, making sure not to slip and begin mumbling the words loud enough for all to hear. That would cause a stir in the synagogue. "You have the most beautiful eyes I've ever seen. And the sweetest smile."

Mary, who is pure of heart and has been praying for an end to wickedness and sin, and for the restoration of David's royal lineage, catches him staring. She blushes and turns away. Then Mary's eyes glance back and meet Joseph's gaze. A sense of deep connection passes between them.

Mary looks away first. Joseph forces himself to focus on the words of the elder, but he finds it almost impossible. He longs impatiently for the wondrous life that he and Mary will build together once they are man and wife. Joseph is not a man of great vision; even if he were, he still could not possibly imagine how extraordinary their lives will soon become. Every bit of his faith in God will be required to understand what is about to happen.

Dust blows through the streets. The sound of marching feet is heard, then the clatter of metal. Swords, shields, and battle armor glint in the hot Judean sun as a body of Roman soldiers moves in lockstep up the empty lane. They have come to collect tribute to Rome, and they soon go house to house, emerging with bales of cloth, leather goods, sacks of fresh fruit and grain, and even small animals.

As Mary walks home on a day like any other day, an angel of the Lord stands before her on the road. "Mary," he says softly, "I am Gabriel. Don't be afraid. The Lord is with you. You have found favor with God. Soon you will give birth to a child, and you are to call him Jesus. He will be great and will be known as the Son of the Most High."

"How can that be?" she asks. "I am still a virgin."

"The Holy Spirit will come upon you. And the power of the Most High will overshadow you."

Mary's hands press against her midsection, as if she can already feel an energy there. "I am the Lord's servant. May it be to me as you have said," she says to Gabriel.

After Gabriel vanishes, she runs her fingertips over her abdomen. "Jesus," she whispers. "I am to name him Jesus."

———

Mary hides her pregnancy for as long as she can, not knowing how she can explain it to Joseph. For the first few months she moves away to live in the hill country with her cousin Elizabeth, who is also pregnant and will become the mother of John the Baptist. When she returns, it is obvious that she is with child, and Joseph notices.

"Tell me what's going on, Mary. Please."

"Not here," she insists with tears in her eyes.

"Then where?"

It is forbidden for the two of them to be alone together until marriage, but she has no choice. She leads Joseph to her father's sheep shed and closes the door. She removes her robe ever so slightly, revealing her pregnant stomach to Joseph, confirming what he has suspected. His eyes squeeze shut.

"Mary? Who did this to you? What on earth have you done?" He feels angry, betrayed, confused, and then a fool.

"Joseph, let me explain." Mary struggles to control herself. She's never seen Joseph like this. Normally he's quiet and strong; now he's on the verge of tears. She grabs hold of his calloused hands. She is so desperately in love with this man that it hurts to see his heart so broken. She forces him to look in her eyes. Their future hangs on the words she is about to say—along with the fate of all mankind. "Joseph," she whispers. "There has been no one. I swear to you. I am a virgin. This is God's work. An angel of the Lord appeared to me, telling me that I would be with child. He is to be the Messiah."

He looks at her in horror.

"This is the truth."

Joseph breaks away. He circles the room like an animal in a cage.

She reaches for his hands again. "My love, please believe me. I am telling you the truth."

"I want to believe," he says softly. "But God would not send the Messiah to people like us." He opens the door, walks out, and doesn't look back. Only then does this mountain of a man let himself cry.

Joseph has a house to build out on the edge of town. But it can wait. He wanders the streets of Nazareth alone, mumbling to himself. "What do we say? What do we tell our parents? Of course, I must disown her. There's no other choice." But the grief that comes with the mere thought of a life without Mary soon sits on his chest. The weight is like an elephant, and it takes away his breath. The hard truth is that if he leaves Mary, both she and the child will become outcasts. They will live on the street, begging for handouts and fending for themselves. "God help me," Joseph prays. "Help me find a way to do the right thing." Joseph leans against a wall, lost in his thoughts. People stare at him. He doesn't care. Joseph's head droops and his shoulders sag. Joseph closes his eyes in prayer and falls into a dream state.

"Joseph," a voice says. "Joseph." The angel Gabriel now stands powerfully before Joseph, the hood of his cloak pulled around his soft and tender face. His eyes seem to peer straight into Joseph's soul. Gabriel reaches for Joseph's hands. "Take Mary as your wife," commands Gabriel. "She is telling you the truth. She is pure. The child that she carries is from God."

A stunned Joseph stares into the divine beauty of the angel. The weight upon his heart is gone. He wipes a tear of joy from his eye, and in that instant Gabriel is gone. Joseph emerges from his dream, elated, and races to Mary's home to tell her that he believes her. It's just the two of them against the world. That's the way it's going to be. Their baby will be named Jesus.

One translation of the name is "God rescues." It also means "God saves." To many in Israel, the notion of a Messiah is a conquering king like David, a savior who will deliver them from Roman oppression. God, however, has something far bigger in mind. God will remain God, yet also become human in Jesus. He will save not just Israel but the entire world.

Periodically the Romans demand a census. No matter where they are residing, citizens must return to the town of their family lineage and be counted. Now happily married, Joseph and Mary strap their belongings to a donkey and set off for the town of Bethlehem, the city where King David was born. The sun has not yet risen, and the morning air is cold. Mary is far too pregnant to walk the eighty-mile journey, so Joseph helps her onto the donkey, where she will ride. Normally it is a four-day trek, but the threat of bandits on the highway has Joseph planning on taking a slower, safer, and circuitous route that will add an extra three days. He leans in to kiss her belly, grabs the reins, and leads them out onto the dusty road at the edge of town.

They soon clear a low rise leading away from Nazareth, where they come upon a sight so utterly astonishing that Joseph's eyes widen. It is the most brilliant star he has ever seen, shining clear and low in the southern sky. Its brightness is a lamp unto their feet, and a light unto their path. Joseph squeezes Mary's hand. This is a sign God is with them.

Mary and Joseph are not alone admiring the star. Just outside faraway Babylon, a sage and astrologer named Balthazar gazes out at the amazing heavenly light hovering over Jerusalem. He is wealthy beyond measure, dressed in fine silk clothing. Soldiers surround him on this hillside, there to protect him against bandits on his long journey. Balthazar has followed the star all the way from Persia, riding his camel up and over the mountains into Babylon. They ride by night and sleep by day so that they may more easily follow the star.

Balthazar is a learned man who has studied the prophecies of many faiths, and he believes the star to be a sign from God. His escorts are quickly bored by the unusual sight, which they consider a mere cosmic fluke. Balthazar studies it at length every night, certain that two great forces are coming together before his eyes: first, God's command of the heavens; second, and equally powerful, the words of God's prophets. "A star shall come out of Jacob," Balthazar recites the record of Moses in the Book of Numbers. "And a scepter shall rise out of Israel." Balthazar is certain this star portends the arrival of a great leader. He feels blessed to be alive for such a momentous occasion. "Perhaps it is true. Perhaps the prophets of Israel were right," he says in awe. He hurriedly rallies his men, climbs back on his camel, and sets off into the night. He is bound for Jerusalem, eager to deliver the Good News.

But Balthazar is taking the Good News to the one man in Israel who doesn't want to hear it: King Herod. The man who rules Israel for the Romans, dominating his fellow Jews under his iron will, clings to power with a paranoid desperation. Even the slightest rumors about an attempt to take away his throne are dealt with immediately. All dissent is crushed. All dissenters are killed.

Now he waddles through his palace, down a marble and gilt corridor lined with rich tapestries. Herod wears velvet slippers, his feet splayed and shuffling. Each step causes him extreme pain. His breathing is labored, and his bald head is shiny with sweat.

Herod's captain of the guard follows close behind, careful not to step alongside the slow-moving king. For that would be seen as an attempt at equality, which would enflame Herod and might result in this career soldier losing his cushy, powerful position.

"You bring me news?" asks Herod, gasping for breath between each word.

"More trouble from the God-fearing fanatics, I'm afraid," replies the captain.

"Fine," Herod says, issuing a death warrant. "If they love God so much, send them to be with Him."

Mary and Joseph are well aware of Herod's evil—and that their journey to Bethlehem will bring them within just five miles of the royal palace. It is dusk now. Joseph makes camp on a barren hillside, even though there's enough daylight to travel a few more miles.

"I could go on," Mary insists, her face lined in weariness and the discomfort of yet another long day riding the donkey.

Joseph smiles and adds another piece of kindling to the fire he's building. "You need to rest. I'm tired and so is the donkey. Let's stop here."

A boy steps forth, carrying a bundle of kindling. He wordlessly hands it to Joseph, who accepts it, and sees the boy's father tending a flock of sheep in the distance. Joseph nods to the shepherd in thanks, even as the boy scurries away.

Their journey has been filled with a dozen such kindnesses. Mary and Joseph are both coming to grips with her imminent motherhood of the Messiah. From now on, all generations will call her blessed.

She curls up by the fire as a hard gust of wind rakes the hillside. Joseph sits down at her side and covers her with a rough blanket. She falls asleep, even as the great star once again rises into the night. Joseph will stay up most of the night, making sure the fire stays strong and keeps his beloved and her unborn child warm.

Herod gazes out into the coming night. He sees the unusual star shining in the east, but thinks nothing of it until the lavishly dressed Balthazar is escorted into the royal chamber. "So what brings you here, oh prince?" Herod demands, his voice echoing off the marble pillars.

"I just want to know if there is an official word about these signs?" Balthazar asks, trying to be as deferential as possible. He knows Herod's reputation for whimsical evil.

Herod stares at his guest, deciding how best to deal with him. "What signs?" he asks.

"The star. The new star rises in the east. I have followed its progress. The star is a sign that a great man is coming."

Herod glares at him. Not wanting to ignite Herod's legendary temper, Balthazar quickly motions for his men to lay out their elaborate charts of the stars on the marble floor. He then goes on to explain how he was guided by the star to Jerusalem.

But Herod isn't listening. He stares intently at Balthazar. "Every week," he finally says, "someone claims to be the chosen one. But those are mostly madmen in the marketplace—easily ignored, and just as easily silenced. So are you telling me that I should take your charts and your belief in a chosen one seriously?"

"Very seriously, sire." Balthazar once again motions for his men to step forward. This time they hold gifts in their arms. "We bring this chosen one presents fit for a king," he tells Herod.

That gets Herod's attention. "King?"

"Yes, Majesty. This man will become King of the Jews."

An awkward silence fills the chamber, making it quiet enough to hear a snake slither. Balthazar realizes he has just said something wrong.

Herod's eyebrows rise "Really?" he says through pursed lips.

"Yes, Majesty. This is from God. This is prophesied. The heavens testify to his arrival."

Herod smiles warmly, feigning a religiosity that he does not possess. "It has been testified? Really? If that is so, then we must do something immediately to pay homage."

Herod summons the captain of the guard and whispers in his ear. "Bring me the priests and scribes. I need a word with them." Then Herod dismisses Balthazar with a wave of his hand, walks to a terrace, and gazes out over Jerusalem. There, in the midst of darkness and turmoil, rises the star.

Herod curses. "I am king of the Jews. And I will forever remain king of the Jews," he vows to himself. "I will keep my throne."

Joseph wakes Mary from a deep sleep and loads the donkey. He walks quickly, leading the animal down the rocky hillside by its rope.

Mary groans. "It won't be long now, Joseph," she says.

"We're getting close to Bethlehem. I'll hurry," he replies, picking up the pace.

Mary is in agony, clutching her stomach and trying not to cry out in pain. To their shock, the streets of Bethlehem are a sea of people, all of them looking for someplace to sleep. They've all traveled there for the census. The young couple look around, overwhelmed by the numbers.

"Thousand upon thousands," Joseph exclaims. "Why do they make us all register at once?" He pulls the donkey under an archway, where others already huddle. Mary's stiff cold fingers spasm as they lock around his arm.

"Joseph?"

He says nothing.

"Joseph!" There is a desperation to her words: the baby is coming.

"I'll find a place," Joseph responds. He leaves Mary and the donkey, and then runs, searching for someplace warm and private where she can deliver the baby.

But no such shelter exists in Bethlehem tonight. Joseph is turned away time and time again. The innkeepers are kind but insistent: there is no room in Bethlehem for Mary and Joseph.

The shepherds stand watch over their flocks, waiting for the moment when the clouds will part and reveal the brilliant star they have become used to seeing each night.

And there it is.

The sheep calm down as the night settles into a time of quiet. And the shepherds, shivering from the damp of night, sit back and stare at the star, wondering what it means.

Herod is also studying the star, though not with the same sense of tranquility as the shepherds. Thanks to Balthazar's alert, he now demands to see all that has been written about the prophesied "King of the Jews." A half-dozen priests and scribes furiously tear through pages of sacred texts in the temple library as Herod paces. His blotched and bloated face is red with fury. "Find it!" he screams again and again. "Find it!"

The scribes anxiously drag piles of scrolls from the shelves. Sweat pours from their faces in the fetid head and dust.

"Here!" one priest yells with excitement. "In Micah."

"Read it," demands Herod.

" 'He shall feed his flock in the strength of God, and they shall live secure.' "

"Is that all?" asks a puzzled Herod.

Another priest has found a different reference in scripture. "No, lord. There's more. This is from Isaiah: 'Therefore the Lord himself will give a sign . . . the virgin will conceive and give birth to a son, and will call him Immanuel.' "

An elderly priest, suddenly unafraid of speaking up, adds another sentence: " 'And he will be called Wonderful Counselor, Mighty God, Everlasting Father, Prince of Peace.' "

The priest finishes, and looks over to see Herod staring at him intently. "*I'm* the one who brings peace," the king snarls. "Do you think some child can do that?"

Silence.

Then the elderly priest clears his throat. "It is written," he says solemnly.

Herod charges at the man, grabbing him by the robe. "Is it? Is it now? Well, then, is it written where this mighty prince, this answer to all prayer and problems, will be born?"

The elderly priest is unruffled. "In Bethlehem. It will be Bethlehem. Micah says, 'You Bethlehem . . . out of you will come a ruler who will shepherd my people, Israel—' "

The captain of the guard comes to drag the elderly priest away. But the old man will not be silenced, and even as he is pulled from the temple library, soon to meet his fate, he keeps reciting prophecy. " 'Israel will be abandoned until the time when she who is in labor gives birth. And the rest of his brothers return to join the Israelites. He will stand and shepherd his flock in the strength of the Lord.

" 'And his greatness will reach to the ends of the earth.' "

Mary goes into labor. All that matters to her is safely bringing her child into the world. Joseph still hasn't found a place for her to give birth. A local takes pity on them. He directs Joseph to a small cave used as a barn—called a grotto—smelling of animal waste and grain. Sheep and cows clutter the small space. Joseph and Mary eagerly step inside.

This baby is coming.

Herod has returned to his palace from the temple library. The words of the priests ring in his ears as he makes his way across his courtyard. As if the visit from Balthazar had begun a long series of very bad news, Herod is shocked to see another entourage enter his palace to offer their regards. Two Nubian potentates, dressed in elaborate robes and headgear, point to the star in wonder.

"More of them," Herod mutters to himself. "More of them. What's going on? Is the whole world in on this? These people come here to my country, to my palace, and ask me about the king who is coming to take my place."

But Herod's mind is devious, and by the time he reaches the Magi, his tone and expression have changed. "Gentlemen," he says sweetly. "You are most welcome. I have the most amazing news for you: the boy king that you are looking for will be born in the town of Bethlehem." He smiles broadly. "When you find him, please come and tell me precisely where he can be found so that I can go pay homage. More than anyone, it is my solemn duty to do so."

Suddenly the king coughs hard. Blood comes from his mouth. His face grows pale. It is quite clear that Herod is seriously ill. His body is ravaged by infection.

"But should you be traveling in your condition?" asks one of the Magi.

"Yes," Herod says solemnly, wiping his mouth with the back of his hand. "Even in my condition."

Joseph holds the tiny newborn baby up to the light. A smile of wonder crosses his face, for he has never known such joy. He brings the child to Mary. As she holds her son, the baby Jesus, her face transforms from tired and drained to radiant joy.

A crowd starts to gather. The star has led many to this site. The same angelic intervention that brought Mary and Joseph to Bethlehem has also spread the news to those who need to hear it most: locals, shepherds, neighbors, and ordinary people. These are the ones whom Jesus has come to save, and for them to be standing in this small barn on this cold night is a moment unlike any other in time. They are witnessing the dawning of a new era—the fulfillment of the new covenant between God and humanity.

Between Herod's palace and Bethlehem, Prince Balthazar, atop an adorned camel, greets and falls into step with the Nubian wise men. They ride elegantly on their camels, ecstatic about the prospect of meeting this great new savior. Not one of them completely realizes who Jesus is and what he represents, but on this night, in their hearts, Bethlehem feels like it is the center of the universe.

In the grotto, the crowd offers prayers and small gifts to the child. Some bow, while others weep with joy. A young shepherd—the same boy who gave Joseph a bundle of kindling just hours earlier—now steps forward to offer something far more precious: a lamb.

Joseph is thankful, but the truth is that he doesn't fully appreciate the gift. He smiles at Mary. She is so taken with her child that she can't stop staring at Jesus. Mary has never has never seen anything so precious, nor anything that fills her heart with such love.

A reflection near the grotto door catches Joseph's attention. His smile fades. The mass of farmworkers, children, and shepherds part as royal attendants quietly and very efficiently clear a path. The crowd backs away, their eyes lowered in deference.

Joseph is uneasy. The last thing he wants is trouble.

Balthazar steps forward. He has changed into his finest robes and wears a gold headdress. His behavior is not regal, however. "I am humbled," he murmurs, as he drops to his knees. He has brought gifts for the newborn child. Balthazar looks to Mary and says to her, "Lady, I believe your son is the chosen king of his people." Joseph realizes that he should bow to Balthazar, but before he can, Balthazar prostates himself on the ground. "What is his name?" he asks Mary.

Mary gently kisses her child on the forehead. "Jesus," she tells Balthazar, surprised to see that the Nubians have also come to see their child. "His name is Jesus." These fine kings all bow down on the dirty ground before the newborn Jesus.

The crowd departs well into the night. The Magi do not return to tell Herod what they saw, or where they found Jesus, because they learn in a dream that Herod has cruel intentions. They return to their homeland by a very different route.

Exhausted, Mary and Joseph are alone for the first time since Jesus' birth. The animals in their stalls are sound asleep, and the new parents soon fall into a deep slumber, too. The infant is swaddled and lying atop a feeding trough. The trough, which rests on a pile of hay, is called a manger. Joseph lies on the floor next to her, his muscles aching from the long days on the road. It feels good to get some rest, and even better to know that their son has entered the world safely. In the morning they can be counted for the census. Soon they can return home to Nazareth, where Joseph's carpentry business awaits.

This routine of sleep and recovery in the grotto goes on for several days. Then one night, Joseph has a dream: he hears a child screaming and Mary calling his name. He looks down and realizes that his feet are soaking wet. But they are not drenched in water; blood flows through the streets. That blood becomes a torrent, raging through the city like high tide. Joseph battles to stay on his feet. That screaming of a single child becomes the wail of hundreds. Joseph sees Herod's soldiers. He screams out for baby Jesus. He cannot be taken.

Joseph wakes up in a panic. The dream felt so real that he is actually stunned to behold Mary and Jesus sound asleep, the picture of serenity. But Joseph knows better. He is a changed man since the angel appeared to him. Joseph's belief in the words of the prophets has become far deeper since he became a vital player in the fulfillment of prophecy. He knows God speaks to prophets in many ways, including dreams. Joseph is absolutely sure God has given him the dream, and he knows what he must do next.

He stands and gathers their belongings. When everything has been packed for travel he rouses Mary from her much-needed sleep. Joseph doesn't realize how panicked he seems, nor how he's behaving. Mary looks at him, completely unsure what has happened to her calm and easygoing man.

Joseph doesn't have time to explain himself. "We have to leave immediately. Just trust me, Mary."

She pulls Jesus closer, holding him tightly, then nods to Joseph and hurries out.

The same people who visited Jesus at his birth come to the aid of Mary and Joseph. Their departure from Bethlehem does not go unnoticed, and even in the dead of night, total strangers approach them and press parcels of food into their hands. These same strangers offer up prayers for them, making sure to get a last glimpse of this very special child before he disappears.

Soon Mary and Joseph reach the edge of town. Before them lies danger and uncertainty. They turn to look back at Bethlehem one last time. This small city will always have a special place in their hearts, even though they were there for just a few short days.

Turning again to look at the road in front of them, they see the torches atop the city walls of Jerusalem burning in the far distance. In another direction, to the east, the great star shines upon them like a compass beacon. Joseph pulls on the donkey's rope, choosing the eastward road. Within a few moments, Bethlehem isn't even visible in the distance, which is good—for Mary, Joseph, and Jesus, have gotten out just in time.

Dawn. Herod's soldiers ride into town. The captain of the guard, a man who never seems to grow tired of carrying out Herod's acts of barbarism, leads the charge. Teams of soldiers split up and scour the city streets.

Without a specific location for Jesus, or even a description of his parents, from the Magi, Herod has sent his army into Bethlehem to slaughter every male child less than two years of age. He believes that is the only way he is sure to murder the right one.

Houses are broken into. Soldiers drag infants from their mothers' arms. The killing is beyond gruesome. Herod's soldiers kill without a second thought. No one counts how many innocents are slaughtered in Herod's purge, but the one child Herod wants has already escaped.

Joseph undertakes an audacious plan to save Jesus: he will traverse a vast desert to take his family to Egypt. Joseph knows that it's a bold move, and he can only hope that the Pharaoh is kinder to his family than Herod. But the Romans also occupy Egypt, and a number of like-minded Jews have returned there, making for the second-largest Jewish community outside of Israel. He is retracing the footsteps of Moses in reverse: from the Promised Land, into the great wilderness where Moses wandered forty years, and then on into Egypt.

But someday Joseph wants to go home. He loves Nazareth, and he longs to raise Jesus there. But this young family cannot and will not return until Herod is either dead or no longer king—whichever comes first.

They make a home for themselves in Egypt and wait. Joseph prays that word will come soon when it is safe to go home. He doesn't have long to wait.

Herod has lived a life of debauchery, and it catches up with him. His face bloats and becomes covered with running sores; his joints become inflamed with gout and his liver fails, making it hard for him to eat or drink without discomfort; poor circulation has led to swelling and gangrene in his lower legs, making it almost impossible for him to walk. His mind is also failing. He lies in bed, waiting to die. A table strewn with pestles, mortars, herbs, and snake heads stands nearby. Herod's doctor makes him drink from a jar containing a potion designed to ease the king's pain. Herod's head lolls to one side. He is moments away from standing before God to explain himself.

Decades of resentment about Herod's treatment of priests, his subservience to Rome, his excessive taxation, and his brutality toward his subjects soon boils over. A collective rage engulfs Jerusalem. Statues of Herod are toppled. Images of his likeness are desecrated. Herod's kingdom is soon split between his three sons, who lack their father's brutal ability to control a nation. Anarchy ensues. Three thousand pilgrims attempting to prevent the looting of a sacred temple are murdered by authorities. Riots and revolts soon follow, which leads Rome to send in their own troops to restore order.

The Romans have a history of allowing people to embrace their own religions, but political dissent is the one thing they will not tolerate. The penalty for political dissent is crucifixion. A man is lashed to a tall pole, which features a horizontal crossbar. The arms are stretched wide on the crossbar and tied in place. His feet are nailed to the vertical pole. In some cases, spikes are driven through the hands to increase the pain of the punishment.

By the time Rome has quelled the disturbances brought on by Herod's death, more than two thousands Jews have been crucified. Their bodies hang in silhouette on hills surrounding the city as warning to those who might also be considering dissent. The Romans' patience with Herod's sons has worn quite thin, so they assume more and more control of Jerusalem.

Jesus is a five-year-old boy as Mary and Joseph make their way home from Egypt. The land is burned. The road is lined with the bodies of the crucified. "Oh, God. What have they done?" Mary gasps quietly. She is worried as never before. She looks back toward Egypt, wondering if it would be better for them to turn around and wait a few more years before returning home. Mary pulls young Jesus close and tries to cover his eyes with her shawl. They move forward, pushing on.

"We must trust in God," Mary sighs. "He has placed trust in us."

As Jesus rides with his mother atop their donkey, he is fascinated by all these bodies hanging on crosses. Jesus is completely unafraid of the journey ahead. He is compassionate and calm. Meanwhile, Joseph is not so tranquil. He urges on the donkey, staring grimly ahead the whole while.

Joseph's family returns to Nazareth, the quiet city in the backwater region of Israel known as Galilee. Both parents know Jesus is destined by God to do something special. His prodigious knowledge of scripture can be a little startling at times, because it is so complex and thorough for his young age, but otherwise he behaves just like a normal boy. He does chores. He helps his father at work. He loves animals. He spends part of each day with Mary, his beloved mother, who carried the Son of God and knows his life will be extraordinary. Sometimes he's such a normal child that it's hard for Mary and Joseph to remind themselves that an angel once proclaimed to them that he is the promised King of the Jews.

When Jesus is twelve years old, Joseph decides it is time to further his son's education. Just as he once placed Mary on a donkey for that long trip to Bethlehem, now he mounts up Jesus and Mary for an equally arduous trek to Jerusalem. Even in the depth of the Roman oppression and despair, faith in God grows in Israel each day. The people make time to celebrate God's greatness. Now, more than ever, they need the ritual and celebration of worship to lighten their burden.

That is why Joseph brings his family to Jerusalem. They travel to the great Temple for the celebration of the Passover. It is the biggest festival of the year in Judea, and thousands of like-minded pilgrims make their way into the city every year to celebrate.

Mary's face bursts into a broad smile as they ride through the great ancient city, once home to such heroes of their people as David, Solomon, and Daniel. People fill the narrow streets and great plazas, and both she and Joseph are swept away in the euphoria.

It is this way throughout Passover, one delight after another. This is their happiest time as a family. But once the holiday is over, as they set out for home, something goes horribly wrong: Jesus is missing.

"I don't see him," Mary cries to Joseph. One minute they were packing to leave, and the next Jesus was gone.

"I don't either. Joseph frantically looks over the masses for a sign of Jesus.

But Jesus has vanished, and he could be anywhere. Mary and Joseph have reason to be concerned, remembering that just a dozen short years ago soldiers were hunting him down.

Mary studies the face of every child she sees. There are so many of them. No Jesus. "Please God," she prays, "please. Give me a sign. Keep him safe. Let him know I'm coming, and that I will find him."

Mary sees a group of boys carrying doves and sheep to a place where animals are being sold. "Animals," Mary cries to Joseph. "He loves animals!"

They follow the boys and are soon led inside the Temple. Mary thinks she spots Jesus and runs up to a young boy holding a dove, but when she turns him around she discovers that it is not her son. The startled child releases the dove. It flies away, straight into the center of the great Temple. Her eyes follow the flight of the dove. The delicate bird lands near a circle of people, all of whom are listening to a great teacher give a lesson. The crowd around him is so thick that Mary and Joseph can't see who it might be.

"Someone's teaching," Joseph points out to his wife. "Jesus will want to listen to the words of a wise and learned teacher."

Mary and Joseph hurry to the edge of the circle, just as an old priest questions the unseen teacher. "What does God say about justice?" the man asks.

They hear a very familiar voice give the answer, and they begin pushing through to the center of the crowd. "It is written in Isaiah," says the youthful voice of the teacher, "that a king and his leaders will rule with justice. They will be a place of safety from stormy winds, a stream in the desert, and a rock that provides shade from the heat of the sun."

Mary and Joseph break through to the center of the circle. They freeze in shock. There, standing in the very center, is Jesus. He doesn't seem to notice them as he continues the lesson. "Then everyone who has eyes will open them and see, and those who have ears will pay attention," says their son.

"Jesus," Mary says angrily. She realizes that her son is no ordinary child, but he has scared her half to death.

Jesus turns and offers his mother a reassuring smile. He mouths the word *Mother* almost imperceptibly. Their eyes connect. And as she gazes into these eyes, Mary sees a depth she has never noticed before. These are not the eyes of a child. These are eyes that have witnessed the beginning of time, and everything since then. Mary is humbled by this vision.

She's also Jesus' mother. And in relief at finding him, her anger fades. "Where have you been? We couldn't see you anywhere. Do you know how worried we were? We have been anxiously searching for you!"

"Why were you searching for me?" he replies calmly. "Didn't you know I had to be in my father's house?"

Mary looks again into Jesus' eyes. She is caught for a moment, unsure of how to react. Then she takes his hands and kisses them, in an instinctive act of homage. She then looks around at the faces of her son's audience and realizes his wisdom and maturity have touched them, too. *Oh, my child, you're not my child anymore. How can I take you away? This is where you belong. These people need you,* Mary thinks. But she says nothing. Instead she kisses Jesus on the cheek and backs away to let him finish his message. Joseph stands with her, marveling at him.

The old priest takes this as a sign to continue his questioning. "How then will we know that justice is coming?"

"Malachi," Jesus responds. "I will send the prophet Elijah to you before that great and dreadful day of the Lord comes."

The old priest is stunned by this succinct and immediate response. He looks with admiration at Jesus, and then to Joseph. "Are you a teacher?" he asks.

Joseph can't help but smile. "No, sir. I'm a carpenter."

From the Temple, Jesus will return to the quiet village of Nazareth with his parents and later experience the passing of Joseph. For almost twenty years he will grow physically, emotionally, and spiritually.

Jesus' voice is unique. But to fulfill his destiny, that voice must reach more than a small circle of believers in the Temple. That voice must be heard throughout Israel and, beyond that, to the entire world. That's why God has sent someone to prepare the way, to start opening the hearts and minds of the people. He is strong in spirit, intensely driven, and pure of heart. He has been a preacher all his life. His clothes are made from the hair of a camel, and he eats locusts and wild honey for food. This new prophet shuns the corruption of the towns and cities for the purity of the wilderness. He lives as he preaches, in simple and uncompromising terms. What he demands from his growing legions of followers is that they change their lives, repent unto the ways of the Lord, and commit themselves to His path. His goal is nothing less than to light a new fire in the hearts and minds of thousands of Jews. The prophet's name is John. He is called John the Baptist because he baptizes followers of God by immersing them completely in a river—the Jordan is his favorite—symbolically cleaning away their sins.

Now he stands alone in the desert near Jericho. John has a wild look about him, with a thick beard and a tangled mat of hair. He is powerfully built, and he dispenses truth.

A group of young men approaches John, who is in an ornery mood today and pretends to ignore them. One of them races ahead to be the first to pepper John with questions. "Please teach us," the young man implores. His face is open and his eyes shine with an eager zeal. "We know you talk about the Messiah and the kingdom of God, and of the importance of repentance."

"So repent," John answers impatiently.

The young man and his friends look confused. John sees they have no intention of repenting and turning to God. He hadn't planned on spending the day teaching. "Come on," he chides them and starts to walk away. "You've come this far. Are you ready to go all the way?"

The tongue-tied men have no choice but to follow. "Is the kingdom of God near?" the young man asks tentatively, appointing himself the group's spokesman.

"Nearer than you can imagine," John replies.

"Then it's true: you are the Messiah, returned to earth by God?"

"No, I'm not the Messiah. Remember what Isaiah said," John responds, growing even more irritated. He picks up the pace. They hasten to keep up. "I am the voice in the wilderness. I will prepare a way for the Lord," he calls over his shoulder. "And the glory of the Lord will be revealed, and all mankind will see it!"

"Wait," the young man yells. "Where are we going?"

John leads them to the Jordan River. It gleams in the sun as he reaches the water's edge. "We are going in here. This is your journey's end—and its beginning."

But they don't follow. "What are you talking about. Are we here to bathe?"

"You must be cleansed of your sins to prepare yourself for God's kingdom."

"But we're already prepared."

John stoops and selects a large smooth rock from the mud along the riverbank. He angrily holds it up, thrusting it close to the man's face. "No, you're not. You think that just because you have Abraham as your father, that's enough? God can raise this stone to be a child of Abraham if He so desires." John hurls the stone into the river. Only then does his tone soften, for he is not truly angry with these young men, but merely frustrated. He desperately wants them to not just know God, but to truly understand what it means to follow Him. He reaches out his hand. "To be worthy of God's deliverance, you must repent your sins and give yourself to Him completely."

Slowly, the young man closes his eyes and relaxes his body, letting John guide him backward under the water's surface. "I, John, baptize you for repentance . . ." is all he hears before the water rushes over his ears and his head is submerged. But even though he cannot hear the rest of the prayer, something inside him is suddenly changed. He feels different. He also feels it in his heart, as if there is now a direct connection between him and God. John guides him back up out of the water. The look on the new believer's face says it all: he has given himself to God. Without being told to, the young man hastily splashes ashore and pulls one friend after another into the river. John baptizes them all.

John baptizes people from miles around, helping them cleanse their hearts in joyful preparation for the coming of the Messiah, bringing them back to God, one baptism at a time. But many don't just come to be baptized. Many who step into the Jordan at John's behest believe that John himself is actually the Messiah.

"There is one to come, more powerful than me, whose sandals I am not fit to carry," John always tells those who ask. "*He* is the Messiah. Trust me, you'll know him when you see him."

But John sees him first. From out of the crowd steps Jesus, now ready to begin his life's work. John is stunned. His entire life has been building to this moment.

The crowds along the shore notice the look in John's eyes. They turn to Jesus, wondering what makes him so special.

"Surely I need to be baptized by you," John says humbly. "And yet you come to me?"

Jesus gently takes hold of John's hand and places it atop his own head. "Let this be so now, John. It is proper for us to do this to fulfill all righteousness."

John nods in understanding. With all the people along the shore looking on, John the Baptist immerses Jesus in the cold waters of the Jordan. And in that moment, the weight of John's ministry becomes lighter. He is no longer a prophet, foreseeing the distant coming of the Messiah.

The Messiah is *here. Now.* His head and body are submerged in a baptism that he does not require, for Jesus has no sin. But the ritual sends the symbolic message that a time of renewal for all mankind has begun. He is on the threshold of the greatest mission in human history. All of the world's imperfection, suffering, and pain will soon be laid upon him. Mankind will receive God's salvation.

As Jesus emerges from the water, the heavens open. The Spirit of God descends, and a voice from heaven says, "This is my beloved son with whom I am well pleased."

First the purification of baptism. Now the contemplative solitude of the desert, where Jesus must fight the greatest battle he has ever fought. He has traveled alone into the farthest reaches of this stark and waterless region. For forty days, he fasts, meditates, and prays. His mind is focused on nothing but the will of God.

Buzzards circle overhead. The sun beats down on Jesus, burning his skin and cracking his lips. He walks along a rock-strewn hillside, knowing that he is beginning his ministry at a time when the unflinching might of the Roman Empire and its puppet kings stands ready to destroy any and all opposition, and where a man's physical existence can be extinguished on a whim.

Yet the power of all the legions and all the emperors in the world is nothing compared to the one true enemy who stalks human emotions and human minds. Before Jesus can take on the spiritual leadership of all mankind, he must confront and overcome that opponent—Satan.

Jesus staggers as he walks, on the verge of collapse from his fast. The hem of his filthy robe drags along the ground. His face is swollen, and thirst is driving him mad. He is consumed by hunger; his muscles and stomach turn inward for nourishment, and starvation sets in as his body begins to feed on itself. It has been forty days and nights since Jesus entered the desert—his personal wilderness. Forty days, one day for each of the forty years that Moses and the Israelites wandered in their own wilderness, seeking the Promised Land.

A snake slithers past, its tongue flicking at the dry desert air. Jesus recoils. The serpent is thick and powerful, poised to coil and strike in an instant. Jesus bends down carefully and selects a large rock. He grasps it firmly in his fist. He stands, and as he does, a shadow appears.

"If you are the Son of God," Satan speaks from the shadow, "tell the stones to become bread."

"Man shall not live by bread alone," Jesus calmly informs Satan, "but on every word that comes from the mouth of God."

Satan turns away in disgust and simply vanishes.

Jesus enters a dreamscape where everything and nothing is real. He dreams that he stands atop the roof of the great Temple in Jerusalem. Soon, the shadow of Satan stands next to him once again. "If you are the Son of God, throw yourself down so that angels can save you."

"Do not put the Lord your God to the test," Jesus warns Satan.

Jesus turns away from the edge. He dislodges a roof tile, which plummets to the cobbled courtyard below and shatters into a hundred pieces.

Now he awakes from the dream to find himself standing atop a mountain cliff. The desert stretches out far below him, as vast and wide as the eye can see, seemingly stretching to infinity. The shadow is next to him. "I will give you the whole world," promises Satan, "if you will bow down and worship me." The shadow extends his hand for Jesus to kneel down and kiss.

Jesus pushes it away. "Get away from me, Satan. It is written, 'Worship the Lord your God and serve Him only.'" The Spirit of the Lord has come upon Jesus. He defiantly turns his back on Satan.

Rugged, upright, and sure, he walks out of the desert in the power of the Spirit to begin his mission. A single venomous snake slithers back into a hole in the ground.

Cold water is pulled from a deep, clear well. Nothing has ever tasted so good to Jesus. He takes his water in sips as his body once again grows accustomed to drinking. The wind blows, whipping dust through the backstreets as he steps away from the well. Joseph passed away many years ago, and he knows that his mother waits anxiously at home for her son to return. But even as he enters his hometown of Nazareth for the first time in months, Jesus does not go straight to see Mary. Instead, he makes his way to the synagogue.

He soon stands before the congregation, reading from the Torah. "The Spirit of the Lord is upon me," Jesus begins. The synagogue is small and cramped, filled with dozens of faces looking back at him. He sees Mary entering through the door at the back, a smile of pride on her face as she sees her son.

It is normal for members of the congregation to read lessons aloud on the Sabbath, and reading the words of the prophet Isaiah is common, but it's clear from his confidence and knowledge that Jesus is no mere member of the congregation, or even a learned student of scripture. He is the teacher. The ultimate teacher. He speaks the words of a distant prophet as though he has written the words himself: "'He has anointed me to preach good news to the poor. Everyone who has eyes will open them and see, and those who have ears will pay attention. He has sent me to proclaim freedom for the prisoners. And to proclaim the year of the Lord's favor.'" Jesus rolls up the scroll. He grasps it firmly in his right hand as he looks out over the synagogue. "Today," he proclaims, "this scripture is fulfilled in me."

There is a collective gasp. Jesus' behavior is *not* usual. These words are blasphemy.

Mary's smile is replaced by a look of worry and concern. A pang of fear shoots through her heart, knowing what is sure to come next. Time slows as the weight of her son's words press down on the congregation.

Then the room explodes. "Who do you think you are?" one man in the audience screams. "How dare you stand there pretending to be the Messiah?" demands another.

Mary tries to force her way through the crowd, hoping to protect her son. But the mass of the congregation has erupted into a rage. The crowd empties out of the synagogue and into the streets after Jesus, meaning to punish him for his blasphemous words. She is terrified. But he has slipped away, and neither Mary nor the congregation can find him anywhere. Mary is relieved; for the time being, at least, he is safe. Her knees grow weak, and she sinks to the ground. "Keep going, my son," she whispers, knowing that Jesus will somehow hear her words.

Mary's fears are well founded. For she knows, just as Jesus knows, that they live in a world where making waves and challenging the status quo is met with unrelenting violence.

John the Baptist, who has long delighted in thumbing his nose at authority, is about to learn that lesson firsthand. The sun sinks low over the hills, casting the banks of the River Jordan into shadow. The water swirls as John stands in the center of the current, baptizing a new believer. Neither man knows that this is the last person John will ever baptize in the name of God.

The moment is sacred and quiet. A long line of men and women wait on shore for their turn. Word has spread far and wide about John's demand that Israel repent and observe the sanctity of God's law. They not only embrace these teachings, but they also hunger for more of John's spiritual teaching. It is a hunger he is more than happy to fulfill.

Then, soldiers on horseback approach from the distant shadows. John sees them before anyone else, and he knows precisely why they have come. He has publicly confronted Herod Antipas, the son of the great and feared king. John has scolded the younger Herod for marrying his brother's wife, a violation of God's law. Now Antipas's soldiers are coming to enforce Antipas's law. John helps the devoted new believer escape before he himself is surrounded by soldiers, who swing clubs and grab at him. But John is wily and slips underwater, only to be caught and beaten. He escapes one more time, forcing Antipas's men to call for reinforcements. They finally capture John, put him in chains, and force him to walk to the road. He turns and looks lovingly at the river where he has changed so many lives, and then he leaves it behind forever.

Jesus will be told of John's imprisonment, which is perhaps a warning to him. But none of them will ever see John again. The dusk is clear and golden, and the Jordan rolls on so effortlessly. John is in shackles, soon to stand before Herod to answer for the crime of speaking the truth.

On a body of water far more turbulent than the Jordan River, three fishermen—Peter, James, and John—finish a long night of trying to fill their nets. They have nothing to show for it. They guide their boats to shore, looks of exhaustion smearing their faces.

They care little for the concerns of prophets or kings, or Rome, or the brutal methods of Herod Antipas's soldiers. They live in Galilee, the same area as Jesus, and their fishing village of Capernaum is also a sleepy backwater. The routine of their lives is simple, predictable: fish all night, mend nets in the daytime, sleep, and then fish some more. They are happy, despite these nights where the nets come back without a single fish to show for hours of backbreaking labor—casting their heavy nets into the sea, then hauling them back in, hand over hand. Fishing is what they do.

As the fishermen guide their boats up onto the sandy beach, a distant figure can be seen walking their way. Jesus' incendiary appearance in the Nazareth synagogue was a sign that he needs to preach to people who have not known him all their lives.

Peter, the most burly and rough of the fishermen, notices Jesus watching their labors. Andrew, Peter's brother, has taken it upon himself to help pull the boats ashore, and to drag the heavy nets up onto the beach to dry. Peter pretends not to notice Jesus, though it's hard not to. Andrew, a well-meaning and bright young man, is clearly captivated by Jesus.

"Who's that?" Peter finally says in a gruff tone.

"John says he is the Messiah."

"Oh, really? Can he teach you to look after your boat instead of leaving me to do it? And can he teach you to find fish?"

"Yes, I can," Jesus replies.

Peter glares at him. His hands are great mitts, calloused and rough from years at sea. His face is lined and sunburned. His back aches from hauling nets. The last thing he needs is a "teacher" to tell him how to fish.

But before he can stop him, Jesus walks over to Peter's boat, takes hold of the hull and shoves it back out into the water.

"Hey!" Peter barks, staring with openmouthed incredulousness at the sheer nerve of this stranger who clearly knows nothing about fishing, for if he did, he'd know this is not the time of day to catch anything. "What do you think you're doing? That's my boat. And you're not allowed to launch it all by yourself."

"You'd better help me then," Jesus calmly replies.

Peter runs into the water and grabs the hull. But Jesus won't be stopped. He looks Peter in the eye and keeps pushing the boat out into the Sea of Galilee. Something in that look startles Peter. He doesn't know whether he's looking into the eyes of a madman or the eyes of a king.

But something in his gut—and Peter is well known for his intuition and discretion—tells him to do as Jesus orders. Peter stops trying to pull the boat back toward shore and starts shoving it out to sea. When the water is waist deep he pulls himself up into the boat. Jesus climbs on board, too.

"What are we doing here?" Peter asks.

"Fishing."

Peter stares into those eyes one more time. "There are no fish out here."

"Peter," says Jesus, "I can show you where to find fish. What have you got to lose?"

Peter reaches for his nets, preparing to cast.

Jesus shakes his head. "Go farther," he commands.

Peter looks at him. "You've never fished here. So listen when I tell you—there are no fish out there at this time of day."

"Please."

So Peter guides his boat into deeper waters.

"Blessed are they who hunger after righteousness," Jesus says. "For they shall be filled."

"Who are you?" Peter demands. "Why are you here?"

"Ask and it will be given to you; look and you will find."

What follows is a day of fishing unlike any other in Peter's life. Thousands of fish fill his nets. His shoulders burn from the strain of pulling them all into the boat. His nets begin to tear. But Peter casts again and again and again, and every time the nets come back full. Other boats soon set out from the shore as Peter is forced to call for help.

"See?" Andrew says when he arrives. "What did I tell you?"

Peter doesn't answer. He merely studies Jesus and wants to know more about this outrageous individual. As the day ends, too exhausted to steer his boat to shore, Peter collapses atop the pile of fish filling the hold. "How did this happen?" he asks Jesus in a tone of desperation. He can feel a tear welling in his eye. Something in his gut tells him that the direction of his life has just changed.

Jesus does not respond, although he is quite aware that this rough-edged fisherman has just become his first true disciple. It is a beginning of a new world for the both of them.

"Teacher, I am a sinner," Peter tells Jesus. "I am not a seeker, just a mere fisherman."

"So follow me," Jesus finally responds. "And don't be afraid. Follow me and I will make you a fisher of men."

"But what are we going to do?" asks Peter.

"Change the world," Jesus answers.

PART SEVEN

MISSION

The marketplace is crowded. The midday sun beats down hard, and flies alight on the fresh meats hanging in the butcher's stall. One booth over, the wife of a fisherman tries in vain to keep the sun off last night's catch, quietly praying that someone will buy the fish before it spoils. Vegetables, honey, and dates are for sale. The baker is the busiest vendor of all, with crowds lining up to purchase their daily bread, the symbolic reminder of God's ultimate authority over their future. It would be foolish to buy "monthly bread." It would spoil. They buy it day by day, living in the moment, not fixated on a future they cannot control. That gives the people of Israel an important sense of peace at a time when their nation is tormented.

A foreign army still controls the country. People suffer from taxes and the excesses of the Roman rulers. Some days their bodies and spirits are sapped of energy, and they can't remember a time when they weren't drained and beaten down. This simple marketplace of friends and neighbors, and food for sustenance, offers a few moments of peace.

For one woman in the crowd, there is no peace. Her mind has snapped and she is tormented by inner voices. Her face is dirty and contorted from her suffering, and she sweats profusely. She behaves like a mad dog, her eyes wild and mouth snarling. No one makes eye contact with her or offers her help.

A group of Roman soldiers strut into the marketplace and immediately begin to abuse the woman. They steal fruit from a vendor, who is powerless to stop them, then form a circle around the crazed woman and throw fruit at her. The game becomes more fun as she bobs and weaves to avoid their throws.

"Get out of my way!" she screams at the Romans. "Stop spying on me! Stop it—leave me alone!"

After a few moments the Romans grow bored and move on. But another man approaches her, offering help. It is Peter, the newly anointed fisher of men.

"Stop following me! Get out of my way!" she screams, weaving her way through the crowd.

When Peter reaches out to help her, she spits in his face and lunges into the mass of people.

"Leave her!" someone yells to him. "She's possessed by demons. You can't help her."

Peter doesn't give up. He presses through the crowd, right behind the woman. She breaks through into an open space, grabs a pot from a stall, and then hurls it at Peter. She turns to run once again, but finds herself standing face-to-face with Jesus. "What do you want?" she bawls at him, completely unafraid. Her are eyes are clouded with confusion and rage.

When Jesus says nothing, she marches right up to him, raises the broken pot above her head, and stares defiantly into his eyes—imbued with a profound wisdom and peace.

"Come out of her!" Jesus commands the demon.

Violent energy whooshes out of the woman. Her face freezes in shock, her body loses its taut posture, and she collapses. She sobs, her shoulders heaving and torso shaking as the demons leave her, one by one. Her shaking slows. She looks up into Jesus' eyes once again and finds herself transformed by the divine spirit that pours out of him. The woman tries to speak, but she is too overwhelmed to make a sound.

Jesus gently places his hand on her forehead. "I will strengthen you and help you," he tells her.

She smiles. Her mind is clear, as if she has just emerged from a nightmare.

"What is your name?" Jesus asks.

"Mary. Mary of Magdala."

"Come with me, Mary."

Peter watches Jesus approach him. The fisherman shakes his head in wonder. He knows that she has just learned what Peter and the other men who have joined him as disciples of Jesus already know: Jesus embodies God's promise of salvation. But the world has yet to discover who this extraordinary, charismatic man truly is.

Peter studies the faces of others in the crowd. They express wonder at the instant change that has come over the madwoman Mary. He hears their whispers: "It's him. . . ." "It's that preacher . . ." "It's the prophet . . ."

Others are cynical. They've seen it all before. They're suspicious of this quiet carpenter. They don't believe he's a prophet.

The Roman soldiers study Jesus as if he is a threat. Their job, should this be the case, would be to subdue him immediately.

But Jesus doesn't give them cause to do so. His every action is one of peace. "Love one another," he tells his followers. "By this will all men know that you are my disciples, if you love one another."

Word of Jesus' miracles—as some are calling his healing powers—spreads quickly through Galilee. Everywhere he travels, crowds gather. Hundreds flock to his side, shuffling for position in the moving tide of humanity that instantly engulfs Jesus when he enters a town with his disciples.

The phenomenon grows with every mile and every footstep, every village and town. The disciples do their best to shield Jesus, but people long for a look from those powerful eyes, or merely to touch the hem of his cloak. "Mercy, mercy, Lord have mercy," Peter mumbles again and again as he sees this growing adulation. "Where do they all come from? So much hunger. So much need."

In one small town the scene grows even more bizarre. Knowing that they cannot get to Jesus through the throngs, four young men clamber from roof to roof, carrying another man on a stretcher.

For a practical man like Peter, the decision to follow Jesus brings tests and challenges he never imagined—tests like the one that unfolds when he attempts to get Jesus away from the crowds by drawing him into a small empty house for a few moments of peace. No sooner do they enter the home than Peter hears the sounds of roof tiles breaking, and those four young men dragging their paralyzed father to a perch on the roof.

Peter goes outside to wave them away, but the men pretend not to hear him. They punch a hole in the thatch roof. Daylight appears in the room. From inside the open doorway, silhouetted against the mass of sunlit followers outside, Jesus begins to speak to the crowd outside. "Come to me, all you who are weary and burdened, and I will give you rest.

"Take my yoke upon you and learn from me," he continues, even as Peter tries in vain to keep the intruders out of their house. But it's too late. One young man has already dropped into the room, and his father has been lowered into his arms. Even if Peter had the power to reverse this situation, there's no going back.

"For I am gentle and humble in heart," Jesus continues, "and you will find rest for your souls."

Only now does Jesus acknowledge the ruckus behind him. He turns to see the paralyzed man lying on the floor, surrounded by Peter and the man's four sons.

Jesus walks toward the man. Peter stands back to make room. The paralyzed man cannot walk, but he can move his arms. He reaches up his fingers to touch Jesus.

Jesus does not extend his arms to the man. Instead, he slowly pulls his hand away. As he does so, the paralyzed man, so desperate to touch Jesus, reaches out farther and farther—and the more he reaches, the more Jesus pulls back.

The look on Jesus' face is one of complete calm. He sees the struggle in the eyes of the man, a struggle that he quietly encourages. Finally, Jesus touches his fingertips to those of the paralyzed man. "Your sins are forgiven."

Mary Magdalene, who has followed Jesus along with the disciples, knows firsthand what Jesus can accomplish. She thought she had seen everything, but her mouth opens wide in shock at what is taking place.

The man realizes he is no longer lying down, unable to move. He is sitting completely upright. Jesus says nothing. The man is emboldened and tries to stand. Everyone in the village knows this is impossible; he has been completely handicapped for years—his sons have had to care for him around the clock. His eyes fixed on Jesus, the man stands.

The crowd closest to the doorway backs away in shock. Those farther back press forward to see what has happened. Heads crane upward to get a better look. Some close their eyes in prayer.

The once-paralyzed man is swept away in euphoria. He hops and jumps like a child, dazzled. These simple movements soon become an impromptu dance, and his sons soon join in. The disciples dance, too. Hands start clapping in the small room, and soon the crowd outside joins in. Men start singing as the crowd sways to the beat of this unlikely and profound miracle. They know that this proves Jesus' real connection to the power of God.

The healed man is exhausted. He stops dancing and comes to Jesus, who softly places his hand on the man's forehead. "Go home now, friend," Jesus tells him. "Your sins are forgiven."

These are not the words the man expected to hear. He shuffles his feet and looks at the ground. His friends stop dancing, the smiles gone from their faces. Soon, the entire crowd has gone silent. Jesus' words could be viewed as an act of blasphemy. Only God can forgive sins. To condone his words would be to act against God's authority.

Those in the crowd who belong to the religious sect known as the Pharisees understand that Jesus' words are more significant than his casting out demons or healing broken bodies. Devoted students of God's law, they distinguish between the powers God assigns to men and those He keeps for Himself. Pharisees listen to every teacher in Israel, paying close attention to their words for signs of either truth or blasphemy. No man equals Jesus. The claims he makes and the command with which he speaks is unsurpassed. The masses have never rallied around a teacher so quickly and with such enthusiasm. Jesus knows what the Pharisees are thinking in their hearts.

One of the Pharisees speaks up. "You can't do that."

"Do what?" Jesus asks.

"Forgive."

Jesus looks at him. Then he looks at the man he has just healed.

Peter leans over and whispers to Jesus, "Don't these people understand what you just did?"

Jesus looks calmly upon Peter. For the world to understand his mission, Jesus must begin by making those closest to him understand. "Which is easier to say: 'Your sins are forgiven,' or 'Take up your bed and walk'?" he asks rhetorically.

The leader of the Pharisees, a man named Simon, shakes his head in disgust and leads his men away. He knows Jesus has become someone to follow very closely. They will deal with him some other day.

"Come on," Jesus tells his disciples. He leads them out the door and into the crowd, in the opposite direction from the Pharisees. "Our work here is done. We have a long way to go. We'd better get moving." Then he turns and begins walking out of town, leaving the people of the village to wonder what exactly they just witnessed.

Jesus' disciples have chosen to be brothers and sisters in Christ. Though they may not yet realize it, this puts them in the vanguard of a revolution—a religious revolution, one not found in ancient texts or in Jewish oral history. Rather, it is a new promise that connects God's will to people's daily lives. This is a difficult concept to grasp, but if the disciples are ever to lead, they need training.

Jesus takes the time to teach his disciples during their daily walks from city to city. His simple, poetic words are delivered casually and gently. Jesus prefers to explain a difficult concept over time, never talking down to his followers, patiently letting the words soak in until they understand them fully.

But Jesus doesn't just preach to the disciples. His revolution is a grassroots movement: he preaches on dirt roads, in fields and villages, to farmers and fishermen and all manner of travelers. These working-class people of Israel form the backbone of his growing ministry. He stops often, standing on a hillside or by a river to address the thousands who flock to hear him, and preaches his new vision for the relationship between God and man. His goal is to liberate these oppressed people, who suffer so dearly under the Roman tax burden. But Jesus has no plans to form an army to save the Israelites from Rome. He wants to free them from something far more dire: sin.

Many don't understand. When Jesus says, "Blessed are they who hunger for righteousness, for they shall be filled," it sounds like a call to arms against Rome.

But then he says things like, "Blessed are the peacemakers, for they shall be called Sons of God."

While many in the crowds hear his words as those of a political radical, many more are coming to understand Jesus' message of love. One evening, he stands on a rocky hillside as the sun sets. He has chosen this moment because his audience of farmers, shepherds, laborers, and their families do not have the financial luxury of taking time away from their occupation during working hours. They stand before Jesus, their long day finished, hands and arms sore from backbreaking labor, and listen to his words. They experience peace washing over their bodies, minds, and hearts. His loving presence touches them.

The evening sun is a dull orange, and the crowd is silent as Jesus tells them about his Father. He teaches the people how to pray, and even what words to say: "Our Father," Jesus begins, "who is in heaven, hallowed be thy name."

Jesus prompts them to really think about what this new prayer says. It begins by praising God's name. It continues with a plea for their daily bread, so that their bellies will be full. Then it turns to a request for forgiveness, because sin will keep them out of heaven. "Forgive us our trespasses," Jesus says, "as we forgive those who trespass against us."

He continues, and the crowd goes right along with him, memorizing the words so that they may say them in their own time of prayer. "Lead us not into temptation, but deliver us from evil."

So there it is. This is the new way to pray: Praise God. Depend upon him for your daily needs. Ask forgiveness. Forgive others. Ask God to keep you from trouble, and the pain that comes with sin.

The people know they can pray like this. But it all seems so . . . easy. Where is the animal sacrifice? Where is the need for a grand Temple, since they can say this prayer anywhere, and at any time?

The sun is almost set by the time Jesus is finished. His audience presses forward to touch him. Their souls have been renewed by this new approach to prayer and God. They are strengthened, encouraged, and comforted. They go back to their homes, brimming with new hope for their future, thanks to Jesus' insistence that God has prepared a place in heaven for all of them. This life of toil and strife and Roman oppression will end someday, but the peace and love of heaven will be forever. To the people of Galilee, Jesus' words feel like a spiritual rebirth.

To the Pharisees, they sound dangerous.

It is daytime, in a small town in Galilee. Hundreds of Israelites wait in line for the mandatory audience with the taxman to pay their tribute. The sound of coins being dropped onto the counting tables fills the air.

The first portion of these monies go to Rome. That much is decreed by law. Failure to pay can mean imprisonment or death. But Rome has long had trouble collecting taxes, so they have farmed out the work to a group of freelance collectors. These men are all Jews, just like the people lined up to pay. So what they're doing is an act of extortion against their own people. For to impose additional fees upon the burden that the already overwhelmed Israelis are suffering is not just onerous, it is treason. The covenant between God and Abraham does not exist between these cruel men and the people they extort. Those who gather taxes are thought worthy of nothing but contempt.

Jesus and his disciples now pass by the lines of sullen men who wait to pay their taxes. "Collaborators and traitors. Taking money from their own people. Sinners all," Peter grumbles beneath his breath. Criticizing the tax collectors is the same as criticizing Rome. He could pay for this indiscretion with his life.

The disciples are stunned to see Jesus carefully scrutinizing one of the tax collectors, whose hands count coins more slowly, his eyes, unwilling to look directly at his victims, betray sadness and doubt. The man's name, the disciples are soon to learn, is Levi. Despite appearing soft or even supportive to his fellow Jews, he is a taxman nonetheless.

"What do you see, Lord?" asks the disciple named John—not John the Baptist, who is still interred in the grisly jails of Herod Antipas.

Jesus doesn't answer. So John tries to see Levi through the eyes of Jesus. What he sees is the look of a man lost in sin, longing for a way out but not believing that such a path exists. Jesus' gaze has been so hard and so direct that soon Levi raises his head to stare back at this powerful energy he feels. His eyes soon connect with those of Jesus, just as the Son of God issues the following order: "Follow me."

In the blink of an eye, Levi understands the summons. "Follow me" is the same as saying, "Believe in me." Free from sin and doubt and worry and faithlessness. *No matter what else happens in my life, I am free to choose.* The moment Levi places his faith in Jesus and follows him, his sins are forgiven and he is free. Levi stands up and walks away from the table, leaving piles of uncounted coins in his wake. The clink of coins from the other tax collectors goes on undiminished until they see what Levi has done. Struck dumb, they stop their work and stare openmouthed at the utter stupidity of Levi walking away from a life of wealth and ease...and for what? To follow this revolutionary named Jesus?

The disciples are incensed. Peter glares at Jesus, enraged that the new disciple is the lowest form of life known to the people of Israel.

"You don't like that I talk to tax collectors and sinners," Jesus says to Peter. "But search your heart and hear what I have to say: It's not the healthy who need a doctor, but the sick. I'm not here to call the righteous. I'm here for the sinners."

Peter has no response. His name means "Rock," and it fits. He is as sturdy and hard as the day is long. His hands are calloused and his ways are not always polite. Following Jesus is a huge gamble, meaning the loss of income during those times when they are not out fishing. Levi becomes a follower disciple, and will from now on be called Matthew. Like it or not, Peter is loyal to Jesus and follows him to the next town on their journey.

———

Jesus squats in the town square, drawing in the dust with his finger. He is not drawing a picture, but a series of letters. He is not alone, nor is the scene tranquil. Directly behind him, a crowd is gathering to watch a stoning. A woman is forced to stand in front of a high wall, facing this crowd. Between the woman and the crowd rises a pile of smooth large stones. When the time comes, each man in the group will be asked to lift a stone and throw it hard at her face. They will do this again and again until she is unconscious, and then keep throwing stones until she is dead—or the pile is depleted, whichever comes first. Death always comes before the pile is used up.

The Pharisees have seen Jesus' popularity grow and watched with dismay as their own followers have taken up with him. They firmly believe that he is a blasphemer, and they have been searching for a way to prevent their entire populace from following him.

At one of his sermons, Jesus quite clearly told the crowd to uphold the law, knowing that to ignore Roman law would mean a wave of punishment against his new followers. In Israel, Roman law and religious law are closely intertwined. If the Pharisees can catch Jesus in the act of breaking a religious law, then they can try him before a religious court. Based on the words of the Pharisees, if Jesus is also shown to be a radical or a revolutionary whose teachings will incite rebellion against Rome, he could also be tried before a Roman tribunal. But there is absolutely no evidence that Jesus has committed a crime nor broken the Law of Moses. A test is their last refuge.

The young woman standing before the wall has been accused of adultery. She is an outcast in the local society. Absolutely no man or woman will stand and come to her defense. Her guilt is assumed. Her fate is sealed.

The men in the crowd grasp their stones, eager to throw. The disciples and Mary Magdalene stand to one side, with Mary holding the condemned woman's sobbing infant daughter. The Pharisees lord over the proceedings, eager to spring their trap.

Jesus, meanwhile, scribbles in the dirt.

Simon the Pharisee steps before the crowd. He is grandstanding, making a very public point. So when he speaks, it is not to the terrified woman standing behind him. His focus is on Jesus, always Jesus, even as the man from Nazareth continues on dragging his forefinger through the dust. "Teacher," he says to Jesus, "this woman was caught in the act of adultery. In the Law, Moses commanded us to stone this woman. Now what do you say?" He is using the question as trap, looking for a basis to accuse him.

Jesus ignores Simon.

The disciples cry out to Jesus: "Please, say something to help her."

Then, to the shock of all who watch, Jesus reaches down and selects a fine throwing stone from the pile. Mary's face shows utter bewilderment, and there is a mild gasp from those who are gathered. Jesus walks over and lines up next to the Pharisees, each of whom now hold a stone, facing the condemned woman.

Now the Pharisees and each of the men so eager to draw blood see the words Jesus has written: JUDGE NOT, LEST YOU BE JUDGED.

As they stare at the words, letting them rest upon their hearts, Jesus strolls back and forth in front of the throwing line. He holds his rock up in his hand for all to see as he scrutinizes the rocks held by the others. "Let the man who is without sin throw the first stone." Jesus offers his rock to each man, even as his eyes challenge them all with the utter certainty that they have all sinned.

Even the Pharisees cannot look Jesus in the eye.

Jesus walks over to the woman. His back is to the throwing line, leaving him vulnerable to attack. Just one angry throw could end his life. "Have they thrown anything?" Jesus asks the woman, his voice thick with mercy and grace. Behind he hears the dull thuds of rocks hitting the earth. But the rocks are being dropped, not thrown. All the men turn silently and walks quickly to their homes as their own sins—theft, adultery, and much more—nag at their consciences.

"Go," Jesus tells the woman. "Go and sin no more."

She doesn't need to be told twice. Breaking past him in a second, she grabs her baby from Mary's arms and runs quickly into the distance.

Simon the Pharisee looks angrily at Jesus. But there is no stone in his hand.

"I desire mercy," Jesus explains to him with his palms upraised, "not sacrifice."

But Simon is not done with him. Jesus has saved a sinner, but the chances of his reconciling his differences with the Pharisees recede with every sinner that he saves. Unless they do, however, Jesus is sure to come out the loser. The Pharisees are politically connected and powerful. One day they will set a trap for Jesus that he won't escape.

———

The Pharisees now focus on ensnaring him in a debate about the scriptures—theological ambush. Two things the Pharisees don't realize: their trap could catch either side; and as a devout Jew, Jesus knows scripture better than anyone. The Pharisees now begin to follow Jesus, watching his every move. They even invite him to break bread with them, on the pretense that both sides can talk and get to know one another better.

Jesus and two of his disciples dine with the Pharisees inside a small room at Simon's home. Jesus sits by the door, listening as Simon expounds on his latest religious theories. On the other side of the table sit a small group of Pharisees. Their faces are a study in rapt attention as they give Simon their complete respect.

Mary Magdalene slips quietly into the room, doing her best to be unobtrusive. The last thing she wants to do is interrupt Simon or to become the center of attention. But that's precisely what she does, for Mary is not alone. She leads a young woman, who is a sinner, into the room. The woman carries a small stone jar. Its contents are a gift for Jesus, and her eyes instantly seek him out in the soft light of the room.

When Simon sees the woman with Mary, he thunders, "You have no business here! Go and offer your body elsewhere!"

Utterly humiliated, the woman moves toward the door. She desperately wants to leave. Her shame is complete. But before she can leave, Jesus reaches out a hand and gently touches her arm. She stops. "Please," Jesus tells her. "Do what you have come here to do."

The words of Jesus give her courage to endure the torment of social scorn. What she planned to do won't take long. She will get it done and then hurry off. Kneeling in front of Jesus, she removes his sandals. A tear falls onto his bare, dirty feet. She uncovers her long dark hair and wipes her tear away with it. Then, hands shaking, she reaches for the small jar and unstops the lid. The scent of perfume, fragrant and delicate, blossoms in the air. The woman pours a few drops of the precious liquid on Jesus' feet, and rubs it in with her bare hands.

Simon can barely believe what he is seeing. His first instinct is to throw these heretics from his home, but then he realizes that this is the perfect moment to lecture Jesus on his impudence. "They say you are a prophet," Simon sneers. "Your friends certainly treat you like one. Well, let me tell you this: if you were a real prophet, you would never let a woman such as this touch you."

Jesus doesn't respond. He has been moved by the woman's kindness and humble servitude, and he knows that this moment means everything to her.

Simon continues: "Look at her. She's a sinner!"

Jesus gently lays his hand atop her head. "Whatever sins she has committed, she is forgiven."

Simon puffs himself up and points a long finger at Jesus. "This is my house. Do you understand? And in my house what matters is God's law. We are devoted to it."

Jesus smiles at Simon and turns back to the woman. "Thank you," he says as she picks up her jar and leaves. The woman is consumed with joy and a sense of peace, but just as eager to flee from Simon and his angry tirade about her character.

"Cursed is anyone who does not uphold the law," blusters Simon, but now his words are intended for Jesus. "To this," he concludes, "all people should say, 'Amen.'"

Incense rises in a thin wisp, spreading its sickly sweet aroma slowly over the dimly lit interior of the synagogue. The congregation bow their heads in attendant worship as Simon stands before them, teaching. The Torah rests before him, and his fingers slide slowly across each line as he reads.

Simon is at peace in his synagogue. It is more than just the meeting place where he can preach to the community, but also a spiritual home. A place where he can lead his followers in devotion to the law—a gift from God. That tranquility is interrupted as Jesus and his disciples step through the door. Simon keeps teaching, even as he carefully tracks Jesus' movement toward the congregation. The bearded carpenter seeks out a man with a withered hand, and leans close to have a word with him.

Peter, always pragmatic, moans to himself, for he knows what is coming. "Surely," he mumbles, "he wouldn't dare. Not here. Not today."

This is the Sabbath, a time God has prescribed for rest and spiritual reflection. Absolutely no work or other exertion can take place on this holy day. Peter looks toward Simon, the Pharisee, who is staring at Jesus. The synagogue has grown silent. All teaching has stopped. All are eyes on Jesus and the man with the deformed hand.

"Today is the Sabbath," Jesus says to no one in particular, though his words are quite clearly aimed at Simon and the Pharisees. "Tell me: is it lawful to do good or to do harm on the Sabbath—to save a life or to kill?"

Simon's face is beet red. His eyes bore into Jesus. "Neither," Simon says under his breath.

Jesus asks the man to stand. Slowly, the man rises. He looks uncertain and self-conscious.

"Most of you have sheep," Jesus says to the congregation. "If on your way here, you saw that one had fallen into a ditch, would you not reach down and pull it out?"

He then takes the man's hand in full view of the entire room. "Then is this man worth less than a sheep?"

The crowd gasps as the man's hand is no longer a withered claw. Instead, he is completely healed. His work done, Jesus immediately turns and heads for the door.

"How dare you!" Simon roars, grasping hold of his robe with two hands and ripping it open in full view of the congregation. The Pharisees standing nearby do the same, making it clear that they have seen something unclean and wish God's forgiveness.

Jesus doesn't see any of this. Only Peter who realizes he's been left behind and races to catch up.

Simon isn't far behind. Enraged by Jesus' behavior, he races into the street and grabs the healed man's hand. He jerks the man to a halt and then raises the new hand into the air. There is no escaping Simon's grip, particularly when other Pharisees come to gather around, so the man is soon paraded through the streets like a trophy. He is evidence to one and all that Jesus has violated the scripture.

Or worse. "This healing is the work of demons," screeches Simon.

Those standing nearby are in awe. They have known this man their whole lives. How is it possible that his hand is completely healed? This is a source of wonder, not shame.

Simon ignores their looks and pleads his case. He knows his audience.

"He's never studied the law, but he's happy to break it," adds Simon.

Despite their amazement about the healing, the crowd is now aghast.

Simon presses on. "He recruits tax collectors and sinful women to do his bidding. He defiles God's law, and His synagogue—your synagogue."

The crowd becomes agitated and unruly. It begins to feel dangerous. Jesus is unruffled and as calm as ever. "Love your enemies," he cautions Peter. "Love those who persecute you."

"We're just supposed to take it?" Peter asks incredulously.

Jesus, the disciples, and Mary Magdalene battle their way through the mob. The city's streets are now in a state of unrest. Roman soldiers wade into the fracas, grabbing the Pharisees and dragging them back toward the synagogue. The Romans are only too happy to mete out punishment with fists and clubs. Jesus goes one way, leading his followers to safety. The Pharisees go another. In the streets, it escalates into a bloody scuffle between the oppressed Jews and the Roman legionnaires. Afterward, as tensions continues to mount, the Pharisees plot how they might kill Jesus.

Jesus has no intention of waging a battle for religious power. But as his ministry grows, he finds himself wading into a complex quagmire of political and religious movements. God, Rome, and religion are intertwined throughout Israel, and two rival factions fight for control. Accepting only the written word of Moses as law and rejecting all other subsequent revelations, the Sadducees think of themselves as the Old Believers. The Pharisees additionally believe in the resurrection of the dead, as well as an afterlife of either heavenly rewards or eternal damnation, taking the Mosaic tradition and the remainder of the Torah as their authoritative text. Politically the Sadducees are a stronger, more powerful force. They represent the priestly aristocracy and the power structure of Israel. Their religious duties are focused on the Temple. The Pharisees represent the common man. The Sadducees view worship in the Temple as the main focus of the law.

The most powerfully religious in Israel make up the Sanhedrin. This council is the supreme court for all Jewish disputes, and it even has the power to hand down death sentences. Despite the Sanhedrin's power, the Romans are still their masters. It is led by a high priest appointed by the Romans, and Rome can just as easily remove him. Caiaphas, the middle-aged high priest, is in the awkward position of balancing the material demands of his Roman masters with the spiritual demands of the Jewish people.

At the moment, Caiaphas is faced with an even greater dilemma. Military banners bearing the Roman eagle have been hung overnight in the great Temple. They brazenly and publicly flaunt God's ban on the use of idolatrous images in the Temple's precinct. All Jews know this is an invasion of their sacred place.

What is Caiaphas to do? If he makes a stand against the Romans he will be stripped of his power. If he does not, his own people will see him as a puppet and a figurehead—a man who pretends to have power but lacks authority. He knows he must make a stand, and to only one man—Pontius Pilate.

Since the breakup of Israel following the death of Herod the Great, Roman prefects have governed the province of Judea. In Rome, Judea is seen as nothing more than the graveyard of ambition. Four prefects have come and gone within twenty years. Pilate is the latest to attempt to control this fractious, troubled backwater. Feeling the need to make a name for himself and stamp his authority on the region, Pilate has moved a new squadron of troops to Jerusalem. As is common practice within the Roman Empire, the arrival of a new group of soldiers also means the arrival of their unit's standard. Hence the eagle banners.

Caiaphas is afraid of Pilate, and with good reason: the new prefect is known for his tough demeanor. He has no trouble oppressing the Jewish people, for he believes the full force of Roman power is sometimes necessary to keep the peace.

But the longer Caiaphas delays his confrontation with Pilate, the more dire the situation becomes. Word of the idolatrous banners, and of the defiling of the Temple, spreads like wildfire throughout Judea. Thousands soon gather in the main square of Caesarea, Pilate's home, to protest.

Caesarea is fifty miles from Jerusalem, on a coastal plain caressed each day by cool Mediterranean breezes. It is the hub of Rome's government in Judea, built by Herod the Great but now the home of Pontius Pilate. He can live anywhere in Israel he wants, but Pilate prefers the tranquility of Caesarea and smell of those ocean breezes to the crowded, manic pace of Jerusalem.

Pilate looks down on the mob from his marbled residence. His well-muscled chest is bare and covered in sweat. As a Roman soldier himself, Pilate knows the value of physical conditioning, and he's spent the last hour sparring with wooden practice swords. Though smaller than a war sword, they are just as heavy, and Pilate can feel the heaviness in his forearms and shoulders from the exertion.

An aide hands Pilate a tunic. Outside, the crowd's roaring and chanting is deafening, as if they have the privilege of saying and doing anything they like without punishment. Perhaps they are unaware that the Roman Empire operates through a mix of enlightened self-interest and overwhelming force. Pilate must put an end to this. He wraps the tunic around his chest and steps into the window so that the crowd can see him. In an instant, the noise stops. Pilate turns to his aide. "Have the men seal the square. Immediately."

"Yes, sir," says the aide, rushing off to deliver the order.

The crowd gazes up at their prefect, waiting for him to speak. But Pilate says nothing, preferring to watch the lines of soldiers assembling in the streets just off the square. A second group of soldiers is now working its way into the front of the crowd, separating the leaders of the protest from the rest.

Only then does Pilate speak: "Go home. In the name of the Emperor, I order you to go home. Leave now and no harm will come to you."

The crowd is still.

Up front, its leaders kneel.

The officer in charge of the soldiers glances up to Pilate for instruction. Pilate responds with a simple nod of his head.

The officer draws his sword, and his men immediately do the same.

The leaders of the protest, still on their knees, pull their robes off their shoulders to expose their necks. They are willing to be beheaded.

Roman intimidation relies upon fear. The soldiers are clearly uncomfortable slaughtering these protesters. Word of this will get back to Rome, if he murders this crowd. It will reflect poorly on his job performance, for Pilate has been sent to govern the Jews, not butcher them.

He steps back from the window, knowing that today the Jews have gotten the best of him. Pilate tastes the bile of humiliation in his throat, and longs to run out into the crowd and run a sword through each of those protesters. Even better, he should have them crucified. That's how the Romans deal with troublemakers: nail them to the cross. Maybe next time. Pilate retreats into the privacy of his home and orders the removal of all banners from the temple.

Far out in the countryside, miles from Caesarea and the Mediterranean, Jesus and his disciples clean up after their afternoon meal. They lounge next to a stream, enjoying the warmth of the sun on their faces and the tickle of fresh green grass against their bare feet. It is a wondrous day, and despite their meager possessions and the possibility of yet another run-in with the Pharisees when they get to the next town, they revel in these simple pleasures.

Peter spies a young man approaching the group. He bears an offering of fruit. The man's clothes mark him as a city boy—too bright, too new, not rugged enough for long days in the fields or on a fishing boat.

But they have no reason to doubt his sincerity, so Matthew gratefully accepts the fruit and leads the young man to Jesus.

"I'd like to learn from you," the young man stammers. "To follow you, if you will let me. And to serve in any way that I can."

Jesus has already shouldered his bag and is beginning to move on down the road. But he invites the young man to walk with him.

Peter eyes the man with suspicion. "We went through all sorts of trials to become disciples," he mutters to Matthew. "Now this guy just walks in from who knows where and gets to join?"

Jesus calls Matthew, former tax collector and professional book-keeper, to walk with him and the new disciple. With just a few words and the transfer of a money bag from Matthew's hand into those of the stranger, Jesus makes the new disciple the group treasurer.

Peter is outraged. His instinct is to rely on logic, not faith. But what Jesus has done is clearly an act of reckless and rather spontaneous faith.

"What's his name?" Peter asks Andrew.

"Judas," he answers. "Judas Iscariot."

It's dusk as Jesus and the disciples walk up a long hill that leads to the next town. Children run to greet them, but otherwise it appears that they are in for an ordinary evening. They'll find a place to sleep and get a meal. Perhaps Jesus will teach, or maybe he won't. All in all, they're just glad to be sleeping with a roof over their heads after many a night sleeping outdoors.

But as Jesus leads the way up and over the top of the hill, the apostles gasp in shock. Thousands upon thousands of people fill the valley below. They stand on the shores of a silvery sea, waiting anxiously to hear the words of Jesus.

The instant the crowds catch sight of him, they rush up the hillside, all trying to get a spot in front when Jesus begins teaching.

"Would you look at all those people?" gasps Peter.

"Yes," Jesus answers. "How are we going to feed them all?"

"Do what?"

"Feed them. It's late. I don't see any cooking fires. They must be famished," Jesus replies.

Judas, trying to show his practical nature, shakes the money bag, and a small handful of coins clank inside. "You'll need a bit more than this," he tells Jesus.

Peter shoots Judas a look.

"Go out into the crowd," Jesus tells his disciples. "And bring back as much food as you can."

They come back with almost nothing: five loaves of bread and two fish. There's not enough to feed the disciples themselves, let alone roughly five thousand. The crowd consumed the contents of their food baskets hours ago, as they waited patiently for Jesus. Now those baskets are quite empty.

Jesus seems unbothered. "Thank You, Father," he prays over the little food they have gathered. "Thank You for what You bring us."

The disciples begin to distribute the food, and the empty baskets overflow with bread and fish—so much that the crowd has seconds, and then thirds.

Peter, that practical man, is once again humbled by Jesus' greatness. As he watches the people eat, he remembers his own miraculous first meeting with Jesus, and how his boat soon groaned from the weight of all that fish.

Jesus comes to Peter and looks him in the eye. There is a loving warmth in Jesus' gaze, once again reminding Peter to let go of his practical nature to put all his trust in God.

The crowd is soon demanding more food, and clamoring to proclaim Jesus as the new King of the Jews. But he sends them away, knowing that the miracle they observed will be more than enough to fortify their faith for some time to come.

In the morning, when it comes time to sail across the sea to their next destination, Jesus is nowhere to be seen. He has told them to go to the far side without him, so that he can go alone into the mountains and pray. Led by Peter, the disciples take their boat and begin the long sail across the vast sea. The small boat is packed to the gunwales with disciples and their small bags of belongings. Peter is the man of the sea, so he commands the helm. His eyes scan the darkening sky anxiously, for he knows a coming storm when he sees one. The wind blows hard and cold. Waves smash against the hull, forcing the small boat to pitch wildly.

"Where are you?" Peter mutters as sea spray covers his face. His eyes scan the horizon, brows knitted into a frown. The weather is only getting worse. The gusts have grown to gale force, making it almost impossible for Peter to look forward into the wind. He has reefed the small sail to ensure that the boat won't capsize, but that also means the boat can't be steered. The disciples row furiously, and Peter has one hand on the tiller, but it's no use: the tiny boat bobs like a cork atop the furious seas, as directionless as a sinner who doesn't know God.

"Oh, mercy," Peter moans. "Why did we leave without Jesus? He would know what to do." Lightning flashes. In the distance, he sees a solitary figure. *Perhaps we're closer to land than I thought*, Peter says to himself, staring into the blackness. Another bolt of lightning. And again, Peter sees a man standing straight ahead, although much closer this time. Peter squints his eyes to see what's out there and feels the wind blast his face. If this man is standing on a dock, Peter should keep a sharp eye, otherwise the boat will be smashed on the rocks.

A new bolt of lightning is followed immediately by another. Peter is blinded by the light, but forces himself to search for this mystery man. Peter gasps. He has seen Jesus. Peter is sure of it. He tries to stand up in the boat, but it's like standing on the bare back of a bucking mule. The other disciples have seen Jesus in the darkness and also try to stand for a better look. "Sit down," Peter orders.

His eyes peer into the darkness for Jesus. "Teacher," he cries out, his words almost swallowed by the wind. "Talk to me!"

And just like that, he can clearly see Jesus standing atop the waves. That's right: standing on the water. Peter knows that he's not hallucinating. What other man can do such a thing? Is Jesus merely a man? Peter thinks of all the times that Jesus made mention of "my Father," as if God were truly his parent. But maybe it's all true. Could it be? In the depths of his heart, Peter finds a new kernel of faith. He tries to wrap his mind around this novel concept that Jesus is who he says he is: the Son of God. Not just a charismatic teacher. Not just a prophet. But the one and only Son of God.

"It's a ghost," Thomas, one of the disciples, cries out in terror.

Peter stills his troubled thoughts. "Lord," he shouts, "if it is you, tell me to come to you on the water."

"Come to me, Peter."

Peter has two hands on the gunwales and vaults himself up and over the side. He is not drenched by waves or gasping for breath in the water. He is standing. A terrified smile flashes across Peter's face at the absurdity of it all. He laughs, a great belly laugh in the middle of the all-consuming storm, and walks confidently toward Jesus, his eyes locked his teacher's. His heart swells with newfound faith, and Peter knows that he will never look upon Jesus the same way again. *The Son of God*, Peter thinks. *I am looking into the eyes of the man who is truly the Son of God.*

Suddenly, the practical side of his mind tells him it is impossible to walk on water. He looks down into the depths, and the one thing that has led him to follow Jesus all this while—his faith—suddenly disappears. Peter sinks. His robes weigh him down, and he plunges farther under the water. He keeps his mouth closed, desperate not to feel water rushing into his lungs, but his chest feels like it will explode from lack of breath. Then Peter feels Jesus pulling his hand, lifting him from the water. In an instant he is out of the waves and lying on the pitching deck, soaking wet. Peter opens his eyes to see a loving Jesus standing over him, his face filled with kindness.

"Peter," he says. "Oh, you of little faith. Why did you doubt?"

Peter is now a changed man, and he desperately wants Jesus to know it. "I have faith, in you. You are my Lord."

Then Jesus calms the storm. He orders the wind to stop, and to the waves he says, "Be still." At his command, the wind dies down, and all is still. The disciples look at him with the same reverence Peter displayed. "Truly you are the Son of God," they say, bowing down in worship.

The sight of Jesus appearing in the middle of the storm, and then walking upon the waves, is not quickly forgotten. Upon reaching the shore, the disciples sit on a hillside, watching the sun rise over the Sea of Galilee, and they cannot stop recounting their individual memories of what they saw. Jesus has set himself apart from them once again, praying alone within sight of their camp. From their lofty perch, they can see from one side to the other of this once tempestuous inland body of water and marvel that it is now as placid as a village well. Their cooking fire is small, for there is little wood in these parts. Peter is still drenched, so he sits as close as he can to the heat in order to dry himself.

John sits beside Peter, who is obviously distraught.

"I let him down," Peter tells John. "I let you all down. I'm sorry."

"No, that was just a moment—a moment we could have never been prepared for."

"Do you think it was a test?"

"I think that this is all a journey, Peter. You can't get there in one step."

Peter laughs. "Where is 'there'?"

It's a rhetorical question, for they both know Peter is alluding to the Promised Land. John looks off to where Jesus is praying. His is a different kind of Promised Land, one not of this earth. John quietly marvels at their teacher's immense powers of concentration.

Jesus' eyes open. He looks directly at John. It's as if he's looking straight into his soul. In that instant, John is reassured. He knows that Jesus is truly the King of the Jews, sent by God to save Israel, but not from the Romans.

———

Rivers of blood flow through the gutters of Jerusalem. The high priest Caiaphas watches over the cleanup of this crimson tide, his face a mask of concern and his heart full of grief. Pilate has had his revenge on the Jews for their riot in Caesarea. When a new aqueduct needed funding, Pilate had requisitioned the Temple coffers. The people of Jerusalem rebelled, and this time Pilate did not turn the other cheek. Hundreds of Jews were put to the sword. Caiaphas is powerless to stop the Roman oppression.

In his ornate palace in Caesarea, Pilate revels in his triumph. The marble floors gleam as the Mediterranean sun shines in through the large windows. Herod built this palace, but to Pilate it's as if the place was designed with his own personal needs in mind. Far from the fanatics of Jerusalem, close to a port from which he can embark for Rome on a moment's notice, and most of all, a bastion of civility in this wretched post with its quarrelsome population. Some days he can even pretend that he's back in Rome.

Pilate sits at his desk as a scribe brings him a stack of official documents. As he signs them, Pilate congratulates himself on how well he handled this latest Jewish rebellion. He knows his behavior will be carefully scrutinized in Rome, and he is certain he had more than enough justification for his brutal response. In his official report, he will honestly tell Emperor Tiberius his no-nonsense approach to the Judean troublemakers is working.

Pilate's signet ring comes down hard on a pool of wax, sealing his official report. If it's rebellion the Jews want, it's suppression that they'll get.

In these these harsh times, it becomes obvious to many Jews that they cannot put their faith in Caiaphas and the Sanhedrin, the Pharisees, or any others of the Jewish religious hierarchy. All eyes focus on Jesus. Some even say that he has power over life itself. He has restored sight to the blind, cured the lame, cast out demons, healed the handicapped, and raised the dead. Some say that if a person has enough faith in Jesus and his teachings, the sick can be healed, the physical body can be made whole, and life itself can be restored.

Caiaphas can't make that claim. Nor can the Pharisees. Jesus is soon put to the test, as he and his disciples walk through a village, enjoying the games played by the young children and the generally festive atmosphere of the day. A messenger comes running with a desperate plea. He tells Jesus that his friend Lazarus, who lives in a neighboring town, lies dangerously ill. Mary, the woman who anointed Jesus' feet in the home of Simon, and her sister Martha had given up hope until they heard that Jesus was nearby. They see this as a sign from God. They know Jesus can save their brother, and they ask him to come quickly and help them in their hour of need.

Jesus knows her brother Lazarus well. Yet he does nothing. Lazarus lives in a region of Judea whose people had tried to stone Jesus and the disciples. They would risk their lives returning there. The disciples assume this risk must be on Jesus' mind, although it is not like Jesus to back down from a challenge. "Aren't we going to see Lazarus?" they ask him.

"This sickness will not end in death," Jesus tells them. "No, it is for God's glory, so that God's son may be glorified through it."

Two days pass. Finally, Jesus tells the disciples, "Our friend Lazarus has fallen asleep, but I am going there to wake him up."

The disciples are unclear of his meaning. "Lord," they tell him, "if he sleeps he will get better."

"Lazarus is dead," he says bluntly, forced to spell it out to them. "And for your sake I am glad I was not there, so that you may believe. Let us go to him."

"Let us go so that we may die with him," Thomas says glumly, thinking of the Judeans' previous attempt to stone them.

———————

Some days later, Jesus and his disciples make the short walk to Lazarus' village. They find a town consumed in grief. "Are you coming for show?" Mary cries at him through her tears. "You could have saved him."

Jesus says nothing as he keeps on walking toward Lazarus' home.

"We believed in you! We trusted you!" Mary sobs. "You're the healer. You could have saved him. Why didn't you come? Why? Tell me."

Martha, bereft, simply moans when she sees Jesus.

An angry crowd of mourners soon surrounds Jesus and his disciples. The mood is hostile. "Fool," says an unidentified voice in the crowd. "If you were so powerful you should have saved Lazarus from dying." The disciples stiffen.

"I am the resurrection and the life," Jesus tells Martha and Mary. "If anyone believes in me, he will live, even though he dies. And whoever lives and believes in me will never die. Do you believe this?"

"Yes, Lord. I believe that you are the Christ, the Son of God who was to come into the world." Mary weeps as she speaks, and Jesus is deeply moved.

"Where have you laid him?" Jesus asks. By now Lazarus has been dead for four days.

They lead Jesus to their brother's tomb to grieve.

"Take away the stone," Jesus commands when he arrives at the tomb.

"His body will smell too bad for us to go near it," protests Martha, because it's well known that bodies begin to decompose after three days, and smell. Horribly.

The disciples and the men of the village obey Jesus' order and roll back the stone that covers the entrance to the tomb. Word has spread throughout the village that Jesus is at the tomb, and now hundreds have gathered, curious.

"Lazarus," Jesus shouts.

Peter can't bear the tension and steps away from Jesus. To conceal his discomfort he absentmindedly grabs a long grass stalk and winds it around his hands. This time Jesus has promised too much, Peter thinks. The man has been dead *four* days.

Jesus with boldness yells, "Come out!"

Lazarus' sisters sob, worn out from false hope, then days of mourning. Then a uniform gasp erupts from the crowd and many fall on their faces in worship, as they stare at Lazarus, wrapped in his burial garments. His head is uncovered, and he squints as he steps into the sunlight. He is alive.

Jesus speaks again, but in a voice so loud and authoritative that it can be heard a hundred yards away. "Whoever believes in me shall never die. *Never!*"

Martha collapses in shock. Her sister Mary is shaking. John laughs, incredulous. Tears run down Peter's cheeks. "It's true," he tells Jesus. "You really are the Messiah."

Jesus turns and strides through the throng. Hands reach out to touch him, and voices call him names like "Lord" and "the King."

Peter runs after him. John follows.

"Lord," Peter yells, "where are you going?"

"It's time, Peter," Jesus tells him.

"Time for what?"

"How long have we walked together, preaching my message?"

"Three years, Lord."

"Don't you think it's time, Peter, that we finally go to the one place that needs to hear my message more than any other?"

Peter opens his mouth in shock. He knows that Jesus is referring to a place where Rome and the Jewish high priests have total control. They are, in fact, walking straight into danger.

Jesus smiles. He stares at Peter. "That's right, Peter. We're going to Jerusalem."

PART EIGHT

BETRAYAL

It is the week before Passover, that holy day that marks the time in Jewish history when its people were spared from death and led out of slavery from Egypt. Ironically, they celebrate their freedom from past oppressors, while suffering under the yoke of new pagan masters—the Romans. It seems to never end.

Right now, even as all of Israel prepares to celebrate this most important and sacred occasion, one very select group of pilgrims is making their way to Jerusalem. Jesus walks at the front of the single-file line, leading his disciples and Mary Magdalene.

They are not alone on the dusty road leading into the city. Thousands of people walk dutifully in from the countryside and desert—children on their parents' shoulders, the elderly. Men pushing handcarts, women leading the family donkeys. Now and again the crowd parts to let Roman soldiers through, knowing that to obstruct their path might lead to a sudden act of brutality.

One family's cart has a broken wheel, and the cart is blocking the road. The wife grasps their small children and the husband desperately rushes to get the cart off the road before it blocks the oncoming Romans, but the columns of legionnaires are forced to come to a halt. Their commander, a decisive man named Antonius, takes control. "Throw it down the bank," he barks.

Everything the family owns is loaded on that cart, but the Romans follow orders and shove it into a ditch. The wife cries softy. The children wail as their precious belongings are strewn over the hillside. Then the couple notices one of their children isn't moving. The cart has fallen on their youngest daughter, and she lies crushed by its weight. As the devastated parents cradle their dead baby, the legionnaires move on. They don't even notice.

The pilgrims know this is no ordinary group of soldiers. There are too many of them, their shields and breastplates are highly polished, and they march with a precision and snap not usually seen in the Jerusalem garrison. They watch as Antonius gallops his horse down the line to a regal figure on riding a black stallion. It's Pontius Pilate. This impressive procession is made up of his handpicked soldiers. Their job is to protect him and serve him. They will stop at nothing to ensure Pilate's safety.

"What's the delay this time?" Pilate impatiently asks Antonius.

"A broken cart, sir. We pushed it off the road."

"These filthy people and their wretched festival," Pilate responds. "Every year it's the same thing. I'd outlaw the thing if only Rome would allow me."

Pilate is returning to Jerusalem to take personal control of the city. As governor of this remote Roman province, it's his duty to maintain order during this potentially explosive period.

"How much longer?" asks Pilate's wife, Claudia. She rides alone in a horse-drawn sedan, fanning herself to keep cool in the midday heat.

"We'll soon be there," replies Pilate. The sedan jerks forward as the procession resumes its progress.

Claudia peeks out between the curtains. All she can see are horses' rumps and polished shields. She sighs and leans back, hating every minute of the journey to Jerusalem. Oh, that she could be back in Caesarea, lounging in her favorite chair. She hears wailing and sees the hysterical cart owner cradling his dead, bloodied child. Claudia, a believer in omens, recoils at the sight. Clearly it's a very bad omen to start to their time in Jerusalem by killing an innocent child. "Nothing good will come of this," she mumbles, trying to shut the image out of her head.

For Jesus, however, the week is off to a rousing start. The people of Jerusalem have heard about him for years, and they now celebrate his triumphal entry into their city. He rides a donkey, which is most unusual for a man who walks everywhere, but it is the traditional way a king would come to visit his subjects if he came in peace. Hundreds of people line his path, throwing palm branches onto the ground to carpet the road. They chant "Hosanna," which means "save us," for even more than a spiritual teacher, these people hope that Jesus is the new King of the Jews. They believe he has come to save them from the Romans. "Hosanna," they chant. "Hosanna, hosanna, hosanna, hosanna." The roar is deafening, and Jesus acknowledges them all with a smile and a wave. The disciples walk on either side of him, somewhat dazzled by the excitement. This is their payoff for three years of sleeping on the ground and tramping through backwater fishing villages. Tonight they will sleep in a nice bed, eat a hot meal, and wash. The welcome is overwhelming for the disciples. This first big test of Jesus' popularity since he left Galilee is a success far beyond any expectation.

"Look at all the people," marvels Mary Magdalene.

"I never, in my wildest dreams, thought we would ever see something like this," John agrees.

Thomas can't believe what he's seeing, and even Peter, that most practical of all men, is dazzled. "This," he gasps, "is incredible."

It is also audacious. Jesus has chosen to make his entry into Jerusalem on the donkey because scripture foretells that the King of the Jews will enter Jerusalem as a humble man riding on a donkey. The symbolism is not lost on the crowd, who know their scripture well.

"It is written!" they cry in the midst of their hosannas, clapping and chanting and waving palm fronds as a sign of fealty. Their faces are alight with hope as they imagine the day when they will throw off the Roman yoke. This is the One, the man who will bring a new peaceful age, free from poverty and suffering.

Peter acts as a human shield as the crowd grows more and more fanatic. He is fearful that someone will be trampled under the donkey's hooves.

"Hosanna! Hosanna!"

"Save us! Save us!"

It is written.

"Hosanna."

"A donkey?" Caiaphas, leader of the Sanhedrin, fumes when a servant tells him of Jesus' mode of transportation.

The elders of the Temple stand with him, shaking their heads. Jesus' arrival represents a direct challenge to the Jewish authorities. Claims that Jesus is the Messiah have outraged and incensed the Sanhedrin, the Sadducees, and the Pharisees. Only they can anoint the new Messiah, and this carpenter from Nazareth is clearly not such a man.

" 'See your king comes to you,' " Caiaphas sarcastically quotes from scripture. " 'Triumphant and victorious, humble and riding on a donkey.' "

The elders say nothing.

"And where is he headed?" Caiaphas asks the servant.

The servant lowers his head. What he's about to say next will not be the words that Caiaphas or the elders want to hear.

"The Temple," he says.

"The Temple!"

One of the elders, a man named Nicodemus, quotes another verse: " 'To lead his people to victory and throw out the oppressors.' "

"The crowds," Caiaphas demands of the servant. "How are they responding?"

The servant's name is Malchus. He had hoped to impress the Sanhedrin by racing to tell them Jesus' whereabouts. Yet it seems that every word that comes from his mouth is just another variation of bad news. So he says nothing.

Caiaphas knows precisely what that means. He paces animatedly. "And the Romans," he says, worried now. "Have they made a move against this man yet?"

Malchus shakes his head.

"Not yet," says a concerned Caiaphas, who remembers only too well the massacre of his people. "We don't need Pilate feeling threatened, or intervening in this situation, particularly during Passover. If we have a repeat of those executions there's no telling what kind of anarchy will erupt."

Nicodemus agrees. "Last time Pilate felt threatened, hundreds of Jews were killed by the Romans," he says, stating what everyone in the room knows all too well.

Caiaphas nods to Nicodemus. "Go with Malchus. If he enters the Temple, you watch him. I want to know every move he makes."

Jesus urges his donkey on toward the Temple's outer wall. Peter, John, and the other disciples quicken their pace to keep up. The crowd continues chanting as they part to let Jesus through. The apostles grow tense as they realize that the people are expecting amazing things from Jesus. This time it's not miracles, but a complete revitalization of Israel. "It is written," voices cry out from the crowd. "He will be called 'Wonderful Counselor, Mighty God, Everlasting Father, Prince of Peace.'"

Jesus would normally shy away from such profound benedictions. Instead, much to the apostle's shock, he is riding straight for the heart of his own people's national identity: the Temple of Jerusalem. This can mean just one thing: the situation is about to explode. John scans the crowd nervously and sees for the first time that their actions are being monitored. He sees the hard eyes of spies and messengers, their faces bereft of the joy possessed by so many others in the crowd. Peter's eyes dart from face to face. He sees Nicodemus in his priestly robes, strategically analyzing their progress. Then, as he glances down a side street, Peter's heart sinks at the sight of Roman soldiers following them on foot.

A manic thug bursts from the crowd. His name is Barabbas, and as he leaps directly in front of Jesus, he yells the word "Messiah." He does not speak with reverence. Rather, he taunts Jesus, forcing Peter to move quickly to protect Jesus. He grabs at Barabbas's robe, which falls back to reveal the hilt of a long knife.

But Barabbas is too strong for even the rugged Peter. He shakes him off and gets close to Jesus. "If you're the Messiah, then confront the Roman scum. Prove it." All Jews want freedom from Roman rule, but anarchists like Barabbas believe that God wants them to use violence to attain this goal. "Make us free," he challenges Jesus, even as Peter once again tries to intervene.

Peter, John, and Thomas work together to form a human shield. "We come in peace," says Peter.

Barabbas looks directly at Jesus, whose serene eyes lock with his. Then Barabbas stops talking, as if mesmerized. He lowers his gaze and steps back into the crowd. He doesn't know what has affected him, but he feels Jesus' gentle power.

At last Jesus reaches the temple. He dismounts from the donkey and begins climbing the staircase to the Temple's outer gate. Not even his disciples know what he will do next.

The Romans are watching his every move. One wrong step will surely prove fatal for this Jesus. They saw Barabbas, a known revolutionary, approach Jesus. Ready as always to crush any sign of political dissent, the Romans wonder whether or not Jesus might be a coconspirator. But there are no Romans inside the Temple complex as Jesus enters. The great palace of worship is filled with Temple officials and money changers. The mood is tense, a stark contrast to the reception Jesus enjoyed just moments ago. The disciples are concerned that things could get out of hand. This is a time to remain completely calm, not upsetting anyone or otherwise inviting trouble.

Jesus reaches the outer court of the great Jerusalem Temple complex— the Court of the Gentiles, as it is known. He walks ahead of the disciples. There is purpose to his every footfall and a determination in his eyes.

"Now what happens?" Peter asks.

"I don't know," answers John.

Judas is frightened. "I don't like the looks of this," he says in a hushed voice. His fascination with being a disciple has been wearing thin lately, and he's not as eager as the others to lay down their lives for Jesus.

"Stay together and we'll be fine," Mary Magdalene adds firmly.

All around them, the great court is filled with human activity. Lambs, doves, and goats are for sale, and their sounds and smells add to the human cacophony. There is the familiar clink of coins being counted and changing hands. The climax of Passover is a ritual animal sacrifice. Poor pilgrims traveling into Jerusalem from all over Israel must part with their hard-earned money to buy the animals. But their coins bear images of Roman emperors or Greek gods, images that are thought to be idolatrous by the Temple priests. So pilgrims must change all coins into temple currency. A portion of the proceeds from the exchange goes to the Temple authorities, part goes in taxes to the Romans, and the rest is pocketed by the corrupt moneylenders, who prey on the pilgrims by charging more than the law allows for making the currency exchange.

The disciples stay close as Jesus stops walking and studies all that is going on around him. His face and eyes are the picture of sadness. He sees more than just animals and money changers: an old man being shooed away by an angry moneylender, a poor family trying to buy a lamb but having only enough for doves, a frail old woman being jostled, and a lost little girl crying. The commotion makes it impossible for anyone to engage in devout prayer. Jesus' face clouds with anger and resentment. He walks calmly toward the stall where the moneylenders have set up shop. Coins are piled on the tables. Their hands are dirty from counting money. They banter with one another. Jesus grabs the table edge with two hands and flips it over. Then he goes on to the next table and does the same. All heads in the Temple court turn to the sound of spilling coins, and onlookers immediately race to scoop up the fallen money. "What are you doing?" shrieks one money changer.

"Rabbi!" Judas pleads, scooping up some coins in his palm. "No!"

But Jesus is not done. He cannot be stopped. On to the next table.

Jesus flips another table, which bounces against a birdcage and sets loose a flock of doves.

Judas sees a band of Roman soldiers lining up like riot police near the entrance to the Temple complex. "Jesus! Please!" Judas pleads. He doesn't have the stomach for Jesus' brand of revolution. Judas wants to be safe and protected. He fears he will be thrown into prison along with Jesus and all the disciples. Unlike the other disciples, he is an educated man who knows the way of the big city. "If only you would listen to me," laments Judas.

But Jesus doesn't listen to Judas. He isn't listening to anyone. Another table gets flipped.

"Why?" asks one vendor, disconsolate about all his earnings scattered about the Temple floor. "Why have you done this?"

"Is it not written?"

"What on earth could you possibly mean?"

"Is it not written?" Jesus repeats, but this time in a booming voice that echoes throughout the chamber. In an instant, the entire court is silent.

"My house . . . My house shall be called a house of prayer," Jesus continues. "But you have turned it into a den of thieves."

Peter and John hold back the angry merchants as they attempt to punish Jesus, who has finished this task and is marching out of the court. In his wake are tipped tables, angry traders, and a scene of total chaos.

Nicodemus from the Sanhedrin steps forward. Judas is so impressed by his expensive robes that he almost trips over himself in his hurry to bow down to the temple elder.

"Who are you to tell us this? How dare you. It is *we* who interpret God's law—not you."

"You're more like snakes than teachers of the law," Jesus replies in a heated tone.

Nicodemus is beyond shocked. "Wait. You can't say that! We uphold the law. We serve God."

"No," Jesus replies. "You pray lofty prayers. You strut about the Temple, impressed by your own piety. But you are just hypocrites."

Nicodemus is stunned. Men of his rank are simply not spoken to in this manner.

Jesus reaches out and gently lifts the fine material of Nicodemus' robe, rubbing the fine threads between his fingers. "It is much harder for a rich person to enter the Kingdom of God than it is for a camel to go through the eye of a needle," Jesus tells him, letting go of the robe.

Everyone in the temple has heard Jesus' words. The Jewish pilgrims who have traveled so far to be here for Passover are inspired by such a courageous stance against the rich and powerful men of the religious establishment, who have oppressed their own people as much as the Romans have. Only they've used threats and God's law to control the people instead of brute force.

Nicodemus looks about uneasily. He feels trapped. The crowd is definitely on Jesus' side. At the far end of the chamber, he sees the Roman soldiers prepared to move in if the situation gets out of hand. Such an intervention would further discredit the Temple elders and Sanhedrin, so Nicodemus says nothing as Jesus strolls away. He will deal with Jesus another day.

Nicodemus notices that one of the disciples, Judas, seems more impressed by the ways of the Temple than by Jesus. He calmly eyes the man, and is rewarded with a deferential gaze.

"Messiah," the crowd chants spontaneously, as Jesus continues on his way out of the Temple. "Messiah!"

Jesus shows no fear as he walks past the line of Roman soldiers at the entrance, their shields braced for signs of trouble.

———

Jesus' actions in the Temple have confirmed Caiaphas's worst fears. He and a handful of elders have been watching the action from a balcony high above the Temple floor. The chant of the crowd still vibrates throughout the great chamber long after Jesus has left. The people have been energized by Jesus. That makes the elders very nervous.

"This is outrageous," fumes Caiaphas. He normally prides himself on his stoic behavior, preferring to come across as unruffled and untroubled at all times. So for his peers to see Caiaphas looking upset is extremely troubling.

A slightly breathless Nicodemus comes up the steps and joins them.

"You weren't much help," says Caiaphas.

"He's clever," Nicodemus counters. "The crowd worships him. There's something unusual about him that is easy for people to draw near."

"There's absolutely nothing unusual about him," Caiaphas snaps. "Except for his ability to create havoc."

Caiaphas turns back to view the scene. Just in time to see one of the disciples approach his favorite servant, Malchus. There is an exchange between them. At first Caiaphas fears that their words will be angry, but whatever this particular disciple is saying surprises Malchus. The two clearly reach an agreement and then part ways. As the disciple hurries to catch up with Jesus, Malchus cranes his head upward to where Caiaphas stands. The look on his face is all Caiaphas needs to see. Judas will betray Jesus.

Caiaphas turns to the elders. "We may have found a way to deal with this Jesus."

As he leaves the temple, Jesus is followed by the disciples, a crowd of excited new followers, and a few Jewish elders who want to know more about Jesus' teachings. Malchus trails far behind, working as Caiaphas's spy.

Jesus leads this unlikely procession of old friends, new friends, elders, and a spy down the Temple steps, then suddenly stops, turns, and faces them.

Malchus does his best to appear as if he's there accidentally, but his purpose is now clear.

Jesus ignores him. Instead, despite the huge crowd, he speaks to his disciples as if no one else is there. "Do you see this great building?" he tells them. "I tell you that not one stone of this place will be left standing."

Peter and John look at one another. Did Jesus really say what they thought he said? Is he really threatening to destroy the Temple?

A Jewish elder has heard Jesus' words and questions him. "Who are you to say these things?"

Jesus continues talking to his disciples: "Destroy this Temple and I will build it again in three days."

"But it took forty-six years to build," replies the shocked elder. "How is this possible?"

Jesus doesn't answer him. He abruptly turns and continues on his way, leaving his disciples scratching their heads about what Jesus means by his comments.

"What does he mean?" asks the one they call Thomas, the one who is constantly so doubtful. "Destroy the Temple? I don't get it."

John has a gift for vision and insight that is unparalleled among the disciples. "He's saying that we don't need a stone temple to worship in. *He* will be our access to God."

"Really?" Thomas questions him, once again showing his unerring ability to question every little fact.

With that, John and Thomas hurry to catch up with Jesus.

———

Pontius Pilate's Jerusalem residence is far more sumptuous than his home in Caesarea, which is a good thing, because he rarely feels comfortable venturing outside when he's in Jerusalem. The city is totally Jewish, which is in stark contrast to the Roman design and Roman population of Caesarea. He feels like a complete foreigner when in Jerusalem, living in a small world with a completely different set of rules and way of life.

As Pilate and his wife Claudia take lunch on the veranda, Antonius, his top military commander, enters and salutes. News of Jesus' confrontation with the money changers spread through Jerusalem in a matter of minutes, but it's only now that Pilate is about to hear of Jesus for the first time.

"We are eating," barks Pilate.

"So sorry to bother you, sir. But a Jew has been causing trouble in the Temple."

"You interrupt our meal for that?"

"Sir, he attacked the money changers and said he will destroy the Temple."

Pilate laughs. It is the first time Antonius has ever seen Pilate laugh, and the sight makes him uncomfortable. "He has a very large number of supporters," Antonius hastens to add.

Pilate's smile disappears. "What's his name?" he asks.

"They call him Jesus of Nazareth."

This catches Claudia's attention. "My servants talk about him," she says.

Pilate looks at her quizzically and then back to Antonius. He has made up his mind. "This Jesus is Caiaphas's business, not mine. But keep your eye on these crowds following him. If they get out of hand, I will shut down the Temple, festival or no festival.

"I mean it."

Caiaphas and the high priests are gathered, discussing the situation with Nicodemus, his servant Malchus, and his handpicked group of elders.

"He said what?" asks an incredulous Caiaphas.

Malchus is the first to reply: "That he would destroy the Temple."

"I am shocked. He claims to be a man of God, and then says he plans to destroy the House of our Lord?"

Caiaphas remains silent, steadying himself against the shock waves pounding his body. This is far worse than he thought. Finally, he speaks.

"We must act fast. Very fast. But with care. We cannot arrest him openly. His supporters will riot, and then Pontius Pilate will crack down." Caiaphas pauses, thinking through a new plan. "We must arrest him quietly at night. Before Passover. Malchus, what was the name of that friend of his, the one who approached you?"

"Judas, High Priest?"

"Yes, Judas. Bring him here. Discreetly."

Malchus nods and makes a hasty exit.

———

Jesus and his disciples camp on the hillside of the Mount of Olives, surrounded by pilgrims who have made their way to Jerusalem for the Holy Day. Smoke from the many campfires rises into the evening sky, and row upon row of tents cover the hill. Jesus drinks water from a small stream, as Peter tries in vain to gather the disciples to have a discussion.

"Has anyone seen Judas?" Peter asks aloud.

They all shake their heads. Jesus looks to Peter but doesn't offer an answer.

A figure steps out of the coming darkness and cautiously approaches Jesus.

"Judas," Peter calls, seeing a shadow by the olive trees, "is that you?"

A man whose face is covered by a hood steps into the light of the campfire. He wears a discreet cloak covering his temple robes. When he pulls back his hood, the face of Nicodemus is revealed. Nicodemus is a member of the Sanhedrin and a Pharisee, but he has come down under the cover of night to see for himself what Jesus is about.

"What are you doing here?" Thomas demands.

"I think you're lost, sir," adds John. A man of Nicodemus' position would never normally associate with ordinary people.

Nicodemus appears tense, but then Jesus steps forward. "Welcome," he says warmly.

The Temple elder is clearly troubled. He turns over thoughts and well-prepared speeches in his mind, unsure of where to begin explaining why he has come. But Jesus' kind welcome disarms him, and he joins Jesus by the fire.

A full moon shines down through the olive grove. Nicodemus starts: "Rabbi, they say you can perform miracles. That you have seen the Kingdom of God."

"You, too, can see the Kingdom of God," Jesus tells him. "But you must be born again."

"Born again. Whatever do you mean? How is that possible? Surely we cannot enter our mother's womb a second time."

"You must be reborn—though not in the flesh, but of water and spirit. That which is born of flesh is flesh; and that which is born of the spirit is spirit."

A sudden wind blow Jesus' hair across his face and rustles the tree branches. Nicodemus looks up into the branches. When he looks back he sees that Jesus is staring at him intently.

"The wind blows where it wishes," he tells Nicodemus. "You hear its sound but don't know where it comes from, or where it goes. So it is when the spirit enters you. Believe in me, Nicodemus, and you will have eternal life."

"Believe in you?"

"For God so loved the world that He gave His one and only son, that whoever believes in Him shall have eternal life."

Nicodemus is torn. Could this be the Messiah? Or is this just another false messiah, a deluded individual claiming to be God?

Jesus knows his thoughts. "Everyone who does evil hates the light for fear that their deeds will be exposed. But those who live by the truth come into the light."

Nicodemus feels a great peace wash over him. The moonlight shines brightly, and the breeze blows gently.

Judas skulks in the shadows, his head and face covered with a hood. He is on his way to meet Caiaphas, and he knows it would be disastrous if he were seen. At the entrance to Caiaphas's palace Judas removes the hood so that the Temple guards will allow him to enter. Judas is led into Caiaphas's inner sanctum, where he immediately feels ill at ease.

"One cannot deny that he has followers," Caiaphas begins. "Especially among the less-educated elements of our society. But you, Judas... why, you intrigue me. You don't seem to be one of them. Why follow this man?"

"I can't explain Jesus to you. He has power. It's hard to put into words."

"Power to stir things up? Or, perhaps, to cause trouble?"

Judas looks embarrassed. "He says things... things that other people don't even think, let alone speak."

"Things like destroying the Temple?" Caiaphas reasons.

Judas is extremely uneasy. "Well, I suppose that if he was the Son of God—*if*—then he could truly destroy the Temple. But why would he abuse the House of God? Surely the true Messiah would seek to unify Israel, not divide it?"

"Maybe we should just talk, he and I? Straighten things out."

"Jesus won't come here."

"Judas, your friend Jesus doesn't know—he can't possibly know— where all this will lead. If the Romans step in, the slaughter will be beyond belief. They have done it before, and they can do it again. It will be the end of our Temple—and possibly even our faith. Do you want that?"

Judas remains silent as the high priest continues his argument.

"It's important that you help," says Caiaphas. "A friend like you could lead him here—discreetly, of course."

And now the high priest gazes straight into Judas's eyes as he delivers his summation. "Help him, Judas. Help your friend. Save him from himself while you still can."

"And if I do? What's in it for me?"

If Caiaphas had any doubts that Judas's initial approach was one of betrayal, those doubts have immediately vanished. Caiaphas reaches over to a table, on which rests a small purse. He holds up the purse.

Judas swallows hard. This is a moment of choice. "I'll do it," he says. He grabs the bag, and the silver coins clink inside.

Jesus returns to the Temple the next day, performing miracles and preaching to the crowds. The Jerusalem crowds swell. The people are liberated and energized by his words, and use the term *Messiah* almost casually, as if it is an acknowledged fact that Jesus is Lord. The groundswell of popular support, particularly during Passover, terrifies the high priests and the Temple guards. At all costs, they must avoid a riot. They know what Pilate would do, for this would be viewed as a revolution. But the religious authorities cannot stop Jesus. He's too beloved, too charismatic, and too authentic for them to make a move against him.

The same cannot be said for Pontius Pilate. The fervor of the crowds at the Temple are unlike anything he's ever seen, and he's sure that the situation is about to explode into full-scale rebellion against Rome. He calls High Priest Caiaphas to his palace and makes it all quite clear: "Stop the disturbances or the Temple will be shut down. There will be no Passover." The rage with which Pilate speaks the words is a reminder that he is more than just a random administrator, sent by Rome to govern the Jews. He is a soldier, a physical man of action who thinks nothing of spilling blood. His disdain for the Jews is complete, so giving the order to slaughter and crucify those guilty of dissent will be an easy decision for him to make. Pilate is the law in Israel. Caiaphas and the priests owe their power to him, and him alone.

Caiaphas heads straight to his priests, then addresses the subject that is on all their minds. "We can't wait any longer. It's almost Passover. We must arrest this troublemaker—this false messiah—tonight."

"And how do we know he is a false messiah?" asks Nicodemus.

The room grows stone silent.

Caiaphas resists the urge to berate Nicodemus in front of the others. "Has he fulfilled any of the signs of a true messiah, as it is written in our laws?" he asks coolly.

Nicodemus remains quiet. There is no sense arguing with Caiaphas.

"Well, Nicodemus," Caiaphas sputters. "Has he?"

Nicodemus holds his tongue. There's so much that he wants to say, and so many points he would like to debate, but not in front of the Temple authorities.

"He must be tried by our laws," Caiaphas demands. "Either we eliminate this one man, or the Romans will step in and destroy everything we have worked our entire lives for."

Nicodemus can't believe his ears. "Eliminate? Are you talking about executing this man?"

"What is the life of one deluded peasant when our people's lives are at stake?" Caiaphas asks, as he walks off leaving a stunned Nicodemus alone in the huge chamber.

On the other side of Jerusalem, the streets are calm and the night air cool, as Peter and Judas approach a small home and knock on the door.

"What does he want us for?" asks Judas.

"He wants us to take supper," Peter tells him.

"To eat together? Before Passover? That's strange."

The door opens. Mary Magdalene answers. She warmly welcomes them inside. "Everyone's upstairs," she tells them, motioning up with one arm. Mary remains downstairs as the disciples climb the stairs and enter a small room. A single long, low dining table fills the space. There is a place for each of the twelve disciples to sit.

"Rabbi," Judas asks Jesus, who seems to have something weighing heavy on his mind. "Why do you want to share a meal today?"

Jesus looks at him, and then looks around the room at the other disciples, but does not reply.

The group prays together, asking that God bless their meal and their fellowship. The unleavened bread in front of them is hot from the oven, and its fresh-baked smell fills the room. After the prayer, the disciples relax, reclining on cushions, tearing off pieces of bread. But before they can eat, Jesus stuns them with devastating news.

"This will be our last meal together," he says calmly.

They all look at Jesus, thick pieces of bread clutched in their fingers.

"What about Passover?" Judas asks a little too quickly.

"I will be dead before Passover," Jesus replies.

Stunned silence.

"What do you mean?" demands Peter.

Jesus doesn't answer, but John leans forward and whispers in Peter's ear. "Do you remember that discussion on the road to Jerusalem, where he prophesied that he would be betrayed, arrested, and condemned to death?"

John doesn't need to continue. Peter remembers. The thought fills him with dread.

Peter has given up everything to follow Jesus, and he has been as loyal as any man can be. The thought that Jesus might die crushes Peter's spirit and pierces his heart.

"Don't worry," Jesus commands them. "Trust in God. Trust in me, also. You already know the way to where I am going."

Thomas is close to tears. "We don't know where you are going. How can we know the way?"

"But Thomas, I am the way. I am the way, the truth, and the life."

The disciples are not all educated men. Like Peter, most of them made their living with their hands, and attended school only long enough to learn the basics. So this concept that Jesus is introducing is hard for them to comprehend.

Then Jesus makes it even more confusing. He tears off a piece of bread and hands it to John. "This is my body," he tells them all. "Take of it and eat."

John has tears streaming own his cheeks, but he understands. He opens his mouth and Jesus places a morsel of the bread on his tongue.

Then Jesus raises a cup of wine. "This is my blood. I will shed my blood so that your sins may be forgiven."

Bread and wine pass from hand to hand around the room. "Remember me by doing this. Soon I will go to be with the Father, but when you eat my bread and drink from my cup, you proclaim my Glory, and I am with you always."

Judas tears off a piece of bread. Thoughts of his thirty pieces of silver dance through his mind. He is torn when he vaguely hears Jesus tell the disciples to "love one another, as I have loved you." Judas snaps back to attention when Jesus shares a new morsel of information.

"But now I must tell you," Jesus says, as the disciples pay close attention, "one of you here in this room will betray me."

The wine is passed to Judas. He struggles to keep his composure, his eyes now riveted on Jesus.

"Who is it?" asks John. "Which one of us would do such a thing?"

Jesus tears off a piece of bread and passes it. "Whoever eats this will betray me."

All the disciples stare, transfixed, as the piece of bread is passed to Judas. "It's not me," Judas protests, holding the bread in his hand, but not eating. "Surely, I would never betray you, Lord."

Jesus' eyes stay fixed on Judas. Looking straight back at him, Judas takes the bread. He eats it and shudders.

The disciples are all staring at him with a look of pure horror.

"Do it quickly," Jesus commands Judas.

Terrified, Judas scrambles to his feet and makes for the door. A disgusted Peter chases after him, not sure whether he will beat Judas to within an inch of his life or merely follow to make sure that Judas does not carry out this betrayal.

But Jesus calls Peter back. "Peter, leave him. You will all fall away. Even you, Peter."

"Never, Lord. I am loyal. I would never betray you."

"Peter," Jesus tells him, "before the cock crows at dawn you will have denied knowing me three times."

Before Peter can protest, Jesus rises to his feet. "Come. Let us all leave."

Caiaphas stands tall in his palace with anxious Nicodemus. The high priest is in a calm and deliberate mood, while Nicodemus is deeply troubled by what is about to happen. The law says that a man must be tried in the light of day, yet Caiaphas clearly wants to condemn Jesus this very night.

"Judas is bringing him to us before dawn," says Caiaphas.

"But the law does not allow it," insists Nicodemus. "A trial must be held in daylight!"

"And does our law allow riots? Does our law invite Romans to spill Jewish blood? You were there. You heard what Pilate said."

Judas bursts into the room.

"Where is he?" Caiaphas asks.

"I don't know." Caiaphas fixes a stare on him, and he admits, "But I do know where he is going."

Caiaphas points to Malchus. "Lead my servant to him."

As Malchus leads Judas from the room, Nicodemus confronts Caiaphas. "Why would he come here?"

"Oh, he will come, Nicodemus. One way or another, he will stand before me tonight and account for his lies and acts of rebellion."

Torchlight flickers on Judas's face as Malchus, Caiaphas's servant, and ten men armed with clubs and swords walk with Judas. Judas is in way over his head, but even if he had doubts, it's far too late for that. The rogue disciple has no choice but to lead them to Jesus. He is on his way to Gethsemane.

"Where are we going?" asks Malchus.

"The garden," Judas says glumly. "We're going to the garden."

The Garden of Gethsemane is deserted, save for Jesus and his disciples, who knows the time to leave his disciples, and this world, is fast approaching. He has spent the last hour in fervent prayer, but if the disciples are anxious about Jesus, they have an odd way of showing it—curled up on the ground, fast asleep.

"The spirit is willing, but the body is weak. Wake up," Jesus demands after observing them for a moment. He needs them to bear witness. "Stay awake. The hour is at hand."

Peter has tucked a long dagger into his belt. He double-checks to make sure it is there, making quiet plans to put it to good use should anyone attack Jesus.

Jesus leaves them, walking slowly back up the hill, once again to be alone with his Father. He knows Judas is almost here, leading a group of men who will arrest him by force. To endure what is about to take place, Jesus needs strength. As he arrives atop the hill, he immediately falls to his knees in prayer, presses his forehead into the dusty ground, clasps his hands together, and prays: "Father, if You are willing, take this cup from me. Yet not my will, but Yours be done." He is beset by confusion because he is both human and divine. Sweat falls from his brow as if it were great drops of blood pooling in the dirt. He is wracked with human fear of the horrific beatings and great pain he will soon experience. He will die a human death and after three days, his body—the Temple—will be raised from the dead, so that all humankind can be saved from the penalty of death. The divine Jesus knows, but the human Jesus questions and fears. Those three days seem so far away. The earthly Jesus pleads for God to spare him the suffering and death, a form of temptation, similar to when Satan tempted him in the desert three years ago. Indeed, Satan now lurks in the garden, watching Jesus cling to the hope that his life might be spared.

Jesus hears the sound of an approaching mob. Their torches light the base of the hill, and their manic voices cut through the night. Jesus' head is still bowed, as he now prays for the strength to carry out God's plan. Sweat continues to fall. Now that God's will is confirmed, resolve washes over him. Not peace, for what he is about to endure cannot bring the gentle calm of peace, just resolve. "Your will, Father, is mine."

Jesus rises from his knees and stands alone in the grove of olive trees. His disciples suddenly burst over the rise and surround him protectively. A line of torches looms in the darkness, marching steadily toward Jesus.

"The time has come," Jesus says to everyone and no one.

Judas steps forth and kneels down behind Jesus, as if in prayer. Then he leans in and kisses Jesus on the cheek.

Jesus does not feel anger or contempt. He tells Judas, "Judas, you betray the son of man with a kiss?" Jesus understands that Judas's role is necessary for God's plan to be fulfilled.

A furious Peter draws his dagger and races toward Judas, who tries in vain to escape. Peter stabs at him, but misses. Malchus arrives with the Temple guard, and Peter swipes the knife, severing Malchus' ear. "Run, Jesus," Peter yells. "Run while you can!"

Malchus spins away in pain, blood flowing down the side of his face. His severed ear falls to the ground, as a circle of torches surrounds Jesus and the disciples. Jesus calmly lifts Malchus' severed ear from the ground and reaches for his bloody head. Malchus flinches, as if Jesus means to hit him. He is caught off guard when Jesus defies his defensive stance and gently touches his wound. When Jesus pulls his hand away, Malchus is stunned and confused that the few moments of indescribable pain are like a momentary dream. His ear is healed.

"Take him away!" a guard shouts, as Malchus stands stunned, fingering his ear.

"Jesus," moans Peter.

"It is my Father's will, Peter. It must happen this way."

A horrified Peter watches as Jesus is shoved forward, grasped on both arms by strong men and surrounded by a half-dozen others, hooded, and dragged off.

The terrified disciples run off into the night, knowing their lives are on the line, fearing they will soon be arrested. Only Peter ignores John's pleas to come with him, and instead of running, he surreptitiously follows the line of torches down the hillside, desperate to see where Jesus is being taken.

Judas trails behind, as if in a trance, on the long walk in from the olive groves.

PART NINE

DELIVERANCE

It is the middle of the night in Jerusalem. Jesus has been beaten. Blood pours from his broken nose. His body is bruised. His hands are bound and held by a guard. The Temple guards lead Jesus by a length of rope to Caiaphas, the high priest.

"Cover him up," cries Malchus. A heavy blanket is thrown over Jesus to conceal his face from the many pilgrims who support him. "Tell Caiaphas we have Jesus," barks Malchus as they lead Jesus into the high priest's home.

Judas follows the procession into Caiaphas's house. Malchus, however, places a hand firmly on Judas's shoulder and pushes him out the door.

"Not you," Malchus says with a sneer. "We're finished with you."

Judas walks off into the night, haunted by emptiness.

The door closes. Caiaphas stands waiting. The Temple guards march Jesus into the center of the room. Malchus removes the blanket covering Jesus and steps back into the shadows. Jesus and Caiaphas square off, though nothing is said by either man. The two are a study in contrasts. Jesus is bruised and bloodied, his hands tied together, and his simple yet elegant clothing dirty and torn. Caiaphas wears fine colorful robes, his body clean. Caiaphas looks into Jesus' eyes and is momentarily frozen. That gaze will haunt Caiaphas for the rest of his days. Caiaphas postures, an attempt to regain his lost authority, as Jesus stands alone, not a friend in the room, surreally in command as he awaits the inevitable.

Nicodemus and the elders enter the room. Because he has been beaten so badly, Jesus' face is horribly disfigured. Nicodemus and some of the elders gasp at the horrific sight. "You can't go through with this," Nicodemus tells Caiaphas. "This is not legal. Our laws say that a capital trial should be held in court, in daylight, and in public."

"This is necessary," Caiaphas fires back.

"Why the rush?"

Caiaphas turns on Nicodemus. His rage is a mixture of envy and anxiety. "You heard what Pilate said," he snarls. "He'll shut down the Temple if there's any more disruption. We must be rid of this Jesus—or God will punish us all."

"But what if he really is who he says he is?" asks Nicodemus. "What if he *is* the Messiah?"

"*We* will decide that!"

"*God* decides that," replies Nicodemus.

"God's guidance will be upon us," Caiaphas replies.

"But how can it?" questions Nicodemus. "For God commands that we obey His laws."

Jesus is led by a rope down a long hallway to the room where his trial will take place. The elders trail behind.

"Let me remind you what the law says," Caiaphas lectures Nicodemus, as the two men walk together. "It says that anyone who shows contempt for the judge or high priest is to be put to death. Anyone..." They stop.

The two men size each other up, then continue on in silence.

The hostile courtroom is packed. In the room where Caiaphas normally spends time alone, unwinding at the end of the day, the elders who comprise the Sanhedrin have gathered for the trial of Jesus. Makers and keepers of Israel's religious laws, whatever these men decide is binding. The sun is about to rise. "Brothers," Caiaphas begins, "thank you for coming at this hour. You know I wouldn't ask if this was not such a serious matter." Then he waves his hand and cries with mock reverence, "The one and only Jesus of Nazareth."

Jesus does not look up or speak.

"Jesus of Nazareth," Caiaphas intones solemnly, "you are suspected of blasphemy. Now let us hear from our witnesses." Caiaphas beckons the first witness.

"In the Temple," says the man who steps forward, clearly intimidated. "He healed a lame woman in the Temple."

Nicodemus can't bear to look at Jesus. It's clear that this whole thing is going to be a charade. A second witness is asked to speak.

"He said he would destroy the Temple!"

"I heard him say that, too," chimes in a Temple elder.

Caiaphas points his finger at Jesus. "You would destroy the Temple! How dare you. That is rebellion against the Lord our God. Tell me, how do you answer these accusations?"

Jesus says nothing. Nicodemus stares hard at him, willing him to speak up. But Jesus remains impassive. The outcome is already decided. Jesus gathers his strength for the ordeal that is soon to come.

"The witnesses' evidence is clear and unequivocal. My brothers, we have faced false prophets in the past and we will face false prophets in the future. But I doubt we will face one as false as this!"

The room fills with murmurs of agreement.

A new voice cries out, that of an elder. "A prophet brings us new words from God. Does he not?"

Nicodemus is stunned. Finally, someone agrees with him.

"If every new voice is crushed, how will we ever know a prophet when we hear one?" the elder continues.

Caiaphas is thrown off. He chooses to deflect the question. "You are right, Joseph of Arimathea. How will we? I will tell you how: we must listen and then judge. So I invite this man—this 'prophet'—to speak." He turns to Jesus. "Are you the Christ, the Son of God?"

Jesus' head is bowed. He remains silent. Blood trickles from his wounds.

"Nothing to say?" Caiaphas asks.

Jesus slowly raises his head. His body stiffens. He stands tall. He looks Caiaphas directly in the eye. "You will see the son of man sitting at the right hand of God and coming on the clouds of heaven."

"Impostor!" Caiaphas cries, ripping his robe open to seek forgiveness from God for hearing such words. "Blasphemer! We must vote and we must vote now!" Caiaphas is so enraged he has lost his senses.

Jesus knows the verdict and the sentence that will be read before the vote is taken.

Joseph of Arimathea and Nicodemus shake their heads at the sham, feeling helpless to stop it.

"The sentence is death," Caiaphas cries out.

"This is wrong," yells Joseph. "This verdict brings shame on this council."

Caiaphas ignores him.

Jesus' followers have gathered at the Temple, the normal place for Jesus to be brought, which is exactly why Caiaphas had Jesus led to his home instead. Disciples Mary and John make their way through the crowd of tents and sleeping, uneducated, largely unsophisticated pilgrims. The Temple guards glare at them, recognizing them from their many appearances with Jesus.

Mary Magdalene notices the distraught face of Mary, the mother of Jesus. She wanders through the crowd. They rush to her side.

"Mary! John! Where is my son?"

"Jesus has been arrested, but we don't know where they've taken him," responds Mary Magdalene.

"Arrested?" replies Mary. "At night?" Ever since that day the angel Gabriel told her she was going to give birth to the Messiah, Mary has known this day would come.

John glances around at the crowds. "He's not here. They must have taken him someplace secret. So they won't have any protests."

The sun rises low and red over the Temple.

The doors of Caiaphas's palace swing open. Peter is standing just outside as Jesus is dragged out. Throughout the night, his own life has been in jeopardy as he has waited to hear what has happened to Jesus, hoping somehow he can help.

Others have come to stand outside Caiaphas's door, as word of Jesus' arrest has quickly traveled. This crowd of supporters is devastated by the sight of Jesus' battered body, with blood caked on his face and bruises around his eyes.

Malchus reads from a proclamation: "Let it be known that Jesus of Nazareth has been tried by the supreme court of Temple elders. He has been found guilty of blasphemy and threatening to destroy the Temple. The sentence is death."

The crowd gasps. Judas, who has remained outside all night long, hurls the bag of silver at Malchus. "Take back your money!" he screams, distraught. This is not at all what he intended. The coins clatter to the cobblestones, at the feet of Malchus.

A large guard approaches Peter. "You . . . I know you."

Peter doesn't scare easily. "I don't know what you're talking about."

"You know him," says the guard, grabbing at Peter. "I saw you call him Rabbi."

"No," says Peter. "He's nothing to do with me."

"He's one of them," a woman screams, pointing at Peter.

He spins around and confronts her. "I tell you, I don't know him."

Peter sees Jesus being hauled away, and he is frustrated by his inability to help Jesus, who means so much to him. The rooster crows, and Peter remembers Jesus' words that he would deny knowing his beloved friend and teacher before dawn. The rough, gruff man sobs in agony. He looks for Jesus, summoning all his courage. Peter means to approach Jesus, even though he is surrounded by guards, and make his apologies—even die trying to free him from the guards. But he searches in vain. The Temple guards have already taken Jesus away.

"Where is my son?" asks Mary. She stands over Peter. The crowd has dispersed, and she has found the sobbing fisherman lying alone the gutter.

"They've condemned him."

Mary gasps in shock.

"They've taken him. I don't know where, but he's gone." Peter slowly rises to his feet, aided by John. A look of humiliation is etched across Peter's face. John notices but says nothing to his friend.

"I told them I didn't know him," Peter says, inconsolable. He breaks away and disappears down the street.

Mother Mary sinks to the ground, as the sun glints off the high walls of the temple complex. Her mother's heart clearly understands that the break of day brings little new hope. The disciples are broken and powerless against the authority of the high priest.

But Caiaphas is having problems. As he changes into his special ornate Passover robes, Caiaphas knows that he cannot execute Jesus, for such a public execution by the Jewish high council will enrage Jesus' followers and create just the kind of disruption he wants to avoid. But the Romans can do anything. "I need to speak to Pontius Pilate," Caiaphas barks to Malchus.

Pilate stands before a washbasin in his residence. As he finishes washing his face, a servant hands him a towel. "Where's my wife?" asks Pilate. "It's past dawn. She should be up by now."

Just then, the maidservant of Pilate's wife appears in the doorway. "Master, come quickly. Please."

Pilate follows her immediately. They run down the empty corridor to his wife's room, where Claudia lies on the bed drenched in sweat and hyperventilating. He goes to comfort her.

"I saw a man," says Claudia. "In a dream."

Dreams are serious business to the Romans, portenders of the future that should never be ignored. "Tell me about this dream," says Pilate.

"I saw a man being beaten and killed. He was an innocent man. A holy man," she says, then adds: "A good man."

Pilate looks to the maidservant. "Help your lady back to bed."

Claudia resists. "My beloved, pay heed to this dream. I believe it is a warning."

"And why is that?"

"Because in my dream, it was you who killed this man."

The branches of a giant ancient olive tree swing in the early morning breeze as Jerusalem greets the day. Its gnarled thick branches rise to a lofty height. Judas Iscariot sits atop the branch that he has chosen, in a hurry to get this done. He has located a horse's halter. The fit won't be as snug around his neck as a hangman's noose, and he may struggle for longer before losing consciousness than with a rope, but every slow, miserable pain he endures will be deserved. Will God have mercy on his soul? he wonders.

Judas slips the halter around his neck. The leather is rough against his skin. He then loops the other end of the halter around a thick branch and tugs on it to make sure the connection is taut. He takes one last look at Jerusalem. Then Judas leaps.

Nicodemus exits the Temple, staggered by the hypocrisy and arrogance he has just witnessed. It is early morning, and the pilgrims camped on the premises are cooking their morning meals, hurrying to prepare for the Passover feast.

"You know where Jesus is!" calls out a voice.

Nicodemus whirls to the sound. This is most unusual. The citizens of Jerusalem don't normally challenge a Temple elder. Nicodemus doesn't recognize the voice of John, the disciple, and keeps walking.

"Wait," John cries. "Please, we know you. You came to see him. I was there. You spoke to him."

Nicodemus stops and turns. "He's gone."

"Where . . . please. Please tell me."

"The Romans will have him soon."

"Romans?" John asks, confused. "He's never said anything against Rome."

"Caiaphas is going to hand him over to the Romans," Nicodemus explains with a heavy heart. "And there's nothing we can do to get him back."

As the stunned John contemplates what this means, Nicodemus walks on. For what he has said is a most simple truth: once a man has been handed over to the Romans, the chance of him avoiding prison or execution is almost none.

Pilate is tending to governmental matters inside the Roman governor's residence when Caiaphas is announced. The high priest is prepared. He knows that his next words must be phrased as precisely as possible.

"Prefect, we need your help," says Caiaphas. "We have convicted a dangerous criminal and sentenced him to death."

"And? When is his execution?"

Caiaphas moves closer, spreading his hands as if in explanation. "We—the Sanhedrin—cannot. It's Passover, you see. Its against our law." Caiaphas punctuates his tale by bowing his head deferentially. Pilate looks at him with distaste.

"So do it after Passover," says Pilate. "Surely the man can live a few more days."

"Normally, I would say yes. But this man is an urgent threat—not only to us, but also to Rome. He claims to be our king, and is using that lie to whip my people into rebellion. This man could very well tear Jerusalem apart."

Pilate looks at Caiaphas. He wonders how such a pompous individual became the leading voice in the Jewish religion. Pilate's patience with the man is at a breaking point. "I am quick to punish criminals," he snarls, "but only if they break the law. I need proof that this man has done so—or Rome will not be pleased."

"He has broken the law, Prefect. I assure you," Caiaphas replies.

"You had better be right," snarls Pilate, fixing Caiaphas with a deadly gaze. "If you're wasting my time, you'll pay for this." He looks at his guards. "I'll see the prisoner."

A ragged, bloodstained hood hangs over Jesus' head as he languishes in the cells located within Pilate's residence. This was once home to Herod the Great, who banished his own sons to these same cells. Their fate, as decided by their father, was death. The same fate befell John the Baptist. Now Pilate will decide whether Jesus should face the same punishment.

The Roman governor enters. A guard pulls off Jesus' hood. The Messiah slowly raises his eyes and looks directly at Pilate, who is unnerved, just as Caiaphas was unnerved by these same eyes.

"So," Pilate begins after a very long pause. "Are you the King of the Jews?"

Jesus says nothing.

"They say you claim to be King of the Jews."

"Is that what you think, or did others tell you this about me?" Jesus replies calmly, for he fears no man. Pilate takes a step back and momentarily averts his eyes.

"Your own people say that," Pilate replies, regaining his composure. "So tell me: are you a king?"

"My kingdom is not of this world," answers Jesus. "If it was, my servants would fight my arrest."

"So you are a king?"

"You say rightly that I am a king. I was born to come into the world and testify to the truth; everyone who is of truth hears my voice."

"Truth? What is truth?" demands Pilate.

Jesus says nothing. He smiles and looks up into the single shaft of light that penetrates the dark cell. It bathes his face. The enraged governor feels like slapping the insolent prisoner—but something stops him in his tracks. He looks at Jesus for what feels like an eternity. Then he turns and leaves. There is something unusual about this prisoner.

Claudia greets him as he returns to his office. "Well?" she asks.

"They want him crucified," answers Pilate.

"You can't. I beseech you."

"Whatever for? This man is only a Jew. They say he wants to start a revolution."

"I tell you, my love, this is the man from my dreams. The man you killed. Please don't do this. His blood will be on your hands."

"And if I don't? How will I explain a rebellion to Rome? Caiaphas will surely testify that it was my fault. If there is an outburst Caesar will blame me. He has already warned me once. He is not going to warn me again. I will be finished... *we'll* be finished."

Pilate walks to the window. His wife's pleas adding to the pressures of his office, pressures he's never felt before. He sees the pilgrims in the streets below, with their newly purchased sacrificial animals. Pilate starts to wish that he had stayed in Caesarea, if only to be away from that wretched Caiaphas and his political maneuverings. But if he had, this Jesus character might very well have caused a riot, and by the time Pilate responded in force, Jerusalem might have burned to the ground. It had happened before, and it could happen again. No... Pilate is glad he is in Jerusalem, determined to survive the next few days and return to his villa by the sea. But Claudia is right: Pilate doesn't want Jesus' blood on his hands.

Claudia places a hand on his shoulder, though she doesn't say a word, knowing that her husband often needs to focus his thoughts before taking action.

"Get me Caiaphas," Pilate says after a moment. "I have a plan."

———

Pilate greets Caiaphas and the elders with thinly veiled contempt. "I have met your Jesus and have come to the conclusion that he is guilty of nothing more than being deranged. That is not a crime in Rome."

"He's broken the law," Caiaphas protests.

"*Your* law," Pilate replies smoothly. "Not Caesar's." The governor stares hard at Caiaphas. "Teach this man some respect. Give him forty lashes and dump him outside the city walls. That is my decree."

"Nothing more? Prefect, I cannot be held responsible for what the people will do if you release a man who has broken our sacred laws. Especially on this day, when our eyes are on God."

"The people?" Pilate responds sarcastically. Pilate knows his next move, even as Caiaphas tries to take control. But Pilate speaks first. "Caesar decrees that I can release a prisoner at Passover. I shall let 'the people' decide which of the prisoners in my jails shall be crucified, and which shall be set free."

Caiaphas knows he's been tricked. He's too stunned to speak.

"Send for the prisoner," Pilate orders.

A crowd is now gathered at the gate outside Pilate's residence, peering through a large steel grate into the empty courtyard. Word has gone out that Jesus will be lashed. Many like to witness public brutality and revel in the carnival-like proceedings that accompany a good beating.

Jesus is dragged into the courtyard by two Roman soldiers. His face is crusted in blood, and his eyes are now swollen shut by a fresh round of beatings.

Mary, his mother, gasps. She stands outside in the crowd, peering into the courtyard through the grate.

Jesus is tied to the whipping post. His robes are ripped from his back, exposing the flesh. The soldiers now retrieve their whips. A single lash is an exercise in agony, sure to scar a man for life.

Jesus is about to endure thirty-nine.

"They're going to kill him," whispers Mary to Mary Magdalene, her heart breaking. John looks down at the two women protectively. The two soldiers stand ready to whip, one on each side of Jesus. They will take turns. A third soldier enters the courtyard, carrying an abacus. It will be his job to make a careful tally of the blows and report back to Rome that precisely thirty-nine were inflicted.

Jesus looks across to his mother. Her pain is enormous, but his eyes lock with hers and she feels a strong connection with him. It is as if he is reassuring her and reminding her that this is how it must be.

The lashings begin. Jesus does not cry out, even as the crowd gasps at the severity of what they are witnessing. The harrowing punishment and ordeal Jesus is to endure has been preordained. Isaiah, the prophet, once wrote that there would come a savior who "was pierced through for our transgressions. He was crushed for our iniquities. And by his scourging, we are healed."

From a window overlooking the courtyard, Pilate and Claudia watch the ghastly proceedings. She winces with each flay of the lash, but Pilate has seen many such beatings. "Its as if he knows this must happen," marvels Pilate.

One last abacus bead slides from left to right. Thirty-nine lashes are now in the books.

Jesus hangs on the pole, barely alive but definitely breathing. When his hands are untied, he does not slump to the ground but stands upright, beaten but unbroken.

Now he is taken back to the dungeon. The guards, never known to show kindness toward their prisoners—especially Jews—have been busy while he was away. To have this delusional Jesus in their midst claiming to be a king is the stuff of folly, and they can't wait to take advantage. One guard has woven a crown out of thorny branches. It is gruesome to behold, with long spikes sticking out at all angles. He now presses it down hard on Jesus' skull, drawing blood as those sharp tips bite into bone. "King of the Jews!" the soldier exults, bowing deep in front of Jesus, then dancing a little jig.

One of the soldiers who beat Jesus has just wiped the blood from his hands. He drapes the crimson towel over Jesus' shoulders as if it were an ermine robe. All the jailers find this quite hilarious.

Pilate orders that the palace gates be opened. The crowds pour in, not sure what is about to happen. They know Pilate is allowed to release one man of their choice before Passover, in one of the many events held during Passover. They wonder who will be set free. Surely, Jesus is no longer a consideration. He has paid his penalty and has probably already been released. That's how the law works. So they wait patiently for their options.

Pilate has skillfully deflected Caiaphas's demand that he crucify Jesus, and given the final verdict to this mass of pilgrims.

Caiaphas remains undeterred, however, and is ensuring that the pilgrims allowed into the courtyard will vote against Jesus. The mainstream Jewish people are not given a choice in the matter. Malchus, his servant, and the Temple guards now stand at the gates, denying entry to anyone who supports the man from Nazareth. Scuffles break out as many in the crowd vent their frustration for being denied entry. They howl in protest—howls that are completely ignored by the Roman soldiers guarding the palace.

Mary, John, and Mary Magdalene are among those kept away. They watch in disbelief as a mob of pro-Caiaphas sympathizers stand ready to determine Jesus' fate.

Pontius Pilate appears in an upstairs window and the crowd silences to hear what he has to say. "Today," Pilate begins, "Passover begins. Caesar makes you a gesture of goodwill through the release of a prisoner chosen by you."

A bald-headed murderer is marched into the courtyard, followed by Jesus, still wearing his crown of thorns.

"I give you a choice," Pilate tells them. "You may choose between Barabbas, a murderer. Or you may choose this other man—a teacher who claims to be your king."

Laughter and jeers spew forth from the crowd. Caiaphas, who now stands at Pilate's side, yells, "We have no king but Caesar."

Temple guards now move through the crowd, whispering instructions and receiving nods of agreement. "Crucify him!" is spontaneously shouted by members of the crowd who have remained silent until now.

Mary, mother of Jesus, is horrified. Her hands go to her face, and she covers her mouth in dismay.

Pilate sees the look on Caiaphas's face and knows that he has an answer.

"Decide!" Pilate shouts to the crowd.

"Barabbas," they roar back. "Free Barabbas."

Outside the gates, Mary, John, and Mary Magdalene all shout in Jesus' defense, as do many around them. But their voices cannot be heard over the roar "Barabbas! Barabbas! Barabbas!" from the courtyard.

Pilate is mystified. He looks at Caiaphas and then back at the crowd. "You choose a murderer," he tells them with a shake of his head, then holds up a hand to silence the mob.

"Do it," he says to his guards. The bewildered soldiers reluctantly unlock Barabbas's shackles. The crowd cheers; the insurrectionist's eyes are wild with delight.

"And this wretch," Pilate yells to the crowd. "What shall I do with him?"

"Crucify him! Crucify him!"

"Save him," comes the chant from outside the gate. "Save him."

"Crucify! Crucify! Crucify!" yells the courtyard.

Pilate silences the crowd. "How can you condemn this man and spare a murderer?"

"Crucify! Crucify! Crucify!"

"Very well," he tells them. "Crucify him."

Pilate reaches for a nearby bowl of water and washes his hands. This is a deliberate gesture, mirroring a custom of the Hebrews and Greeks to show that he is not responsible. "I am innocent of this man's blood," he says, hoping to shift blame.

Pilate knows Jesus is innocent and that he can prevent his death. He has the power, and should simply disperse the mob. But instead of standing up for truth, he is taking the easier route of political expediency. It is a dangerous time in Jerusalem, the home to more than a million Jews and less than a thousand Roman soldiers. Pilate cannot risk the sort of tumult, as it would make its way back to Rome and Caesar.

Pilate dries his hands. This crucifixion is no longer his affair.

It has been just six days since Jesus was welcomed into Jerusalem. Now he is to be crucified on a hill outside the city walls, for Jewish law does not allow executions inside the city. Two criminals will also be crucified at the same time.

Crucifixion—the act of nailing a man to a wooden cross—is the standard Roman form of capital punishment. It is brutal. A man can take days to die, hanging alone on the cross until he wastes away. To this heinous death for Jesus is added the torment of dragging the cross through the streets of Jerusalem. He staggers, trailed by a guard on horseback prepared to whip him if he falls or drops the cross. Many who were denied the chance to spare Jesus' life line the streets, forced back by a phalanx of Roman soldiers who ensure that no one helps Jesus escape.

Jesus is in agony as he struggles toward his death. His body is bent by the weight of the cross, and the crown of thorns inflicts a new burst of pain whenever the cross bumps against it. The many beatings he has endured in the hours since his capture make it hard to breathe, for his jailers have kicked and punched him in the ribs again and again.

Yet he sees everything. Both the sympathetic and not-so-sympathetic faces in the crowd. He also sees Mary, his mother. Jesus stumbles and feels the lash of a Roman whip as he falls. He reaches out to steady himself, pressing his hand flat against a stone wall. It leaves a bloody print. As Jesus moves forward to continue his grueling march, a woman in the crowd places her own hand against Jesus' handprint. She weeps; she knows who Jesus truly is.

The ground is cobbled, so the cross bumps along rather than drags smoothly. The distance from Pilate's palace to Golgotha, the place where Jesus will die, is five hundred yards.

Jesus knows he cannot make it. He spits out a gob of blood and falls to his knees. He drops the cross and crumples to the ground. Roman soldiers are upon him in an instant, raining kicks and punches on his helpless body. Mary races forward to save her son, but a Roman guard grabs her roughly and throws her back.

"Please," John says, risking his life by stepping from the crowd. "She's his mother!"

Tears stream down Mary's cheeks. The Roman guard steps toward John with a menacing glare on his face, but the disciple is undeterred. "Have mercy. Please!"

Mary can't help herself. She flings herself forward and falls onto her knees, next to her son. She wraps her arms lovingly around him in what will surely be their last embrace. Jesus' eyes are swollen shut, and he can hardly react.

"My son," Mary sobs.

Jesus forces his eyes open. "Don't be afraid," he tells his mother. "The Lord is with you." Repeating exactly what Gabriel had told her when he visited her as a young virgin. His words give her strength, and his look of love fills her with courage. She tries to help him up with the cross. If she could she would carry it for him, but she knows this is what he came to do.

Then suddenly Mary is pulled away from her boy. The soldiers whip the fallen Jesus, but it is clear that he cannot carry the cross any farther. A man, Simon of Cyrene, is chosen for his broad back and obvious strength, and he is forced to shoulder the cross for Jesus. Their eyes lock, and then their hands link to lift the heavy wood. Together, they share the burden. Step by painful step, the two complete the long walk up to the crucifixion site.

Back in his palace, Pontius Pilate continues his running battle with Caiaphas. Roman law dictates that every condemned man should have a sign placed on their cross to indicate their crime. Pilate dictates the wording for Jesus' sign. "Post these words in Aramaic, Latin, and Greek," he tells a scribe. "JESUS OF NAZARETH: KING OF THE JEWS."

"He was never our king!" says Caiaphas, who stands by the window watching Jesus' progress toward Golgotha. "Surely, it should read that he *claims* to be the King of the Jews."

"*The* king," Pilate corrects him. "It stays as I have commanded." He stares across the room, daring Caiaphas to respond. But the high priest says nothing.

The crowd thins as Jesus leaves the city walls behind. Mary, John, and Mary Magdalene walk to the side of the road as it curls steeply upward, just out of Jesus' sight but always there. This hill is known as Golgotha, or "Place of the Skulls," because it is believed that the skull of Adam is buried here.

Choking dust fills the air, and Jesus can barely breathe. He trips and is immediately whipped. He rises and then trips again. And once more, he immediately feels the sting of the lash.

"My Lord," cries a woman as she steps into the street. Despite the threat of punishment by the guards, she lovingly washes his face with a cloth. But when she urges him to drink from a small cup of water, the guards snatch it away and hurl it to the ground.

Jesus and Simon of Cyrene finally arrive at the place of crucifixion. Simon drops the heavy cross and quickly leaves. Jesus, no longer able to stand, collapses into the dust. The Roman guards spring into action. Coils of rope are unwound and laid flat. Spades dig out the excess earth from the holes in the ground so often used for crucifixions.

"I want to see him," Mother Mary murmurs as she strains against the arms of a Roman guard who prevents her from getting close to Jesus.

Mary Magdalene sinks to her knees and starts to pray. Mother Mary stands resolutely upright, keeping a distant vigil over her son. John stands next to her, ready to catch her if she collapses from the stress.

Jesus is laid on the cross. The guards stretch out his arms and hammer nails into his hands. His feet are nailed to the cross, one over the other. The sound of his bones breaking fills the air, and Jesus gasps at each new burst of pain. After everything he's endured today, nothing hurts like the moments the nails pierce his feet.

Pilate's sign is nailed into the cross above Jesus' head: JESUS OF NAZA-RETH: KING OF THE JEWS.

To raise the cross, ropes are attached, one end to the cross and the other to the horse that will pull it to an upright position. The crack of a whip, and the horse walks forward. Jesus no longer sees just the sky above. Now he sees all of Jerusalem in the distance, and his loving mother standing vigil at the base of the cross.

He can barely breathe. His outstretched arms make it almost impossible to draw a breath. Jesus knows he will suffocate. It is not the nails that kill you, but the steady weakening of the body until it becomes impossible for the lungs to expand.

The cross is upright. Jesus hangs from it. The executioner's job is done. Those soldiers who crucified Jesus divide his clothes among them and cast lots for his garments.

Meanwhile, those who have watched the crucifixion step forward.

Mother Mary weeps with unbearable grief.

"Come to save others, can't even save yourself," mocks a Pharisee.

Jesus hears it all. He moans, and then speaks to God: "Father, forgive them, for they know not what they do."

The two criminals have been crucified on either side of him. The first taunts Jesus: "Aren't you the Messiah? Why don't you save yourself and us?"

The second criminal responds, "Our punishment is just. But this man has done nothing wrong." He turns to Jesus and speaks softly. "Remember me, Messiah, when you come into your kingdom."

Jesus turns to him. "Truly, I say to you, today you will be with me in Paradise." He grimaces in pain. The Romans may have finished their work, but they won't go home until all three of the crucified men are dead. Now it's just a matter of time.

Mary, John, and Mary Magdalene stand at the base of Jesus' cross. He is immobile and seems dead. It is now midafternoon, almost time for the start of Passover, just before sunset. The Roman soldiers know that his body must be taken off the cross by then, and are contemplating break-ing his legs to kill him quicker, but they will not need to do that.

"My God," Jesus cries suddenly. "My God, why have You forsaken me?" This is the opening line of Psalm 22, King David's lament for the Jews and a cry for help. Jesus looks down at Mary. "Mother, this is your son," he tells her, referring to John as he stands at her side. "John," he adds. "This is your mother."

Mother Mary stands, silent tears running down her face. John places a protective arm around her.

Jesus looks away, consumed by the pain in his mortal body. He looks to heaven as a hard wind kicks up. A rumble of thunder sweeps across the land. "I thirst," Jesus says. In response, a soldier soaks a sponge and raises it up to his lips on a spear.

Peter hears the thunder, as he sits alone in the room where his last sup-per with Jesus took place less than twenty-four hours ago. His eyes are rimmed in red from exhaustion and tears, for he cannot forgive him-self for denying Jesus. The coming thunder terrifies him, and he doesn't know where to run.

Pilate hears it, as he awaits sunset inside his palace. Claudia does, too. She's certain it's an omen that her husband did the wrong thing by kill-ing Jesus, and is furious at him. "I told you not to kill him," she hisses as the thunder breaks.

"Hardly the first Jew we've killed," Pilate responds. He lies facedown on a bench, his torso bare and a towel around his waist as a servant rubs oil into his back.

"He was different," Claudia rails. "I told you that."

"Trust me," Pilate tells his wife, ending the conversation, "he'll be forgotten in a week."

Jesus, in a barely conscious fog of pain, hears the thunder. Black storm clouds now fill the sky as he knows that the time has come to leave this world. "It is finished," Jesus says aloud. "Father, into your hands, I commend my spirit."

The thunder strikes. This bundle of energy, vibration, and sheer power explodes upon Jerusalem. In the Temple, the great curtain is ripped in two, and panicked crowds race to flee the building, leaving their hard-earned sacrificial animals behind.

Mother Mary knows it is the signal that her son has died. She stares up at Jesus with a look of utter calm. All the pain she has been suffering is gone, replaced by the peace of realizing that her son will suffer no more.

The terrified Roman guards believe the thunder to be an omen, and they hurry to break the legs of the crucified so they can remove their bodies before Passover. They hastily grab metal rods and swing them hard against the two criminals on either side of Jesus. But they see that Jesus is already dead. To make sure, the Roman commander runs a spear through his side.

"He's dead," the commander confirms, pulling his spear out of Jesus. He looks across at Jesus' mother, then back up at Jesus, and slowly says, "Surely this man was the Son of God."

Normally, the bodies of the crucified are left to rot or are thrown into shallow pits. But Nicodemus and Joseph of Arimathea have secured special permission from Pilate to take the body down and bury it decently. Tombs overlooking Jerusalem are normally reserved for the wealthiest citizens, but Joseph has arranged for an expensive, newly hewn tomb to be the final resting place of the Messiah. Normally, a tomb contained the bodies of several family members, but Jesus' body would be the first and only body to be laid there.

The two stately elders, the older Mary and the younger Mary, and

John gingerly retrieve the mangled Messianic body and prepare it for burial and, unwittingly, for its forthcoming bodily resurrection. His mother lovingly washes him with a sponge, cleaning away all the dirt and dried blood while the other Mary tears strips of linen. Mother Mary places one over Jesus' face. Nicodemus anoints each cleansed portion of the body with fragrant oils. Nicodemus prays over Jesus the entire time. Then the process of wrapping his body in linen begins. It is a long, emotional process, the official beginning of Jewish mourning.

A vast slab of stone is the opening of a cave, and Jesus' body is placed inside. The body of Jesus, immaculately wrapped in linen, lies alone on a hewn rock. Strong servants of Nicodemus and Joseph of Arimathea roll the rock over the opening of the tomb to make sure that the body won't be disturbed. Night has fallen, so the burial party lights torches to guide their way back down the path. As the group begins to leave, they are surprised to see a pair of Roman guards stepping forth to stand sentry. Pilate is fearful that if the body of Jesus disappears, all of Jerusalem will riot. Better to make sure it doesn't leave the tomb.

All over Jerusalem, the people are celebrating the Passover. But in the small upper room where Jesus and his disciples took their last meal, the mood is somber. The disciples expected the Kingdom of God to come when they entered Jerusalem six days ago. Now everything they believe in has been destroyed. Their hope is gone. They have lost everything. They eat a small quiet meal together, certain that within moments Caiaphas or Pilate will send soldiers to arrest them.

The morning of the third day after Jesus' death, Mary Magdalene takes it upon herself to go visit the tomb. She misses Jesus enormously, and even the prospect of sitting outside his burial site is a source of comfort. Her eyes are tired as she ascends a small hill. She knows that even in the early morning fog, she will be able to see the tomb from the top, and she begins looking once she gets there. The entrance to the tomb stands open. The rock has been moved aside. She gasps. Someone has stolen Jesus' body. Mary fearfully takes a step toward the open tomb, but she doesn't dare enter.

Perhaps grave robbers are still inside, prepared to beat her for interrupting their labors. Then, an unrecognizable, distant figure standing on the ridgeline catches her eye. "Teacher?" Mary asks in a small and terrified voice. For a moment, Mary thinks she sees Jesus alive. But she can't be sure. Soon the figure disappears from sight. The fact remains that the tomb is open and the body isn't there.

Where is Jesus?

PART TEN

NEW WORLD

Mary weeps at the empty tomb and then, still sobbing, takes a deep breath and conquers her fears. It's pitch-black, but her eyes soon adjust. She sees the slab where Jesus' body was laid. The linens that were bound tightly around his body now lie in a pile. Mary smells the sweet perfume that was poured onto Jesus' corpse to minimize the smell of decay.

"Why are you crying?" says a man's voice at the tomb's opening. "Who are you looking for?"

Mary can't see who's talking. Terrified, she finds the courage to call out from the darkness: "If you've taken him, tell me where he is."

"Mary."

It is the calm and knowing voice she knows all too well. Mary's heart soars as she realizes who is talking to her. "Jesus!" Her eyes swim with tears of joy and amazement as she steps out into the sunlight.

"Go and tell our brothers I am here."

Mary stares at Jesus in awe. She can see the marks on his hands where the spikes pierced his flesh. A quick glance at his feet reveals the same. There is an aura about Jesus, something far more heavenly than anything she has experienced in all their many days together. It is as if she is looking at two sides of the same being: God and man. Then he is gone. Mary, overcome with joy, sprints back into Jerusalem to tell the disciples the good news.

———

The disciples have been terrified since Jesus' execution that the religious authorities and Romans are working in unison to end all traces of Jesus' ministry—and that means snuffing out his disciples as well. They are hiding, fearful of that knock on the door in the dead of night telling them that they've been discovered.

Peter glances out a window. He is a shell of the man he once was, and no one would confuse him for the gruff fisherman Jesus recruited three years ago. Roman soldiers march up a nearby alley, breastplates and swords glistening in the early morning sun.

There is no knock at the door. Instead, a clearly delusional Mary Magdalene bursts inside, screaming at the top of her lungs, "I've seen him! I've seen him!"

"Close the door," barks John.

Mary slams it shut. "The tomb is open," she gasps. "He's gone."

"He's dead and buried," says a morose Peter. "That's impossible."

"You have to believe me. I saw him!"

"I think you were at the wrong tomb," mutters Thomas. "It must have been someone else."

"You don't think I know what Jesus looks like? Do you think I'm mad?"

"It's been a stressful time, Mary. For all of us."

This infuriates her. She grips Peter's wrist hard and pulls him to the door. "Come with me. Now."

Peter looks to John. Then at the other disciples. It wouldn't be safe for all of them to venture out, but perhaps maybe just two of them.

Peter nods. Mary leads John and Peter out into the sunshine.

⸻

They stare in shock and disbelief at them empty tomb. Peering sheepishly inside from a few feet back, they can't see footprints or any other sign that tomb robbers have been here, but they know that's the obvious answer.

"Thieves," says Peter.

"That's right: tomb robbers," adds John.

Peter steps closer to the opening. A white circle of light suddenly shines inside. Peter moves toward the light and sees the unmistakable

Jesus. "My Lord," he says in a hushed voice. Peter reaches forth to touch Jesus. And then Jesus disappears.

A stunned Peter steps back out of the tomb. Mary sees the look on his face. "Now do you believe me?" she asks.

Peter hands John a strip of linen from the tomb. "But he's gone," John says, mystified.

"No, my brother," Peter assures him, that old confidence suddenly returned. "He is not gone. He's back!" An exuberant Peter takes off and races down the hill. On the way, he purchases a loaf of bread from a vendor.

"What happened?" asks Matthew as the three of them step back inside the hiding place.

"A cup," Peter answers. "I need a cup."

Peter gives a piece of unleavened bread to John, who puts it slowly into his mouth. "His body," Peter reminds him. A cup is found and thrust into John's hand. Peter fills it with wine. "And his blood," Peter says.

Peter, suddenly transformed into the rock of faith Jesus always knew he could be, looks from disciple to disciple. "Believe in him. He's here. In this room. Right now."

John drinks deeply from the cup as Peter continues talking. "Remember what he told us: 'I am the way, the truth—'"

Jesus finishes the sentence: "'—and the life.'"

Peter spins around. Jesus stands in the doorway. The disciples are awestruck as he walks into the room.

"Peace be with you," Jesus, the risen Messiah, tells them.

"No," says Thomas. "This is not possible. There is no way you are Jesus standing here with us. This is all a fantasy, an apparition brought on by our insane mourning for a man we loved so very much."

Jesus walks toward Thomas and takes his hand. "Thomas," Jesus tells him. "Stop doubting and believe." He places Thomas's fingers into the gaping holes in his hands, and then to the hole in his side. Looking down, Thomas can clearly see the awful marks atop Jesus' feet where the spikes passed through flesh and bone, then into the wood of the cross.

Thomas doesn't know how to respond. He has traveled far and wide with Jesus, and he knows Jesus' voice and appearance as well as he knows his own. But what Jesus is asking of him is impossible. Thomas is a man of facts—a man committed to truth that cannot be disputed by emotion or trickery. He is being asked to believe that he is touching Jesus, as alive as the last time they all broke bread together in the upper room. It seems impossible. But it is real. This is Jesus, not some dream or vision. Thomas touches the wounds and hears his teacher's voice. Overwhelmed, Thomas looks into Jesus' eyes. "My Lord and my God," he stammers, tears filling his eyes. "It *is* you."

Jesus looks at his disciple with compassion. "You believed because you see me. But blessed are those who have not seen me, and yet have believed."

Faith floods Thomas's entire being as he slowly accepts what it means to believe that anything is possible through God. This is the faith in Jesus that will transform lives. Not seeing and yet still believing.

Jesus soon passes on some sad news to his disciples: He is not here to stay. His work on earth is complete. He has died on the cross as a sacrifice for the sins of all men. Throughout history, a lamb has been slaughtered for the same purpose. Jesus has been the Lamb of God, who takes away the sins of the world. He has conquered death.

He appears to his disciples one last time before ascending into heaven. Peter has been fishing all night and pulled in more than 150 fish. The other disciples had spent the night on shore. As Peter pulled in his nets, Jesus invited them to share breakfast. When they were finished eating the small meal of bread and fish, he spoke to them of the future. He twice asked Peter, "Do you love me?"

The response came back as a surprised yes every time. And on both occasions, Jesus instructed him to feed his lambs and take care of his sheep. But when Jesus asked a third time, Peter was hurt. Peter also knew he had denied Jesus three times, so these responses were his moment of redemption. "Lord," Peter sighs, "you know all things. You know that I love you."

"Feed my sheep," Jesus tells him a third time. "Follow me!"

Jesus says good-bye to his disciples after forty days back on earth. For three full years he has trained them, equipping them with the skills to lead others to follow in his footsteps and worship God. "You will receive power when the Holy Spirit comes to you," he tells them. "My body can be in only one place, but my spirit can be with you all wherever you are. Go into the world and preach the gospel unto all creation."

The disciples listen intently, knowing that this is the last time they will see Jesus. He is not saying that the Holy Spirit will come into them right now, so they know they must wait for this great moment. Jesus stands before them and gives them peace. Everything he said would happen has come to pass, and it is clear that the power of God extends much farther than they even dared to believe. They have nothing to fear—even death. It is a proper and fitting way to say good-bye. Peter is anointed as the new leader of the disciples in Jesus' absence.

"Peace be with you," says Jesus.

The words echo in the disciples' ears. This peace pulses through them, infusing them with energy and calm resolve—this is the peace that will fortify them as they do God's work.

He then ascends into heaven.

The disciples feel the loss, as Jesus' physical presence among them is no more. Peter's eyes fill with tears. He tilts his head upward, as if squinting into the sun. Peter blinks away his tears and feels his breath return. He stands and addresses the disciples. He knows that Jesus will always be with them, and with all people. He has accepted Jesus' command that he follow him, no matter what the physical cost. Now it is time to go out into the world and let the people know about the greatness of God.

"Be strong, my brothers," says Peter, his voice sure and brave. "We have work to do."

This moment Jesus departs the disciples—now also known as "the apostles"—becomes forever known as the Ascension. Ten days after this happening, thousands of pilgrims once again flood into Jerusalem for the feast known as Pentecost. This is a time of thanksgiving, when the Jewish people remember the bounty of the harvest and the provenance of the laws given to Moses.

For Caiaphas, this means a return to normal after the upheaval of Passover. From the temple steps, he watches with pleasure as daily life revolves around him: pilgrims chatting in the streets, walking with sheaves of wheat, baskets of bread, and bundles of fruit and olives. These are the fruits of the harvest—fruits that will soon be lavished upon his temple. And, by proxy, upon Caiaphas.

"Anything I should know about?" Caiaphas asks his servant Malchus.

Roman soldiers can be seen on the fringes of the crowd, but there is no sign of the rebellion or rioting that marked Passover.

"The crowds are quiet," Malchus tells him. "The Romans are merely keeping watch."

"As it should be," he says, then pauses. "Any sign of Jesus' followers?"

"None. One can only assume they've fled back to Galilee."

"You assume? Really? Make sure the Temple guards stand ready. If they return, you will have to deal with them. I cannot go to the Romans for help a second time."

But Jesus' disciples are not in Galilee. They are gathering in Jerusalem, easily concealed among the hordes of pilgrims. Jesus has promised them that the Holy Spirit will come to them, but they're not quite sure what that means. So they remain in their hiding place, waiting. Peter now kneels in the middle of the room, eyes closed in prayer. Thomas paces nearby, muttering aloud, oblivious to Peter's quiet moment with God. "What form will this spirit take?" he asks again and again. "What is a Holy Spirit and when will it come?"

An irritated Peter opens his eyes. "Jesus said that all we have to do is ask. I've been asking every day. In fact, I'm asking right now. The Holy Spirit will come when the time is right."

Mary Magdalene joins the argument. "Thomas," she says patiently, "Moses waited forty days to receive the commandments. Our people wandered forty years in the wilderness, waiting. So be patient. Jesus promised it will come—and the Holy Spirit will come."

John, James, Matthew, and Stephen step into the room. "There are Romans everywhere," says John.

They sit and look to Peter, who clearly sees the anxiety on their faces. "I know it's dangerous for us all to be here at once, but Jesus said that when two or three gather in his name, he would be with us." He sees that his words are having little effect. "Come, let us pray." Peter shuts his eyes. He reaches out and takes hold of the hands of the two disciples sitting on either side of him. "Our Father, who art in heaven, hallowed be thy name..."

John and the others pick up the words, and all join hands. "Your kingdom come, Your will be done, on earth as it is in heaven."

Thomas can't help himself. In the midst of the prayer he doubts their safety, and opens his eyes to peer out into the streets for signs of approaching Romans. Seeing none, he returns to his prayer. "Give us today our daily bread..."

The lamps in the room flicker and smoke as the prayer continues. The room grows suddenly dark. The wind outside rises and the sound fills the room. Shutters bang open. Scared but unbowed, the disciples continue praying. Tongues of fire enter the room and settle upon each apostle. The Holy Spirit fills them. Soon each of them is praying in different languages, even though none of them have ever understood those tongues before. In this way, they are being prepared to go out unto all nations and preach the Word of God.

Their prayers and their foreign words now miraculously reach out across the city. People can hear the apostles, even though they cannot see them. In Jesus' final days he had promised to pour out his spirit on all the people of the world, and now it is taking place. The prayers of the disciples are heard and understood by all the people gathering for the festival—Israelite and foreign ears alike, drawing these people to the Word of God.

The wind howls across Jerusalem. Even a Roman soldier understands the simple phrase now ringing in the ears of every man, woman, and child in Jerusalem: "Everyone who calls on the Lord will be saved."

Caiaphas stops and looks up, then pulls his shawl around him and enters the Temple.

Even as the disciples continue their unlikely prayer, a commotion can be heard in the streets outside their upper room. Crowds are gathering, though they are not sure what is drawing them to this place.

"We'll be discovered," laments a panicked Thomas.

"No. This is good," says Mary Magdalene. "The people must feel the same spirit that we do. The Holy Spirit is drawing them near."

Peter stands. "We must speak with them, and let them know that this is a sign from God."

Empowered and renewed, the disciples march down the stairs and open the door. They scan the crowd for signs of Romans or Pharisees or Temple guards. "People of Israel," says Peter, with a sense of poise and command that surprises all of the disciples. Peter has been radically changed by God's saving grace.

"God promised King David that one of his descendants would be placed upon his throne. A man whose flesh could not be corrupted. Now God has raised Jesus to life. Jesus of Nazareth is the Messiah. He is the Christ. Come join us!"

John chimes in. "Join us!"

The crowd roars their approval, chanting, "Jesus is the Lord." They clamor for Peter's blessing, reaching out to touch him. But the upheaval does not go unnoticed. Within moments, a Roman centurion hovers on the edge of the people.

"We're taking our chances here," John whispers to Peter.

"Jesus risked his life every day," responds Peter.

More Romans arrive. Their hands hover over their swords. The crowd presses in more tightly around the apostles, on the verge of turning rabid.

"We cannot spread the Word if we are dead," John reminds Peter.

He's right, and Peter knows it. With a nod, he guides the disciples away down a narrow side street.

It is morning in Jerusalem, and yet another of the city's many beggars begins his day. The man's legs will not support him, so he uses his arms to drag himself to his usual sport. His knuckles are calloused and his skin filthy from years of the same ritual—dragging and then squatting, his body all too often coated in the grit and dust of a busy city going about its day.

A stranger drops a coin into his hand. The beggar nods in thanks, but does not make eye contact.

Peter approaches. The beggar does not know him and holds out his hand, palm up. Peter stops and crouches down. The beggar looks at him with curious eyes, as if some great evil will befall him next. Peter has been trailed at a distance by a small crowd of new believers, and they edge closer, eager to see if Peter will do what they hope he will do. Peter and the beggar lock eyes. "I don't have silver or gold," Peter tells him. "But what I have, I will give to you." Peter raises his own palm to the sky. "In the name of Jesus Christ, our Lord and savior, I want you to stand." Peter places his right hand in that of the beggar. He lifts gently, but then lets go. The beggar rises to his feet on his own power.

"It's a miracle," cries a voice in the crowd.

Peter responds by turning to face these new believers. "Why are you surprised? Do you think that he is healed by *my* power? Or by that of my fellow apostles? No. It is by Jesus' power that this man walks. Jesus is the Messiah!"

The beggar has a dizzy smile on his face, and walks around for the first time in his life.

"Jesus did this!" chants the crowd. "Jesus did this!"

Not far away, inside the great Temple, the high priest Caiaphas hears the roar.

"What are they saying?" he asks Malchus. As always, his servant hovers just a few feet away. But Malchus doesn't get the chance to answer, for a furious Caiaphas has deciphered the sounds for himself. "Why are they chanting that wretched man's name?" Caiaphas demands. "Why!"

Malchus remains silent as Caiaphas launches into a furious rant. "We'll have the Romans down on us any minute. I told you to deal with these people before this could happen. And now it is done, and I am once again forced to deal with it. Bring the ringleaders to me!"

Within the hour, the Temple guards have bound and beaten Peter and John. They drag them into Caiaphas's chamber and hurl them to the floor. The healed beggar, now clearly terrified, is led in by the arm.

"Stand up," Caiaphas says crisply, entering the room. He's just received word that more than five thousand people have become followers of Jesus since hearing the beggar was healed. This is an enormous figure. This must be stopped.

John and Peter struggle to their feet. They face Caiaphas, faces defiant.

"Tell me," demands the high priest, "what makes you think it acceptable to preach in the name of that dead criminal?"

"Jesus lives," Peter informs him.

"Impossible."

"This man walked because of the power of Jesus Christ," Peter reminds him.

"Really?" responds Caiaphas, trying to sound bemused. "Is this true?" he asks the beggar.

Malchus whispers to Caiaphas, "I have seen this man on the street for years. He has been lame his whole life, and High Priest . . . It is true."

Caiaphas pauses for an eternity, never moving his focus from Peter and John. Then he finally speaks: "I forbid you to speak of your so-called Messiah from this day forward."

"Judge for yourself whether it is better in God's sight to obey you rather than God," Peter responds.

"I have a duty to our temple, our nation, and our God!" Caiaphas responds angrily. "I repeat: you are forbidden from speaking about your Messiah!"

"We cannot help speaking about what we have seen and heard," says John.

"Then you will be beaten," Caiaphas threatens. "Either remain silent or suffer the same fate as your Jesus."

"We must obey God, rather than men," say the disciples, almost in unison.

No matter what code of silence he might try to enforce, Caiaphas senses he is powerless to stop this movement. People are turning their hearts to Jesus in record numbers. Caiaphas can't stop the five thousand, but he will silence the apostles, one by one—though not now. Reluctantly, Caiaphas lets Peter and John go. He will see them again soon.

Pilgrims line up on a street to hear a young disciple named Stephen preach about Jesus. Despite threats by Caiaphas, the followers of Jesus refuse to be silent. "Be baptized in the name of Jesus Christ for the forgiveness of your sins," urges Stephen. "He was crucified, but he rose from the dead."

The crowd hangs on his every word, enamored with all that he has to say.

"Impossible," cries Saul. He is a tough man, an intellectual, and a Pharisee who speaks several languages. His father was also a Pharisee and his mother was a Roman. Stephen would be a fool to debate him publicly. Saul is concerned about this "new" way of looking at the God of Abraham. Unlike Caiaphas, whose primary concern is the power he derives from religious leadership, Saul's faith in Jewish law and tradition is so passionate that he considers anyone who deviates from it a traitor.

And even though Saul is Jewish, he is a Roman citizen, which grants him special privileges throughout the empire. Saul is zealous in his belief.

Stephen has Jesus on his side, so he pushes aside his own fears and launches an attack. "Why do you resist Jesus? He is your savior, the way to everlasting life."

"Jesus is dead," Saul shouts back, trying to rally the crowd to his argument. "And you shall soon go the same way, blasphemer." Saul pushes through the crowd and stands toe to toe with Stephen.

Stephen is unafraid. "No. Jesus is alive. They killed him. But he conquered death. He is our true Messiah!"

"What do you know about prophets? Your Jesus put himself above the law—and no man is above the law."

"I know the scriptures promise the Messiah and Jesus—" Stephen attempts to respond.

"Really?" Saul interrupts, relishing the moment. "If you know scripture, then you'll know Deuteronomy: 'because he sought to entice you away from the Lord your God, your hand shall be first against him.'" Saul turns to the audience, where three men have discarded their cloaks, picked up stones from the ground, and are hurling them at Stephen. "'And you shall stone him until he dies,'" Saul continues reciting, as the rest of the crowd turns vigilante and begins to hurl rocks. As he draws closer to his death, Stephen speaks, "Lord, please forgive them for this sin." Saul stands to one side and picks up their cloaks as they continue to stone Stephen, the first Christian martyr.

Caiaphas sends for Saul and questions him. He is concerned about the riot that might have ensued if Saul's zealousness had let things get out of control. But he also admires Saul's like-minded enthusiasm for rooting out this new breed that he considers heretics—and Caiaphas tells him so. When Saul asks for money and letters of introduction so that he might continue this work, Caiaphas is only too happy to comply.

Soon, thanks to Caiaphas's blessing and ample resources, Saul begins brutally rooting out any trace of Jesus' followers. Doors are kicked open. Men and women are dragged into the streets by Saul's handpicked army of Temple guards. The message Saul is sending to the streets is quite clear: it is no longer safe for anyone to follow Jesus.

"Where are the others?" Saul shouts to one man who is accused of being a believer. It is midday in the center of Jerusalem. The hapless man has been retreating backward from Saul and his henchmen, but had the bad fortune to stumble over a trough. He sits helplessly on the edge of the trough, unable to rise as Saul steps forward to keep him down.

"Suddenly, no one's talking about Jesus," Saul says. "But I don't think they've just forgotten about him. I think they're in hiding. And I think you know where they are."

Saul shoves the man backward into the trough. He pushes the man under the water with his bare hands, keeping him there until the flailing man is on the verge of death. Only then does Saul pull him out of the water.

"Damascus," the man sputters. "Someone said they're in Damascus."

Saul makes his way north, to the cultured and beautiful city of Damascus. Despite the dangers of being a believer in Jesus, tiny pockets of his followers have been slowly growing within Jewish communities. A man named Ananias is a leader within this secret movement, and he is breaking bread in a walled garden on the outskirts of the city when he hears a noise behind him.

"Welcome, friend," Ananias tells him. A small group of Christians are about to eat their meal, and are just now praying over their small feast. "Would you like to join us?"

"Trust me. I am not your friend," Saul responds. "Take them!"

Saul's men stream into the garden. Some inside manage to scatter in time, but most are caught and beaten. Ananias is beaten, and then dragged toward the door for later interrogation. But one of his captors becomes distracted, and in that moment Ananias breaks free and runs. Saul's men give chase to Ananias and those who have fled the scene. "Tell all your friends," Saul crows to one man lying helplessly in the dust, "that I will find all the followers of Jesus. Wherever you go, wherever you are, I will find you. For God is on my side. He will lead me to you, as He has led me here today." Saul then mounts his horse for the ride into Damascus. He feels just in his persecutions, for he knows that he is saving these wretched souls from God's judgment. It is a long ride, and Saul spends hours thinking about how he will track Jesus' followers down within Damascus.

Suddenly, Saul's horse veers side to side for no reason. There standing in the road before Saul is Jesus. Saul does not know it is him. A brilliant light shines around Jesus.

"Who are you?" Saul demands, struggling to control his horse. Then Paul's horse rears up and he is thrown to the dirty highway. Saul hits the ground hard.

Jesus crouches down in front of Saul as he lies on the road.

"Why do you persecute me?" Jesus asks.

Saul cannot make out who it is. "Who are you?" he demands. He tries to roll away from Jesus, but finds that Jesus is there. He tries again, but wherever he turns, Jesus is still there.

"Why?" Jesus asks again.

"I demand that you tell me who you are!"

"I am Jesus, whom you persecute."

A blinding light strikes Saul's eyes. "No!" he insists. "No." He holds up his hand to protect his eyes from the withering white light, but the light envelops him before flaring out.

Saul's men have seen their leader fall to the ground, and now race to his aid. They find him broken and defeated, not at all like the surly Saul that they know so well. Something else they soon learn when he stumbles and gropes his way to his feet is that the light has blinded Saul.

News of Saul's persecutions has spread. Even in Damascus, where Jesus' followers were once considered safe, believers are going into hiding. Among them is Ananias, whose worship group was recently ambushed by Saul's army. The streets of Damascus were once so comforting to him. But now, as he carries his bedroll down an empty street on the outskirts of town, Ananias peers anxiously into the shadows, unsure when or where the next attack will take place.

"Ananias."

He turns toward the voice that calls out to him, making Ananias tremble with fear, but his entire body relaxes as he sees the Messiah standing to one side of the road. The piercings on his hands and feet are all too clear, making it obvious who Ananias is looking at.

"Lord?" he cries, falling to his knees.

"Please, rise," Jesus tells him.

Ananias, trembling with joy, stands. His worries are suddenly gone, and his faith has become a deep well that will never go dry.

Jesus walks toward him, gently placing a hand on his shoulder. "You must go to the street called Straight. There, ask for a man they call Saul of Tarsus."

"Lord," Ananias says hesitantly, "Saul beats us and arrests us. Our followers are being persecuted by this man." Ananias knows in his heart that Jesus is already aware of these facts, but it seems important to repeat them.

"Go." Jesus smiles at him as he commands him, his voice smooth and reassuring. "I have chosen this unlikely man to proclaim my name to the world. To the Gentiles, to their kings, and to all the sons of Israel."

Ananias is incredulous. Surely Jesus is mistaken. The mere thought of saying Saul's name out loud fills Ananias with dread. Saul is going to stop his persecutions and spread the Word of God to all nations?

Jesus disappears just as quickly and mysteriously as he arrived, leaving Ananias alone to ponder and to summon his courage.

Ananias does as he is told. He finds Saul and is startled to learn that he is blind and helpless. Rather than take him back to Jerusalem, Saul's men have left him in Damascus, hoping a few days of rest will restore his sight. Ananias finds him alone in a rented room, curled up asleep in a corner. The innkeeper opens the door and hastily retreats, leaving Ananias alone with his tormentor.

It is a pitiful sight. Saul hasn't touched the meal provided for him last night, and he has knocked over a bowl as he groped in the darkness. The spilled food litters the ground, and the sleeping Saul has rolled over into it.

Ananias feels a rage bubbling inside of him. His fists clench and unclench. He looks down upon Saul and is shocked to compare the sad sight before him with the cruel persecutor who confronted him in the garden not so long ago. Ananias remembers the screams as his friends and fellow believers were kicked and beaten. Ananias hasn't told any of those people that Saul is here now. Despite their abundant faith, there's every chance they might seek revenge for their suffering. It's a revenge that Ananias would also like to exact.

Saul wakes up with a start. "Who's there?"

"You are Saul?" asks Ananias, his throat dry and words measured. He picks up a nearby water jug. It is clay and heavy. Smashing it down on Paul's head would be such an easy way to kill this miserable man.

"Who are you?" demands Saul. "Speak!"

"I am one of those you long to destroy."

Saul rises to his knees. "Forgive me. Please forgive me."

Ananias puts down the jug.

Saul reaches out, his hand fumbling to take hold of Ananias's. His body is convulsed by remorse. "Please forgive me! I have wronged you. I have wronged God. My soul is on fire. Help me! Save me!"

Ananias places his hands on Saul's face. Saul winces as if he's been stung, and tries to push Ananias's hands away.

Then he stops.

For the touch of those hands has restored Saul's sight. He blinks away tears as sunlight bathes the room. A succession of faces flashes before his eyes. These are the images of those men and women he has persecuted. He feels regret for pain he has inflicted, but that suffering is soon replaced by God's healing forgiveness. He realizes this, and breaks down sobbing.

"Shhh," Ananias tells him. "I am sent by God. For you."

Saul looks up at the voice offering him such comfort. He recognizes the face of the man before him. "I know you," he says.

Ananias nods.

"Don't leave me," Saul begs. He clings desperately to Ananias's cloak.

Once again, Ananias reaches for the jug of water and now pours it over Saul's head. "I baptize you, Paul of Tarsus, in the name of the Father, the Son, and the Holy Spirit."

Saul is a new person. Even his name is changed. From this day forward, Saul is gone. The man named Paul, the apostle who will fearlessly go out into the world and share the Good News about Jesus, now takes his place. The water runs over Paul's head and into his eyes and mouth. He coughs, chokes, and gasps for breath.

Ananias continues: "For he has chosen you to change the world in his name."

Slowly, Paul brings his hands up to his own face. A calm has come over him. "Why me?"

Ananias shrugs.

Paul stands. "Please forgive me for what I have done to you."

"You are already forgiven."

Caiaphas stands in the sacrificial courtyard of the Temple. The other members of the Sanhedrin have just approached the high priest with the most outrageous news. "Saul has done what?"

"He's joined Jesus' followers," his servant Malchus informs him. "He has even changed his name. They now call him Paul."

Caiaphas stares at Malchus. He says nothing.

Malchus is once again eager to take on the role of henchman. "I'll find him for you," he says, eager to get away from the Temple and be granted autonomous power. "I'll assemble the men."

Caiaphas's eyes flash with hope. He rounds on Malchus, as if to hand over the mission to him, as he has done so many times before. But not this time. "And then . . . ?" asks Caiaphas. "What happens when *you* join them? Will I have to send someone after you? And then someone after him?" Caiaphas looks to heaven. He sighs.

"Let them be," Caiaphas speaks softly the words of the Sanhedrin leader, Gamaliel: "If this is man's work it will not succeed. If it is God's we cannot fight it." With all eyes on him, Caiaphas climbs the enormous steps of the Temple. He walks inside and closes the door behind them. Life had once been so simple here, so orderly. It was a world that he controlled. But now everything is changing. Caiaphas shuts out that world and all its new confusions. He will never be the same man again.

But the threat to Jesus' followers does not end with Caiaphas. The Romans and Herod Agrippa are stamping out all challenges to the status quo. The elder brother of the disciple John, James—also a disciple—is arrested and sentenced to death by Herod. His beheading is meant to be a word of caution to all who follow Jesus—and it succeeds.

The apostles meet secretly to regroup. Along with Mary Magdalene, they assemble in the small upper room that has marked their gatherings so many times. But this is not a time of peace or even connection. The disciples are engaged in a heated debate as to their future. A frightened Thomas can't take the conflict, and he is on the verge of leaving just moments after his arrival. John, on the other hand, is in a particularly foul mood, eager to do battle.

"It's getting too dangerous," says Thomas. "If we stay in Jerusalem we will die—all of us. Just like they killed James."

"I'm not afraid of death," John says defiantly.

"None of us are," says Peter, taking on the role of peacemaker. "But now is not the time. We cannot spread his word if we are dead."

The disciples stop their bickering. Peter has their attention.

He takes a deep breath and begins to explain himself. "Jesus said, 'Preach to all creation.' Our job is now to spread the Word."

"I thought that's what we were already doing," challenges Thomas.

"And we have," Peter reminds him. "But now we must go out into the world, far beyond merely Jerusalem."

"Where will we go?" asks Mary.

"Where the spirit leads us," says Peter.

"I feel called to travel north—perhaps to Ephesus," says John. His eyes swell with tears as he recalls his brother's sacrifice—and knows that such a death might also await him once he steps out alone into the world.

The disciples arise. They take on another's hands and pray. This will be their last moment as a group. After so many years and so many world-changing experiences, their work now will be solitary and dangerous, without the comfort or support of this band of brothers.

John, with his gift for insight, offers perspective. "We will meet again," he tells them all. "On earth or in heaven."

One by one, the disciples say their good-byes, shedding many a tear and sharing more than one vivid memory. They have never considered themselves merely friends, but lifelong companions who have come together and given up everything in the name of Jesus. Their bond runs deep, which makes the good-byes all the more difficult.

They step out into the street and scatter.

Their travels take them far and wide. The Roman Empire is vast. Persecution is swift for those who attempt to bring forth change, but the disciples seek to change the religious fabric of this culture, one believer and one soul at a time.

Peter confines his travels to the Jewish communities in and around Israel. It is exhausting work, and he has never felt so alone. But there

is comfort in remaining so close to Galilee, to home. Despite his calling
to lead the disciples, Peter is a very simple man. He does not speak the
worldly languages like Latin or Greek. There is simplicity in preaching in
the backwater hamlets and burgs throughout the countryside. He takes
a room at the end of one particularly draining day. He has little money
for food, so his stomach barks at him as he stumbles into the dark space
and lies on the bed.

"Peter," says a voice. Peter would recognize that voice anywhere. He
turns and sees Jesus. "You have done so much."

Peter's eyes open wide in shock. He sees Jesus standing before him,
with those wounds still marking the piercings on his hands and feet.

"I'm proud of you, my fisher of men," Jesus adds.

"My Lord," says Peter, sitting bolt upright on the bed.

Jesus smiles.

"I miss our work in Galilee, Lord. I'd go back with you in a moment
if you asked."

"No, Peter. That time has passed. I must ask something far more
from you."

Peter knows what Jesus is about to say. The sentiment has been on his
heart for some time, but he has been afraid to recognize this hard truth.

"You have to move on," Jesus tells him.

Peter doesn't respond. He's so afraid. So very afraid.

Jesus continues: "You are hungry right now, and yet you are afraid to
travel into Caesarea to find food."

"It's a Roman town," Peter protests. "The food and the people will be
unclean."

"Are there no souls in Caesarea worth saving?"

"But cleanliness keeps us close to God."

"Peter, you could not be closer. I am with you always. And it is I who
make all things clean."

Peter is confused. All along, he has been thinking that only Jews can
be led to faith in Jesus. It is a radical notion to believe that anyone, of
any faith or nationality, can also receive God's blessing.

There is a sharp knock at the door. Peter turns in shock. "What do I do, Lord?"

"Answer it, Peter. Go with them. The door is open to everyone."

The fisher of men rises to answer the door. Every step forward is in agony, for he knows what awaits him when he pulls it open. Peter opens the door. Three Roman soldiers stand there. Peter instinctively backs away, even though there's nowhere to hide from Rome. "You are Peter?" asks the tall one in the center.

Peter turns and looks back for Jesus, but the Messiah is no longer there. "I am he," Peter says with a lump in his throat.

"You must come with us," the soldier tells him gruffly. "Centurion Cornelius awaits you."

Knowing that it is useless to fight, Peter picks up his satchel and staff, and then walks with the Romans to meet the centurion Cornelius. He knows better than to question God's plan for his life. But right now, Peter just wishes it were a little easier.

———

Romans have dominated the land is Israel for as long as Peter can remember. They conquered it before he was born, and there is a good chance it will be in their hands long after he dies. They bring with them a constant presence of fear and control. The imposition of Roman will on the Israelite people is stifling and oppressive. Dispensing justice the Roman way is their penalty for disobeying Rome.

Peter ponders all this as he is led into the courtyard of Cornelius' oceanfront villa. This is not a sight the plainspoken Peter is used to, for he is surrounded on all sides by the sort of opulence and wealth a fisherman could never imagine in a million years. Even the slaves are better dressed than Peter, and the soldiers now gathered around him seem even more educated and polished.

"Lord, why am I here?" Peter prays.

In the center of the courtyard, surrounded on all sides by servants, sits a Roman family. Parents and children alike dress in immaculate white togas, and the centurion Cornelius is also draped in shining gold necklaces. He is an imposing man, having earned his position through politics and the battlefield. Cornelius rises to approach Peter. As he does so, every soldier and servant in the courtyard bows and then descends to one knee.

Peter remains standing. The kneeling soldiers place their hands upon their swords, prepared to leap forward and kill Peter on a signal from Cornelius. But the centurion issues no such snap of the fingers. Instead, he steps toward Peter, sizing him up. Cornelius is taller than Peter, and perhaps even broader in the shoulders. It will be easy for him to inflict physical punishment on this rabble-rousing preacher. But Cornelius gets down on his knees and prostates himself at Peter's feet, much to the disciple's embarrassment. Peter's feet are filthy and dusty from his long day on the road, yet Cornelius kisses them. "An angel of the Lord," the centurion explains himself, "came to me and told me to find you. And to listen to all you have to say. Please, save me." Cornelius looks up at Peter, who returns his gaze.

"Please stand," Peter tells him. "I am a man, just like you."

Cornelius is reluctant. "The angel's words were powerful and forthright."

"I cannot save you," Peter tells him. "But Jesus can. If you believe in him, your sins will be forgiven." Peter takes Cornelius by the hand and pulls him to his feet. Then he steers the Roman to a pool in the center of the courtyard. Peter is well aware that this is a moment to be seized, for this is a God-given chance to bring the first Roman to Jesus.

He and Cornelius step into the pool. "Jesus' message to all people everywhere is that everyone who repents and believes in Jesus can be forgiven their sins," he tells Cornelius and all within earshot, his words echoing across the courtyard.

The Roman nods, and Peter immerses him in the water, baptizing him. "I, Peter, baptize you, Cornelius, in the name of the Father, the Son, and the Holy Spirit."

The courtyard bursts into applause. A dripping Cornelius, his white robe now drenched, beckons to his family. "Come with me, all of you. Be filled with the Holy Spirit," he tells them joyfully.

One by one, they step into the pool. As they do, the words God spoke to Abraham so long ago continue to become reality: "I will give you descendants as numerous as the stars."

Thus the gospel, as the words of Jesus are known, enters the Roman world. Peter is tireless in his work, as are all the other disciples. But one man does more than any other to take the Word to the empire. It is the man who once tried hardest to crush Jesus' disciples: Paul. His past as a hunter of Christians is not easily forgotten. Whenever he meets with fellow believers, he hears the same charges over and over: Murderer. Oppressor. Unbeliever. Many are doubtful of his claims that he has changed, and rightfully so, for their memories of loved ones spirited away in the night or trampled before their own children are all too vivid. But Paul repeats his story again and again, knowing that God's love flows through him, and will change hearts. "I've changed," he says again and again. "I once was blind, but now I see."

In one small church, a woman steps forth and spits into his face. "Liar!" she screams at him.

Paul does not wipe it off. "Please," he tells her and the others in the small room. "Listen before you judge."

The room goes silent, but the suppressed rage has a sound all its own that rings in everyone's ears and lays heavy upon their hearts. Fists curl and uncurl. Feet tap the ground impatiently as men debate within themselves whether or not to set aside the peace of their beliefs just long enough to kill this awful man standing before them.

Paul continues, afraid and yet also unafraid, knowing that he has no choice but to say what he is about to say. "I did what I did because I was certain that I was right. I was certain that I knew the will of God. As certain as you are now."

He looks around the room, knowing that he's bought a little time.

"But then Jesus came to me. Not in righteous anger or in judgments, but in love. His love."

Eyes moisten. Heads nod. Yes, they've felt this, too.

"Without love we are nothing," Paul tells them. "Love is patient. Love is kind. It is not jealous. It does not boast. It is not proud."

There are murmurs of discontent. What does this man know about love?

But Paul continues. "It keeps no record of wrongs. It rejoices with the truth, bears all burdens, believes all things, hopes all things, endures all things. When everything else disappears, there still remains faith, hope, and love. But the greatest of these, by far, is love."

One by one, members of the congregation rise from their seats and walk to Paul. It is difficult for them at first, touching this man whose fists have so often brought forth pain. But they soon reach forth and hug him, accepting him and his teachings.

One man holds back. He is a learned man, clearly disturbed by Paul's words, and he wants to have an intellectual discussion of what they mean.

Finally, Paul addresses him. "You don't believe in God's love?" he asks.

"I do," says the man, whose name is Luke. "But I am a Greek. A Gentile. I know there are laws and rituals which I must follow to first become a Jew."

Paul's face grows stern. He shakes his head. "No. No. You don't need to become a Jew in order to know God's love. It is available to all."

"But the laws," Luke reminds him.

"If you could be saved just by following laws, Jesus would have died for nothing. But Jesus died to save you from sin. To save all of us from sin."

Once again, Paul addresses the entire congregation. "There is no longer Jew or Greek, male or female, slave or free man. We are all one in Jesus Christ."

These are world-changing words, and the congregation shouts back a heartfelt "Amen" in agreement.

"Join us," Paul tells Luke. "God will be with you."

Paul is a radical and a revolutionary, preaching this new gospel of Christianity with a fervor that puts his life in danger and sees him thrown into prison time after time. This new faith spreads across the Roman Empire, thanks to Paul's selfless and tireless zeal.

But once again, it is Peter whom God calls upon to do some of his hardest chores. Peter accepts the arduous task of traveling to the hub of the empire to change hearts and minds. Peter, the unlearned and uneducated fisher of men, is on his way to Rome. Like Daniel wandering into the lion's den. To a rational man, Peter's fate will most certainly be death. But as he walks slowly through the empire on his way to Rome, Peter reminds himself of the story of God and all of us. The words and stories give him strength and serve as a reminder of his purpose.

"In the beginning, God embraced Abraham. From him came a family that became twelve tribes, which became a people and a nation. Now, through Jesus Christ, we must embrace the entire world."

Thus fortified, Peter enters Rome. The city is exotic and exciting, with smells and spices from around the world wafting through the winding streets. He feels out of place, and at first believes that his simple dress and foreign appearance mark him as an outsider. But then he realizes that as the hub of the empire, Rome is home to men from around the known world. All manner of dialect and mode of dress can be seen all around him. Peter may be an outsider, he realizes, but he is not alone.

Empowered, Peter approaches a line of manacled slaves. They lean against a colonnade, waiting to be marched off to perform some chore or other. He offers them water from his goatskin. "Please," he tells one of the chained men. "Take some water."

The slave looks at him thankfully and slurps a greedy drink. "I have good news," Peter tells him. "News that will relieve your suffering. It is about a great teacher named Jesus."

Chains clank as the slaves stand and gather around Peter. They come near for the water Peter offers, but he also adds a message of hope. "Jesus said that if anyone is thirsty, they should come to him and drink from the well of salvation."

Such behavior doesn't go unnoticed long. Soon, Roman soldiers are keeping a sharp eye on Peter. The Roman emperor Nero has accused Jesus' followers of starting a fire that has burned much of Rome. It is a dangerous time. Persecution has broken out once again. Yet the disciple who once knew such fear and lack of faith does not stop preaching. "The Romans crucified Jesus. But he rose from the dead, and in his infinite love, gave his followers the keys to the Kingdom of Heaven. Believe in him, and the gates will be opened to you."

The slaves fall to their knees, one by one, accepting Jesus.

But in a sudden burst of violence, Peter is sent sprawling as Roman soldiers are now upon him. They rain blows down on his back, his kidneys, and his head. The slave traders join in, not wanting their precious cargo to become polluted with dangerous new ideas and emotions. The end comes soon for Peter. He is jailed, then tried in a Roman court of law and found guilty of fomenting rebellion. The Romans crucify him. But just as they are about to nail him to the cross, Peter protests. He has already been beaten, stripped of his clothes, and has carried his cross to the hill where he will be hung on the cross. "I am not worthy to die in the same manner as Jesus," Peter tells them, struggling to make himself understood in the Roman tongue. "So please, crucify me upside down."

The Romans are only too happy to oblige.

Wherever the disciples travel, they pay this ultimate price. Peter is crucified in Rome. Matthew is butchered in Ethiopia. Thomas is slaughtered in India. And John also falls victim to the Romans, but ultimately survives. Of the original group of men that set out from Galilee with Jesus, all are executed as evangelists. And of that number, all of the disciples saw Jesus' face once more as they stood before him in heaven.

———

Luke, the new follower whom Paul has recruited for Jesus, like Matthew and Mark before him, is fervent about writing down the story of Jesus so that it will be passed on through all generations. He sits alone in an upstairs room in Rome when he hears the thunder of an approaching army. Luke knows what this means, and instantly races into the room where Paul sits in prayer.

"Paul," Luke warns him. "They're coming for you."

Paul has been expecting this moment for years. Despite his many times in prison for his faith, something tells him that this will be his final journey. "Take them," he nods to Luke. "These words and letters need to survive." Luke grabs the scrolls and writings from the table.

Paul rises up, as fearful and defiant as the day he once persecuted Christians. Roman footsteps can be heard charging up the stairs. "Go," he orders Luke. "Get out of here. You need to stay alive to continue our work."

Luke hesitates, but then nods and climbs out through the balcony.

Paul is alone. For nearly three decades he has preached the Word of God. It has been a hard life, full of deprivation and suffering. Yet in all the chaos and carnage that has marked the growth of the Christian church, Paul knows that the Word will survive him. The Word is love. "I have fought the good fight," he reminds himself as he sits down to await his fate. "I have finished the race. I have kept the faith." He sighs. His time has come. He hears the soldiers on the stairs, and he turns to face them as they rush into the room

Paul will be beheaded in the Mamartine Prison.

The parchment scrolls escaped with Luke and form a large part of the New Testament.

John is the last disciple standing; the one who owns the gift of intuition is a living miracle. He has refused to accept the Roman emperor as his god, and somehow survived all Roman attempts to kill him. He lives out his days in a small cave on an island off the coast of Asia Minor. It is a sparse home, but it is enough for this elderly disciple. The Romans could have killed him any of a number of ways, but they have exiled John to the remote island of Patmos. His face is weathered from the wind and sun, and his lips are chapped from sunburn and thirst. The Romans assume that his isolation will mean death—that they will work him to death, as they have so many others, in the Roman mines on the island. But John knows how to fish. He lives off the sea, knowing that his life's work means descendants as numerous as the stars. The Romans may have sent him away, but like Christianity itself, they cannot wipe away his memories. Or his gift of intuition.

At his lowest ebb—and there are many in these final, lonely days— John has a revelation of hope. He looks back on the past, on all that has happened in the years since he met Jesus. He hears Jesus' voice as a memory, but the memory becomes more and more clear. His vision shifts from the past to the present, and then to the future—a future infinitely greater than anything which has come before. Jesus stands before him.

"I am the Alpha and the Omega," Jesus says, appearing to John in the small cave. A fish rests on the coals, waiting to be turned. "The first and the last, the beginning and the end."

John's face is transformed into joy. "Lord, forgive me. I have been expecting death, but it is you."

Jesus smiles. His hand beckons to John, leading him out of the cave. "There will be no more death or mourning or crying or pain," Jesus tells him. "I will make everything new." He offers John a cup of water, which the disciple slowly lifts to parched lips. "To him who is thirsty, I will give water from the river of life. Behold, I am coming soon. For I am the light of the world."

An ecstatic John understands fully what Jesus is telling him.

"Blessed are those who read the words of the book," Jesus tells him. "And heeds the words that are written in it. May the grace of the Lord be with all God's people."

"Amen," John whispers. He looks into Jesus' eyes, eyes that saw the beginning of time. They saw Adam and Eve, they saw Noah and Abraham and David. They also see the future, billions of Jesus' followers—as numerous as the stars in the sky—repeating the words that John has just whispered.

"Amen."

A Special Thanks to
David Young
Rolf Zettersten
and the team at FaithWords

All our scholars and advisors, your wisdom is abundant.

Our entire production team on *The Bible* series

We couldn't have done it without:
Jan Miller
Shannon Marven
Bob Beltz
Richard Bedser
Randy Sollenberger
Mishy Turner

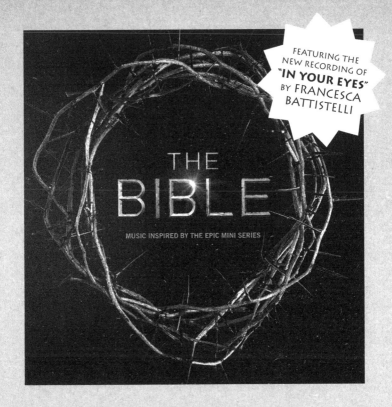